Karolinum Press

MODERN CZECH CLASSICS

Beyond
the World of Men
Women's Fiction
at the Czech
Fin de Siècle

Edited and translated from the Czech
and German by Geoffrey Chew

KAROLINUM PRESS 2024

KAROLINUM PRESS
is a publishing department
of Charles University
Ovocný trh 560/5, 116 36 Prague 1
Czech Republic
www.karolinum.cz

Cover image from Felix Tèver, *Duše nezakotvené* (1908),
illustrating the beginning of 'Solitude'
Copyediting by Martin Janeček
Graphic design by Zdeněk Ziegler
Set and printed in the Czech Republic
by Karolinum Press
First edition

A catalogue record for this book is available
from the National Library of the Czech Republic

ISBN 978-80-246-5617-5
ISBN 978-80-246-5631-1 (pdf)
ISBN 978-80-246-5632-8 (epub)

CONTENTS

*Dedicated to the memory of Edith Birkett (1879–1946),
a splendid and loving great-aunt for whom some
of these stories would have had painful resonance,
and in commemoration of the many successes achieved
by the women of her period, despite the difficulties
they had to overcome.*

It is a great pleasure to thank those who have been generous with their help with this volume, especially Martin Janeček and his colleagues at Karolinum Press. Michael Tate originally suggested this translation, and I am grateful for the help and criticism I have received from readers, especially Rajendra Chitnis, Peter Zusi, Robert Vilain, John Fallas, Carleton Bulkin and Václav Mlčoch. I am also grateful to Mark Cornwall, Julia Sutton-Mattocks, Jack Coling and Carleton Bulkin for help in gaining access to some of the original texts. All remaining errors are mine.

The sources of the texts from which these translations were made, listed in the order in which the stories are presented in this volume, are as follows:

Marie von Ebner-Eschenbach, 'He Kisses Your Hand': 'Er laßt die Hand küssen', in her *Ein Buch, das gern Ein Volksbuch werden möchte* [A Book that Would be Glad to Become a Popular Book] (Berlin: Gebrüder Paetel (Dr. Georg Paetel), 1911), 207–33

Teréza Nováková, 'A Kaleidoscope': 'Kaleidoskop', in her *Z měst i ze samot: povídky a črty* [From Cities and Lonely Places: Short Stories and Sketches], 2nd edition (Prague: Jos. R. Vilímek, 1890), 41–9

Božena Viková-Kunětická, 'Confirmed Bachelors': 'Staří mládenci', in her *Staří mládenci a jiné povídky* [Confirmed Bachelors, and Other Stories] (Prague: F. Šimáček, 1901), 7–38 (originally published in the journal *Lumír*, 1891)

Růžena Svobodová, 'Life's Sorrow': 'Smutek života', in her *Povídky Růženy Svobodové (1891–1895)* [Short Stories by Růžena Svobodová] (Prague: Libuše, Matice zábavy a vědění, 1896), 73–82

Tereza Svatová, 'A Visit to His Parents': 'Návštěva u rodičů', in her *Selské črty* [Peasant Sketches] (Prague: Libuše, Matice zábavy a vědění, 1894), 128–31

Tereza Svatová, 'The "Práže" – A Prague Bastard': 'Práže', in her *Selské črty* [Peasant Sketches] (Prague: Libuše, Matice zábavy a vědění, 1894), 99–108

Vladimíra Jedličková, 'Tales About Nothing, nos. 5 and 14': the untitled chapters 5 and 14 of Edvard Klas, *Povídky o ničem* [Tales About Nothing] (Prague: Moderní revue, 1903), 17–19 and 40–41 respectively

Marie von Ebner-Eschenbach, 'Daily Life': 'Das tägliche Leben', in her *Genrebilder: Erzählungen* [Genre Pictures: Narratives] (Berlin: Gebrüder Paetel (Dr. Georg Paetel), 1910), 379–402

Anna Maria Tilschová, 'A Widow': 'Vdova', in her *Na horách – Vítr: dvě knihy povídek* [In the Mountains, and Wind: Two Books of Short Stories], Anna Maria Tilschová: Spisy, 2 (Prague: Fr. Borový, 1928), 27–69

Anna Maria Tilschová, 'A Rose for Uncle: An Unserious Tale of a Very Young Coquette, With a Moral': 'Lehounká povídka o koketním děvčátku s mravním naučením', in her *Na horách – Vítr: dvě knihy povídek* [In the Mountains, and Wind: Two Books of Short Stories], Anna Maria Tilschová: Spisy, 2 (Prague: Fr. Borový, 1928), 121–7

Božena Benešová, 'Theories': 'Teorie', in her *Myšky: povídky z let 1909–1913* [Little Mice: Short Stories from 1909 to 1913] (Prague: Edice Sever a východ, 1926), 99–106 (but in manuscript, 1906, and originally published in the journal *Národní obzor*, 1906–7)

Marie Majerová, 'A Tale from Hell': 'Povídka z pekla', in her *Povídky z pekla a jiné* [Tales from Hell, and Others] (Prague: Tiskový výbor českoslovanské sociálně demokratické strany dělnické, 1907), 89–101

Marie Majerová, 'Marriage': 'Manželství', in her *Povídky z pekla a jiné* [Tales from Hell, and Others] (Prague: Tiskový výbor českoslovanské sociálně demokratické strany dělnické, 1907), 123–6

Božena Benešová, 'A Loyal Wife': 'Pýří', in her *Myšky: povídky z let 1909–1913* [Little Mice: Short Stories from 1909 to 1913] (Prague: Edice Sever a východ, 1926), 73–96 (but originally published in the journal *Zlatá Praha*, 1908)

Anna Lauermannová-Mikschová, 'Solitude': 'Samota', in Felix Tèver, *Duše nezakotvené* [Souls Unanchored] (Prague: Jos. R. Vilímek, 1908), 195–224

Helena Malířová, 'Three Points of View': 'Tři kapitolky', in her *Ženy a děti: rozmarné příběhy z jejich světa* [Women and Children: Whimsical Stories from Their World] (Prague: F. Topič, 1908), 120–30

Růžena Svobodová, '. . . And Music will be Playing Outside Your Windows Every Day!': '. . . a denně bude hrávat hudba pod vašimi okny!', in her *Černí myslivci: horské romány* [The Dark Huntsmen: Mountain Stories] (Prague: Jan Laichter, 1908), 245–86

Růžena Jesenská, 'The Death of Ophelia': 'Smrt Ofélie', in her *Mimo svět: prosa* [Beyond the World] (Prague: Pražská akciová tiskárna, 1909), here quoted from Tereza Nejtková, 'Růžena Jesenská: Mimo svět – ediční příprava a komentář k souboru povídek' (dissertation, Charles University, Prague, 2017), 175–87

Růžena Jesenská, 'A Truthful Tale of a Stone Statue': 'Pravdivá historie kamenné sochy', in her *Mimo svět: prosa* [Beyond the World] (Prague: Pražská akciová tiskárna, 1909), here quoted from Nejtková, 'Růžena Jesenská: Mimo svět', 113–17

Lila Bubelová, 'The Child': 'Dítě', from Lila B. Nováková, *Nad její drahou zachmuřenou . . .* [Over Her Dear Gloomy Path] (Prague: Antonín Reis, 1912), 30–33

Marie Majerová, 'A Thorny Question': 'Těžká otázka', in the journal *Lumír*, 45/1 (1917): 29–38

Anna Maria Tilschová, 'A Remarkable Incident': 'Podivuhodná příhoda', in her *Černá dáma a tři povídky* [The Black

Lady, and Three Stories] (Prague: Šolc a Šimáček, 1924), 130–40

Lída Merlínová, 'Marie and Marta': 'Marie a Marta', in the journal *Nový hlas*, 4/2 (1933): 59–61

The selection of shorter fiction by Czech women writers presented here centres on texts dating from the two decades between 1890 and 1910, with a few earlier and later outliers chosen for their interest or rarity. They are presented in chronological order of writing, so far as I have been able to establish this. I make no claim that all these stories are of equal literary merit (some are primarily of historical interest), and I have not restricted the choice to stories with a feminist ideological slant, while including many that do display such a slant. Nor have I made any attempt to provide comparative material from regions of the Habsburg empire beyond the Bohemian lands, as has been impressively done in recent years for both Cisleithania and Transleithania, particularly by the Hungarian-Canadian academic Agatha Schwartz.[1] I have, however, included two stories originally in German by the aristocrat Marie von Ebner-Eschenbach – who was born Dubská, from an ancient Bohemian noble family, at Zdislavice near Kroměříž in Moravia, was competent in Czech, and is increasingly celebrated as an important Austrian writer of her period. The stories of hers translated here are relevant to themes treated by writers in Czech, quite apart from their considerable merit as literature. In the following paragraphs, I attempt to identify some representative themes in this body of writing; the titles of stories that are included in the present collection are distinguished in **bold type**.

CZECH WOMEN'S WRITING IN THE LATE
NINETEENTH CENTURY: PERMISSIBLE GENRES
To readers familiar with the European modernism of the same period, comparisons might seem best in order with

---

1 See the items listed under her name in the Bibliography below.

fiction reflecting themes and styles commonly associated with *fin-de-siècle* 'Jung-Wien', such as Decadence, alienation, sexual anxiety and the fragmentation of identity, and more specifically the new developments in psychology and psychiatry associated with Freud among others.[2] And such themes are not absent in the writing of the women represented in the present collection; indeed the ironizing narrative technique of Ebner-Eschenbach in **'He Kisses Your Hand'** has been directly compared with a similar technique employed by Hugo von Hofmannsthal in his dramatic writing, though she avoids Hofmannsthal's echoes of French Symbolism, and the comparison, even if justified, may mask some of her originality.[3] As for Decadence, Růžena Jesenská boldly orients it towards women, especially in her collection Beyond the World (*Mimo svět*, 1909); her **'The Death of Ophelia'**, from that collection, explores psychological breakdown. The title story of the same collection, replete with Decadent imagery, skirts around the themes of lesbian love and necrophilia, though without endorsing them.[4] (Positive accounts of lesbian relationships seem absent in women writers until some years later, as in Lída Merlínová's **'Marie and Marta'** (1933), included in this collection on account of its rarity. It tells of the breakup of the relationship between two women, with two alternative en-

2 Especially those discussed in Carl E. Schorske's influential *Fin-de-Siècle Vienna: Politics and Culture* (New York: Alfred A. Knopf, 1980).
3 See Lore Muerdel Dormer, 'Tribunal der Ironie: Marie von Ebner-Eschenbachs Erzählung "Er lasst die Hand küssen"', *Modern Austrian Literature* 9/2 (1976): 86–97.
4 This story, with its title translated 'A World Apart', is not included in the present collection but is available in translation in Kathleen Hayes, ed. and trans., *A World Apart, and Other Stories: Czech Women Writers at the Fin de Siècle* (2nd edn., Prague: Karolinum, 2022), 51–64, and Hayes's translation is reprinted in Agatha Schwartz and Helga H. Thorson, *Shaking the Empire, Shaking Patriarchy: The Growth of a Feminist Consciousness across the Austro-Hungarian Monarchy* (Riverside, CA: Ariadne Press, 2014), 198–209.

dings, of which only one is of conventional tragic despair.[5])
Vladimíra Jedličková's collection of fourteen brief prose
poems published under the male pseudonym Edvard Klas
as **'Tales about Nothing'** (1903; two are represented here)
also develop a Decadent mood in their celebration of Nature; she was praised by the leading Czech Decadent writer
and critic Jiří Karásek ze Lvovic as the 'poet of longing *par
excellence*',[6] though praise may have been two-edged from
as explicit a misogynist as Karásek.

Perhaps partly under the influence of Decadence, women
writers sometimes adopted an extreme Naturalism in sexual
matters, which to some degree foreshadows twentieth-cen-
tury psychological realism. It appeared sensationally in
popular German-language novels of the period published in
Berlin or Vienna, such as Grete Meisel-Hess's *Fanny Roth:
Eine Jung-Frauengeschichte* (1903), with its description of
marital rape, Margaret Böhme's *Tagebuch einer Verlorenen*
(1905), a fictional diary of a prostitute, and Else Jerusa-
lem's *Der heilige Skarabäus* (1909), set in a brothel.[7] The
explicitness of such novels is echoed in the blazing rage of
'The Child', from Lila Bubelová's collection Over Her Dear
Gloomy Path about masculine brutality (*Nad její drahou
zachmuřenou . . .*, 1912).[8]

<hr>

5   My thanks are due to Mark Cornwall for supplying me with a copy of this
short story. It is not an excerpt from Merlínová's later 'Marie a Marta' novels,
in which the women of the titles are sporty, emancipated sisters, rather than
lesbian lovers.

6   Preface to Edvard Klas (Vladimíra Jedličková), *Povídky o ničem* (Prague:
Moderní revue, 1903), 6.

7   An extract from Meisel-Hess's *Fanny Roth* (the notorious rape scene) is
included in translation in Schwartz and Thorson, *Shaking the Empire* (n. 4
above), 166–73.

8   Bubelová wrote at this period under the pseudonym Lila B. Nováková. In
the afterword to her drama The Maidservant (*Služka*, 1933) she apologizes,
needlessly, for her writing of this earlier period: 'As a young girl I used to write
poetry [...] I am enormously glad that these books (there were five of them, but

However, most Czech women writers worked out another kind of modernism under the shadow of the celebrated and canonic *Grandmother* (*Babička*, 1855) by Božena Němcová, whose themes were arguably drawn on by many of them. (Němcová is usually regarded as the greatest nineteenth-century Czech woman writer, and a founding figure of the National Revival in Czech literature. In a comparable way, male Czech writers returned constantly to the language and imagery of the nihilistic poem *May* (*Máj*, 1836) by K. H. Mácha, another foundational text of Czech Romanticism.) And the genre choices open to Czech women writers were usually strongly limited by the expectations of their patriarchal society, and followed Němcová in being 'concentrated primarily in the realm of the domestic idyll, in didactic writing, and [. . .] autobiography'.[9] This was the case even with the novelist Karolina Světlá (1830–99), a spokeswoman in her fiction for the underdog, who, inspired by the example of George Sand, in her turn inspired some of the authors represented in this collection.[10] Women writers could accordingly adopt a kind of 'ethical realism', often ironic, 'an engagement with the problems of contemporary society, aimed at altering the reader's outlook and moral values';[11] some, such as Jedličková and Lauermannová-Mikschová in

very slim volumes!) have disappeared; I am very embarrassed when any of my old friends remind me about them.'

9   'Das weibliche Repertoire war vor allem auf den Bereich des Häuslich--Idyllischen, des Pädagogischen und [...] des Autobiographischen konzentriert': Gudrun Langer, 'Babička contra Ahnfrau: Božena Němcovás "Babička" als nationalkulturelle Immatrikulation', *Zeitschrift für Slavische Philologie*, 57/1 (1998): 133–69 (this quotation at p. 139).

10   Karolina Světlá was the pseudonym of Johanna Mužáková née Rottová; she was a leading member of the so-called *májovci*, contributors to the *Máj* almanac founded in 1858 and so named in honour of the poem *Máj* by K. H. Mácha, whose aesthetic the almanac hoped to revive.

11   Charlotte Woodford, 'Suffering and Domesticity: The Subversion of Sentimentalism in Three Stories by Marie von Ebner-Eschenbach', *German Life and Letters* 59/1 (2006): 47–61 (this quotation at pp. 48–9).

the present collection, published their work under male pseudonyms.[12]

SOME VERSIONS OF PASTORAL: BIGOTED GRANDMOTHERS AND WELL-MEANING ARISTOCRATS

In Němcová's *Grandmother*, the notional female narrator is Barunka, granddaughter of the Czech peasant woman of the title, who is apparently now grown up as an infant teacher. Didactically and expertly, she depicts an ideal Czech landscape in which all social classes live in harmony. This society is still held together in Barunka's memory by the universal controlling wisdom of her grandmother, who had grown up in the second half of the eighteenth century, and is fondly remembered as fanatical in her traditional Catholicism, distrustful of the city ways and German language of 'Pan Prošek', her son-in-law, but very comfortable in dealing with royalty and nobility. In the traditional pastoral terms of the story, she is able, out of her simplicity as a peasant woman, to instruct the local noblewoman (and, by extension, Countess Eleonore Kaunitz, the aristocratic dedicatee of the novel) in correct behaviour. Nevertheless, she is evidently unable to handle some of the social problems endemic in her own class – she can do no more than wring her hands when Viktorka, a young peasant woman, is fatally, and supernaturally, compromised through yielding her virginity to a 'dark huntsman', and when Viktorka, driven out of her mind, drowns the infant she bears to this malignant figure and spends the rest of her sad life sleeping rough.

The motif of the controlling grandmother recurs in two of the most successful and well-known works by a Czech

---

12 Lauermannová-Mikschová's pseudonym, 'Felix Tèver', refers to Rome, where she lived for a time (happily beside the river Tiber or Tevere).

woman writer later in the century, the first two plays of Gabriela Preissová, not represented here, which both deal with problems of marriage and illegitimacy in rural society. The first of these, 'The Boss Peasant-Girl' (*Gazdina roba*), with a stereotypical bigoted Catholic grandmother, is a dramatic adaptation (first performed 1889) of a short story of that year with the same name.[13] The second, 'Her Foster-Daughter' (*Její pastorkyňa*, first performed 1890) adds Němcová's motif of infanticide by drowning; it provided the libretto for Janáček's opera known in English as *Jenůfa* (1904). The central conflict of the play, and of the opera, arguably lies in the impossible situation faced by the elderly and ultra-pious Kostelnička, Jenůfa's foster-mother, who is driven to the brink of insanity in feeling herself forced to risk damnation by drowning Jenůfa's illegitimate child.

A very different development of the same theme, in another pastoral context, is seen in the multiple layers of irony in Ebner-Eschenbach's savage story, **'He Kisses Your Hand'** (1885). Ebner-Eschenbach's fictional aristocratic narrator is, once again, a grandchild; his grandmother, a widowed noblewoman and the absolute ruler of her domain, had been as strict, and domineering, a Catholic as Němcová's grandmother, and had been raised in the same period and the same landscape. The framing narrative in Ebner-Eschenbach's story shows the aristocracy and the Czech peasantry, unlike those imagined by Němcová, essentially in continual conflict. Ebner-Eschenbach's grandmother, like Němcová's countess, intervenes paternalistically in the lives of her subjects, ostensibly with the best of intentions. But her mind is fatally occupied with other things. As an accomplished poet, she has composed and rehearsed a clichéd Renaissance pastoral in 'impeccable Alexandrines',

---

13   Preissová's short story 'The Boss Peasant-Girl' is available in translation as 'Eva', in Hayes, ed. and trans., *A World Apart* (n. 4 above), 119–52.

Les adieux de Chloë, for the aristocratic guests attending her birthday celebrations, in an uncomfortable parallel with Marie Antoinette before the French Revolution, and in doing so she has failed to see the real pastoral unfolding before her eyes, initiated by her own repressed sexuality, until it is too late to forestall the more catastrophic *adieu* with which the story ends.

THEORIES, THEORIES . . . :
THE 'WOMAN QUESTION' AND THE PROMOTION
OF WOMEN'S RIGHTS

The 'woman question' (*ženská otázka*, *Frauenfrage*), addressing the injustice of patriarchal society in the Habsburg empire, is unsurprisingly a constant theme in these texts.[14] Women were debarred from voting, as also from participating in the public sphere through membership in professional or political groups. With few exceptions, they were virtually confined to the private domestic sphere, when married, inescapably under the control of their husbands – although the noted feminist Božena Viková-Kunětická, represented in the present collection, was proud to be the first woman to be elected to the Bohemian Diet within Austria-Hungary in 1912. When unmarried, they had few opportunities for

14 Outside the sphere of literature, though by a prominent woman writer perhaps best known for her operatic libretti, see the political essay 'The Czech Woman Question' of 1881: Eliška Krásnohorská, *Ženská otázka česká* (Prague: Edvard Grégr, 1881), excerpted in translation in Schwartz and Thorson, *Shaking the Empire* (n. 4 above), 210–27. Krásnohorská links the call for justice for women with Czech nationalism, appealing to prehistory and medieval history, and the memory of Czech warrior princesses, though the national question and the 'woman question' were usually kept separate. Krásnohorská was also responsible for founding the Minerva school in Prague in 1890, the first Gymnasium opened there for girls: the eighteen-year-old 'daughter of a rich, decent family' in Helena Malířová's story **'Three Points of View'** is an old girl of that school. It should be added that some male writers concerned themselves sympathetically with the 'woman question', notably J. S. Machar and the future Czechoslovak President T. G. Masaryk.

independent behaviour, and women teachers were required to remain entirely celibate as a condition of employment (this was the situation of the author Růžena Jesenská, and also of the young fictional teacher in Růžena Svobodová's **'Life's Sorrow'** (1891–5).[15]

Though such restrictions on women's participation in public affairs affected bourgeois women in particular, the same constraints applied to women of all social classes.[16] Writers represented in this volume taking the 'woman question' as a main theme indeed range from the conservative aristocrat Ebner-Eschenbach to the young anarchist and later well-known communist Marie Majerová; I have chosen Ebner-Eschenbach's **'Daily Life'** (1904) and Majerová's **'A Thorny Question'** (1917) as an obvious pair, both concerned from their different points of view with seemingly inexplicable female suicides that result from intolerable and unjust pressures imposed on women, whether or not Majerová is directly using Ebner-Eschenbach's tale as a model for the plot of her story. (Majerová had foreshadowed Socialist Realism in her earlier **'A Tale from Hell'** (1907) – an admittedly tendentious story of the re-education of the resident physician at the Kladno steelworks and coalmine.)

---

15 Women had been entirely debarred from the teaching profession in the Habsburg lands, except in a very subordinate capacity, until an Act, passed in 1869, which allowed the establishment of institutes for training women teachers but enforced celibacy on women teachers (except teachers of handicrafts) as long as they continued in the profession. Even when qualified, women were paid only 80% of the salary of male teachers with equivalent qualifications. The enforcement of celibacy was abolished only in 1919, after the establishment of the First Czechoslovak Republic.

16 Even labouring women were subject to such constraints in the workplace (for telling examples, see Rudolf Kučera, 'Marginalizing Josefina: Work, Gender, and Protest in Bohemia 1820-1844', *Journal of Social History* 46/2 (2012): 430–48), although 'by 1880 Bohemia and Moravia-Silesia accounted for approximately two-thirds of Cisleithania's industrial production' (Hugh Agnew, *The Czechs and the Lands of the Bohemian Crown* (Stanford, CA: Hoover Institution Press, Stanford University, 2004), 140).

As for the political and sexological theories spawned during this period about the essence of those strange beings called Woman and Man, ironically deflated by Božena Benešová in her brief story **'Theories'** (1906), it will suffice merely to quote a couple. In his first aphorism on the subject, expressed in 1878, Nietzsche advanced one such theory:

Perfect Woman is a higher type of human being than perfect Man, but also much rarer. The natural history of animals offers a means of demonstrating the probability of this proposition.[17]

In December of that year, perhaps provoked by this, Ebner-Eschenbach wrote, in a pointed letter to a male friend who was personally in correspondence with Nietzsche:[18]

A newly invented natural history among us has made the discovery that Woman is nothing in and for herself, that she can become something only through Man – to whom she belongs in love – to whom she submits in humility – in whose life her own life is absorbed. A being as perfect as that self-evidently does not possess a perfect talent. Her efforts to develop one have something gratuitous

17   Friedrich Nietzsche, *Menschliches, allzumenschliches: Ein Buch für freie Geister* (Chemnitz: Ernst Schmeltzner, 1878), aphorism 377 (my translation). On Nietzsche reception in the Habsburg empire more generally, see Alice Freifeld and others, eds., *East Europe Reads Nietzsche*, East European Monographs 514 (Boulder, CO, and New York: Columbia University Press, 1998).

18   Her correspondent was the Hungarian nobleman Emmerich von Du Mont, and he was interested enough in the subject to write a book, *Das Weib: Philosophische Briefe über dessen Wesen und Verhältnis zum Manne* (Leipzig: Brockhaus, 1879). The extract from the letter (here in my translation) is quoted from Anton Bettelheim, *Marie von Ebner-Eschenbachs Wirken und Vermächtnis* (Leipzig: Quelle & Meyer, 1920), 277ff, in B. J. Kenworthy, 'Ethical Realism: Marie von Ebner-Eschenbach's *Unsühnbar*', *German Life and Letters* 41/4 (July 1988): 479.

and mistaken about them: at best they arouse pity, and at worst disgust.

But how would it be if Woman were first and foremost a human being and only secondly female? if she were to possess just as much individual life as Man, and were to need complementation through him no more than he through her?

Her own marriage was one in which her husband had disapproved of her literary activity and her leading role in a Viennese women's literary association, the Verein der Schriftstellerinnen und Künstlerinnen in Wien, and had tried to restrict them. Her **'Daily Life'**, published only after her husband's death, fictionalizes the situation of her marriage, though it is hardly autobiographical in its detail.

More notorious as a theory of Woman was Otto Weininger's *Sex and Character* (*Geschlecht und Charakter*, 1903).[19] This deeply misogynistic and anti-Semitic work invokes Woman and the Jew as symbols in a 'grandiose attempt to explain the modern world on the basis of the putative opposition between male and female principles, and the struggle between the Aryan and the Jewish mind'.[20] It gave rise to considerable discussion at the time, and may have resonated with some of the anti-Semitism evident in Czech women writers of the time, further discussed below, though it scarcely represents a defining influence on them.

---

19 Otto Weininger, *Geschlecht und Charakter: Eine prinzipielle Untersuchung* (Vienna and Leipzig: Braumüller, 1903); English translation as *Sex and Character: An Investigation of Fundamental Principles* (Bloomington, IN: Indiana University Press, 2005).

20 Christine Achinger, 'Allegories of Destruction: "Woman" and "the Jew" in Otto Weininger's *Sex and Character*', *The Germanic Review* 88/2 (2013): 121–49, this quotation at p. 122.

'Czech men! We're not satisfied with you either!' was the title of a pamphlet published in 1897 by the feminist Jaroslava Procházková,[21] and the constructions of inadequate masculinity (and femininity) in women's writing of the period, reflected in this collection, are varied and sometimes comic. Two stories in the present collection are taken from the 1916 collection *Myšky* by Božena Benešová, whose title means 'little mice' – their heroines are middle-aged petit-bourgeois women, more or less frustrated, who experience epiphanies that enable them to transcend their tedious lives, while their men remain in blissful ignorance of what has happened. (There is a further twist in her story **'A Loyal Wife'**, not its original title, first published in 1908, which stops well short of the unhappy end that must inevitably be awaiting its heroine.)[22] A variant of the 'little mouse' is Ebner-Eschenbach's Myška (in the German, 'Mischka'), a peasant boy of guileless Czech simplicity, in **'He Kisses Your Hand'**. Another is the Johann Myška, a ne'er-do-well who falls in with itinerant strolling players, in the story 'Myška, Man of the World', not included in this collection, from Anna Maria Tilschová's *In the Mountains* (1905).

A more consistently comic variant of male inadequacy is found in Božena Viková-Kunětická's splendid mock-fairytale, **'Confirmed Bachelors'** (1891). Though her three ridiculous, aging bachelors have apparently foresworn sex in their enchanted castle, a magical princess intervenes, at

---

21 Jaroslava Procházková, *Českým mužům: 'Ani my nejsme spokojeny s vámi!'* (Prague: J. Baštář, 1897).
22 Another story by Benešová is translated as 'Friends' in Hayes, *A World Apart* (n. 4 above), 30–50, and two more were published in translation in Geoffrey Chew, *And My Head Exploded: Tales of Desire, Delirium and Decadence from Fin-de-Siècle Prague* (London: Jantar Publishing, 2018). For further details of the dating of the original stories, see Dobrava Moldanová, 'Rané povídky Boženy Benešové', *Česká literatura* 20/2 (1972): 115–30.

last setting their libido free and allowing them to indulge in extreme erotic – but ultimately sterile – fetishism. In this story Viková-Kunětická, unlike other women writers, limits her feminism – but reinforces her position as a politician – by suggesting implicitly that the ideal relationship between the sexes is to be found in marriage.[23]

A ROSE FOR UNCLE: OLDER MEN AND YOUNGER WOMEN, AND THE MARRIAGE MARKET

Another recurrent topos in women's writing is the mismatch between young, nubile women and girls and the older men, often predatory, but in any case with an advantage of power owing to their gender, who show an interest in them. This situation is hinted at in Teréza Nováková's curious semi-comic **'A Kaleidoscope'** (1890), a conversation at a society ball between an evidently middle-aged gentleman and a very young débutante, in which he gives her eye-opening gossip about a number of the dancers present and, implicitly, explains the society she is entering, without revealing what his own interest might be in her, and without allowing her to speak a single word. It is more obviously central to Anna Maria Tilschová's **'A Rose for Uncle'** (1906; not its original title), in which a paedophile 'uncle', a family friend, seduces a girl about ten years of age. This story is cast as a kind of Aesopian fable, with a moral apparently directed entirely at young girls rather than at the men who pose a danger to them. And Helena Malířová offers a light-hearted account of the sexual politics of marriage as viewed by the young daughter of an affluent family and by the two men attracted to her in her **'Three Points of View'** (1908).

23   On this story, see in particular Robert B. Pynsent, 'Neplodní "Staří mládenci" jako výplod feministické ideologie Boženy Vikové Kunětické', *Slovo a smysl / Word & Sense* 1/1 (2004): 66–87. Pynsent foregrounds Viková-Kunětická's political commitment to marriage as an instrument of nation-building.

Class conflict had not been a traditional topic in women's writing, but emerges in those stories in this collection that take as their subject-matter the social problems of the peasantry. (Ethnography was an acceptable occupation for some women, such as Teréza Nováková, who published her findings in scholarly journals after her marriage and her move to Litomyšl.[24]) Some of these stories are, in effect, fictionalized ethnography, and include not merely conflicts between aristocracy and peasantry, but also conflicts within peasant village communities between wealthy tenant peasant farmers (those who held title to their house and land) and poorer 'inmate' peasants (those who resided in titleholders' households). It is largely these conflicts that underlie the griefs and complaints of the characters in Růžena Svobodová's **'Life's Sorrow'**, though the story suggests fatalistically that the griefs are a universal aspect of humanity – an inescapable part of a Nature beyond human control.

The uneasy relationship between wealth and poverty among the peasantry, without reference to the aristocracy on whose lands they lived, is developed more comprehensively in Tilschová's **'A Widow'**. This is the most substantial of the very varied stories in her remarkable collection, In the Mountains (*Na horách*, 1905), which she wrote at Kameničky in the Českomoravská vrchovina, the hilly region between Bohemia and Moravia, when she and her husband were on holiday there in 1904 with the historian Jaroslav Goll and the painter Antonín Slavíček.[25] There were dai-

---

24   See Libuše Heczková, *Píšící Minervy: vybrané kapitoly z dějin české literární kritiky*, Mnemosyne 1 (Prague: Filozofická fakulta Univerzity Karlovy, 2009), 167–8.

25   Another of the stories from Tilschová's In the Mountains is available in English translation as 'A Sad Time' in Hayes, *A World Apart* (n. 4 above), 209–16.

ly discussions about Goll's theories of the persistence of archaic religion and archaic customs among the local peasantry,[26] and she weaves these into her psychological study of the unforgettable Adna, a strong-willed, rich widow of a tenant peasant farmer, her passively hostile relationships with the local inmate peasants, with her ineffectual and illegitimate son Francek, with her teenage orphan servant Lojza, and with her three very imperfect men: Drahoš, her abusive husband; Kaplan Humperský, with whom she has a brief sexual relationship; and the symbolically named Svoboda ('liberty'). In nineteenth-century rural Bohemia, some rich widows of tenant peasant farmers (like Tilschová's Adna, but unlike most other women) were potentially able to enjoy a remarkable degree of freedom and independence.[27]

Admittedly, Tilschová's story may disappoint a modern readership in suggesting finally that an elderly widow, even one as independently minded as Adna, is unlikely to survive in the Czech countryside without a male partner, even one with as lurid a history of criminal violence as Svoboda. This story bears comparison with Anna Lauermannová-Mikschová's **'Solitude'** (1908): its central character is another widow, Teza Uvarová, also living in the countryside. Like Tilschová's Adna, Teza is rich, but unlike Adna, she is mid-

26 See Miroslav Heřman, *Národní umělkyně Anna Maria Tilschová*, Knižnice Národních umělců československých (Prague: Ministerstvo informací, 1949). One of the obscure nineteenth-century survivals of folk myth among heterodox Protestants that is referred to in the text is footnoted in the translation.

27 See, in particular, Alice Velková, 'Women between a New Marriage and an Independent Position: Rural Widows in Bohemia in the First Half of the Nineteenth Century', *The History of the Family* 15/3 (2010): 255–70. Němcová's fictional grandmother supplies no precedent for the widows of these stories, and cannot be placed in the context of real history at all. In the mountain village from which she moves, she is clearly rich enough to be independent, but even if she is a widowed tenant, it is inconceivable that she should be able to leave her 'modest cottage' permanently, at a moment's notice, merely at her daughter's request.

dle-class; she feels herself on the verge of old age at 35, as the menopause approaches. She has reluctantly taken up 'philanthropy' as her only realistic future prospect, and knits for charity, but she receives a proposal of marriage from a longstanding friend, an aristocratic parliamentarian with the ominous name Peklín ('peklo' meaning hell), and he thus offers her an opportunity to escape from her 'philanthropy'. She is fond of Peklín, but puts him to the test by visiting a remote estate of his, a property in the inhospitable mountains. There she sees the fate of the females, human and canine, who, once of use to him, are now cast aside, and particularly that of Fanynka, an orphan girl whom he had fancied as a young man, had provided with an education for his own amusement, to the consternation of his mother, but had later forced into marriage with his boorish farm manager. We do not find out explicitly whether Teza finally rejects marriage with Peklín in favour of her 'philanthropy', nor what the authorial attitude is to the remarriage of widows more generally, but the story ends with her retreating into 'Solitude', her house, and slamming the door.

JEWS, GERMANS, CZECHS, ORIENTALS, AND OTHERS

Society in the nineteenth-century Bohemian lands was not merely patriarchal but also classically colonial, with a dominant group seeking to legitimize its control over other groups defined both racially and linguistically. For those Czechs seeking independence, this was a particular concern as a result of the *Ausgleich* (the so-called Austro-Hungarian Compromise) of 1867, under which a dual monarchy had been established, with a considerable degree of independence for the Hungarians but not for the Czechs. Unsurprisingly, with tension between Germans and Czechs increasing markedly towards the end of the century, much literature by writers of both sexes in all linguistic and racial groups draws on images of the Other, often stereotypical, sometimes Orientalist, and sometimes hostile, in depicting members of other groups.[28] Some Bohemian-German writers, even those like Ebner-Eschenbach who were not essentially hostile to the Czechs, draw on stereotypes that masculinize Germans and feminize Czechs;[29] some Czech writers make a similar construction to distinguish Czechs from Jews.

Anti-Semitism in fiction by Czech women writers has been discussed in recent years by Robert Pynsent and Jitka Malečková;[30] as for the present collection, the Jewish characters in tales by non-Jewish writers may be mentioned in particular. These sometimes draw on stereotypes without ideological implications, as in the incidental Jewish characters (the merchant, and the chancer Kaplan) in Tilschová's **'A Widow'**. The young anonymous Viennese-Jewish woman in Tilschová's later science-fiction tale **'A Remarkable Incident'** (1924) bears closer scrutiny, however: her stereotypical amorality and love of luxurious excess are essential parallels to the 'nothingness' of the Ohnes men in the story. She is very comparable to the Viennese-Jewish capitalist

28 For a particularly thoughtful introduction to this topic, see Ritchie Robertson, 'National Stereotypes in Prague German Fiction', *Colloquia Germanica* 22/2 (1989): 116–36.

29 It does not yet seem possible to judge whether male writers were more liable to do this than female. For an example of a novel where the stereotypes prove damaging, see Robertson, 'National Stereotypes in Prague German Fiction' (n. 28), 118 ('in [his] *Ein tschechisches Dienstmädchen* [Max] Brod inadvertently confuses his pro-Czech message by uncritically adopting stereotypes which by 1909 had been current for so long as to pass for knowledge').

30 Robert B. Pynsent, 'Czech Feminist Anti-Semitism: The Case of Božena Benešová', in *History of the Literary Cultures of East-Central Europe: Junctures and Disjunctures in the 19th and 20th Centuries*, ed. Marcel Cornis-Pope and John Neubauer, 4 (Amsterdam: John Benjamins, 2010), 344–66, and Jitka Malečková, 'Czech Women Writers and Racial Others: (Un)Timely Reflections on the History of Czech Nationalism', *Central Europe* 13/1-2 (2015): 4–18.

Jindřich Frank in Svobodová's unusual tale of late-awakening female sexuality, ' . . . **And Music will be Playing Outside Your Windows Every Day**'. Anča, the heroine of Svobodová's story, is a version of Němcová's Viktorka who, attracted by the dangerous violence of a Czech 'dark huntsman', marries him and tries her best to settle down with him, only to find that the danger was overestimated, and he is frigidly uninterested in sex or romance. She herself has become a Sleeping Beauty, and is awakened to sensuality by her Jewish prince, who is joyfully oversexed and exotically Oriental – and, far from receiving the punishment for this which a reader might expect, she is happy to leave her Czech husband and live in sin with him for ever.[31]

SOME REMARKS IN CONCLUSION

I hope that this selection illustrates some of the great variety of approaches that Czech women's writing displays in the *fin de siècle*, in a period when Czech literature, written by authors of both sexes, was particularly lively. The survival of serious literature in Czech was no longer in question at this period, as it arguably had been earlier in the Czech National Revival, with a substantial reading public now supported by a solid base of publishing houses, and with literary journals prepared to publish challenging material.[32] (Some such journals catered specifically for women.) Fur-

31   The story is one of Svobodová's *The Dark Huntsmen* [*Černí myslivci*], stories loosely linked together in what the author calls a 'mountain novel' [*horský román*]. Svobodová's narrator glosses the 'dark', 'black', of the title by having the huntsmen dressed in black. Another of the stories from this collection, variations on a theme, is translated as 'A Great Passion' in Hayes, ed. and trans., *A World Apart* (n. 4 above), 182–208.
32   'However ferociously the nationalities conflict [sic] in Austria was raging [by the 1890s], writers no longer feared for the future of the literary language': Robert B. Pynsent, 'Czech Women Writers, 1890s–1948', in Celia Hawkesworth, ed., *A History of Central European Women's Writing* (London: Palgrave Macmillan, 2001), 126.

thermore, some women hosted salons in which literature was discussed by both men and women; the principal such salon in Bohemia, and one of the longest-lasting, was hosted by Lauermannová-Mikschová.

Clearly, the present selection invites comparison with the outstanding, and pioneering, anthology of English translations of shorter fiction by Czech women writers edited by Kathleen Hayes and published by Karolinum Press almost a generation ago, and now fortunately available in a second edition.[33] In some respects the two selections are complementary, since there are still a good many texts – and authors – that are unfamiliar but deserve to be unearthed. But in including a couple of German-language stories, I have attempted also to point towards the reassessment of Czech literature that may be imminent in the present climate – in which, one may hope, Czech literature may come also to be imagined in territorial terms as the common inheritance of all the writers who lived and worked in Bohemia and Moravia, rather than merely those who wrote in the Czech language or who were patriotically Czech. Moreover, there has been interest in recent years in exploring 'indifference to nation', the rejection of patriotism or narrow identity politics, as a response to modernism rather than as a symptom of backwardness or insularity, and some texts by both women and men may merit analysis along these lines in the future.[34]

Moreover, the women of this period, whether writing in Czech or in German, seem to share styles and approaches

33   Kathleen Hayes, ed. and trans., *A World Apart* (n. 4 above).

34   A symposium at Edmonton, Alberta, in 2008, examined 'Sites of Indifference to Nation in Habsburg Central Europe', and volume 43 of the *Austrian History Yearbook* contained articles based on material presented there. For an overview see Pieter M. Judson and Tara Zahra, 'Introduction', *Austrian History Yearbook* 43 (2012): 21–7.

that divide them from contemporary male writers.[35] Not only does their social comment often seem more trenchant than that of the men, but they also seem able to spice their writing with both comic and sentimental elements with a degree of humanity, and of subtlety, that escapes their male colleagues. Even as harrowing a story as Ebner-Eschenbach's **'He Kisses Your Hand'** is made more palatable by its comic touches. And the preference for social comment may to some degree explain why some of these women – notably Tilschová and Majerová, of those represented here – later came to be regarded as better models for a literature fit for a socialist society than their Decadent male colleagues.

So I hope that readers may be pleasantly surprised by the wide variety in the body of writing represented by the present collection: these authors had interests that included, but that also went well beyond, themes reflecting the oppression suffered by their gender. But I also hope that readers should not be surprised to know that it has been a great pleasure to seek out these stories – some of them extremely rare survivals – and to translate them.

Geoffrey Chew
Egham, April 2023

---

35 Admittedly, even the most prominent of the male authors of the period, such as Jiří Karásek, Julius Zeyer, and more generally those writing for the influential modernist Czech periodical *Moderní revue*, will probably not be familiar to an English-speaking readership; a selection of fiction written by such authors is offered in Geoffrey Chew, trans., *And My Head Exploded* (n. 22 above).

Abrams, Lynn. *The Making of Modern Woman: Europe 1789-1918*. Edinburgh: Longman, 2002.

Achinger, Christine. 'Allegories of Destruction: "Woman" and "the Jew" in Otto Weininger's Sex and Character'. *The Germanic Review: Literature, Culture, Theory* 88/2 (2013): 121-49.

Boyarin, Daniel. *Unheroic Conduct: The Rise of Heterosexuality and the Invention of the Jewish Man*. Contraversions: Critical Studies in Jewish Literature, Culture, and Society. Berkeley, CA: University of California Press, 1997.

Brown, Hilary, ed. *Landmarks in German Women's Writing*. British and Irish Studies in German Language and Literature 39. Bern, etc: Peter Lang, 2007.

Denisoff, Dennis. 'Feminist Global Decadence'. *Feminist Modernist Studies* 4/2: 'Global Decadence' (2021): 137-45.

Disch, Lisa, and Mary Hawkesworth, eds. *The Oxford Handbook of Feminist Theory*. New York: Oxford University Press, 2015.

Dormer, Lore Muerdel. 'Tribunal der Ironie: Marie von Ebner-Eschenbachs Erzählung "Er lasst die Hand küssen"'. *Modern Austrian Literature* 9/2 (1976): 86-97.

Fábián, Katalin, Janet Elise Johnson, and Mara Irene Lazda, eds. *The Routledge Handbook of Gender in Central-Eastern Europe and Eurasia*. New York: Routledge, 2021.

Freifeld, Alice, Peter Bergmann, and Bernice Glatzer Rosenthal, eds. *East Europe Reads Nietzsche*. East European Monographs 514. Boulder and New York: East European Monographs/Columbia University Press, 1998.

Harriman, Helga H. 'Women Writers and Artists in Fin-de-Siècle Vienna'. *Modern Austrian Literature* 26/1 (1993): 1-17.

Harrowitz, Nancy A., and Barbara Hyams, eds. *Jews and Gender: Responses to Otto Weininger*. Philadelphia, PA: Temple University Press, 1994.

Hawkesworth, Celia, ed. *A History of Central European Women's Writing*. Studies in Russia and East Europe. Basingstoke, London and New York: Palgrave Macmillan in association with

School of Slavonic and East European Studies, University College London, 2001.

Hayes, Kathleen, ed. *A World Apart, and Other Stories: Czech Women Writers at the Fin de Siècle*. Translated by Kathleen Hayes. 2nd edition, Prague: Karolinum Press, Charles University in Prague, 2022.

———. 'Images of the Prostitute in Czech Fin-de-Siècle Literature'. *Slavonic and East European Review* 75/2 (1997): 234–58.

Heczková, Libuše. *Píšící Minervy: vybrané kapitoly z dějin české literární kritiky*. Mnemosyne 1. Prague: Filozofická fakulta Univerzity Karlovy, 2009.

Horská, Pavla. *Naše prababičky feministky*. Knižnice Dějin a současnosti 11. Prague: Lidové noviny, 1999.

Janeček, Petr. 'Eschatologická a profetická motivika ve folkloru českých zemí v 2. polovině 18. a na počátku 19. století: písně o králi marokánovi'. *Český lid* 93/2 (2006): 153–77.

Jusová, Iveta. 'Gabriela Preissová's Women-Centered Texts: Subverting the Myth of the Homogeneous Nation'. *The Slavic and East European Journal* 49/1 (2008): 63–78.

Jusová, Iveta, and Jiřina Šiklová, eds. *Czech Feminisms: Perspectives on Gender in East Central Europe*. Bloomington, IN: Indiana University Press, 2016.

Langer, Gudrun. 'Babička contra Ahnfrau: Božena Němcová's "Babička" als nationalkulturelle Immatrikulation'. *Zeitschrift für Slavische Philologie* 57/1 (1998): 133–69.

———. *Das Märchen in der tschechischen Literatur von 1790 bis 1860: Studien zur Entwicklungsgeschichte des Märchens als literarischer Gattung*. Frankfurter Abhandlungen zur Slavistik 28. Giessen: Wilhelm Schmitz Verlag, 1979.

Lantová, Ludmila. 'Cesta Marie Majerové k velkému sociálnímu románu (Studie k monografické kapitole Dějin ceské literatury)'. *Česká literatura* 7/3 (August 1959): 249–78.

Ledger, Sally. *The New Woman: Fiction and Feminism at the Fin de Siècle*. Manchester: Manchester University Press, 1997.

Luft, David S. *Eros and Inwardness in Vienna: Weininger, Musil, Doderer*. Chicago, IL: University of Chicago Press, 2003.

Malečková, Jitka. 'Czech Women Writers and Racial Others: (Un) Timely Reflections on the History of Czech Nationalism'. *Central Europe* 13/1–2 (2015): 4–18.

———. 'Nationalizing Women and Engendering the Nation: The Czech National Movement'. In *Gendered Nations: Nationalism and Gender Order in the Long Nineteenth Century*, edited by L. Blom, K. Hagemann, and C. Hall. Oxford and New York: Berg, 2000.

Málek, Petr. 'Babička Boženy Němcové, od idyly k elegii: k některým aspektům adaptace klasické literatury'. *Česká literatura* 61 (2013): 183–217.

Maxwell, Alexander. 'Nationalizing Sexuality: Sexual Stereotypes in the Habsburg Empire'. *Journal of the History of Sexuality* 14/3 (1 July 2005): 266–90.

Moldanová, Dobrava. 'Rané povídky Boženy Benešové'. *Česká literatura* 20/2 (1972): 115–30.

Nejtková, Tereza. 'Růžena Jesenská: Mimo svět – ediční příprava a komentář k souboru povídek'. Dissertation, Charles University, Prague, 2017.

Neudorflová, Marie L. *České ženy v 19. století: úsilí a sny, úspěchy i zklamání na cestě k emancipaci*. Prague: Janua, 1999.

Oates-Indruchová, Libora. 'Unraveling a Tradition, or Spinning a Myth? Gender Critique in Czech Society and Culture'. *Slavic Review* 75/4 (Winter 2016): 919–43.

Pachmanová, Martina. *Neznámá území českého moderního umění: Pod lupou genderu*. Prague: Argo, 2004.

Pallasvuo, Katri Ilona. 'The Formation of the Female Self in Czech Literature, 1890–1945'. M.Phil in Czech Literature, University College London, School of Slavonic and East European Studies, 2013.

Parker, Sarah. 'The New Woman and Decadent Gender Politics'. In *Decadence: A Literary History*, edited by Alex Murray, 118–35. Cambridge: Cambridge University Press, 2020.

Patton, Paul, ed. *Nietzsche, Feminism and Political Theory*. New York: Routledge, 1993.

Putna, Martin C., ed. *Homosexualita v dějinách českého umění*. Prague: Academia, 2011.

Pynsent, Robert B. 'Czech Feminist Anti-Semitism: The Case of Božena Benešová'. In *History of the Literary Cultures of East-Central Europe: Junctures and Disjunctures in the 19th and 20th Centuries*, edited by Marcel Cornis-Pope and John Neubauer, 4 (Types and Stereotypes): 344–66. Amsterdam: John Benjamins, 2010.

———. 'Czech Women Writers, 1890s-1948'. In *A History of Central European Women's Writing*, edited by Celia Hawkesworth, 126–49. London: Palgrave Macmillan, 2001.

———. *Ďáblové, ženy a národ: Výbor z úvah o české literatuře*. Prague: Karolinum, 2008.

———. 'Neplodní "Staří mládenci" jako výplod feministické ideologie Boženy Vikové Kunětické'. *Slovo a smysl / Word & sense* 1/1 (2004): 66–87.

———. 'Obchod a smyslnost: české spisovatelky a židé okolo přelomu století'. *Sborník prací Filozofické fakulty Brněnské univerzity, studia minora / Facultatis philosophicae Universitatis Brunensis* D43 (1996): 23–39.

Robertson, Ritchie. 'National Stereotypes in Prague German Fiction'. *Colloquia Germanica* 22/2 (1989): 116–36.

Schorske, Carl E. *Fin-de-Siècle Vienna: Politics and Culture*. New York: Alfred A. Knopf, 1980.

Schwartz, Agatha. 'Sexual Cripples and Moral Degenerates: Fin-de-Siècle Austrian Women Writers on Male Sexuality and Masculinity'. *Seminar: A Journal of Germanic Studies* 44/1 (February 2008): 53–67.

———. *Shifting Voices: Feminist Thought and Women's Writing in Fin-de-Siècle Austria and Hungary*. Montréal and Kingston, ON: McGill-Queen's University Press, 2007.

———. 'The Crisis of the Female Self in "Fin de Siècle" Austrian Women Writers' Narratives'. *Modern Austrian Literature* 40/3 (2007): 1–19.

Schwartz, Agatha, and Helga H. Thorson. *Shaking the Empire, Shaking Patriarchy: The Growth of a Feminist Consciousness across the Austro-Hungarian Monarchy*. Studies in Austrian Literature, Culture and Thought. Riverside, CA: Ariadne Press, 2014.

– – –. 'The Aesthetics of Change: Women Writers of the Austro-Hungarian Monarchy'. In *Crossing Central Europe: Continuities and Transformations, 1900 and 2000*, edited by Carrie Smith-Prei and Helga Mitterbauer, 27–49. Toronto: Toronto University Press, 2017.

Showalter, Elaine, ed. *Daughters of Decadence: Stories by Women Writers of the Fin-de-Siècle*. Virago Press, 1993.

– – –. *Sexual Anarchy: Gender and Culture at the Fin de Siècle*. London: Bloomsbury Publishing, 1991.

Vocílková, Petra. 'Černí myslivci Růženy Svobodové'. Dissertation, Masarykova univerzita, Brno, 2016.

Warner, Marina. *From the Beast to the Blonde: On Fairy Tales and Their Tellers*. London: Chatto & Windus, 1994.

– – –. *Once upon a Time: A Short History of Fairy Tale*. Oxford: Oxford University Press, 2014.

Wingfield, Nancy M. *The World of Prostitution in Late Imperial Austria*. Oxford: Oxford University Press, 2017.

Woodford, Charlotte. 'Suffering and Domesticity: The Subversion of Sentimentalism in Three Stories by Marie von Ebner-Eschenbach'. *German Life and Letters* 59/1 (2006): 47–61.

Worley, Linda Kraus. 'Telling Stories/Telling Histories: Marie von Ebner-Eschenbachs "Er lasst die Hand küssen."' In *Neues zu Altem*, edited by Sabine Cramer, 43–56. Munich: Fink, 1996.

Zirin, Mary, Irina Livezeanu, Christine D. Worobec, and June Pachuta Farris, eds. *Women and Gender in Central and Eastern Europe, Russia, and Eurasia: A Comprehensive Bibliography*. Vol. 1: Southeastern and East Central Europe. Armonk, NY: M. E. Sharpe, 2007

MARIE VON EBNER-ESCHENBACH

'So, in the name of God,' said the countess, 'have your say! I shall listen to you, but I shall not believe a single word.'

The count leant back comfortably in his large armchair. 'And why not?' he asked.

She shrugged briefly. 'Probably you are not inventive enough to be convincing.'

'I am not inventing at all – I am remembering! Memory is my leisure activity.'

'What a one-sided, servile leisure that is! You remember only the things that suit you. And yet there are many interesting, beautiful things on earth besides – nihilism.' She had lifted her crochet hook, and fired off the final word like a rifle shot at her old admirer.

He took it without flinching, stroked his white beard easily, and regarded the countess from his shrewd eyes almost with gratitude. 'I wanted to tell you something about my grandmother,' he said. 'It occurred to me in the middle of the forest while I was on my way here.'

The countess bent down over her work and murmured, 'It will be a story about robbers.'

'Oh, nothing less! And as peaceable as the creature that stirred the memory in me when I saw him – namely, Myška IV, a great-grandson of the Myška I who gave my grandmother cause for a little hastiness that she seems later to have regretted,' said the count with slightly affected carelessness, and he then quickly continued, 'A careful gamekeeper, my Myška – one must grant him that! But he was not a little frightened when I stepped unexpectedly into his path – and I had already been watching him for a while. He was crawling around like a beetle collector, his eyes fixed on the ground, and what do you think he had stuck in the barrel of his rifle? Imagine! It was a bunch of strawberries!'

'Very sweet!' replied the countess. 'Get yourself ready – soon you will be meandering over the steppes to me, because you'll have been deprived of the forest.'

'At least Myška isn't preventing that.'

'And you're making sure of that?'

'And I'm making sure of that. Oh yes, it's terrible. That weakness is in my blood – inherited from my ancestors.' He sighed ironically and cast a sidelong glance at the countess, with a degree of malice.

She suppressed her impatience, forced herself to smile, and attempted to give her voice as indifferent a tone as possible, saying, 'How about having another cup of tea and leaving the shades of your ancestors unsworn for once? There is something else I should be discussing with you before I leave.'

'Your lawsuit with the municipality? – You are going to win that.'

'Because I am in the right.'

'Because you are completely in the right.'

'Make the peasants understand that. Advise them to withdraw the lawsuit.'

'They won't do that.'

'They would rather bleed to death and give the lawyer their last penny. And, good God, what a lawyer he is . . . a ruthless sophist. They believe him and not me, and I think they don't believe you either, in spite of all your seeking after popularity.'

The countess drew herself up and took a deep breath. 'Confess that it would be better for these people, who are so stupid both in trusting and in mistrusting, if they were prevented from choosing their own advisers freely.'

'Naturally it would be better! They should have an appointed counsellor, and their trust in him should also be appointed.'

'What idiocy!' said the countess, angrily.

'Why? Perhaps you mean that trust cannot emerge to order? . . . I tell you, if I had ordered a servant of mine to receive a dozen lashes forty years ago, and had then told him to go to the officials to receive them, it would never have occurred to him, even in a drunken stupor, that he could do anything better than follow my instructions.'

'Ah, your old line! – And I had hoped that for once I could engage you in a rational conversation!'

The old gentleman took some pleasure in her annoyance for a while, and then said, 'Forgive me, dear friend. I confess I was teasing you with nonsense. No, trust cannot emerge to order, but obedience without trust unfortunately can. That was the misfortune of poor Myška, and of so many others, and it is for that reason that people insist nowadays in being miserable, at least in their own way.'

The countess raised her eyes, as dark as the night and still beautiful, to heaven, before lowering them over her work once more, and saying, with a sigh of resignation, 'Tell me the story of Myška, then.'

'I shall keep it as short as possible,' said the count, 'and begin at the moment when my grandmother first took notice of him. He must have been a handsome lad; I recall a picture of him that was painted by an artist who was staying in the castle once. To my regret, I did not find it in my father's estate, and yet I know that he kept it for a long time as a memento of the times in which we were still exercising the *jus gladii*, the right to impose the death penalty.'

'O God,' the countess interrupted him, 'does the *jus gladii* play a part in your story?'

The narrator made a gesture of courteous protest, and continued, 'It happened at a harvest celebration, and Myška was one of those bearing wreaths. He offered his up in silence, but without lowering his eyes; in fact he looked the noble lady in the eye, seriously and at ease, while an overseer was reciting the usual speech on behalf of the field labourers.

'My grandmother inquired about the lad, and was told that he was the son of a cottager, twenty years old, quite well-behaved, quite industrious, and so quiet that he had been thought dumb as a child, and was still considered stupid. – Why? the noble lady asked; why was he thought stupid? . . . The village elders lowered their heads, cast furtive glances at one another, and could not be induced to say more than "Yes, well, so it is," and "After all, that's how things are."

'Now my grandmother had a valet – a real pearl of humanity. Whenever he spoke to the nobility, his face was so transfigured with joy that it virtually shone. The next day, my grandmother sent him to Myška's parents with a message telling them that their son was being promoted from field labourer to garden labourer, and that he should begin his new work the following day.

'This most eager of all servants flew back and forth and was soon standing once more before his mistress. "Now then," she asked him –, "what did the old people say?" The valet extended his right leg, which was turned outwards, far forwards . . .'

'Were you present on that occasion?' – the countess interrupted her guest.

'Not precisely then, but on other occasions when the good Fritz was present,' replied the count, without being put off his stride. 'He pushed his leg forward, sank right down in reverent submission, and told her that Myška's parents were drowning in tears of gratitude.

'"And what about Myška himself?"

'"Oh, him" – came the submissive reply, and now his left leg swung forward gracefully – "oh, him – he kisses your hand!"

'Fritz omitted to mention the fact that it had taken a severe beating from his father to put the idea of hand-kissing into the mind of the boy. An explanation of the grounds for Myška's preference for work in the open fields over that in the garden would not have been decent for a lady to hear. – Enough of that. – Myška took up his new duties and fulfilled them moderately well. – The gardener remarked, "It wouldn't hurt if he were to work harder." My grandmother made the same observation from the balcony once, when she was watching the meadow in front of the castle being mown. She also noticed particularly that, while all the other mowers were taking sips from time to time from flasks they drew out from under piles of clothes and then replaced there, Myška was the only one to spurn this source of refreshment and to take his from an earthenware jug left in the shade of the bushes. My grandmother called the valet. "What do the mowers have in their flasks?" she asked. – "Brandy, your ladyship." – "And what does Myška have in his jug?"

'Fritz rolled his bulbous eyes, tilted his head to one side, exactly like our old parrot, who resembled him like a second pea in a pod, and replied in a tender voice, "Dear God, your ladyship – it is water!"

'My grandmother was instantly seized by a fit of compassion, and gave orders that all the garden labourers should be given brandy at the close of the day's work. "Myška must have it too," she expressly added.

'This order was greeted with jubilation. The fact that Myška refused ever to drink brandy was one of the reasons why he was thought stupid. Now, of course, once the Countess's invitation had been extended to him, there was no further question of personal preference. When in his innocence he tried to defend himself, he was taught manners, to the great amusement of young and old. Some of them dragged him down to the ground, a sturdy lad pushed a wedge between his teeth, which were clenched in fury, and another held him with his knee against his chest, and continued to pour brandy into him until his face had become so red, and its expression so dreadful, that even his enthusiastic tormentors were horror-struck. They gave him a little air, and immediately he shook them off with a furious effort, leapt up and clenched his fists . . . but suddenly his arms dropped, he staggered, and he fell to the ground. There he swore and groaned, attempted several times vainly to pull himself together, finally fell asleep on the spot where he had fallen, in front of the barn in the courtyard, and slept until the next morning. When he was wakened by the rising sun shining on his nose, the servant who had administered the brandy to him the previous day happened to be passing. He was about to take to his heels, expecting nothing less than revenge from Myška for the previous day's abuse. Instead, the lad stretched, gazed at him dreamily, and slurred, "One more sip!"

'His hatred of brandy had been overcome.

'Soon after that, my grandmother happened to be on a Sunday afternoon drive, and, tempted by a pretty country lane, alighted, and during her walk became the witness of an idyllic scene. She spied Myška sitting under an apple tree at the edge of a field, with a baby in his arms. Like him, the child had a head of dark brown curls, but its sturdy little body was light brown in colour, and the threadbare little shirt that barely covered it was halfway between these two shades. The little urchin was positively crowing with delight each time Myška lifted it up, kicking his breast with its little feet, and trying to poke him in the eye with its outstretched forefinger. And Myška was laughing, apparently just as entertained as the child was. A young girl was watching the goings-on of the two; she was also a brown creature, and as delicate and dainty as if she had been cradled by the Ganges. Over her short patched skirt she was wearing an

(41)

apron, also patched, with a small collection of ears of corn in it. Now she broke one of these off its stalk, crept up to Myška, and let the ear slide down his neck under his shirt, next to his skin. He shook himself, set the child down on the ground, and ran after the girl, who escaped lightly and swiftly, and as deftly as if in ballet; now as straight as an arrow, now circling around a rick of sheaves, full of fearfulness and yet also teasing, and at every moment extremely graceful. It is true that a certain inborn grace is not rare among our country folk, but these two young creatures offered so diverting a spectacle in their innocent merriment that my grandmother enjoyed it with genuine pleasure. Her appearance, however, made a different impression on Myška and the girl. Both stood as if petrified at the sight of the lady of the manor. He, the first to react, bowed almost to the ground; she lowered her apron, together with the ears of corn, and hid her face in her hands.

'At supper, which (like every meal) was attended by the *Hofstaat*, comprising a few poor relations and the head officials of the court, my grandmother said to the head manager, who was sitting next to her, "The sister of Myška, the new garden labourer, seems to me to be a nice, nimble little girl, and I would like a post to be assigned to her so that she can earn a crust." The manager replied, "At your command, immediately, your ladyship . . . although to my knowledge Myška does not in fact have a sister at all."

'"To your knowledge!" responded my grandmother. "That is something else, your knowledge! . . . Myška has a sister and also a little brother. I saw all three of them out in the country today."

'"Hm, hm," came the respectful reply, and the manager held his napkin in front of his mouth to muffle the tone of his voice. "It will have been – I beg your ladyship's pardon for the indecent expression – Myška's mistress, and, to say so with all respect, her child."'

The reluctant listener to this narrative was finding it more and more difficult to restrain herself, and now she exclaimed, 'You are claiming that you were not present when these remarkable utterances were exchanged? How then can you report, not merely on every word, but also on every facial expression and gesture?'

'I knew most of the people involved, and I know – something of a painter, something of a poet, as I admittedly am – I know to perfection how they must have behaved and expressed themselves in a certain situation. Believe me, as a true reporter, that my grandmother felt a surge of anger and contempt for humankind after the manager had imparted that information to her. From what you have heard so far, you can be in no doubt that she was good and caring for her subjects. In the matter of morals, however, she maintained the utmost strictness, towards herself no less than towards others. She had frequently found that she was unable to control corrupt morals in grown men and women, but corrupt morals in adolescent creatures had to be restrained. – My grandmother again sent her valet to Myška's parents. An end must be put to the lad's love affair. That was a disgrace for a boy like that, she said; such a lad should have other things occupying his mind.

'Myška was at home when the message came. The shame penetrated under his skin . . .'

'But it is rather rich that you are now claiming to have got under Myška's skin!' scoffed the countess.

'Up to my ears!' replied the count. 'I am under it more than up to my ears! I feel as though the consternation and shame that seized him was my own. I can see him writhing in fear and embarrassment, casting a nervous glance at his father and his mother, who were also at a loss to know which way to turn in their terror. I can hear the pitiful sound of his laugh at the words of his father, "Be merciful, sir! He will break it off, of course he will, he will break it off immediately!"

'This promise satisfied the worthy Fritz. He returned to the castle, reporting with satisfaction on the successful accomplishment of his mission, with his usual genuflections and with the usual expression of joyful humility in his avian physiognomy, "He kisses your hand: he is going to put an end to it."'

'Ridiculous!' said the countess.

'Completely ridiculous!' agreed the count. 'My good, credulous grandmother regarded the matter as settled with that, and gave no further thought to it. She was much occupied with the preparations for the great festival that was celebrated in the castle each year on 10 September, her birthday, and was preceded and followed by smaller festivities. The entire neighbourhood was in attendance, and a joyful succession took place of al fresco lunches on the green carpet of the meadow, hunts, drives in the park grounds, suppers with the most beautiful outdoor illuminations, balls – and so forth . . . One has to admit that the older generation knew how to cut a figure and make themselves heard in the world. God knows, our present-day life in the castle would have seemed tedious and barren to them.'

'True, they were great lords,' replied the countess bitterly. 'We are fathers of paupers, retired into the country.'

'And – mothers of paupers,' added the count, with a gallant bow, which was not received very graciously by the one to whom it was addressed. The count, however, did not take the displeasure he had aroused to heart in any way, but resumed the thread of his story with lively pleasure in the narrative.

'As numerous as the retinue of servants in the castle was, it was not enough for the duration of the festivities, and people from the village always had to be enlisted to supplement it. How it happened that Myška's mistress was among them on this particular occasion I don't know, but, enough, that was the case, and the two who should have been avoiding one another were brought together more often than had occurred when they were working together in the fields. If he were entrusted with an errand, he would be going from the garden into the kitchen, or she would be going from the kitchen into the garden – they would often meet each other on the way and linger chatting for a quarter of an hour . . .'

'Extremely interesting!' mocked the countess – 'if only one could know what they were saying to one another.'

'Ah, how curious you have now become! – but I shall disclose only what is essential to my story. – One morning, the lady of the castle was strolling in the garden with her guests. By chance the company directed its steps to a leafy pathway they had seldom taken, and they noticed a young couple at its end coming from different directions and pausing as if in joyful surprise. The boy, no other than Myška, quickly took the girl in his arms and kissed her, and she accepted this without demur. Roars of laughter broke out – from the gentlemen, and, I fear, also from some of the ladies, whom chance had made witnesses of this little scene. But my grandmother took no part in the general merriment. Myška and his mistress of course fled. I was told –' said the count, jokingly anticipating an objection from the countess, '– that the lad said he hated his poor girl at that moment. But that same evening he was of the opposite opinion, when he discovered that the little girl was being sent off with her child to another estate owned by the countess; it was two day's journey for a man, and for a woman who had additionally to take an eighteen-month-old child with her, at least twice as much. – Myška could say nothing but "O God! O God! O dear God!", and he wandered around as if in a dream, not understanding what was required of him when it was time to go to work – he flung the rake which a servant had given him (together with an awakening kick in the ribs) on to the ground, and ran off into the village, to the cottage in which his mistress lived with her sick mother – or rather, had lived, for that was now over. The little girl was standing, ready to leave, beside the old woman, who was entirely crippled, unable even to lay her hand on the girl's head in farewell benediction, and weeping bitterly. "Stop weeping now," said her daughter, "stop, dear mama. Who will be wiping away your tears when I have left?"

'She dried her mother's cheeks, and then her own, with her apron, took her child by the hand, placed a bundle with her few belongings on her back, and went on her way past Myška, not even daring to look at him. He followed her at a distance, however, and when the servant charged with ensuring that she had started properly on her journey left her on the road beyond the village, Myška was soon at her side, took the bundle from her, picked up the child in his arms, and walked along beside her.

'The field labourers who were nearby were amazed. – "What is that idiot doing? . . . Is he really going with her? Is he stupid enough to imagine that he can simply go away with her?"

'Soon after that, Myška's father came running, gasping and shouting, "O all the saints! Mother of God! I thought as much – he's going after his whore and bringing misfortune on all of us . . . Myška! Son – my boy! . . . Ne'er-do-well! Devil's spawn!" – he was alternately wailing and cursing.

'When Myška heard his father's voice and saw him approaching nearer and nearer, brandishing a stick threateningly, he took to his heels, to the intense joy of the small boy, who screamed, "Run! Run!". Soon, however, he realized that he had left his companion in the lurch, as she was unable to follow him so quickly, and he turned and came back to her. She had already been reached by his father, and knocked to the ground. The furious man was raging madly, attacking her with his feet and with the stick, and venting all his anger at his son on the defenceless creature.

'Myška flung himself upon his father, and a dreadful struggle began between the two, which ended with the complete defeat of the weaker – the younger man. Beaten black and blue, bleeding from a wound to his forehead, he gave up all resistance. The cottager took him by the collar and dragged him off, shouting, "Be off with you!" at the poor little woman, who had meanwhile been struggling to get up.

'Without a word, she obeyed him, and even the labourers in the fields, dull, indifferent folk as they were, felt sympathy with her, and watched her for a long time as she staggered away with her child, so in need of help, and so utterly forsaken.

'Near the castle Myška and his father met the gardener, who was immediately addressed as "esteemed sir" by his father, with the tearful request to have patience with his son for just one hour. Myška would certainly be back at work in an hour, but now he must go home quickly and get washed – and wash his shirt too. The gardener asked, "What is wrong with him? He is all bloody." – "Nothing is wrong with him," came the answer. "He has only fallen off a ladder."

'Myška kept the promise his father had made on his behalf, and was back at work an hour later. In the evening, however, he went to the inn and drank himself dead drunk – his first voluntary intoxication; after that day he was a changed man. He did not exchange a single word with his father, who would have liked to be reconciled with him, for after Myška had been given employment in the castle garden, he had become a capital investment that bore interest; and from the money he earned, he did not bring a single penny home. His money was spent partly on brandy and partly on the support that Myška provided to his mistress's mother – and the cottager thought the latter use to which the lad put his earnings the worst crime his son could possibly commit against him. That the poor devil, who had poor parents, should be giving something away to a stranger –

this thought became the old man's nightmare, his undying worm. The angrier the father became, the more obdurately the son behaved. Eventually he did not come home at all, or at most once in secret, when he was obliged to push his father out in order to see his mother, to whom he was very attached. This mother of his . . .' the count paused a moment – 'You, dear friend, know her as well as I do.'

'Am I supposed to know her? . . . Is she still alive?' asked the countess, incredulously.

'She is alive – not in her original form, admittedly, but in many copies. The tiny, weak little woman, always quivering, with the gentle, prematurely aged face, with the motions of a beaten dog, who subsides in the greatest humility and attempts a smile when a great lady like you or a good-hearted gentleman like me addresses her with "How are you?", and replies kindly, in the utmost humility, "May God reward you – as well as can be expected." – Good enough for the likes of us, she means, for a beast of burden in human form. What else could one wish for, and if one wished for it, who would give it? – Not you, noble lady, and not you, kind gentleman . . .'

'Go on, go on!' said the countess. 'Will your story soon be over?'

'Soon. – Myška's father came unexpectedly on one occasion to his cottage and found his son there. "So you are able to visit your mother, but not me," he shouted, calling both of them traitors and conspirators, and he began to maltreat Myška, which the latter accepted without demur. But when the cottager also began beating his wife, the lad began preventing him from doing so. Strangely enough – why only then? If he had been asked how often he saw his father beating his mother, he would have had to answer, "The number of years I remember it happening, multiplied by three hundred and sixty-five." – And for all that time he had remained silent, and today, at the long familiar sight, an overwhelming anger had suddenly erupted in him. For the second time he was siding against his father on behalf of the weaker sex, and this time he was victorious. He seems to have felt more horror than joy at his triumph, however. With a violent sob he called out to his father, who now wished to submit, and called out to his weeping mother, "Farewell, you will never see me again!", and stormed out. For two weeks his parents hoped vainly for his return, but he had finally vanished. The news of his abscondment reached the castle: my grandmother was informed that Myška had beaten his father half to death and then made off. Now after his contravention of the Sixth Commandment, it was his failure to observe the Fourth Commandment that was condemned the more severely by my grandmother; she showed no leniency to bad, ungrateful children ... She gave orders that a search be mounted to find Myška and to bring him back to suffer exemplary punishment.

'The sun had risen and set a couple of times, and Fritz was standing one morning at the garden gate, looking out into the highway. A soft, warm wind was blowing over the fields of stubble, and the atmosphere was filled with a fine dust irradiated and turned into a golden shimmer by the all-enlightening sun. Its rays produced charming little milky paths in the labile element, in which billions of tiny stars were twinkling. And now a heavy, grey column of cloud approached through the glittering, dancing mass of atoms, moving ever closer and finally rolling so close to the gate that Fritz was able clearly to distinguish who it was that the cloud was enveloping. It was two heyducks and Myška. He looked as pale and hollow-eyed as death, and was staggering as he walked. In his arms he was carrying his child, which was asleep with its little hands wrapped around his neck and its head laid on his shoulder. Fritz opened the gate, joined the small party, made a few rapid enquiries, and then floated into the house, a parrot flying in the guise of a dove, up the stairs and into the hall in which my grandmother was just then holding her Saturday council meeting. The valet, transported with the joyful sensation that the souls of servants customarily feel when they are imparting the latest news, spread out his arms expressively and spoke, almost bursting with ecstasy, "Myška kisses your hand. He is back."

"'Where has he been?" asked my grandmother.

"'My God, your ladyship" – lisped Franz, touching the roof of his mouth with his tongue several times in quick succession, and gazing at his mistress as tenderly as his deepest, most obsequious servility had ever allowed him. "Where would he have been . . . With his mistress. Indeed," he reiterated, while the noble lady frowned, indignant at this insolent disobedience, "indeed, and he resisted the heyducks, and nearly knocked one of Jankó's eyes out."

'My grandmother expostulated, "I am really inclined to have him hanged."

'All the officials bowed in silence, but the head forester, after some hesitation, ventured the assertion, "But your ladyship will not be doing that."

"'How do you know that?" asked my grandmother, putting on the stern noblewoman's countenance that is so outstandingly reproduced in her portrait, and which makes me shudder when I pass it in our picture gallery. "The fact that I have never hitherto exercised my right to impose capital punishment does not guarantee that I shall never impose it."

'All the officials bowed once more, and there was silence again, broken by the inspector requesting the mistress's decision on a matter of importance. Only after the close of the conference did he enquire, and in private, about her high order concerning Myška.

'And now my grandmother committed the over-hasty act of which I spoke at the outset.

'"A flogging of fifty lashes," was her swiftly formulated sentence. "And to be carried out today, for it is Saturday in any case."

'Saturdays were in fact at that time, which you' – the count laid particular, very mischievous, emphasis on the word – 'cannot possibly remember, the days on which executions took place. They used to set up the bench in front of the court room . . .'

'Go on, go on!' said the countess. 'Leave out unnecessary details.'

'Back to work, then! – On that same Saturday the last of the guests were due to leave, and there was a great deal of activity in the castle. My grandmother, busy preparing a farewell surprise for the departing guests, was late in getting herself ready for dinner, and urged her chambermaids to make haste. At this most inopportune moment, the doctor had himself announced. Of all the mistress's officials he was the one who stood least in her favour, and deserved no better, for a more tedious, ponderous pedant never existed.

'My grandmother gave orders that he was to be turned away, but he did not comply, but made a second attempt, most humbly requesting that the noble lady should grant him an audience, as he had only a few words to say about Myška.

'"What more are they asking for with him?" cried the mistress. "Leave me alone – I have other things to concern me."

'The insistent doctor departed, grumbling.

'The concerns of which my grandmother spoke, however, were not frivolous ones, but among the most painful of concerns – concerns, for which you, dear friend, admittedly lack understanding and therefore also lack sympathy – the concerns of a poet.'

'My God!' said the countess in indescribable contempt, and the narrator countered:

'You may despise it all you like, but my grandmother had poetic talent, and this was clearly manifested in the pastoral *Les adieux de Chloë*, which she wrote, and herself rehearsed with the performers. The piece was to be performed after the meal, which was held al fresco, and though she was fairly certain that it would be a success, she was experiencing an unpleasant uneasiness as the decisive moment approached. At the dessert, after a solemn toast to the lady of the house, she gave a signal. The walls, covered with foliage, which had been concealing the view of a semicircle formed by trimmed beech hedges, rolled apart, revealing an improvised stage. The dwelling of the shepherdess Chloë could be seen: the mossy bank bestrewn with rose petals on which she slept, the house altar covered with tragacanth at which she prayed, and the robe secured with a pink ribbon on which she spun the snow-white wool of her little lambs. As a shepherdess in an idyll, Chloë possessed the secret of this art. Now she herself appeared from an avenue of yew, and after her came her retinue, including her lover, the shepherd Myrtillus. All the characters were bearing flowers, and in immaculate alexandrines the sweet Chloë informed the attentive audience that these were the flowers of remembrance, plucked on the meadow of loyalty, and destined to be offered on the altar of friendship. Immediately after this revelation, unrestrained applause broke out in the audience, growing louder at each line. Some of the ladies who knew Racine declared that he would have hidden his head in shame before my grandmother, and some of the gentlemen who did not know him confirmed their opinion. She could have been in no doubt, however, about the enthusiasm that had been aroused by her poetry. The ovations were still continuing as the noble company were entering their carriages or mounting their horses, and rolling or rushing out of the castle gates, some with ceremonial retinues, some in light vehicles, some on nimble steeds.

'The mistress was standing under the main portal of the castle, waving her farewells in gratitude for their applause. She was in a tranquil, cheerful mood such as is seldom enjoyed by an autocrat, even one of the smallest realm. Then, just as she was intending to return into the house, she noticed a little old woman kneeling at a respectful distance in front of the steps of the portal. She had seized the favourable moment, and had slipped in unnoticed through the open gate in the tumult and confusion. Now she was seen by some of the lackeys, and with the good Fritz at their head, they rushed towards the old woman to drag her away roughly. To the astonishment of everyone, however, my grandmother waved the servile crowd away, ordering that the old woman be asked who she was and what she wanted. At the same moment, there was the sound of a throat being cleared and a cough behind the mistress, and the good doctor approached thoughtfully, holding his broad-brimmed hat in one hand and concealing his tin of tobacco in his bosom with the other. "She is, hm, hm, your ladyship will pardon me," he said, "she is Myška's mother."

'"What, Myška again? Are we never to hear the end of Myška? . . . And what does the old woman want?"

'"What does she want, your ladyship? She wants to plead for him, nothing beyond that."

'"To plead for what? There is nothing to plead for."

'"Of course not. I told her that in any case, but what is the use? She is still wanting to plead, hm, hm."

'"Tell her that it is all in vain. Am I not to be able to leave the house without seeing the garden labourers embracing their mistresses?"

'The doctor cleared his throat, and my grandmother continued, "And he beat his father half to death."

'"Hm, hm, in fact he did not do anything to him, and did not even wish to do anything to him, but wished merely to prevent him from beating his mother to death entirely."

'"Is that so?"

'"Yes, your ladyship. His father, your ladyship, is a vile animal, with a grudge against Myška because he often provides the mother of his mistress with a few pennies."

'"Provides whom?"

'"The mother of his mistress, your ladyship, a woman who is unable to earn a living, from whom her means of subsistence have been cut off, so to say . . . in that her daughter has been sent away."

'"All right, all right! . . . Spare me people's domestic affairs, doctor, I do not involve myself in them."

'The doctor tucked his hat under his arm, drew out his handkerchief, and discreetly blew his nose. "So I shall tell the old woman that it is nothing." He made a mock stage exit, what the French call *une fausse sortie*, adding, "Of course, your ladyship, if it were only on account of his father . . ."

'"It is not only on account of his father. He has also knocked one of Jankó's eyes out."

'The doctor assumed a solemn expression, raised his eyebrows so high that his thick forehead was bulging out, and said, "As far as that eye is concerned, it remains intact, and will continue to provide Jankó with good service once the bruise that he sustained with the blow he received has subsided. I would in fact have been surprised if Myška had been able physically to deliver a powerful blow after the treatment he received from the heyducks. The heyducks, your ladyship, did him a great deal of harm."

'"That was his fault. Why did he not simply accompany them?"

'"Of course, of course, why did he not? Probably because they were forcing him to leave his mistress's deathbed – that is why he was very unwilling to depart . . . The girl, hm, hm, was in a bad way; she is said to have been severely beaten by Myška's father before she set out on her journey.

And then – the journey was a long one, and the girl, hm, hm, was never strong . . . it is no wonder that she collapsed at her destination."

'My grandmother listened to every word of these disjointed sentences, although she did her best to give the impression that she was paying only cursory attention to them. "A remarkable chain of misadventures," she said. "Perhaps it was an act of God."

'"Well, well," nodded the doctor, and although his face retained its expression of equanimity, it had gradually turned crimson. "Well, well, an act of God, and if God has already intervened, your ladyship may wish to leave the rest of the matter to him too . . . I am only joking!" he interposed, in excuse for the presumptuousness of his conclusion – "and graciously grant this beggar", carelessly pointing at Myška's mother, "her indigent request."

'The old woman, still kneeling, had attempted to follow the conversation, but had not uttered a word. Her teeth were chattering in fear, and she sank closer and closer to the ground.

'"What does she actually want?" asked my grandmother.

'"Postponement of the punishment imposed on her son, your ladyship, for eight days, is what she is asking, and I too, your ladyship, support her request; if it is granted, justice will be better served than it can be today."

'"Why?"

'"Because the guilty man would hardly be able to endure the full execution of his sentence in his present condition."

'My grandmother made an unwilling gesture and slowly began to descend the steps of the portal. Fritz sprang to her side, wishing to give her his arm. She waved him away, however. "Go to your office," she ordered. "Myška is pardoned."

'"Ah!" sighed the faithful servant in wonder, and hurried away, while the doctor thoughtfully drew his watch out of his pocket and quietly muttered to himself, "Hm, hm, there will still be time; the execution of the sentence will just have begun."

'The word "pardoned" had been understood by the old woman. A whimper of delighted emotion escaped from her lips, and she fell down as the noblewoman approached, pressing her face to the ground as if she were trying literally to level herself to the earth before such grandeur and majesty.

'My grandmother's gaze turned with a certain reserve towards this image of embodied humility. "Stand up," she said, and – flinched and listened . . . And all present were listening with a shudder, some rigidly, and the rest with the foolish laughter of horror. From the area around the court room the breezes had carried a terrible scream. It seemed to have evoked an echo in the heart of the old woman, for she raised her head with a groan and murmured a prayer . . .

'"Well, now?" my grandmother asked Fritz, who had rushed up breathlessly. "Have you done it?"

'"At your service," answered Fritz, and this time was capable only of a mournful grin instead of his usual sweet smile. "He kisses your hand. He is dead now."' –

'Dreadful!' exclaimed the countess. 'And you call that a peaceable story?'

'Pardon the stratagem,' replied the count. 'You would not have heard me out otherwise. But perhaps you now understand why I do not dismiss Myška's gentle descendant from my service even though he is quite negligent in representing my interests.'

A KALEIDOSCOPE

TEREZA NOVÁKOVÁ

My dear young lady, you say you are tired. I am not surprised. You have undertaken more today than a never-tiring dancer at the Paris Opéra might undertake in an evening devoted entirely to ballet. But don't imagine that I shall simply insist on giving you the next dance as you promised me; I pressed you enough before you agreed to have it! Besides, it's a waltz, and I am almost glad that you are disinclined to dance it. I dance the waltz excruciatingly badly, and I would not want you to laugh at me for not having learnt it in Vienna. If you will allow me, I shall take you over to that sofa which is raising its pink velvet arms so seductively over you. I should love to sit at your feet; but what a pity it is that those beautiful, chivalrous times are past when shepherd swains used to sit at the feet of their inamoratas playing the guitar! That's no longer in fashion.

My dear young lady, would you allow me to stay with you during this waltz? – Really, you are infinitely kind! What a beautiful background that pink sofa makes to the pale blue of your dress and to the circlet of white flowers you are wearing! Tilt your little head back so that your curls can rest comfortably on the soft cushion. We have chosen a very good spot; you can watch almost the whole crowd flying around the hall and whirling in a colourful throng. Would you lend me your fan, and keep only that fragrant bouquet? The cool air circulating here will certainly be pleasant for you, and will undoubtedly also help me to entertain you. I should not like you in any way to be regretting the quarter of an hour you are devoting to me.

I shall tell you about – or, rather, I shall unfold before you – a kaleidoscope, with very intriguing pictures, and I shall provide you with a commentary. You are looking at me in astonishment. My dear young lady, do not be surprised; it is neither in my pocket nor under my seat. Simply look in front of you, and imagine that everything you see is behind glass or projected on the wall like the pictures of a magic lantern. If I had an opera glass here, I should give it to you; through those lenses you would see that the mixture becomes more picturesque at a distance. What a delightful kaleidoscope it is!

How do you like dancing? Are you laughing at me? Of course in your mind's eye you are seeing how I would have danced the waltz, and you would certainly have been angry with me. Perhaps you would have thought of someone far better able to waltz, and you would have incited me to enormous jealousy. Now you are taking cover behind your bouquet – but beware, lovely lady, that the demon lurking in your hyacinths does not tempt you with his poisoned darts! It would be better to cast your eye into my kaleidoscope.

The first picture is of a waltz. You will notice that some of the men are dragging themselves across the floor as if they were here on cleaning duty today; some of the others are hopping on one foot, 'à la française', right through the whole hall. Those over there are whirling like a spinning-wheel, so that the mere sight of them is enough to render one blind. Some brave souls have ventured to try the quick waltz, but those are real disasters! Look over there where two couples have collided with one another. There is no more ridiculous sight than when two hundred couples are all dancing in different ways in a confined space. I am very glad, my dear young lady, that you are not dancing! You might damage the beautiful train of your dress, which you wear so gracefully. I love trains on the dresses of beautiful women – they give them a regal look.

Here is another picture. I can offer you a great many; I am acquainted with everyone present here today, and there are not many who are new: friends of mine, just as inquisitive as I used to be, have told me this. Are you surprised at this 'used to be' of mine? Ah, trust me, I have been a guest in these halls for a long time now; you would not believe that this year is now my eighth season. I should not have come here at all if it had not been for a certain young lady of whom you have not the slightest idea. – Why, you have struck me with your glove and left a white streak on my black coat! Really, I have no idea why. I shall not forgive you that, unless you promise that you will give no credence to anyone who tells you that I am blasé! I would only wish to say that I know almost everyone here – so let us direct our attention to a few antiquities.

Now look at those three sisters over there. They are dressed alike; the eldest is still very beautiful – you wouldn't guess that she is almost thirty years old. When I was learning to dance, I was anxious to know what it was like at a real ball, and I went to one incognito. At that time that lady was adored by everyone, and she was so proud that she picked and chose her partners, and altogether refused to dance with young people. They played a trick on her, and persuaded a certain impecunious tailor, who happened to be helping in setting up the ball, to invite her to dance with him. Can you imagine the fury of that lady when the story came out in the papers! These days she attends balls with her grown-up sisters; they operate in tandem with one another. She allows them to borrow her name, and they allow her to borrow their youth and patronage, for they are not pretty, whereas she is renowned for her polychromous eyes, now blue, now green, for the antique features of her countenance, and for her splendid figure. They are true Gypsy maidens!

Near us you will see a man with a monocle in his eye – the model of a blasé man! He is not even an Epicurean, but a nihilist of the most abject kind. You must agree I do not resemble him in the very slightest degree. He has yellowed skin; his sunken eyes stare as insolently as if they were threatening to destroy the entire world. He is not dancing; thank God, there are no ladies here for him. Poor man, he was born too late; he belongs to the era of Nero and Messalina. If you were to go into the dining room after midnight, you would see him sitting in front of the silver pail, filled with ice, in which the champagne is being cooled.

Right at this moment a most beautiful lady is dancing around us. I think you have already drawn my attention to her magnificent attire. I don't understand fashion, but I agree that she is a remarkable spectacle. You are looking at me questioningly; shall I tell you about her? I shall not speak about her past. If you had mentioned her to your mother, she would have forbidden me entry to your house. I shall say only that in her younger years she was a dancer; she became married to a very rich, and not too respectable, husband; she entered, shall we say, into social circles. She does not, however, behave with gratitude to her husband; each year she goes to the spas, she has been several times to Paris, she spends immense sums of money, and she perpetrates such wonderful pieces of mischief as defy belief.

A few weeks ago, her worthy husband fought a duel with an enthusiastic admirer of hers. Look at that gentleman on the right: he has a scar on his right ear. That is the happy spouse of that virtuous beauty. How many of those present are envying her that tiara of fiery topazes and her costly dress! But believe me, my dear young lady: all that, even including its owner, is not worth being trodden on by your little foot. You have heard tell of Aspasia, Sappho and their influence – they at least had the merit of cultivating poetry and science. But ones like this beautiful little madam are worthless.

Let us turn our attention in another direction! Look at that girl in a white dress! You will instantly find yourself on the greensward and not in the seductive warmth enveloping you. Are you laughing at her? Admittedly she is not a phenomenon belonging in the salons. She is a girl whom you city ladies would simply call a 'stupid Podháj goose'.[1] But to me that girl is interesting. She is in good health, with a ruddy, sincere face; it is a pity that she has ventured here, where she is entirely out of place. I would love to see her in a peasant's skirt and bodice, with a garland in her thick braids, which she has arranged like a 'garden' today, weaving a multitude of flower-buds into them. She would be lovely as a peasant girl! Do you agree? I'm delighted to have guessed your thoughts. She is a good girl; I know her father, who is a wealthy landowner. She should not be blamed for failing to understand the Paris journals as you do; that white dress, trimmed with narrow pink ribbons, must certainly seem the model of all toilettes to her. How she loves dancing! She is all out of breath. Now look, a gentleman is approaching her, the riding master of a regiment of hussars, a man who has passed, as we say, through fire and water, and who is now intending to rid himself of his debts and all the miseries of life with the thirty-thousand fortune of this countrified 'goose', as he calls her. The lively country girl is entirely carried away, of course, by the fact that a gentleman in a fine uniform is paying attention to her.

And now we shall observe the beginning of a tale about a spider that spins a fatal web for an unfortunate fly.

A rural admirer has now also come in pursuit of our peasant girl. What a figure he makes! He has large hands, red like a lobster; he has squeezed one of them into a glove, but cannot manage to do the same with the other. His face clearly reveals that its owner was not the inventor of gunpowder. His hair is slicked down; it is a wonder that the pomade is not dripping from it as it did with the dandies in Ancient Rome. By chance I was standing with the staff at the entrance when he arrived, and it was a wonder we

1 'Stupid and provincial': Podháj is a village in western Slovakia.

did not laugh aloud. He wished to leave his overcoat at the cloakroom, and flung it into the hands of the staff; he would have gone into the hall in his muddy clothes if we had not detained him. There was no doubt that he would take something out in any event: before the ball he was smoking a Virginia, and he had forgotten the straw behind his ear. He guards his beauty with the eyes of Argus, and by his clumsiness he has torn and trampled on the trains of five ladies, and broken the bracelet of one. All of them would avoid touching him with a bargepole. You would also have had this fearful destroyer of trains ejected, would you not, my dear young lady? Surely you would? You are too magnanimous; I can see you are unwilling to allow the peasant girl to fall into the soldier's predatory clutches. But I can assure you that this clumsy yokel has his eye equally on her fortune.

Now here we have yet another rural genre. These are the students who are attending a Prague ball for the first time. After the dance I shall show you some of them. They keep together; you will recognize them by their black coats of antediluvian cut and by their spectacles, which are obligatory for all of them, even for those with good eyesight. But they are amiable boys; from sheer modesty they never venture to approach the more sought-after girls, and are the salvation of poor wallflowers and superannuated beauties. A student like that will have only one topic of conversation on a ball night. He will always speak about the types of ball, dance party, conversation, and visitation that are held in his home town. Even today I have been the witness of two such discourses – so I am speaking from experience.

I think the waltz is coming to an end – but no, I'm wrong, so I'm not yet losing my charming auditor. I shall also show you a terror of every man.

Do you see the lady here, carelessly reclining on the sofa? She is certainly thinking that she looks very seductive, and is even presenting her legs for inspection. She is an old coquette! There is no more frightful creature on earth. I respect old age; I am looking forward to seeing you in twenty-five or thirty years' time: you will be a redoubtable matron. But that woman is unable to reconcile herself with the notion that she must grow old. Pity her, my dear young lady! She is a true ruin of her former great beauty. At a distance, of course, she does not appear so terrible; her cheeks are painted red and white, her beautiful hair is false, some of her missing teeth have been replaced artificially, and the whiteness of her shoulders and neck is due to a fine powder. If you do not take account of her face, she looks truly regal. Her magnificent dress has been manufactured with attention to detail and at great expense according to the model of the gown of the Crown Princess of P . . . . Who is paying any attention to her? She has not come with her daughter, whom she married off as a child two years ago so that she should not stand in her way; the poor thing has come as a dancer. Some of the subordinates of her pitiable husband have danced with her; the rest have passed her by. She has a very chequered past, in which counts, princes, actors and swindlers have played an important part, and where her unfortunate husband has been merely a keeper of the purse, or has been a guarantor when the lovely lady has been mired in debt somewhere. However, her youthful years are already past; she is now approaching fifty; yet she is not withdrawing from the world. You will see her everywhere – in the theatre, at concerts, at the spas and on the ice, and always extraordinarily attired. I should not wish to see her in dishabille! Pity her, then, my dear young lady! Think how much labour her transformation from old to young costs her! Let us hope, for her sake, that Cagliostro's elixir of eternal life may finally be discovered![2]

2 Alessandro di Cagliostro was the pseudonym of a celebrated occultist, Giuseppe Balsamo (1743–95), who was usually regarded as a charlatan, and was the subject of Goethe's comedy *Der Groß-Cophta* (1791).

The waltz is at an end; now I must take you back to your esteemed Mama. Listen to the applause! May my narrative have entertained you enough for you not to have missed the dancing! Listen, the signal has been given for a reprise – they are coming for you!

How generous you are! For my sake you are giving me a third chance now; I gratefully accept your kindness. But I shall not dance. Hang yourself in my picture-frame; we shall remain here by the mirror. If you are vain enough, look at the lovely picture to be seen in it, and I shall tell you something more.

This evening we have here a certain noble beast, whom you will certainly have seen in your 'circumnavigation of the globe'. He is close to you now; have you ever seen a more fitting transmutation of an elephant into the realm of humanity? The old measures of length are not adequate to determining the size of his back; it is a good metre broad, and his height and breadth will together make a lovely square. His head is enormous and flattened, his nose bent and large – like a trunk. But his legs are his noblest part: those are two stout Doric columns, to which he owes his income. Now he is moving; are you not afraid that the floor will give way beneath us? And those beautiful hands! He does not deny that his Papa was a blacksmith, of honest workmanship, who left him a great fortune. The son has become a gentleman: his money has opened an office for him in a certain bank, where he presides incompetently, and the little girls are enchanted by him. You are putting on such an incredulous face that I am obliged to assure you that this is unfortunately true. Look over there and see how joyful that pretty blonde is, whom he has approached, and how ecstatic her Mama is! She is the penniless daughter of a judge, and she would be very happy if a rich bank official were to take her as his wife. And now that elephant is dancing! A dancing elephant is such a freak of nature!

His steps are crashing like thunder – turn away from that swollen-headed idiot! –

Now, my dear young lady, I am really obliged to bid you farewell, not only for this dance, but also for the rest of the evening; I have to undertake an official journey, a very important one, at five o'clock tomorrow morning. Please take another look in the mirror! I should like the image in it to be fixed long and deep in your memory. I shall deliver you to your Mama now; do forgive me if I have bored you! If you wish to remember this evening, add a keepsake for both me and the kaleidoscope into which we have been looking together!

My dear young lady, I kiss your hand!

CONFIRMED BACHELORS

BOŽENA VIKOVÁ-KUNĚTICKÁ

All three of them were called Lukeš. There were Jindřich Lukeš, aged sixty, Eugen Lukeš, aged fifty-five, and finally Vilibald Lukeš, fifty years old. From their Christian names it is immediately obvious that their mother had wanted them to be heroes, with names that would give them added lustre. In other ways her dreams had come quite decently true; for the three of them were the owners of a four-storey house, in front of which many people assembled every day to gape in wonder, for the building was both monumental and luxurious.

There was no doubt that the Lukešes were rich, even if they had only the one house and shared anonymous respect from their tenants. They had built the house according to their own taste, which they had kept alive ever since the times when they had been admirers of charming blonde ladies with slender hips. Besides, even after the house was built, a fair amount of capital had been left over, because they had been the legatees of Ivančický, a factory own-er, who was reputed to have left at least a million in his will. It is possible that the Lukešes had not inherited the whole fortune; but it is certain that they had inherited a lot of it.

However, their finances do not come into question here, for I have no interest in writing about them as capitalists, but rather as eccentrics for whom I am now begging the reader's sympathy.

All the Lukešes were, of course, unmarried. This is obvi-ous, for I would already have mentioned right at the outset that they had charming wives, if this had been the case. But by no means: the Lukešes genuinely did not have any wives, even though they had provided the first floor with two balconies, and one might have assumed these to have been built with women's shapely elbows in mind, to provide them with something to lean on.

Every morning – and also every evening – all three brothers used to meet on one of the balconies, just after breakfasting or dining on gastronomic delicacies, smoking long pipes, with Serbian caps on their heads, carefree and replete. From the balconies they would contemplate the blue sky, more than the street, for it held the mystery of life after death, that matter about which one begins to think seriously once one has passed the age of fifty. Besides, many people, completely unknown to them, used to greet them from the street, and the Lukešes were indolent, rather than vain.

Their indolence was expressed in every aspect of their residence, their wardrobe, and their external appearance. Quite possibly it is my duty to describe what my heroes looked like; but it is difficult to find words for that, if only because no one in the world could ever visualize those figures, unusually tall, with broad shoulders, slightly stooping, but as solid as if carved from granite. They were three dandies, who showed in the tossing of their heads, the pursing of their lips, the narrowing of their eyes, that there had once been a time when they had played the coquette with that tossing, that pursing, and indeed also that narrowing. As yet they had not become accustomed to assuming the careless gait, slightly swinging, nor the smile, that we women think hides so much! But the Lukešes were already grey-haired. They were among the people who turn grey already at thirty-five, who have no anxieties, and yet do not in any way possess exceptional intelligence.

Their whiskers were glittering silver, though still very fine. The fine white hands of the Lukeš brothers stroked those whiskers of theirs with tranquil elegance, as if they did not realize that they were symbols of their old age.

Indeed it seemed that the Lukešes were not even aware of what had happened in the past, and that it was only the present and the possible future that occupied their minds. There are many such people, who have no memories, even though they may have had the most colourful of pasts. What is the point of remembering? The only people who do that are those who imagine they have lost a good deal.

But the Lukeš brothers had lost nothing – they had amassed things. They had amassed a house, tranquillity, comfort, old age. One could genuinely say that the Lukešes regarded their old age as a great asset, though they never spoke about how young and attractive they had once been.

My impression is that they were now admiring each other, finding themselves more handsome and dashing than they had once been. Certainly they had a rare gift in lacking nothing and desiring nothing. Mothers usually inculcate these principles into their sons, and the Lukešes had had no mother since their childhood. They had never witnessed tears, and had never heard expressions of grief. I think that they were convinced that everyone is inexpressibly content in himself, and that life is a long continuous span of pleasure and bliss. At least they had never themselves experienced moments in which they had felt the least bitterness.

Moreover, great happiness gives people solidity just as a good nutritious diet does. The Lukeš brothers looked as if nothing on earth would shake or move them.

It was surprising that they had not married, although this could easily be explained by the fact that their love for each other was almost tender; and they were unable to understand the extent to which wives might have given rise to quarrels – which would very surely have awaited them as soon as they had taken such a step.

Still earlier – twenty-five years earlier – they had spoken of the possibility that one of them might marry, but this unfortunate prospect had always scared them, and they had put off pursuing it until it should actually happen.

At that time all three were serving in the army in the same regiment. For elegance, physical strength and pride, no one could equal these Lukešes, who seemed to have absolutely no unfulfillable ambitions, and in whose whole being so much real peace was rooted that it was inconceivable that they could ever be afraid of anything.

And in fact these extraordinary, strange brothers were the inheritors of the substantial estate of Ivančický, the factory owner; in fact – why should I conceal it? – they were his prime inheritors.

And so, replete with honours, amusements, their obligation to the state, and all the rest, they returned to civilian life, with all in their souls now at peace, and without anxieties.

What was the world to them? They had their sumptuous four-storey house, and that constituted their entire world. They did not attend the theatre or the circus, and still less concerts, because music always produces a rather elegiac effect, and the Lukeš brothers knew all too well that it was not advisable to awaken something in the breast that had always been sound asleep there. They had no intention of seeking out any novelty, persuaded as they were that they might here and there encounter new insights or new findings, and that any of these might cause them discomfort.

The life they had set up for themselves was an extremely pleasant one. It resembled an coastal inlet in which no storm ever occurs – whose surface is untroubled by a single ripple. –

Havel, their manservant, always moved around on tiptoe, as silent as a shadow, dust-cloth in hand. With it he wiped off the dust in all three rooms, in which everything was gleaming, magnificent, untouched, and somehow sublime. There is nothing more gloomy than the apartments of confirmed bachelors.

From all sides an anonymous chill stares out as it does in a completely empty church. It is impossible to touch anything without feeling that it will be broken, damaged, desecrated.

To us it seems as if everything has lain there for many centuries, and that all is turned to dust. Even the confirmed bachelor in the midst of his treasures seems strange, as if he lacks any feeling, and any blood – as if he is a mummy who for a while has left its coffin. We might certainly suppose that the mummy will return to its box as soon as we leave, and that it will simply stare numbly at the pipes, the books, as well as everything else around it, in terrible immobility – –

And the rooms of the Lukešes matched the cells of old bachelors to a hair, although there were vases in them, filled with flowers, that were renewed, fresh and fragrant, every day. All their elegance, so rich and silent, lacked soul. Either there was something in those rooms that was freezing them, or they lacked something there that might warm them. But the Lukešes did not know this. They were accustomed to talk loudly, and occasionally to laugh, and they did not notice that some kind of terrible Nothing was standing in every corner and staring into their eyes, into their lips, into their hands, and that it was appalled by their talk and their laughter. –

They were partial to dining on prime English beefsteaks or mutton cutlets in piquant sauce. In the evenings when the frightful Nothing swelled up as if it were trying to swallow everything, the brothers would be dining on choice delicacies and wiping their mouths with their napkins, while listening to Havel recounting the news from their house, which they invariably found of interest.

Indeed the Lukešes listened with great interest to everything, as do those who have no contact with anyone else. The need to occupy one's spirit is well-developed in every human being.

They very frequently enjoyed conversing about things they had never seen and about events they would never at any cost have attended. Most often they spoke with humour, fluently and effortlessly, which in any case was merely the result of their complete contentment.

One day, their servant Havel suddenly announced a visit from a lady; naturally, this had not been expected at all by the Lukešes, for they maintained no contact with women, considering it both indelicate and ridiculous at their age. Besides, their former loves were all married, and their beauty was by now shrivelled up. The Lukešes had never imagined that new flowers might ever start blooming.

'Who is that lady?' they asked Havel in astonishment.

'It is paní Procházková from the fourth floor, the widow of a state official, very short and wizened,' replied Havel, who was acquainted with every detail in the house of its owners.

It was resolved that our Lukešes would receive paní Procházková, though they had not the foggiest idea why this paní Procházková should be coming to visit them.

And before long paní Procházková entered. She was very upset and distraught, nervously clasping her hands while smiling in embarrassment, with tears welling up in her eyes. She was an emaciated old lady, dressed with a mournful elegance, who resembled the weather-beaten monuments on the graves of great personages which leave no doubt that they were once sumptuous and remarkable. Everything about her spoke of times past, as if the poor lady were an old chronicle brought to life. Her silks were full of holes and creased; her hat was gloomy and ridiculous. Her brow was full of wrinkles though it was white and fine. The Lukeš brothers rose from their ample, comfortable armchairs, and asked her what she wanted.

'Ah, excuse me – please excuse me,' cried paní Procházková, forcing herself to be polite, though she was overcome with weeping. 'It is bold of me, but I do not know what to

(71)

do. Dear landlords, I am short of money. I am very worried, and I am all alone in the world without help. Forgive me for weeping, but I find it hard. I've been living up on the fourth floor with my daughter Klotilda for two years now, and I pay my rent as I should.'

Paní Procházková stopped speaking, expecting that the Lukešes would say something in reply; but the Lukešes did not do so. It seemed strange to them that this lady should be weeping if she were able to pay the rent properly.

'I don't want to detain you, dear landlords,' continued the old lady, 'but it is so hard for me to express myself all at once. I need a hundred gulden – a hundred gulden! – oh, I know it is a lot. Oh, and it depends on a lot! I've received a solicitor's letter from the doctor who treated my husband. His demand for payment goes back three years now. I don't think he'd sue me, but a hundred gulden is a huge sum for me. There is nowhere I could get it from! Klotilda is weeping upstairs – – Ah, dear landlords, I'm pleading on bended knee, please lend me that hundred gulden. My daughter and I will save up, and I will repay you in three months at the most – I promise you, by all that is dear to me.' –

'What actually is it that you are asking for?' asked Jindřich, who had not heard her final words properly, because she had spoken them quietly and timorously.

'That you would be so kind as to lend me a hundred gulden, dear landlords. I can give you a pledge for them – yes, so I can. Be assured that I wish to repay you soon.'

'A pledge? – But we aren't moneylenders, dear lady. Perhaps it would be better to go to a pawnbroker –'

'Oh no, no!' cried paní Procházková in horror. 'That's out of the question! We're talking about my daughter's trousseau, which she inherited from her godmother, paní Koncová, the councillor's late wife. I have no other pledge, and I could not consign it to that place, where everything smells so bad and everything is so awful and grubby. –

I shudder at the thought of it. I can't bring myself to talk about it, dear landlords.'

'Are you wanting to give us your daughter's trousseau as a pledge?' said the Lukeš brothers at once, with the smile with which they had once asked naïve little girls, 'Won't you give me those lovely flowers, little girl?'

'Ah yes,' replied paní Procházková. 'It's lovely and clean here.'

'Right, dear lady, we'll lend you the hundred gulden, and Havel will bring the money to you upstairs. Please accept our best regards, paní Procházková,' said Jindřich, and the brothers bowed to the old lady as a sign that she should leave . . .

*   *

The same day, at dinner, which they regularly ate at 7 p.m., it occurred to Vilibald, the youngest of the three, to wonder whether paní Procházková had kept her word and had delivered to them the pledge of which she had spoken.

The brothers, seated in long warm Persian robes and dining on jellied perch, which they occasionally enjoyed, were very obliged to Vilibald for remembering something that neither of the other two had thought of.

Accordingly, they rang for Havel to ask him whether paní Procházková had indeed had something delivered for them.

'Ah, yes, of course,' said old Havel, earnestly. 'A large trunk, and I have the key to it, so that you may be pleased to examine its contents, to make sure that everything is in order.'

'Where is that trunk?'

'In the hall.'

'Would you bring it in here?'

'Yes – I'll get the cook to help me.'

When Havel had left, the Lukešes quickly consumed the rest of the perch, and drank a glass of wine.

Suddenly it occurred to all three of them, though none of them admitted it, that there was something very important and interesting in store for them. By turns there appeared an almost mysterious smile on their faces, so that it was immediately obvious how each of them was struggling separately with his thoughts.

'We shouldn't miss the opportunity,' said Eugen under his breath, wiping his hands.

'No, we shouldn't, on my word,' said the other two, wiping their hands after him.

Havel and the cook brought the trunk in and placed it by the table, then left, bowing as if leaving a church in which divine service was about to begin.

There was silence in the room; there was only a hollow, gloomy sound from the elaborate majolica clock. A cold autumn rain was blowing on the windows, but the warmth in the dining room seemed positively royal against that rain. On evenings like that it is unspeakably blissful to have with us someone who is completely devoted to us. That can be either a man or a woman, though only if we are a woman or a man respectively.

Well, the Lukeš brothers were not feeling the lack of anyone, for they would have had to have been feeling the lack of women.

This trunk seemed mysterious to them. It annoyed them and caused them some embarrassment, which they were unwilling to admit. Jindřich Lukeš spent a long time twisting the little key with its red ribbon in his hand, but finally his brother Vilibald spoke, smoothing his delicate beard with his delicate hand.

'Well, then, open it! We have no intention of stealing or damaging anything.'

No living soul could have failed to read the true meaning of these words, which was, beyond all doubt, 'For God's sake, open it up quickly! Because what we're going to find there will be truly extraordinary.'

Jindřich rattled the key in the lock, and opened the mysterious trunk, which contained the great hopes of the future dream of the young girl. At the same moment it seemed that the silent, terrible Nothing, which had been grinning so appallingly in the room hitherto, was crawling under the cupboards, behind the stove, under the tables, behind the curtains, like an evil goblin expecting and fearing a reprimand.

Eugen turned up the light of the lamp as far as he could. – From the trunk there wafted the delicious perfume of rose oil, and suddenly the room was full of it, as if a woman, the most beautiful on earth, were moving around in it. The Nothing crawled away further and further, so that even the Lukeš brothers noticed its absence.

'Something has disappeared from here with that perfume – a kind of emptiness,' said Vilibald, looking around the room and dilating his nostrils so that he could become intoxicated with that pleasant feminine fragrance.

Jindřich, however, with a quiet smile merely drew back the white linen cloth under which an entire Paradise of enchantments was concealed.

'Ah, upon my word, those are delightful bonnets,' cried Eugen, stroking his whiskers with an epicurean enthusiasm that he had not felt for a very long time.

Here there were white bonnets, pink ones, blue ones, with ribbons, with lace, dainty, tiny, astonishing. They lay on the surface like choice desserts – if I may be excused in saying so – as if fashioned from cream, but miraculous and intoxicating.

'That girl is a redhead, just as paní Dečvová, the major's wife, was. She also loved white, blue and pink,' said Jindřich, who had once courted paní Dečvová, and had therefore paid attention to her bonnets.

Each of the brothers placed three fingers under one of the bonnets, lifting it carefully and delicately, with as much grace as if they were taking the sweetest little hand of a young lady to their lips.

Paní Dečvová, the major's wife – Katina, the merchant's wife – XYZ, the ballerina – all of them had once upon a time worn similar bonnets!

'I swear that girl has lips like cherries!' cried Vilibald, looking under the bonnet in case he could spy those cherry lips there. It seemed appallingly merciless that these bonnets were being lifted up only on three fingers, and that no eyes, tiny nose, lips and cheeks were being revealed! However, Jindřich did claim that he could see all of those things rather than his own three fingers, even if those fingers had very lately been occupied with the perch.

It was resolved that they would not return the bonnets to the trunk, for all of them felt that there was an extremely sweet dream in store for them. The bonnets were set up on the table – in fact, only three of them, because all of them together evoked only three dreams. However, Vilibald Lukeš took his bonnet into their shared bedroom, and hung it on a four-branched candelabra in which there were no candles.

'That's excellent!' said Jindřich, and he burst out laughing.

But Vilibald said, 'Go and have a look. There's a strange light coming from that bonnet, and the whole bedroom is filled with it.'

The brothers got up and went to see what the little blue bonnet looked like in their room, where there were so many pipes, so many books, and such a chill.

'Very good! Paní Lukešová has taken off her bonnet!'

At these words of Eugen's, it really seemed to the poor brothers that a lovely woman was standing in front of the mirror on the dressing table, and that she had hung her bonnet on the candelabra. They left the room almost on tiptoe so as not to alarm or at least disturb the apparition. And returning to the trunk, they were virtually convinced that they were no longer alone in their rooms. At that moment, the dreadful Nothing disappeared from their house entirely, and all that was left was the perfume of rose oil and the perfume of freshly laundered feminine linen. A cold flood of rain was driving against the windows, but in the room there was a warmth, as sweet as if it were proceeding from the presence of a young woman.

Under the bonnets there was a teeming flood of lacework and linen, in which, here and there, there shimmered a ribbon, or some embroidery, like flowers in a snowdrift, and all the more enticing for it. At first glance one could not make out what this drift of snow actually was, which was falling, floating, even moving as if something alive and restless had emerged under it.

Finally the Lukeš brothers perceived that these things were daytime and evening bodices.

'Oh, that's why I thought they were alive,' cried Vilibald, blushing at his own fantasy.

'Ah, that makes an excellent match,' he continued, taking hold of one of these bodices, so adorable and seductive. 'I'm going to hang this bodice on that candelabra, too.'

The brothers were so genuinely tactful that they did not allow themselves any gross jokes except for one, which advanced the fascinating idea that some pretty redhaired paní Lukešová had also divested herself of her bodice. So a bonnet and a bodice were now dangling from the candelabra, and there was no doubt that they were still warm and delectable.

Under the bodices, the brothers found pinafores – but what pinafores! Grace and modesty, coquetry and tenderness gazed forth from them – all this was hidden in those pinafores, which fluttered out of the trunk like multicoloured butterflies, one after another, both serious and mischievous, both simple and elaborate, so that it was possible to see the young woman in almost every moment of the happy life she was leading in her household by her domestic hearth!

'Oh! I have never seen pinafores like these!' whispered Jindřich Lukeš, who had been received by paní Dečvová, the major's wife, when she had not been wearing a pinafore.

'That doesn't matter,' replied his brother Vilibald. 'I'll hang one of them here in the dining room, because paní Lukešová wears pinafores only in the kitchen and at meals.'

He picked out a white lace pinafore of remarkable cut – one of those that seem as lovely and chaste as the daisies in the meadows which we are sorry to pick.

He went and hung it on the sideboard, so that it seemed that some small hand in a great hurry had simply flung it there in passing.

A glow emanated from these pinafores, too, which filled the entire dining room.

'This is so much better than perch,' said Eugen, unable to explain what he was saying.

Under the pinafores there were little embroidered ladies' shoes, which prompted a complete revolution in the minds of the Lukešes.

'That girl is an angel!'

'Yes, so she is. That shoe is one that even U., the ballerina, never wore!'

'Divine!'

With superb elegance, Vilibald leant over the shoe and kissed the pink flower-bud that was attached to it. He was not at all willing to admit how stirred he was, for it suddenly occurred to him that his old brothers might not understand his youthful fit of giddiness. He called to mind the fact that he was ten years younger than the sixty-year-old Jindřich Lukeš. The shoes were placed in the bedroom under the dressing-table mirror, and it seemed to the brothers that paní Lukešová had really retired to bed for the night – –

'And now there are eiderdown covers, towels, table-cloths, sheets,' went on Jindřich.

'Don't bother with those – we have them too,' said both Eugen and Vilibald simultaneously.

But at that same moment the brothers looked at one another in tremendous amazement. For the first time in their lives they realized that today they had witnessed something they had never had before.

It was that woman – the vision of a paní Lukešová, who had left her pinafore in the dining room, taken her bonnet off her head, removed her bodice, slipped off her shoes and retired to bed – –

As the Lukeš brothers fell asleep, they were straining to hear the sound of a woman's gentle breathing, but they could not catch it. Nevertheless, they had dreams that were filled with a glow, filled with fragrance and filled with warmth.

When they awoke in the morning, they smiled tenderly at the pretty blue bonnet. – –

*   *

Reflecting on all this, and growing accustomed to all possible situations, the Lukeš brothers acknowledged that it would be possible for at least one of them still to get married; though by a strange chance they simply could not imagine any paní Lukešová other than the one whom they had imagined that first evening when they opened the trunk – and she was clearly no other than Miss Klotilda Procházková from the fourth floor.

Whatever that Klotilda really looked like, the brothers wanted her to be redhaired, pretty, charming and affectionate. They cared about nothing other than her having the same little cherry lips, the same cheeks, eyes, hands, nose, which they had seen under the bonnet, in the bodice, in the little shoes.

It was virtually settled that she and only she should become paní Lukešová, the wife of any one of them. Perhaps all of them were in love with the charms of her pinafores, perhaps even with the girl herself, but Vilibald was certainly the most in love, because he suddenly felt his fifty years to be very fresh in comparison with the fifty-five and sixty years of his brothers.

Besides, he was aware that he might still be eligible to take a wife, whereas his brothers would need to be content with a sister-in-law. He wanted to become a father, and they would certainly be content to be uncles. He had his fantasies and they had theirs; but it is definite that all of them were thinking about a wife, something they had never done before.

Everywhere, there was an almost desperate effort to see her and to breathe the same air as she did. There were bonnets not only in the bedroom but in the dining room and also in the parlour. Pinafores hung in every possible place, and bodices, like fresh bouquets, were placed in vases and under pictures. It seemed that the fairies themselves had taken their wardrobes apart in these desolate rooms. Suddenly, there were no pipes to be seen, nor maps, nor books, and everywhere there was only linen, lace, ribbons. But it was pleasant. So pleasant, indeed, that Havel himself was bowing to some invisible being, in the most perfect courtesy, in the conviction that even if she were not yet there, she was certainly on the way to him, amiable, cheerful, and beautiful.

It often happened that sweets were now being ordered in the kitchen, even though not one of the Lukešes ate them; but they gave a mysterious air to the table, and suggested many enticing things. In any case there was no doubt that the lady was present somewhere, because the brothers quickly learnt to speak with a certain tenderness and courtesy, with a certain self-discipline, with which men, if they are even only slightly self-aware, respect the society of ladies.

Finally it became almost unavoidable that they should reach a decision on what they actually intended to do.

'If one of us gets married, there will be new conditions for both of the others – certainly more pleasant than the ones before.'

'And who will be the one to get married?' cried Vilibald in some anxiety.

'It won't be me, I promise you,' said Jindřich seriously, because he was sensible rather than foolish.

'It could be me –,' said Eugen, rather hesitantly, acknowledging that it would be an absolutely gargantuan decision.

'You? No. I'll be the one. I'll provide you with a wonderful sister-in-law, who will love you, and with a niece and nephew for you to love,' said Vilibald, carried away by his own daring; and, more seriously, he added, 'In any case it is just a matter of which of us gets married first. It doesn't exclude the possibility that both of you might get married too.'

'Upon my word, it depends in the first place on Miss Klotilda, and all three of us can't marry her.'

With these words of Jindřich Lukeš, the screen was abruptly torn away, behind which all their fantasies had been concealed. So it depended entirely on Klotilda alone, who, with her bonnets and all the rest, up to those unusual little shoes, had filled the monastic cells of their bachelorhood with a charm that even Eden would have lacked if Eve had not been present in it.

So that everything relevant in this conversation should be settled, both Jindřich and Eugen Lukeš invited Vilibald to pay suit to Klotilda as soon as possible, for there was something delightful in the prospect of starting a new life with a new range of possibilities.

Jindřich cried out 'my dear sister' into the void, and Eugen tucked two pins into the pocket of one of the pinafores, laughing very heartily at the prospect of the screams of the charming creature as she pricked her fingers on them.

It was obvious that a revolution was in the offing.

The brothers were in an excellent mood, and there had never been such merriment among them as at that moment, when all three were thinking only of her, occupying themselves only with her, and seeing her everywhere, everywhere, in every corner.

The illusion was complete, for it seemed that the bonnets, bodices and pinafores had not arrived there purely by chance.

* *

One day, Vilibald Lukeš managed to catch sight of Klotilda on the veranda, and he returned home dazzled.

'It's the girl,' he said, laughing in a manner that expressed the highest satisfaction. 'We were not wrong. If you want to see here, go to the kitchen window – she's on the veranda on the first floor. Her hair is like a golden cobweb, she has slender hips, and lips like the glow of rubies. The cook brought her to my attention.'

'Let's go.'

And, in their Persian robes, the brothers crowded around the window, from which they saw her, the lovely Klotilda, who had been walking up and down their room so many times, who had been taking off her bonnets and bodices, for whom they had been providing sweets, and who was due to prick herself on Eugen's two pins. It would not have taken much for Jindřich Lukeš to call out in his powerful voice, 'Listen, dear sister-in-law!'

And Vilibald stood there, proud, dazzled, overjoyed. He resolved to take the first step the very next day that would lead him to the altar.

Back in their rooms, the Lukešes surveyed the little pieces of finery with infinite tenderness, and all three had the same unspoken thought in their minds:

'She's charming!'

Alas, Miss Klotilda already had a fiancé. It was cruel, but it was the case.

Her beauty, her charm and her elegance were reasons why she had acquired a fiancé even before she had attracted the attention of those poor rich Lukeš brothers. It was virtually certain that she would not have accepted a proposal from anyone under the sun other than her 'Moji', who was in her opinion the bravest, most handsome and best man in the world.

Although he was not a millionaire, he had very beautiful handwriting, and there was nothing under the sun that was able to impress Klotilda as much as his words in his letters.

'Ah, my sweet Tylda, I love you. You are the supreme happiness of my life.'

The only possibility was for her to reply, writing with a trembling hand:

'My Moji! I am yours. I live for your love. I've kissed the bottom right-hand corner of this page. Oh Moji, you kiss it too!'

In fact Mojmír Bareš was not in Prague, but he intended to get there as soon as possible, and then to take Klotilda as his wife, and thereby realize the most beautiful dream of his life. He had so far been unable to do so, because he was poor, and had nothing apart from his salary of six hundred as a supply teacher in Ďakovo.[3] But he had excellent hopes, he knew someone who could pull strings – he had a golden key to a golden lock! He knew without a doubt that he would find himself in Prague within a few months

3   Ďakovo (now Dyakovo in southern Ukraine, close to the Romanian border) was one of the remotest villages in which Mojmír Bareš could have found employment.

as a regular teacher who could hope for celestial bliss. And magic for him and also for her consisted in that certainty, which cast a rosy glow on their love.

From all this it will be obvious that Miss Klotilda was really not unhappy at all. The poverty of their life on the fourth floor, in their two tiny rooms, in which everything was shabby and gloomy, did not in any way represent reality for her. Reality for her lay in a future under the gaze of her Moji, in his embrace, with their children – – That is how matters were. That smile of hers, the fire in her eyes, the vivacity and seductiveness of her movements – all these belonged only and exclusively to her Moji. What is more, in fact, her bonnets and bodices, indeed also her tiny shoes, had been kissed a thousand times by them when the two of them had nestled together to defend the happiness of their life.

That was the reason why Klotilda had wept so bitterly when her mother decided to give her trousseau as a pledge to the landlords of the house.

Some days later, after she had mustered enough courage to do so, late into the evening, she wrote a letter, burying her teeth in her lips as if in nameless pain.

'Ah, Moji! Ah, Moji!' she wrote in one passage, 'poverty is so cruel! All my bonnets and the other things too are down with those unfeeling, pretentious people, who have no idea what love and what dreams lie in that simple trunk. I hate them, those mummies in their golden coffins! Oh, my heart aches, and my head aches too, Moji! And it could not be avoided. Mama would otherwise not have done it to save her soul. And here it is suddenly so empty as if our most beautiful hopes have been dashed. Your little future wife has gone away from here, your little wife, Moji, who will love you so much. I will cry my eyes out, Moji, if my – our – trunk does not come back here soon!'

But in no time, poor Miss Klotilda received an answer to this letter, in which was written:

'I can't sleep, Tylda. Just what was your mother thinking of? Giving up your most sacred things to the tender mercies of those three sinners. My whole body trembles when I remember that they could be touching things which you haven't wanted even to show me! I simply can't stay calm, at any price. And you write that she gave them the key. That's awful! They'll desecrate everything with their hands. Oh, my Tylda, that trunk can't stay there. I'll get hold of those miserable hundred gulden in a few days and your mother must immediately, I repeat immediately, get your trousseau back home. Oh, I know you've been crying, my darling! And every tear of yours is burning my heart, believe me. Your loving Moji.'

Once Klotilda had read the reply from her fiancé at least ten times, as she invariably did, she finally grasped that Moji was going to send a hundred gulden to repay the loan from the Lukešes. She was never inattentive in reading his letters, but at the eighth reading she was still not concerned with anything other than seeing the words that spoke entirely of their love. After that she began to grasp things that were less important, less sacred and more prosaic.

'Mama, Mama!' she cried to her mother in the other room, very excited. 'Moji's going to send us a hundred gulden to repay that awful loan, and I'll soon get my trunk back.'

Paní Procházková, with a black lace bonnet on her head and wearing a patched robe with a vast train, appeared in the doorway, more surprised than pleased.

'You wrote that to him?' she asked, like a condemned criminal receiving a life sentence instead of the gallows. 'Whatever will he think? That was too hasty.'

'But Moji is honourable.'

'You don't understand life! The more money there is, the more respect you get. It's really for his sake that I borrowed the money, so that he wouldn't realize the frightful situation in which we live.'

'Ah, Mama, I've not been keeping secrets from him for a long time now.'

'That's bad, very bad. Now I'll be blushing in front of him like a schoolgirl,' said paní Procházková, rapidly sizing up the whole situation.

However, it was now too late for her to think about her wounded pride and the consequences of the reckless trust of her daughter, for Mojmír Bareš was just then, with a trembling hand, sealing an envelope in Ďakova, containing the hundred gulden which he had borrowed from a more fortunate colleague, and repeating over and over to himself:

'Just be quick, quick! It wouldn't be surprising if those old sinners were to fall in love with my beautiful Tylda's bonnets!'

The clear-sighted eyes of his great love might have been reading the hearts of the Lukeš brothers, who at the same moment, resplendent in their Persian robes like the Three Magi of ancient times, were gazing at Klotilda on the first-floor veranda as if at the Infant Jesus and as if at their salvation.

Vilibald Lukeš had his black suit and his white cravat laid out for the next day, and Havel had immediately deduced that he intended to set out – to get her.

*   *

The fact that paní Procházková did not herself go to pay off her daughter's trousseau, and to take the masters of the house the hundred gulden sent to them by Mojmír Bareš in the extremity of his love, was due to one reason and one alone: that the good lady was unwilling even to touch the banknote that had originated from the hand of her future son-in-law, and had detracted from her dignity in so cruel a manner.

'For the whole world I wouldn't accept anything,' she said. 'You do whatever you like in this respect, but I'll never permit Moji to imagine that I was asking for help from him. You pay off the whole sum to our landlords without my knowing anything about it, and write to Moji straightaway today telling him you have done it all without breathing the slightest word to me.'

'But you do know all about it after all, Mama,' cried Klotilda, smiling.

But paní Procházková quickly covered her ears and cried, quite breathlessly:

'I don't know anything, I can't hear anything, I can't see anything. I'll repay my debt in three months' time out of the money I'll have saved by then. You do whatever you want, but it must be without my knowledge.'

'So must I go downstairs by myself?'

'Probably, because I'm not going down there. I don't yet have the money to repay the debt.'

Klotilda of course raised many more objections, but paní Procházková firmly stuck to her guns and to the story that she knew absolutely nothing about the affair of the money into which Moji had intervened.

So there was nothing for it but that Klotilda should put on her pale blue bodice and put fancy pins in her hair, kiss the hundred gulden from her fiancé once more, and then take them to the first floor, to those three demigods who were holding her treasure in thrall.

'Don't stay longer than is decent, and say about me that I have a bad migraine,' called paní Procházková after her, acknowledging in the most secret recesses of her heart that she was extremely relieved.

And the solemn Havel announced Miss Klotilda precisely when Vilibald Lukeš, more resplendent than at any other time, was about to leave his magnificent quarters to ascend to the fourth floor, to visit the charming, beautiful Miss Procházková.

'Is Miss Klotilda here?' cried the Lukeš brothers, in great surprise, for the question immediately arose as to why Miss Klotilda should have come.

It was necessary, of course, to receive her, and all the more necessary because she had already opened the door, being unwilling to put off her important visit any longer. And so Vilibald found himself in front of Miss Klotilda earlier than he had anticipated.

'I'm coming instead of Mama,' said Miss Klotilda, eagerly looking around to find her cherished trunk.

Her charming, large, tender eyes took in only too well all the magnificence surrounding her, which included so much ebony, so much majolica, plush, bronze, alabaster, glass, works of art, so much glitter and also gloom, and they remained wide open for a time as if marvelling at this great splendour, but shortly afterwards, impatient with her own slowness, she explained her first words further: 'Mama has a migraine.'

She looked at the enormous sideboard – by now she had entered the dining-room – which lorded it over the whole room like some monument. She felt some kind of embarrassment under the gaze of the three old dandies, who were staring at her lips, her brow, her cheeks, her hair, her little feet, and who seemed so affable, indeed fatherly, as if all these things had induced ardour in them. And at that moment she became accustomed to the majestic gloom that the plush curtains cast into the dining-room, and she could distinguish objects other than the sideboard more clearly. So she could make out what the bronze statue represented, and what had been painted on the canvas of the large picture.

Suddenly she gave a strangled scream and bit her lips weakly. A slight frisson ran through her body as if her blood were up. Poor Miss Klotilda had seen her bonnet – two of her bonnets, her pinafore! – Ah, for the sake of God

Almighty, were those tobacco pouches, that they should be hung in the most impossible places? Oh, what might these treasures of hers have been experiencing here! - -

'I'm bringing the money Mama owes you, dear landlords, and I want – I want my trunk back,' she said, in an extraordinary, disjointed voice that was intended to make the Lukeš brothers aware that she had seen everything, that she had seen all their unspeakable impudence and shamelessness.

But the Lukešes suddenly saw a wasteland opening up before them, a great wasteland in which even their sideboard, their tables, their majolica and their bronze were reduced to desert sand. They would be losing their bonnets!

'And why so suddenly?' asked Jindřich, first gaining control of his words.

'Oh, it's certainly not too sudden,' cried Miss Klotilda, forcing herself not to cry, 'it's almost too late, dear landlords. My bonnets have certainly been causing you a great deal of inconvenience.'

Hesitantly, Jindřich accepted the money Klotilda was giving him, and at the same time he and his brothers watched her face in horror and anger. It was only then that they realized in a flash that Miss Klotilda had caught them in their unforgivable temerity. They remembered that she had seen her linen strewn around like washing set out to dry.

Something had to be said to her, but that had to be sensitive, tender and serious, something to reconcile their guilt with her offended sensibility. But, for God's sake, what?

Involuntarily the brothers remembered what they had been accustomed to say to little girls who were angry when they were at fault. But all that was simply inappropriate in the present case. It was too foppish, and by now they could be miserable grandfathers of the children of this young creature if they were her fathers.

'Your bonnets are lovely, Miss, and we have been enjoying them,' said Eugen Lukeš.

'It was desolate here before they came, and it will be again after they've gone,' said Vilibald Lukeš, whose only concern was that Klotilda should realize that the entire success and failure of their future lives depended on her.

Miss Klotilda looked at each of them in turn, because she was surprised at their agitation; and seeing these sad, almost pleading, faces, serious and pale as if they were the faces of grandfathers with a granddaughter at the point of death, she brightened up and was suddenly sorry for these three lonely souls complaining of the desolation into which they had been cast, in the midst of magnificent splendour.

'Oh, it's not desolate here, dear landlords,' she cried with a smile. 'It's lovely and warm here.'

'It's lovely here because you and your delightful trifles are here,' replied Vilibald Lukeš, already completely persuaded of their misfortune. 'When you leave and take all these things away from us, there will be a gloomy air here, a hollowness, a desert, Miss Klotilda.'

'Oh, you're certainly joking!' cried Klotilda again, and her laugh, so fresh, bright and unaffected, sped through the room like the song of a nightingale in a night when everything was asleep and everything was gloomy.

It seemed to the brothers that their bronze statuettes were laughing along with Klotilda, that everything was trembling with delight, and that the whole room was filled with a host of angels playing every possible celestial instrument. They were also laughing in the midst of this pleasure. It was clear to them that they were in inescapable need of Miss Klotilda, and this made them content to the highest degree, because they knew what could stimulate them and make them happy. They did not indeed consider whether the lovely girl would want to do all this, because there was nothing on earth which they were unable to acquire!

'We could offer the lady sweets. We have good sweet things that we get from our cook. Would you like to try some, Miss Klotilda?' asked Jindřich, forcing himself not to say, 'Dear sister-in-law, these sweets have been made just for you!'

But Miss Klotilda, remembering that she had been talking longer than was decent, and that her mother on the fourth floor would certainly sustain a real migraine from this, responded in the negative.

'No, thank you, no! You are too kind. I must rush back to Mama, dear landlords. I'll just put everything back in the trunk, so that it can be delivered back to us straight away.'

And not waiting to know whether the Lukeš brothers would allow her to do so or not, she was tearing off pinafores and bonnets, standing unsteadily on tiptoe, laughing when she could not immediately reach them, jumping up and lifting her plump hands on which she had a silver bracelet given to her by Moji.

'And isn't there anything else?' she asked next.

'There are also some shoes and a bodice behind those doors.'

'Oh! – Moji had better not see that my shoes are behind those doors!'

'Moji? – Who is this Moji, Miss Klotilda?'

'May I go in there, dear landlords?'

'Of course, Miss Klotilda! You may go wherever you wish. But who is this Moji you have just mentioned?'

Klotilda slipped into the bedroom, snatched her little shoes, her bodice and her third bonnet, and returned, smiling at the thought of who that Moji was, that Moji of hers, who had thick curly hair and eyes as black as black diamonds. Klotilda knew that black diamonds could only look like his eyes.

'And where's the trunk, dear landlords?'

'There behind the sideboard, behind the curtains. – And who is that Moji?'

'Thank you!' said Miss Klotilda, opening the trunk. 'Moji? Did you really say Moji?'

'Of course, Miss Klotilda.'

'I really don't know whether I should say who Moji is.'

'Why ever not?' asked Vilibald, coming closer to her in some measure of great anxiety.

'What concern is it of yours, dear landlords, who Moji is? You don't know him – –'

'What is he like?'

'Moji?' asked Klotilda again, checking the contents of her trunk with infinite charm. 'Oh, he is very brave! Perhaps even you, dear landlords, were as brave as he is when you were thirty. He has lovely eyes and a lovely voice. For instance, when he talks –' Klotilda put on a deep masculine voice – '"That pink bonnet looks best on you, Tylda!" He calls me Tylda and I call him Moji, but his name is Mojmír. He was the one who gave me these shoes, and also this bonnet and this pinafore. And many other things underneath as well, handkerchiefs, towels and a dozen fancy napkins. All the rest was given me by my late godmother.'

'Who is this Moji, Miss Klotilda?' asked Vilibald again, though the other two had this question only in their thoughts.

'But haven't you guessed, dear landlords?' laughed Klotilda, whose happiest moments came when she was able to tell anyone about Mojmír Bareš.

'Not at all!'

'Well, he is my – fiancé!' said Klotilda, with some pride, expecting a torrent of congratulations from the masters of the house.

But they remained silent, as if petrified – horror-struck.

At that moment Klotilda cried out in pain.

It was a cry filled with anger, resentment, pain and surprise, a cry that was certainly bound to have been heard in the room of the Lukeš brothers.

Eugen Lukeš recognized it instantly and smiled bitterly.

'Did you prick yourself on some pins, Miss Klotilda?' he asked, darkly.

'Yes – and badly! – How did those pins get there?'

'Give them back to me, Miss Klotilda. They should never have got there.'

'And the trunk?'

'Havel and the cook will take it out immediately.'

'Immediately?'

'Of course.'

'Oh, thank you! It's so desolate upstairs without it.'

Miss Klotilda bowed, smiled again so that her teeth sparkled, and disappeared beyond the doors in the corridor.

In her mind she was already composing an important sentence in a letter for her fiancé.

'I've got the trunk home, Moji. I organized it without Mama knowing – she would have been very offended by your help. The landlords of the house are extremely friendly people and have wonderful apartments. The trunk hasn't been touched. – But no, I can't lie,' Klotilda said to herself, 'it's quite enough that I should be telling lies about the affair to Mama.'

At that moment Jindřich was ordering Havel to have the trunk taken back to paní Procházková on the fourth floor.

*   *

And it was evening once more. There were no stars, no wind, no rain. It was desolate, dry and dark. Nowhere was there any sound or glow on which to fix all one's mind, all one's soul, that is wearied by that darkness and silence. Ah, such evenings are like graves in which everything must moulder.

The Lukeš brothers, those poor people without wives, sat at dinner, afraid to speak, to laugh, to think; they were surrounded by a terrible emptiness. The Nothing, more powerful and more intrusive than ever before, crawled out from under the cupboards, from under the tables; it appeared in the windows and behind the curtains, and was as hideous as the head of Medusa, if she is indeed so hideous as it was. It stared the brothers in the eye, and snatched their sighs, their brief words and the rustling of their movements away into some bottomless abyss. Everything disappeared into that void.

The brothers toyed with their capon bones without relish, with a kind of aversion, not hungry, nor with any desire. At times it had seemed to them that a silvery feminine laugh must be heard from somewhere, but on that evening everything was dumb. – And in the room they had no bonnets to sustain their imaginations. Ah, what a fearful evening it was!

Vilibald, being more dissatisfied than either of his brothers, suddenly threw his fork down violently so that it clattered on the plate, and said, filled with anger and sorrow:

'Something must happen if we are not to suffocate.'

And the good Lukešes, brave and calm, satisfied and earnest, as they were, felt that they were poorer than anyone else in the world.

It had been some fragrant trinkets belonging to a charming, vain woman that had clarified the entire unforeseen situation to them.

Now it was necessary that one of them should undertake something to save himself and the other two. It was Vilibald who first summoned sufficient strength to carry out something great. One day he disappeared with Havel for a full three hours, and when he returned, he was smiling with such triumphant bliss that there could be no doubt how seriously and truly he had been occupied for those three hours.

Havel carried in a multitude of boxes, large and small, looking as mysterious as the boxes and packages themselves.

'What is that?' cried Eugen and Jindřich Lukeš, seeing the little procession.

'It's – our wife,' replied Vilibald.

In the boxes there were enchanting bonnets, bodices, shoes, pinafores, petticoats, stockings, lace, ribbons, linen – a snowfall.

'Oh!' cried the Lukeš brothers, flinging themselves at these delicacies with epicurean passion.

And the room, the dining room and the bedroom were immediately filled with bonnets, pinafores and so forth.

But Havel, standing by the door with his eyes filled with tears, said, at a moment when no one was expecting his voice:

'Yes, it's lovely, but it seems as if this is happening here in memory of a dear departed paní Lukešová.'

The brothers looked at one another – and suddenly burst into tears.

LIFE'S SORROW
RŮŽENA SVOBODOVÁ

I travelled out into the mountains and forests. It was June – hot, oppressive June. The days were almost unbearably long; the forests were free, remote, invigorating, with paths in them that were grassy, green, humid; the sky was deep, and white clouds as light as swans' down floated silently and swept over it.

Every morning, as I awoke, when it was still dark in my little room (in a cramped little room, with two little windows over an extensive, untended garden), when something light grey was merely shimmering from the east through the white curtain on the glass door, Žana, the landlord's daughter, would knock on the door sharply, and shout in a loud voice, without tact or tenderness, as if she were rousing some little herdsboy:

'Get up quickly! The sun isn't up yet, but you mustn't fool around so long!'

I got up, half asleep, with my deep sleep rudely interrupted, dressed myself quietly as if I were afraid of something, and went out to the front of the cottage.

The air was usually chilly but crystal clear and delectable, the sky cloudless, high and tranquil, greyish-blue, with only a slight mist in the east.

Although I was slightly fatigued and heavy-eyed, I ran quickly through the high, translucent forest and the wet grass to an open clearing, full of great felled pine trees, bark and white splinters, among the pink flowering hair grass. From there the valley of the plain could be seen, the whole distant landscape, roads darkened and saturated with water, broad fields stretching up to the remote mountains in regular ranks, and also tiny white villages with black roofs of shingle and thatch.

Far off among the mountains, along the whole length of the winding river, over each of its tributaries and also over the ponds by the colourful mills, light, milky mists were rising like breaths.

The low whitish cloud, hanging low above the mountains, turned red and became saturated with a brilliant, heavy, metallic crimson. Behind it appeared a higher section arching into the red of the glowing sun, whose enormous ball of heat and power was penetrating the snowy clouds, filling them in a fan-shaped range of rays of liquid gold, and floating, grown pale and ever clearer, into the pure, milky azure.

Over the whole landscape, not yet flooded with the noise of the day and of labour, the roosters were announcing dawn with their long-drawn-out call. From the slender spire of the little chapel, which towered over the forests as if it could reach to heaven merely through the sound of reveille, small, sweet bells sang their greeting to the new day, over the broad valley and the high pine forests.

Perhaps the villages were now awakening. Tiny white villages, piled together like playthings, so small and quiet, folded into the valley below me, that it was incomprehensible that pain and laughter might be welling forth even in them.

'What sort of pain?' I thought. 'What can agitate the uncomplicated, tough course of the lives of these folk? They labour when they are young and die in old age. Nothing more.' And I was anxious to investigate those tough aspects of their lives, little described in words – as little described in words as are their deaths, simply recorded on birch crosses above their tombs.

'He lived and died,' they seemed to say. 'What more can there be to say?' I longed to understand the sluggish, inert life of the village I saw daily at sunrise as if in an opened palm, and once, on a blustery day when it was unpleasant in the forests, and the wind was howling in the crowns of the swaying trees, I ventured down into the outspread landscape.

It took three-quarters of an hour to get to the nearest village on foot, though it had seemed within easy reach. It lay in broad meadows behind a pheasantry, a mill, and a fishpond. I persuaded Žana to be my guide, a strapping, twenty-year-old country girl who knew every corner of the region.

We went into the valley at one o'clock on a cloudy afternoon. It rained off and on. The clouds banked up in the west and rolled forward strongly. Women in colourful costume were working in a field of rapeseed, half mown, which rippled in the soft pink, verging on orange, of the land, and which lay in regular rows on the other side, binding it up. Out of the dark background of the forests, somewhere through a narrow slit in the clouds, a narrow ray of light broke through and illumined everything. The golden, slanting rapeseed, as well as the blue, red and yellow dresses of the women, saturated with the rain, were irradiated and suffused with the glow.

On the outskirts of the village, between barns with thatched roofs, we encountered an old man. He was walking slowly, and carefully clutching the fences. He was bareheaded. His jaw seemed shrunken, and the sockets of his eyes were black and empty below his half-closed eyelids. Where the fences ended and he had nothing on which to hold, he extended his hands in front of him, with palms outstretched, into the void, and walked slowly in his coarse blue canvas clothes, barefoot, scarcely moving forward. When we passed him he muttered something incomprehensible and fell silent.

Žana took me to the large farm of the village mayor. A large, stout peasant woman with a rectangular face, lazy, dark-haired and dishevelled, led us into her sitting-room. Four of her children and a dog rushed in after her.

She sat down heavily opposite us on a wooden bench behind the table, and breathed out.

'I was asleep,' she said, 'and the children came to wake me! And what is life like in a village? You have to slave away from morning to night, go through hell with these children, with no thought of amusement. I'd run away in a minute. It's no sort of life. You haven't even got anything nice to look at. Listen here, Eva,' she said to her ten-year-old daughter, who was standing in a corner biting her lip, 'go and fetch the teacher lady, and you, Karel, go and look for your Dad!'

The children went out, and the peasant woman went on complaining. She led us into the parlour, which smelt of mould, and showed us pictures of young officers with their signatures and dedications. She told us about her youth. She was from Prague, an innkeeper's daughter, and had been married out without a dowry to the owner of a big farm. She considered it a sacrifice, and had been blaming her husband for years. He came in out of the fields; he was a big man, gaunt, covered with dust, and physically worn out. He had kind blue eyes, fair hair and a face that was sunburnt up to his hairline. He caressed the head of one of his daughters, about four years old, and kissed her. His wife did not stop grumbling.

'When the soldiers came to this place, all the officers told me I was wasted in a village,' she said, placing her youngest daughter, about a year old, on her lap.

He shifted in impatience, looked out of the window, and drummed his fingers on the table, in order to avoid looking at his discontented, overweight, dishevelled wife with her big, lazy eyes, in her untidy, shabby clothes.

'People labour away like cattle till they almost drop! And when they come home they hear nothing but all this.' His eyes darted over the window frame, but his bony, tanned face did not change its expression.

'What are you looking for, ma'am,' said Žana, 'what sort of different life would you want? You have food to eat, praise God, and also someone to look after. And there is happiness in all that already!'

'That's what I say!' interjected the mayor cheerfully. 'Look, you must be content with what the Lord God has bestowed!'

She smiled contemptuously and pursed her thick lips.

Eva entered the room, and after her a young woman, slender and gentle, with a face pale as if from cold or want. She had a high forehead, and features and grey eyes filled with the expression of a sensitive soul, and full of suffering.

She was the village schoolteacher.

'Look, it's Auntie,' said the mayor's wife to her youngest daughter, who was holding out her little hands to the young lady.

The mayor frowned and turned away.

I could not understand why.

The young lady was the daughter of a village schoolmaster, the eldest of twelve children. She was serving as village schoolteacher for an annual salary of 120 gulden. In the mayor's household she was given a little soup at noon, from what they cooked for themselves and for their domestic servants. In return she taught and cared for their children, helped with the domestic chores and sewed for them. She was in poor health and overworked, but modest and quiet, sensitive and proud. The bread she received was repaid a hundredfold. The mayor's wife, strong and coarse as she was, exploited her. She loathed work herself, and placed everything that needed to be done in the frail white hands of the schoolteacher. The latter worked far into the night, to the point of fatigue and illness.

She was in love with an assistant teacher in her native village. The mayor's wife reminded her of this very frequently, with a coarse chuckle. Each time the schoolteacher shivered like a birch in the wind and interjected something serious about some work of hers, in order to divert the conversation elsewhere.

Grandfather came home for afternoon tea – the father of the master of the house, a red-faced, stout old man, quiet and taciturn.

'Run and give him coffee straight away, Miss,' said the mayor's wife, 'and give him the biggest bun, so that Grandpa doesn't think I don't appreciate him. In any case, he ought always to be served!'

'But I . . .' objected the old man inaudibly, smiling in embarrassment, and taking the little four-year-old girl, his granddaughter, on his lap, he pulled her dress down over her bare knees and with a rough, worn hand pressed her blonde, curly head to himself.

A beggar-woman came into the room – a little old lady, quite green in colour, with white wisps of hair under an unkempt green scarf on her forehead. It was the wife of the old blind man. She was also unable to see properly; neither of the two was able to work, and in the small living space that they had on a peasant's pension, a family with five children had moved in, paid them nothing and oppressed them. They tolerated them there, and did not throw them out, only because they were allowing them to keep warm.

'Where can we go in the forest now? We went once. My husband had a fall, and I had a fall, and we took nothing at all home! And so it is as they say: the common folk are worth nothing!' she said, lowering her head and weeping.

'Auntie,' said the mayor's son, who had the temerity to call me that, 'I'd like to have a horse. But only if they have horses in Prague not mounted on boards.'

'I'll send you one like that,' I said. 'Without a board.'

'But will you really? Aren't you just promising?'

'I really will, and I'll send you a whip and a drum.'

'And have you promised all this to Mum as well?' he asked, naïvely.

'And so people are just abandoned in this world like turtledoves!' sighed the green beggar-woman, as if no one had interrupted her lamentations. 'And people waste away, but they have no sympathy! If my old mother were alive, she would still be giving me some potatoes. But now I can scarcely beg for crusts of bread!'

Towards evening we left the village. All of them wanted to walk with us. All of them wanted to complain of their loneliness, so that the others could not hear, to someone to whom their grief would not seem mundane, but important and noteworthy.

Finally it was agreed: the children all wanted to walk, and because their father would not allow it, their mother also had to remain at home. 'So you have seen what village life is like,' she said in farewell. 'Only you townspeople would be able to understand, if I could tell you about everything I have been trying to do here.'

Only the schoolteacher and the master of the house came. The teacher fastened herself on me and urged me forward quickly so that Žana and the mayor should not hear.

The sun had already sunk below the horizon; behind it, the wind had been driving the clouds, and was now silent. The sky was grey in several layers, the fields green, the flowering meadow pink, the pea-field by the mill burning with the flowers of the common poppy.

The village was submerged in a wavy orchard of apple trees.

We walked quietly along the ridge, on which old spreading pear-trees were blooming, with their branches outstretched to the reddened sky.

The teacher was compelled to tell me about her grief. Sadly she whispered to me what I had seen for myself: the unfortunate position she had accepted with the mayor's family, embarrassing and without prospects.

'And if only I had seen that my work was not being done in vain, that I was working for someone who needed my work, that I was producing some benefit. But like this? I never see that anyone is better off from what I do. She merely has more time for complaining and irritating her husband. She should be glad that he forgave her – that he did not drive her out – after what happened . . .'

She was imagining I perhaps knew what had happened.

'But did you see?' she said. 'Poor man, he keeps control of himself; he knows the child is not to blame, but nevertheless when he looks at it, his eyes fill with tears, and he says, "If only it did not look so much like that Doležal, I might have forgotten!" I am so sorry for him that I excuse him for everything. But what is the use when he knows everything, and it is impossible for him to excuse it?'

Then she told me also about her own love affair – that her parents were standing in the way of it, and that he too was unhappy. It seemed to him that he was destined for something better than to be an assistant teacher in a village. He did not have the means to take a course of study at a technical college, so accepted what was on offer. She told me that he had built some sort of remarkable machine, an outstanding invention, but, lacking money, had needed assistance from someone else, and this man had appropriated the invention and exhibited it under his own name.

'And now, now we have fallen out with each other!' she said sadly, and explained why. But however she excused him, and painted the rosiest picture possible, I sensed that he was lying to her, and that he would be glad to escape her – that the reasons she was giving for his failure to write to her were transparent, badly patched together, and flimsy. Yet she was trusting him and failing to see the simple horror of the pretexts thrown up before her. She wept that everyone was thwarting their love, both his close family and hers – not understanding that all the coldness, all the erosion of the relationship was due to him and his own inner being.

'So God knows how things will turn out with us!' she concluded, and fell silent.

The master of the house was walking behind us with Žana. I could hear that he, too, was complaining.

'I'm glad when someone wise excuses my wife for a thing like that,' he was saying to her.

They led us up to the meadow and bade us farewell. Both of them thanked us for something, as if someone had done them the greatest favour, but in so confused and unconscious a manner that they themselves perhaps did not know why they were doing so.

We parted from them. In front of us, a silhouetted pheasant was rustling with the alarmed wings of its crowns, and behind us the life of the village was humming in the importance of proximity, as if we were pressing a conch shell to our ears.

I was recalling the whole of this incomplete, unresolved life, into whose open quarry I had been gazing. Those tough aspects of their life, for which I had been seeking only a few words, were meanwhile teeming with crowds of griefs. And I realized that there is no separate law for a smaller grouping. Society, which, pitiless and ruthless, pursues its own interests, which in the name of goodness destroys and oppresses, has manifested itself here too, as if shared from conjoined vessels. It has imposed its law of negative relationships on the tiny village, piled together, as it had seemed to me from the mountains above, like children's toys – so quiet that it had seemed no life was moving in it at all.

I heard the desires and the miseries of all of them blazing and crackling like the flames of a fire that is continually being fed. And I felt how little they all would lack, if they were to be spared suffering; but the torments they were preparing for themselves were welded together like the masonry of a building, conditioned by each other, and solid.

It was now dark, and the meadows were breathing with the dampness. Somewhere in the darkness above the fishpond, a lapwing screamed with its rough voice from afar, and then was silent.

Far off somewhere behind the fishpond and the little town, in the opaque gloom, as if emerging from the earth in a breath of vapour, long drawn-out singing could be heard. Delicate women's voices were singing a Marian hymn. We stood still and listened.

'A procession!' said Žana. 'They are going to the Holy Mountain and will stop in town overnight.'

The unpleasantness of the whole afternoon, the onset of night and the dampness of the evening, and that long-drawn-out hymn from somewhere in the dark, gripped me with gloomy yearning, in body and soul. I imagined the crowd of weary people somewhere beyond the town, going to find rest in the course of their pilgrimage in discomfort under some unknown roof, and I sensed how different – while equally strong – must be the source of their pain; what the faith and anxiousness that unites them must be, to bring them before the miraculous image of the Madonna for comfort and healing.

In the mirror of my heart, the waves were still tossing with the unsettled and unprocessed impressions of the whole afternoon: the griefs of the schoolteacher and of the mayor, the misery of the old, half-blind beggar-woman, the sad apology of the old pensioner, the longings of the mayor's wife and of her son, the conceptions of the singing penitents, and also their modest woes and prayers. And at that moment I grasped the separate, lonely life of the villages, the murmur of their tiny convergent springs, inaudible at a distance, above which – just as over a river – cares and woes, unseen in the bustle of the day, emerge and rise like white vapours before sunrise. In them, just as in hair nerves, there tremble elements of consciousness and feeling.

A VISIT TO HIS PARENTS

TEREZA SVATOVÁ

The neighbours, noticing the Říha family doing a lot of tidying and cleaning, were muttering, 'That cottage of the Říhas is being turned completely upside down.'

But soon they found out for whom the tidying was actually being done.

'The Říhas are at home waiting for their son Václav to arrive, and with his family too. – I hear he sent his parents a clear hundred to spend!'

Václav Říha was the pride not merely of his family – the entire village was proud of him. And how should they not have been! Václav had gone up in the world. He was sentencing people to death, and that was something to think about! He was the chief magistrate in the regional court.

He had finished his studies by pulling himself up by his bootstraps, as we might say. Although his parents had helped him a little off and on, that would hardly have been enough.

But Václav had always been lucky. Even as a student and later as a clerk, and when he had finally married the daughter of his superior, he had rapidly progressed through promotion at work until he had become chief magistrate of the regional court.

Now he had come back to Bohemia, and had written to his parents that he would come and see them at home, bringing his family too. He had been away from home for fifteen years now, but he used to write several times a year, always enclosing some money for his parents.

The Říha household were completely beside themselves with joy, and making everything ready so as to be able to welcome their son with due honour. They had whitewashed the cottage inside and out, the old man had painted all the doors yellow, re-gilded the rooster on the clock, repaired the fence, and was still fastening and hammering in nails. Říhová and her daughter Marjánka had prepared the eiderdowns. From the hundred gulden that Václav had sent, Říhová had bought white sheets and a lovely red tablecloth.

'I want everything to be in order,' she said to Marjánka. 'In any case I'm afraid his bride might say things about us behind our back.'

They had moved temporarily into the bedroom, only so that the young people would have more room, and had beautified the sitting-room so that it looked like a chapel.

At least, that was what her husband had said, when he surveyed the sitting-room with satisfaction.

On the day which the guests had set for their arrival, it was like the eve of a festival for the Říhas. The old man, in his best clothes, was walking around the building establishing, with an eagle eye, what still needed to be done. Říhová and Marjánka had their cotton aprons starched completely solid, and were bustling around in the kitchen, making sure the food would be ready when the guests arrived.

Říhová had been completely rejuvenated with her joy that Václav was coming, let alone the grandchildren! She simply could not wait.

Only when she remembered his bride, she always checked herself. Perhaps not because his bride was from such a grand family – but Václav's wife was German, and that vexed Říhová.

'I'd have given up ten years of my life if only Václav had brought me a daughter of our own people,' she used to say at every opportunity.

While Říhová was cogitating in this way, Říha was walking up and down in front of the building, gazing into the distance to see whether their guests were coming. Finally he spied a carriage on the highway.

'They're here!' he cried in a trembling voice into the building, and the womenfolk rushed straight out to welcome the guests.

The latter finally arrived and drew up in front of the building.

Out of the carriage stepped a stout gentleman with a serious countenance, perhaps a little greying.

Was this really Václav? The old couple could not believe their eyes. They had imagined him entirely differently. Poor people, they had forgotten that fifteen long years had passed since they had last seen their son, and that time had left its traces on Václav's appearance. In their hearts there still lived a rosy-cheeked youngster, and for that reason this serious gentleman somehow drew them up short.

After him emerged a petite lady, as tiny as a doll, thought Říhová to herself, and finally two angelic little girls all in ribbons and lace.

The old couple embraced them and looked at their son in almost reverential admiration. Marjánka even bent down trying to kiss her brother's hand, though he prevented her from doing so. It had never entered Marjánka's head that this eminent gentleman might be her brother.

The first day passed fairly well at the Říhas. Václav took his wife around the building, the garden, and so forth, explaining it all to her, meanwhile asking questions about everything; one after the after, his parents willingly supplied answers.

However, the second day was somehow awkward for all of them. The reason may have been that Václav's wife did not understand Czech, and nor did the granddaughters. And how glad Říhová would have been to chat with them!

Říha also tried in vain to launch some kind of conversation with his son. He kept clearing his throat each time he addressed his son. Václav answered him affably, but in a somehow inhibited way. It seemed that he was embarrassed to find something to speak about with his parents.

Říhová continually bustled round the room, waiting for her son to start asking all kinds of questions, as he had always used to do when he had come home as a student.

However, he was talking to his wife in German, forgetting that his mother was also waiting in the room.

So Říhová always went outside to work, and it was strange: when the children were in the house, her eyes were continually brimming with tears.

Marjánka did not spend much time at home; she was very uneasy with the guests, and, poor thing, gasped when Václav addressed a word to her now and then. She preferred to go out with the children, with whom she quickly made friends.

After all, children will always be children.

On the third day the guests left.

The old couple could not help loading them up for the journey with everything they could find.

Old Říhová's heart leapt for joy when the children gave her to understand that they wanted to stay with her.

Weeping, she kissed them. But when she bade farewell to Václav, she felt as if she must collapse under the weight of the emotions that were assaulting her.

Even Václav's eyes were misted over as he parted from his parents.

Finally they drove off. The old couple stood on the porch for a long time, gazing sadly at the carriage until it had disappeared from their sight.

Both of them maintained an embarrassed silence until Říhová asked, in a broken voice, 'Don't you think Václav has simply changed?'

Her husband silently agreed. After a while he said, quietly, 'Don't be surprised. He has become used to the life of a gentleman, and we, common folk, no longer suit him.'

'You're right – we don't suit him,' wailed Říhová, and quickly she went into the building to relieve her constricted heart in the bedroom.

Do you know the fable about a simple hen who hatched a bird of paradise?

THE PRÁŽE - A PRAGUE BASTARD
TEREZA SVATOVÁ

When Vondráková returned from church after the service of thanksgiving after childbirth, she said to her husband, 'What would you think, old man, of adopting a "Práže" to bring up as well?'

'Whatever's got into you?' growled Vondrák. 'After all, you're not strong, and our boy's such a complete handful – where will that leave us?' And he looked fondly at the baby which his wife had just laid on the bed.

Bending over the little boy, he said, 'They're wanting to sideline you.'

Vondráková, pretending she hadn't heard, pressed on. 'Look, Horáčková has weaned two children too, and nothing's happened to her, and think of the money she's got from Prague for that! She's told me that if it hadn't been for her Práže, it would have been really bad for them. For the money they got from Prague, they rented a field on a manorial estate, and now they have rye and potatoes for the whole winter.' With a sigh, she added, 'We have it worse!'

'Come on, maybe it won't be so bad for us. After all, we'll be saving a few pence,' countered Vondrák.

'Anything we save before Christmas we'll spend after Christmas, and there won't be anything till the day we die. But if you agree and let me go to the maternity hospital in Prague for a child, it'd turn out quite differently for us. When the gentry rent out their fields in the autumn, we could also get hold of one, and there'd be an end to our eternal scrimping and scraping!'

And Vondráková spent so many hours talking her husband into it, she painted such touching pictures of their future wellbeing, that finally, overcome by her eloquence, he agreed.

A week later she set out for Prague.

Mortally tired from walking and from her exertions, she brought a child home with her, hoping against hope that things would turn out well.

'She's called Jindřiška,' she said, showing her husband a fine, rosy-cheeked girl.

Soon it was not only the people in the house who came to the Vondráks to see the Práže, but also the neighbouring women. Vondráková explained what she had been required to do in Prague, and how she had done it, and showed off some lovely baby-clothes as well as the document giving the child's name.

'Jindřiška Švarcová, born on the fifth of June 1868,' spelt out one of the women.

'She must be some aristocrat's child,' decided the women-folk, when they discovered how much Vondráková was being paid for the child.

'Whoever would have thrown you away, poor little thing?' whispered the widow Slezáková to herself.

Slezáková was the housekeeper where the Vondráks lived. She was one of the women of whom it is said that they have their hearts in the right place.

Although she did not count exactly as rich, for a wooden cottage with a thatched roof and a few small fields cannot be regarded as wealth, she was full of good deeds. 'Love your neighbour as yourself' was always her guiding principle.

But her own bed had not been one of roses.

Her late husband, whom she had loved for the sake of his handsome face, and whom she had married against the will of her parents, had been a cold man with an unyielding heart. He had preferred a grain of wheat to the kindest of words, and thought a penny's worth of money more valuable than the deepest of emotions. He laid more burdens on his wife than she could bear. And yet Slezáková had not complained, and every time she remembered her late husband, she shed tears.

The only child of their marriage not only inherited his father's handsome face, but also exhibited the same strange heart to the world. Things had not turned out for her quite as she would have wished.

'Just think, it'll be hard for a woman like that to justify herself before God – to have brought that poor creature into the world and then to push it away,' said Slezáková, turning to the women.

They nodded silently, and those of them who were holding children in their arms hugged them all the more tightly to their breasts.

*   *

Who would have guessed that Vondráková should have failed to experience everything that she had imagined would be so rosy?

'But that's how it is – man proposes and God disposes,' wept Vondrák, after returning home from his wife's funeral, while the housekeeper had meantime been taking care of the children. 'I always said she was weak, but she wouldn't be talked out of it and that field never stopped tempting her. She struggled, she struggled, and then the two children – and when she began to realize I was right, it was too late . . .'

Vondrák sat down on the chest by the bed where both children were sleeping peacefully, and looked at them sadly.

'What am I to do with you now?' he lamented.

'God help you – it'll be a heavy burden,' said the housekeeper in response.

'And what will happen to Jindřiška?' she asked suddenly.

'I am taking her back to Prague,' said Vondrák dryly.

Slezáková was wounded to the heart.

Jindřiška was her favourite. From the first time she had seen her she had liked her, and the child, as soon as she began to distinguish between people, always stretched out her hands to her.

How delighted Slezáková had been when the child had crawled to her door for the first time and called out, 'Granny'. 'Yes, call me that, poor little one, it will be worse when you find out you have neither granny nor mummy,' she said bitterly. No day passed without her giving the child something, and when she went to church she would always bring back some treat from town . . .

And now she must be parted from her!

Who knows into whose hands the child will pass – she will be beaten, she may also go hungry. –Slezáková knew how a Práže would be brought up, and knew all too well what kind of care she would receive for so little money.

Jindřiška's fate disquieted her so much that she could not sleep at night, and wherever she went, she saw before her the sincere, childish eyes, she heard the sweet little voice, and she felt the warm little hands of Jindřiška embracing her.

'I'll take you on myself,' she decided, when the people in the house had gone out to the funeral and she was left alone in the building.

'I'm not giving you up, I'm not, little one,' she whispered to the child. 'Though I'm old now, I'll at least save you from the worst.' She told Vondrák briefly what she had in mind, and he was completely in agreement with it.

Jindřiška moved into the other room that same day.

The neighbours took it amiss that Slezáková should take on such a burden at her age; they raised objections and suggested good reasons, but nothing would persuade her – Jindřiška remained in the village . . .

'What will Tonička have to say about this?' fretted the women.

Tonička was Slezáková's daughter.

She was a peach of a girl: pretty, lively, cheerful – she had no equal far and wide. But she did have one fault: she was proud and dissatisfied. She did not like village life, and longed for something else . . . The city, the city constantly tempted her.

The reproofs of her friends did not help; even the weeping of her mother failed to soften her. She held to her opinion, and one fine day she went off to Prague – into service . . .

On that occasion, Slezáková stood sadly on the doorstep and gazed for a long time at the departing vehicle. 'I cared for you like the apple of my eye, I'd have shed my blood for you – and yet you're still leaving me!' she whispered.

But that is what children always do.

They cling, cling to the parental nest as long as they need shelter; but a single tempting sound from outside is enough to make them fly off. Although they cast their eyes back in longing and weep, hardly have the tears on their cheeks dried before they are smiling, and they forget that a heart is bleeding deep within the old folk.

Thus it was also with Slezáková.

It was a long time before she began even slightly to forget her daughter. There were sad moments when she was sitting alone on long winter evenings – it was a wonder that she did not cry her eyes out with sorrow then.

The room she lived in seemed empty; no one was there who might bring it to life with singing and happy laughter.

It was empty and gloomy also in her old heart. Years passed. Her daughter came home a few times, but now it was not the same cheerful, rosy-cheeked Tonča in her short frock and with a red kerchief on her fair hair.

Now serious, in her town clothes, a hat on her head, she seemed a different, alien person even to her own mother.

Each time, after her daughter had left, Slezáková had been more gloomy and more taciturn.

Suddenly, everything had changed – the room had come to life. The presence of the child had lighted up the poor dwelling like a ray of sunshine, and the glow from the child's eyes now warmed even her fading heart.

Ever since Slezáková had had the child with her, she had been a changed woman – completely rejuvenated.

And now, more often than previously, she was remembering her daughter, not as the woman in those fancy clothes – that woman never entered her mind – but as the fair-haired, blue-eyed child she had once taken to her heart with love and hope, as if she had returned to her once more in Jindřiška . . .

And before she could say Jack Robinson, the little girl had turned six.

*   *

Sunday afternoon.

All was quiet in the village, with not a soul to be seen. The young people had left for Benediction in town; the older folk were either loitering in the fields or dozing at home indoors or in their gardens, and even the children were keeping quiet because it was so sultry.

Slezáková was sitting in the garden behind her cottage, saying her prayers.

She had not been to church, so had to make up for it at home. But because of the heat, even her prayers were somehow impeded – the old lady kept dropping off to sleep.

Jindřiška skipped around her grandmother for a while and played with Gypsy, the dog; when the two of them were tired, they settled down at her grandmother's feet.

The little girl yawned – yawned – and closed her eyes.

Gypsy growled but immediately closed his eyes again and went back to sleep: he had recognized someone coming.

It was Jedlička, the village postman.

'I have something for you, Auntie,' he said, taking a sealed letter from his leather bag.

'That'll be from Tonča. Anyhow, it's such a long time since she last wrote to me.'

The postman left. –

Slezáková called after him, 'Send Marjánka this evening to collect a few pears – I forgot to give you any, even from the road!'

'Fine, fine, thank you, I'll send her!'

The old lady slowly opened the letter and began reading . . . . 'Dear Lord!' she cried out suddenly, 'whatever can have happened?'

'My daughter! My Tonča!' she wailed.

Surprised, the child looked at Slezáková, but the old lady noticed nothing, merely wringing her hands and weeping.

It was a long time before she began to come to herself. Jindřiška, seeing her grandmother in such a state, also burst into tears.

The people in the house rushed out, and curious faces began to show themselves in the neighbourhood as well – and in a short time the entire village had found out that Tonička Slezáková was mortally ill in Prague and that the old lady would travel there the next morning.

Before sunrise the next morning there was a carriage already waiting outside the building, and the old lady, in her Sunday best, bade the people in the house farewell.

The housekeeper was to take care of Jindřiška and the household in the meantime.

When she saw her daughter, Slezáková thought her heart would break with grief.

Pale and gaunt, she looked more like a corpse than a living person.

It was clear that Slezáková had arrived in the nick of time, for the sick girl was barely capable of speech.

On the day after her mother had arrived, Tonča begged that they should be left alone.

'Mama,' she began, when the others had left the room, 'forgive me, for God's sake, please, please, for the sin I have committed against you.'

The old lady caressed her cheek, for she could not utter a word through her tears.

'Forgive me also this – what I am about to tell you now' – continued Tonča with the greatest exertion.

It was like a wound to Slezáková.

'Mama – I'm not as blameless – as you may think I am; – – I'm – – – I have – I have had a child – –' she added, barely audibly.

The old woman's head was spinning, her knees shaking; she thought she might faint.

Her daughter – her Tonča – dishonoured! 'Ah, Tonča!' she sighed in grief.

The sick girl turned pleading eyes on her mother – and this gaze disarmed her.

These eyes were no longer of this world . . .

'I forgive you,' said Slezáková after a pause. 'Where is the child?'

'Ask at the maternity hospital: they will tell you, here on this document.'

Tonča took out a yellowed folded document from her bosom. 'Take this, Mama – and forgive me this sin!' she begged, in a muffled voice.

She tried to say something more, but her voice failed, and she closed her eyes as if they could not bear her mother's gaze.

Slezáková opened the document mechanically, but had hardly glanced at it before she tottered.

The same name, the same year and date, as were on the document she had at home, which had been brought long ago by Vondráková together with Jindřiška from Prague.

'It is God's doing! – Jindřiška! Tonča! I have the child – do you hear, Tonča?' she cried, completely beside herself.

The sick girl may have understood this, for a slight smile flitted across her face although she did not open her eyes. She breathed more and more weakly, and towards evening died peacefully . . .

And Slezáková, kneeling by her bedside, did not vex the dying girl with a single word.

She did not find out, therefore, who the father of the child was.

From the information she received from the maternity hospital she found out that the child had been well provided for, and guessed that Jindřiška's father had probably been the gentleman who had taken Tonča into service . . .

*   *

Some years later.

Jindřiška has meanwhile grown into a slender girl. Her hair is truly as fair and beautiful as Tonča's once was, her teeth white and her cheeks rosy as Tonča's were; but her eyes are not the same – large and dark. Her grandmother is thinking, 'Perhaps she takes after her father there.'

Singing and laughter are heard once more in old Slezáková's cottage, and the old lady forgets more often how long ago it was that the first girl had left her for ever. After all, she has left such a lovely replacement . . . It is only when people say, 'Just look at that Práže, what a fine girl she has turned into!' – that the old lady turns pale, and caresses and embraces her Jindřiška with still greater love.

She would love to say to people, 'She's my granddaughter', but cannot disturb her daughter's rest in the grave – for nothing in the world would she ever bring her into such dishonour!

For that reason she says a twofold prayer, both for the departed and for the living . . . .

TALE ABOUT NOTHING, NO. 5 (1903)

VLADIMÍRA JEDLIČKOVÁ

It was early morning; in the smithy, iron was sounding reveille, larks were flying from the forest and bees from their hives, and in a garden they had poppies, blooming blue.

The night had been beautiful; fruit had ripened in it, and the air was scented with the fruit.

Before dawn the clouds had been in fog; the sun had broken through them, they were falling on the meadows, which were still dim, they were also caught on the branches, and the maples were damp.

The lime trees were in flower, a faint, broad scent was dripping on the clover, bees were singing in the flowers; it was a protracted, stifled chant coming as if through locked chambers, though the sky was open and was itself singing.

Someone had mown the ridges; long grass was lying on their cut roots – it was wet, mixed with last year's grass; footsteps over it were silent and toilsome.

*　*

The sun had meanwhile risen and the mown grass turned into a soft, clattering pile of cuttings.

He returned home; the bees were singing in the lime trees, the earth was burning in the sun.

*　*

He found some bad mushrooms; they had a pungent scent of benediction. They had been unnoticed under one of the trees; all the strawberries had been picked, women had broken off young branches from the pine trees, children had taken away richly flowering boughs from the lime trees, but no one had taken away the bad mushrooms, and they were so beautiful and so pure – he breathed in their burning scent, and he broke them all in half.

(121)

The clouds were a wonderful blue; the poplars were bathing their new leaves directly in their abyssal depths, set ablaze by the sun.

On the hillside the grass was so suffused with light that it was yellow, even white, with a ray suspended on every blade.

On the low bushes wild cherries were ripening, over them gleamed outgrowths of small larches, a child bent down to kiss them; in the village the poultry was calling, and when it was silent the birds were calling, and the earth could be heard calling.

Below the grove there were meadows; he remembered that somewhere abroad there were graveyards below the forest, and that at the outskirts of the forest, where the trees were slender and sparse, a burial chamber could be seen, pure white, with Doric columns, with covered windows, with graves lying in green stains – he remembered it well.

He looked down through gaps in the trees: the meadows must be damp with dew, and where the sun was already falling, a sultry, steamy heat must be radiating – he could almost feel it.

There are no dead bodies there, he thought, but then he remembered all the insects, from the bees of the meadow to the tiny grasshopper, from the white ant to the greenfly on the caraway – all of them were dead when their time came, and so he saw graves, open and futile, graves in green stains, graves in the meadow.

He picked ears of rye; they were full of grain, they were soft, with the taste of fresh bread, the cornflowers were already turning white. A harmless grass snake was lying on one path; far from it, tall, milk-infused poppies were ripening – they were a splendid green, without intermediate shades, and without flowers.

He returned through the grove; the footpath was narrow, with pine needles. One of the lime trees was in bloom; he found it by its scent – it stood tall in the sun, the bees were singing from it. Suddenly an egg fell from the tree; it was green, he picked it up and carried it in his hand for a long time. It was as cold as stone, and did not even begin to get warm – it was the egg of a wild dove.

He imagined he was carrying a dead bird and quietly repeated to it: the bees are singing, the bees are singing for you, thousands of bees are singing for you.

So he reached home; the clouds were a wonderful blue, the poplars were dark, it was noon.

TALE ABOUT NOTHING, NO. 14

VLADIMÍRA JEDLIČKOVÁ

He could still hear crickets – the green crickets on the hazel bushes.

He bade farewell to the garden; for the last time he saw its wilted foliage, its bees, fruit, hazel nuts, elder trees.

He touched the grass; he also touched the slugs in the grass.

He touched the roses, the cobwebs, the vines, the irises, the earth.

He entered a transparent arbour – the leaves there were white, lying on the paving stones.

He sat down to dream – close by, the hawthorn was rustling; through the vine he saw red dahlias over the milk-weed; he dreamt of roses, of summer, of birds, of bees; he bade farewell to the meadows and to the grove and to the wild roses below a certain hillside.

All summer long he had loved the gardens and the fruit and the flowers and he had loved the heather in the meadow and the pine needles and the fields with ears of corn and with clumps of clover; he had seen the willows and poplars in spring and yesterday he had seen green grasshoppers on the dry sedge and he had recognized the leaves floating on the stream.

So he bade farewell to the Chinese roses; they were the colour of faded dandelions; and he remembered the poplars and the ash trees and he listened to the rustling of the hawthorn close by.

Soon I shall see neither green grasshoppers nor red flybane; I shall search in vain for ants on the paths and for cobwebs and for hazel nuts.

I shall hear neither the birds nor the summer rains nor the music of bees on the meadow and in the lime trees.

He spoke this to the garden and to the vine and to the asters and it belonged to the grove and to the edible wild mushrooms and to the fallen pine needles and it belonged to all meadows and to every field and to all red ants and to all reeds.

He bade farewell to the poplars and to the acacia bushes and to all fruit trees and his hand also touched the elder trees and the hazel bushes and he stroked the red currants and at last he gently pushed apart the raspberry bushes, the raspberry bushes, which were completely yellow.

Finally he drove away; he was carrying a Chinese rose and one ant, one red ant.

MARIE VON EBNER-ESCHENBACH

On the eve of the silver wedding anniversary of a highly respected married couple, which was to have been celebrated by a wide circle of their family and friends, the wife shot herself.

It was a completely inexplicable event. The suicide had lived in the happiest of circumstances, and had been most dearly loved and highly esteemed by all who knew her. She stole away with no farewell, leaving not a single line, no explanatory word, for any of her relatives – nothing that could have been taken even as a hint of leave-taking. She must have gone to her death as one walks from one room to another. On her writing-desk lay the account books, in which she had entered the expenses incurred that day, and the kitchen money for the next day. And, besides, a tribute that had arrived a few minutes earlier from the association of which she had been the president, twenty-five 'La France' roses in a beautiful silver vase, and a packet of telegrams, some of which had already been opened: all of them were full of warm praise and sincere congratulations.

And the lady whom they concerned had been found dead in her chair at the writing desk, and beside her on the floor was the revolver she had used to shoot herself in the heart. Straight in the heart. A well-calculated shot that must have been guided by a steady hand.

The revolver belonged to her: it had been presented to her as a gift the previous year by her soldierly son-in-law. Papa had at that time chosen an isolated house in a rather inhospitable mountain region as a residence for himself and his wife. Presumably the erudite, passionate ornithologist hoped to identify some unusual species of bird there. How everyone laughed when the captain presented his mother-in-law with a revolver before she left for her summer holiday, with the words:

'Take it with you! You will use it in an emergency. Dear Papa forgets to pull the trigger even at the most dangerous moment when some strange bird of the night is flying by.'

The captain was the only one in the entire family who often permitted himself joking references to 'dear Papa' or 'our saintly Grandma', even giving vent a little to his seething impatience with both of them.

The others maintained an ironic silence to their faces; behind their backs they probably made up for that. The little young ones seemed taken with me, even though I hardly knew them. There was no communication between us – we merely exchanged a few polite phrases when we happened to meet somewhere or other by chance.

I entered the house shortly after Frau Gertrud had committed her dreadful deed. It had been arranged that I should fetch her for a meeting of our association. And now I met her family, cast down in grief and horror at her death. The drawing-room to which her parents and her daughters had gone was adjacent to the bedroom in which the corpse had been laid out on the bed. Through the open door came loud sobbing, weeping and wailing, and frequent sudden bursts of laughter, hair-raising and strident. The unhappy husband was abandoning himself unrestrainedly to his despair. He fell to his knees before the bed, sprang up, ran back and forth wringing his hands, paused, and addressed the dead woman:

'Trudel! Trudel! . . . You can't be serious . . . A joke – but such an ugly one . . . Don't play the fool like this . . . Wake up . . . Get up!' . . . And once more the dreadful laughter, and once more an outburst of despair. Meantime, soothing words from the doctor and from her two sons-in-law, who eventually succeeded in leading the poor man away from the corpse and into his own rooms.

All this time I had been reproaching myself. Why was the indescribable grief of this unfortunate man causing me almost unbearable pain, but no genuine heartfelt sympathy? What was the reason for this? Had I suddenly become hard-hearted, or so egoistic that the suffering of others was leaving me unmoved because I myself was feeling deep suffering? – The deceased had meant a great deal to me; our joint activity, which had achieved significant successes after long struggles, had forged a very close bond between us. I had lost more in her than I had been able to gauge immediately, under the impression of the first horror. But I already knew that it would get worse and worse every day; that on every fresh occasion I would miss her influence, her loving, calm guidance, always sure. And yet it was self-evident that it was not my grief, but only hers, that should now be allowed to speak. Where, then, were the grounds for my insensitivity to the outbursts of despair from her unfortunate husband?

The silent desolation of her parents touched me, of course, and also the grief of the younger daughter. She knelt brokenly beside the armchair into which her grandfather had collapsed. The old man pressed the head of his granddaughter to his breast, and softly stroked her tearstained face. If any stray tear from his own eyes fell upon it, he wiped it away carefully with his handkerchief, as if this single heavy drop should not be permitted to mix with the childish tears that were flowing in such unconstrained streams. No word escaped his lips, no appeal not to weep. Indeed not – he knew well that she must cry it out. To cry things out – that art is one practised only by the young; with their tears they overcome their sorrow once it is cried out . . . Then cheerfulness returns; then the lovely blonde woman will again be heard laughing; she will cheer her husband returning home from the parade as Klärchen cheered Egmont;[1] she will delightedly kiss the fingertips of her baby in the cradle and perform antics for him which he is of course not yet able to appreciate. She will sing and rejoice in her insignificant life as though no shadow had ever disturbed the brilliance of its mirror-clear and mirror-smooth uniformity.

It was otherwise with Eleonore, her elder sister. She will not soon recover from the heavy blow of fate that has been dealt to her today. What is expressed in her features, however, is not childish grief for her mother, but sharp accusation – bitter resentment. I could read the question from her face: How could you have done this to me? To me, the wife of a civil servant with a promising future, on the path to a high position in life, who will carry me up to it too! Now a reproach is hanging over me, heavy as lead: You have made me the daughter of a suicide. – Those were certainly the thoughts of the beautiful lady with a heart as hard as steel. She had nothing but reproaches for her mother; she was not asking what had driven her from them, or what had made life intolerable for the poor woman. At this moment, at least, no feeling of compassion was accessible to her.

Her husband came with an assurance that her poor Papa was slightly calmer. He sat down next to her, speaking quiet, tenderly soothing words to her, which she accepted like a shy beggar receiving a far too meagre gift of alms.

Her grandmother was the reverse of this granddaughter. The old lady was sitting in a corner of the sofa opposite the bedroom door, which was now closed, looking at it from time to time with a shudder. She seemed sunk in herself, as if ground down under the burden of an inexorable judgment. Her face, pale as wax, expressed a grief above any other grief. The Virgin Mary, the *mater dolorosa*, wept at

1   Egmont, the eponymous hero of Goethe's tragedy of 1788, and his mistress Klärchen.

the cross of the Redeemer, but was able in spirit to see him resurrected in splendour, to eternal glory ... But this poor mother was weeping for one for whom the Saviour had died in vain. She held a rosary in her hand, which she had taken mechanically out of her bag, but she was not praying. Her daughter was a suicide, and damned to eternity. No one prays for the damned.

For a time I stood facing this silent agony – but finally could no longer endure the sight. I approached the old lady, sat down next to her, bent over, and kissed her ice-cold hands. She flinched, startled by the touch of my hot lips, and tried to withdraw her hands from me. I held them tightly ... I began, at first probably stammering, but then with greater and greater confidence and quite like a habitual liar, to speak of an unfortunate accident ... Accident! – I could not accept any other possibility. It could not have played out more cruelly than as it had happened, it could not have occurred on a day when it had been a heavier blow ... I – indeed, I had always feared it and had always warned against it ... The revolver, in the same drawer as the publications of our association, had always frightened me. She used to handle it so carelessly ... Quite recently I had had to put it away myself, for it was lying on her writing desk with the muzzle against her breast ... My God, how shocked I had been! – I had cried out in absolute horror, 'Frau Gertrud, if by chance one were to bump against the thing and it were to go off ... Frau Gertrud, surely the thing is not loaded?', and she had answered, 'No, I do not think it is.'

Her poor mother listened tensely; her clenched lips relaxed. 'No, I do not think it is,' she repeated softly. 'She did not know it was? ... Did she say, '"No, I do not think it is"?'

I continued with lie after lie, inventing all kinds of moderately probable details ... And I succeeded: I convinced her, I provided her with redemption. Her dry, embarrassingly rigid eyes became moist; a sob convulsed her breast, she wept, and she prayed.

*   *

While I was still weaving my web of lies, the doctor had entered the room and had been listening to me. When I left he accompanied me. For a time we walked next to each other in silence, and then he said, in his abominable manner of making a joke at the most inappropriate of occasions:

'Dear lady, you have been pumping out an impressive smokescreen today.'

To which I replied, 'Blessed be white lies!'

He shook his head, quoting, 'The truth, the truth – even if it should destroy us!'

'Us, you say! – and other people as well? No, no, I am not in favour of things that destroy. Truth dressed in a scarlet hood armed with the executioner's axe, or tender lies of mercy, bringing healing relief to wounds – which of the two do you prefer, Doctor?'

– 'In my own professional capacity, of course . . .' He had become serious; a long pause intervened before he began to speak again. 'For twenty years I have been dealing with this family, and I would have thought anything at all possible rather than that a suicide should take place in it. But I am in no doubt that Frau Gertrud did indeed commit suicide – possibly after a sudden decision, but in complete presence of mind . . . Why should she have done so? – this tranquil, dutiful, seemingly happy woman! . . . Somewhere there must be concealed a terrible secret – it cannot be otherwise.'

I replied that I did not believe in any terrible secret; he held to his opinion, and I did not contradict him any further. Once the imagination of a rational person unfurls its wings, who can restrain its flight? In any case – my lies had been believed, and the truth I thought I knew was very unlikely to find acceptance.

That night I could not sleep. I could not stop thinking about Gertrud, with deep sorrow. No slander had dared to approach her hitherto, but now it had an opportunity to disgorge its poison, and would do so, denigrating the memory of the woman who was of such blessed memory to me. She had contributed to the welfare of thousands of people and had exercised enormous talent as a leader, together with good-natured wisdom; she was the heart and soul of our association, and we had been proud to be able to collaborate in the ambitious projects of a strong-minded woman of genius. I had admired Gertrud particularly for that, and for setting an unattainable example for a weak, compliant person like myself. But when I saw her in her own home, the picture changed for me. Our clear, strong leader seemed distracted, uncertain, and almost shy. One can see so much, and so clearly, at the first glance, with an eye that is still unbiased! My own eye took in immediately, and clearly, that she was alone among her relatives – oppressed between the older and younger generations. Her mother was a heavy burden on her, and her father probably gave her no support. I knew him by sight – the famous lawyer, the combatant and victor. He had exceeded the age limit as a professor, but continued to work boldly and recklessly as a writer.

He was a man of high standing, too high for his family to be able to depend on him. To you, distant things are close, and nearby things remote, I said to myself, as I watched him for a while, and saw the gaze of his big, watery blue eyes glide over the round table, and then suddenly become fixed on an object opposite him, as if ignited by an inner light. For us, that is, it was an object – and merely a coffee machine on the sideboard – but for him it was something invisible, a mathematical point, and the epiphanic gleam in his eyes was the reflection of a great thought springing up in his mind.

The two daughters . . . How had this mother produced these daughters? They were as closely related to her as a couple of birds of paradise would be to a lioness. Thesi, the younger, was a typical little officer's wife, full of admiration for her handsome husband, finding everything that was not concerned with him and 'his regiment' beside the point. The elder was an imposing beauty like Frau Gertrud – an equally tall figure with a noble head, and features replete with the powerful refinement that delights us in Greek representations of goddesses. During lunch, which has remained such an embarrassing memory for me, I sat opposite her, feasting on her appearance and expecting that it would produce the revelation of a soul commensurate with it at any moment. But nothing emerged but a cold, cruel arrogance, in every expression of hers, and in her least utterance, which rendered her beautiful face somehow run-of-the-mill.

Poor Gertrud – there could be no bond and no understanding between her and these two young women . . . In the anxious night after her death, the memory of the insight I had gained into her domestic life returned to me, in a jumble and as it were drop by drop. The conduct of her daughters towards her, unloving and inconsiderate even in the presence of a stranger, must have been more so in private . . .

In front of me it was easy to see that they were acting in unison, but they could not hide their impatience at having to wait for their Papa. The civil servant stoked the embers with pointed remarks. These acquired a slightly poisonous flavour when Grandmother rejected Gertrud's question, whether they should serve up the meal, with horror, as if her daughter had suggested setting the house on fire. Grandfather saw and heard nothing of this; he was wandering, lost to the world, in his own realm of thought. The cavalry officer and his wife had retreated to a recess in the window, and were quietly and eagerly negotiating with each other; she seemed to be asking him for something and he seemed to be making suggestions. Finally he turned and hurried across to Gertrud, clicked his heels, and said:

'Forgive me, Mama, but – the meal is always at the same set time . . .' He made a brief apology and left the room.

Thesi burst into tears, the grandmother grumbled to herself, and the expressions of the civil servant and his wife became more and more contemptuous. Agonized, Gertrud apologized to me, and I wished I were hundreds of miles away, thinking I would never again accept an invitation to a family dinner in this house.

The mood had been irretrievably spoilt when the author of all this havoc entered, or rather crept into, the room. Like most people who are habitually late, he was always in a hurry. In the street the tall, lean scholar could be seen striding along in constant haste, his head bent forward, his eyes searching absent-mindedly, and, even when there was no wind at all, his coat-tails flying.

He was received by his wife and by her parents without a single word of reproach. He greeted them with warm kindness, patted his daughters' heads one after another, disturbing Eleonore's coiffure and getting his cufflink caught in Thesi's hair without noticing that he had pulled some of it out, and he also failed to notice that one of his sons-in-law was absent from the table and that his younger daughter was pouting. But when she expressed her grief in words, he was full of remorse. – Has Kari left, still hungry, without eating! Oh no! Oh dear! Oh, he was really so sorry! . . . No – how awful! Oh dear, oh dear, it would never happen again . . . and had never happened before in any case, today only by chance, because he had come across a book in the library . . . he had been searching for it for so long – a remarkable book . . . he had been immersed in it . . .

And now he was conversing with the professor about the remarkable book, and for all the world I would have loved to listen to the two men making their clever remarks. But the behaviour of the rest of the company spoilt my pleasure in it.

The old lady began performing a concert of sighs and throat-clearing. She suspected irreligion in the subject-matter that the gentlemen were discussing, and with a pleading, wistful smile interjected little weather reports across the table in order to change the subject. Poor, dear, kindly old lady! She should have received limitless honours and – should have allowed herself to be escorted out of the room. I would gladly have undertaken to do the same with the young people, but in their case without the honours.

Thesi continued to sulk, now once more in silence; she and her husband were practising the optical telegraphy that was commonplace between them. Eleonore gave a restrained yawn; her husband cast his eyes up to heaven, displaying his handsome face at full length – it gave the impression of an ornamental garden for the cultivation of a wide variety of beards.

Gertrud participated frequently in the gentlemen's discussion, with a question or with a shrewd, apposite objection. Her father considered these, and nodded kindly to her, saying, with obvious satisfaction, 'I can't deny it, she is quite right!' Her husband waved her off impatiently, repeating several times in an almost tearful tone, 'Trudel – no! No – Trudel!'

He was obviously one of those scholars who do not abide their territory being invaded by even the most beloved woman. Gertrud continued to listen attentively, but from then on kept her thoughts to herself. The occasional cautious attempts that she made to divert the conversation to subjects of general interest misfired. She became embarrassed, blushed, and kept silent, entirely ashamed.

Embarrassed, ashamed – this woman! In front of whom? In front of a couple of dolls who happened by chance to be her daughters; in front of a dandyish son-in-law.

After the meal, when we had adjourned for coffee in the smoking room, the civil servant came over to me and said something kind about my 'activity as a writer'. In doing so he bowed a little and rubbed his hands together as contentedly as if he were washing them in warm water with scented soap. 'I hold your most recent works in especially high esteem . . . .' There followed the titles of a few books, which were very lovely, but unfortunately not authored by me. I was about to draw his attention to this gently when a sound was heard resembling the cracking of a tiny whip. We looked around. What had happened? The master of the house had given the mistress of the house a kiss.

It was not the kiss that was remarkable, but the effect of its sound, and its after-effects were very regrettable. The civil servant, Eleonore and her sister giggled almost openly, and Gertrud blushed once more in front of her children, and the esteemed scholar once more noticed nothing. He sat down next to his wife, took spoonfuls of coffee from his cup with his right hand, and continued to stroke her hand with his left hand (both his hands were grubby). To me she seemed saturated with silent shivers; she had dropped her gaze and clenched her lips, her cheeks changed colour, but she did not withdraw her hand.

I regard that as an act of heroism.

However, there were many other greater deeds that she probably accomplished each day. I had a sample of what may have been the most difficult on the day of that unfortunate family meal.

We had arrived at almost the same moment, her parents and I, and soon after the formal introductions, the professor expressed the wish to view some rare ornithological specimens that were on display in an adjoining room. Gertrud accompanied him, and the old lady and I were left alone.

She was unsure of herself and anxious; she evidently had something on her heart that she was eager to say, but did not know how to introduce. Finally she contrived to assure me that she knew how fond Gertrud was of me. I did not demur and accepted her assurance gratefully, but as something self-evident. Now the ice was broken. Oh, if only I would exert my influence in the only true and good way! She could not believe that I thought the path her daughter was taking was the right one. I did not immediately understand – she was speaking confusedly and softly – that in her eyes there was one, and only one, 'right' path – the path of the Church . . . Why was her daughter placing herself at the head of an anticlerical association? . . . My protestations that our association had absolutely nothing to do with ecclesiastical or religious matters, that it did not take sides for, or against, any system of belief, had the worst possible effects . . . That was indeed it – the essence of the sad, dreadful matter! . . . Not taking sides for – and therefore taking sides against! She repeated the inexorable opinion that condemns so many pure, noble aspirations. And yet it was not done with bigotry, but gently and apologetically. There was no rigidity in her; she spoke in a touchingly pleading tone, with tears in her eyes. Each word emerged from the depths of an anxiety-ridden soul, and even though the reason for her anguish seemed childish to me, that anguish was real and was robbing the old lady's nights of sleep, and her days of peace of mind.

It grieved me, a stranger, not to be able to liberate her from her torment; if I had been her daughter, I might perhaps have yielded to her, whatever my convictions. Gertrud resisted. She had the strength. She held fast to the activity that invested her life with rich content and a noble purpose. But the victory that she won so courageously every day – what must it have cost her!

Every day – that was the point. The bread of affliction dispensed to her every day by Fate finally became inedible to her, the strength of soul she had exercised for years suddenly failed, and she succumbed.

Perhaps the worst would not have happened if she had exercised less self-control; perhaps a temporary failure of her steadfastness might have saved her. – But her silence, her heroic silence – the pride that she would have had to overcome in order to say to me, or some other faithful person, 'See, they are only pinpricks, but they always touch the same wounds: I can no longer bear it!' If one is wringing one's hands, sobbing, and crying out: 'I can no longer bear it!' – then one does bear it.

But to remain dumb and to give no vent to impatience, anger, or pain, means sinning against one's strength. It is as if one were quietly to push back, every evening, the dust that has accumulated during the day, against a wall – as far as one's arm can reach . . . And against the wall the mass piles up, and rises and rises, itself becoming a wall that threatens to fall when more and more impulses shake it; for a long time it merely threatens to do so, but finally it loses its equilibrium and collapses on top of its builder.

The doctor was certainly correct when he said, 'It was a sudden decision.' I am convinced that she had never previously contemplated suicide. But the day came on which her domestic bliss was to be celebrated, the day on which she was to praise it, and to thank God and her relatives for it . . . and from that she shrank. Self-control to the uttermost limit of the possible . . . But hypocrisy – certainly not!

That is how I explain the deed – how it seems to me. Few will find this explanation convincing. I can hear all the objections that will be raised against it as clearly as if they were being shouted in my ears.

'Ridiculous!' daughters will say. 'If we were to shoot ourselves because our Mamas bemoan and oppose our behaviour, we would have been dead long ago!'

'Dear God,' many married women will say, 'if we had nothing to hold against our husbands except that they come late to meals and show affection at inopportune moments, we would regard ourselves as more fortunate than thousands of others.'

And brave, resigned mothers will say, 'Relationship? My dear, let us allow the younger generation to go their own way and follow their own interests! It is their right to do so and was our right too, against our parents. You cannot call the fact that we did not assert it either virtue or guilt – call it rather the spirit of the times. And as for understanding? If we ask for this great gift, we must be able to reciprocate it too, and if we lack the capacity to do so, then we must submit to the inevitable – and the more we can do so with good humour, the better!'

And the mildest of the religious people will shake their heads, saying sadly, 'All that you have adduced there in defending a suicide – for admit, that is what you have been doing – does not excuse it!'

Well, condemn her, then! I shall always remember her as a dear guide who walked ahead of me for a while on a broad, sunlit path. Joyfully and trustingly I followed her, hoping always to be able to follow her to goals that were ever brighter and higher.

And once, when I looked for her again, seeking her sure guidance, she had disappeared, and the path on which she had just been walking so calmly and proudly was empty.

A WIDOW

ANNA MARIA TILSCHOVÁ

I

'Upon my soul, aren't you afraid of dying?' Marjána, the beggar-woman, asked Drahoš, in front of his cottage. Meanwhile, she was rapidly scrutinizing the whole of his filthy body with inquisitive, darting, mouse-like eyes. Drops of liquid were standing in the corners of his dim eyes, he had turned yellow, and his hands were shaking like the hands, white with age, of a hundred-year-old pensioner – God have mercy! And Marjána herself was a cripple from birth. She did not have the use of her legs, and used only her hands to push herself from cottage to cottage and from benefactor to benefactor.

'After all, the blacksmith's already been saying that you were dead!'

'Well, let's be clear, Marjána – out of spite, I'm going to stay alive until I die, like anyone else!'

Marjána bared white teeth in her ruddy face, and pushed herself on into the village on her hands, close to the ground like a reptile. Wooden looms were rattling behind the little windows, and yellowed branches were reflected in the glass panes. Dirty, undersized girls were looking after children tied to scarves in front of bluish, whitewashed cottages, and the older ones were doing netting on the thresholds or winding sized thread on to spools. Scattered clay pots had been put out to dry on the fence posts, and here and there the sunlight was trembling on eiderdowns as red as poppies. Ragged herd-boys were yelling taunts at the cripple, 'Marjána, ever-virgin!', or asking over and over, each time from a different place, 'Are you a good girl? A bad girl or a good girl?' When she had been tiny, her parents had wheeled her on straw in a barrow on pilgrimages and to markets – and now, as bad-tempered as she was poor, she was cursing the boys over the open beaks of their geese from the dust by the fences.

The bare plain stretched out to the point where it met the sky. The village itself seemed to be sunk in it – a couple of grey roofs in thick vegetation, hidden from human eye in hollows and shadows, like a sin that is debarred from being seen in the light of day. In the end house, the husband of a wife had been poisoned with white arsenic for the sake of a horse, and within a week the husband's wife was dead too – better that this had been hidden under a wooden roof rather than in the light of day. Folk were gossiping around the fire in lonely places and in clearings in the neighbour-hood . . . about leaving cakes for patronal festivals unsalted, about keeping their children unbaptized, and about the village clerk, who had himself buried his daughter's infant under the window in his own garden. In truth they were strange folk – today one thing and tomorrow something else. The eldest of them, who still remembered the time of forced labour, neither bought nor sold: they took little pots for tow and oakum from tinkers, and when they ex-changed cottages, they merely transferred wooden boards with numbers to conclude the exchange. Some of them, the poorest and most unsophisticated, had been taken in by the 'Moroccan song', from which they hoped to be freed from all human suffering through King Shalmaneser;[1] so they paid no taxes, but, instead of gaining their freedom, they had their oxen confiscated. And there was poverty – so grinding

1 Eschatological songs about a mythical 'King of Morocco' whose appearance would herald a Day of Judgment and liberation for the peasantry existed among Protestant sects in eastern Bohemia (and more widely) in the late eighteenth century and the first half of the nineteenth, as Tilschová evidently knew. The myth is likely to have originated in a folk memory of a diplomatic visit made to Vienna in 1783 by an envoy of the Sultan of Morocco. See Petr Janeček, 'Eschatologická a profetická motivika ve folkloru českých zemí v 2. polovině 18. a na počátku 19. století: písně o králi marokánovi', *Český lid* 93/2 (2006): 153–77.

that the children of one of the mothers had been crippled from lying naked on the floor when there had been nothing with which to heat the room. There was a little rye; merely reddish pastures, infested with moles, undulating in the distance, and meadows on which reeds grew and marshy ground trembled. All the cottages were huddled together irregularly, askew, on the uneven ground of the hollow, up to the last one, of the Čápek thieves, patched together with birch-bark. And sheer drudgery, and the other things that go with it, were staring the people in the face as they were staring at the houses out of their windows.

The rowan trees were in blossom beside the main road, full of dirty white fluff, when Drahoš fell ill. He had a large farm of his own, a wife and a farm; he kept the inn and had a shop. His peasant pride did not abide a status between the stove and the bench, and, uniquely in the whole village, he was the possessor of a separate sitting-room. But all this was in vain – he was groaning. And this despite the fact that he had had his illness exorcised with spells and with water drawn against the current by Hulánka, an old honey and henbane crone, who preferred her huláns, the cavalry-men, to God. In his own mind, Drahoš was accounting for his illness by explaining that the red blood in his body had somehow gone bad, perhaps through drink, and that each time new blood appeared it was quickly turned bad by the old blood. And since the blossoming of the rowans, he was being asked on every side, aren't you afraid of dying? But Adna, his wife, continued to berate him, in sickness as in health, as a wastrel and a prodigal. And he reciprocated, calling her a slut. Cat and dog as they were, they had been thrown together by their fathers, both peasants and hucksters. But it was Drahoš alone who used to benefit when his attractive wife drew pints for the peasants and the young lads, and he paid little heed when they suggested that Francek, his second son, had eyes of the same colour as those of the stable-boy Štrof. Drunk, he said, 'I'll give her a thrashing – and then so what? Will she be any different?' He did so once, but not for a second time. They called him a wastrel and also called him a skinflint – let God be his judge! He might transport stone in a wagon on the track from Monday to Saturday, never touching liquor, preferring to buy leather for his trousers in town; but against that on Sunday he would sit with the carriers in town in the Jew's inn and not stir until he had turned both pockets inside out. And he said of himself, 'Lads, I'm not to blame . . . if I had a thousand now, I'd go on drinking till dawn! . . .' But he only drank when the season was one of rejoicing; in the days of fasting after Carnival, and in the days up to Shrove Tuesday, he used to say his prayers, avoid swearing, and avoid drink. For the whole of the time of harvest, he was expecting to die, when he could not even raise his finger to touch the bedhead, but each day dawned anew, and he stopped seeing Death stalking over his farms, that grey lady whom no one looks in the eye.

On the festival of St Peter and St Paul, he was visited by the priest, and from that time his hands were shaking so badly that he could not even eat with a spoon from a cup, and he was continually in a high fever – and the servants would set him down on a bench in front of the empty cottage, a scarecrow for the sparrows. On barrows they drove colourful coarse rugs and velvets into town, bringing cloth rash and jute back from town, but little Lojza did not drive the cattle back until six o'clock, and then immediately went for water for the cattle from the cesspool, flapping her bare feet. She was an orphan with only God and kind folk to supply her, and every rag she wore came from the community. Her late mother had put her into service, and her father, a one-legged beggar, was roaming the world. The destitute, like birds of a feather, flock together: Lojza was being taught by Marjána how to sing and pray. She did not go to school, and had already begun serving Drahoš's wife in return for bed and board.

'Lojza!' called a loud, cajoling voice to her from the cottage.

At the sound of the voice, Drahoš craned his head back with difficulty. In the doorway stood Adna, his wife, in an orange skirt. Standing erect, around forty years of age, a red kerchief across, strong-breasted, with flashing eyes and bright teeth – passionate! ardent!

'Look, look . . . look, look . . . stupid Delilah . . . stupid Delilah,' he muttered twice, weakly, hoarsely, out of spite. Since their wedding he had not called her by her real name, knowing how much it annoyed her. She for her part stood there as if he had already been buried, red in clothing and red in the sun as if aflame. 'Delilah betrayed Samson and Eve betrayed Adam,' he began, dully nodding his head. 'Delilah!' he said again, mockingly, 'do you know where the chaffinch sticks its nose?'

No response, not a squeak.

'Well, Delilah!' he shouted, 'if I may be so bold, if I may be so bold as to dare to ask, where've you been? Has it been with some chap or among the potatoes?'

No reply.

'Of course it wasn't with a man – you're a fish out of water! But Delilah! You've been drinking a whole purseful of money with them, and more!'

She bared teeth that were large but white.

'Toothy squirrel, all puffed up,' muttered Drahoš weakly, 'but I'm going to knock out those squirrel teeth of yours!'

'Lojza,' she shouted in answer, 'come quickly! He's trembling all over, his teeth are chattering – let's get him inside!' And the two strong, buxom women took the yellowed invalid between them and pushed him inside like dead meat.

'Lojzička, you little weasel! I'm choking!' moaned Drahoš from his unmade bed at the girl as she went out through the door. Behind him, potatoes were overflowing on the hearth; they reeked of the old pot and of clay, and nauseated the invalid more than the pregnant girl. The two small windows over the garden seemed completely green in the white wall, owing to the low branches behind them, and it seemed to him as if he were looking out of a cave at a place where all was green and happy. The window openings were very small, so that it was cheerless in the room, in which they slept and in which they also served liquor. Just below the shiny black beams, smeared with ox blood, gleamed holy pictures that hung beside one another like a magic circle, encircling the dimly lit space.

'Now, now,' said Lojza apathetically to the master of the house, opening the window. Meanwhile her eyes were laughing, but at nothing at all, as they had done since her birth, as if they saw only ridiculous things in every corner of the room but also of the world. Fresh air blew in through the window, and the wheels rattled, and also the harness, of the empty wagon in which the carrier was lying on his stomach, singing to himself through his teeth, Let's get going, my darling . . . let's get going, my darling . . . until the song sent his bony horse off between the houses.

It was almost dark; only a low, yellow streak of light was cast on the floor from the doors of the tiled stove. The invalid in bed could now see and hear nothing – when at times he opened his eyes, each time he saw the same hunchbacked girl with her extended belly at the corner of the common pasture, and cows bending down in the grass, and then his eyes again went dark.

'Ma'am!' said Lojza outside the door, 'is the master still breathing or not?'

Adna came in, lit a wax candle from a taper, and bent very close over the invalid. He could not have been quieter; only a prominent vein in his neck was swollen. At that, Drahoš opened his eyes, and saw her bending over him with the bright light on her eyebrows and her cheekbones cast by the wax candle she was carrying in her hand. Almost beside himself he half-closed and opened his shrunken eyelids, as he followed the stripes of her skirt up and down with his eyes; finally he said:

'So why all this? Christ Jesus did not grant us the gift of being good to each other . . . I'd love to beat you black and blue, scratch you to pieces with my fingers . . . but this here is a carcass already!' And, with more contempt than at a corpse, he looked at the bulging knuckles of his hands, dried up and shaky – which at the time he married Adna could have strangled her white throat on its beads for a penny or for a trifle. And again he continued to lie silent; only the large vein was twitching under his chin.

'Little weasel!' said Drahoš, humbly and pleadingly – a different man when addressing the orphan – 'what a small light you've got today! Light a bigger one! Fetch a pot from the alcove, and get praying! – Aloud!' he demanded after a moment, 'so that we can both hear, the Lord God and me too!' But the drone of the words in his ears was merely unintelligible, like water from a weir, or the sound of stormy weather. Lojza, with a book of prayers in her hand, crouched by the chair with its attached Frantal candlestick, and Adna, her strong bare arms folded across her chest, stood motionless by her husband, who was going his way to eternity from this passing world. For nine weeks now she had refused to answer his sneering, leprous remarks, and she would not for anything say a word to him – and she still did not do so, right up to the moment of his death. She merely stared at him in concentration with eyes that might have been of molten metal. Until – all of a sudden! Alongside the large vein, a small blue one spun round six times, and his wide mouth fell open for breath. At first, there was silence; and then Adna screamed loudly, 'Holy Virgin! He's dead!', as if that were impossible. And Lojza's eyes were fixed not on the dead man, but on her, as at other times – as if she were still seeing the force of risible, amusing things.

'Off you go, girl, for Francek, and tell him his Dad has died! He'll need to be shaved if that's still possible!' called Adna after Lojza into a night in which dogs were barking, one after another, as Lojza hurried from building to building. The old proverb warned the girl, who might be petting or exciting a strange dog, 'Don't trust a dog or a soldier, my girl!' Then the barking ceased, and the night arched over the village, quiet, clear and chilly, as it is only in September – a night when stars fall from heaven on lads and their girls, and yellow leaves fall from trees on the poor, for bedding for their goats.

II

He was still a forsaken unfortunate, even in death – that is what they said about him in the village. And when the clock at the Drahošes stopped on the morning of the funeral, on the second Marian festival, they added that even the clock, though inanimate and without a soul, would not let its sound disturb the slumber of one still unburied, whose widow was not grieving for him. The ancient clock was remembering the last head of the household, who had been cruel to his people, and it was remembering that daughter and father had been estranged though both of the same stock. Fifteen years previously, he had demanded it back from Adna on Easter Monday, saying it was his rather than hers, and that no one would be looking at it after his death. 'Take it!' she said. 'But who will be the first to trample it underfoot, you or me?'

Now, with his back to the bar, the 'grenadier' was drinking an eggnog with beer, so as to lubricate his singing at the funeral. 'The clock won't go . . . and just this morning I said I'd throw it out!' said Adna to him, with a black widow's shawl of Tibetan wool across her ample bosom.

'Upon my soul!' said Dvořák, the herdsman, putting his cloudy glass on the bar, 'I've taken less time drinking up than your man took dying, not so, Adna, Adnička?' And the joker winked knowingly at the Jew. His woollen scarf was knotted under his chin, and his long greasy hair was evenly cut at neck length. They called him 'grenadier'; they had no idea why, but they simply did so.

'Lord bless us, you're a reprobate!' was Adna's response to this.

Through the window a distant view opened up over the wide, undulating plain towards a sparse cluster of spruce, beyond which the brickwork of solitude gleamed white. Neither men nor oxen were ploughing, and a sky as clear as a polished jewel arched over the clay, great and monotonous without people working in it. Something was gleaming blue near the sun – blue laths around the crucifix at the cross-roads at the place where of old desperate suicides used to be buried, so that wayfarers should trample their sinful bones. The mourners were coming slowly, one or two at a time, those from outside the village, and the poor and the poorest from the village. The men were walking hunched over, with colourful velvet shirts under their coats and pipes in their pockets, and in no hurry. The women, short and stocky, walked faster, heads and shoulders wrapped in large plaid or floral scarves, stiff from labour and from child-bearing, one hand pressed against their sagging breasts, the other holding a white starched scarf.

And they simply entered the room in silence, clattering on the boards with their hobnailed boots. But the old ones at a pace – and indeed almost the first who shuffled into the room, stooping in his coat of lambs' wool, was a miser-ly, centenarian grandfather, who earned his gold selling tinker's toys. And after him: a cobbler's wife, affable, flam-boyant and entirely freckled even to her hands; Svoboda, who had just made his estate over to his son, skin and bone, but so strong that he could lift the rear of a wagon from a kneeling position so that it seemed that the coupling had opened of its own accord; a space remained between the door and the exposed coffin; down near the floor Marjána was cackling, red in her red shawl, scrutinizing the widow's mourning with restless eyes; there was Bureš, the village clerk, who was neither Catholic nor Protestant and said that no religion tended to immorality, even the 'Moroccan', and that any religion was good provided it survived; there was deaf Tonda from the bridge; the vagrant Anyčka Krupicová, three foot high with a head like a vegetable marrow; the bricklayer Moučka, a clown who danced, drunk, at full moon in the fishpond; Jirmásek, the worst rogue apart from Kaplan in the neighbourhood; Dvořák, a cabinet-maker who had returned after six years in America; and crazy Otto who trusted no one under the sun or moon apart from Adna. They came in twos and threes until the bar was full.

All of them were mourning Drahoš, and yet they neither liked nor disliked him. Some of the womenfolk simply came into the doorway, already weeping – not on account of the dead man, but on their own account, about life and death, for they were thinking to themselves, 'When will this overtake us?' A young woman sobbed, an old woman sobbed, and once more there was quiet in the room. Only occasionally did the floorboards creak under Adna, who came pouring glasses of spirits, coloured and clear, for all the mourners. It is an old, old trinity: liquor when a person is born, liquor when a person marries, liquor when a person dies. Although they held off at first, afterwards they drank to the last drop, serious and hostile to the lady hosting them, complete strangers to a man. She had a musician brother in Slavonia, and her parents were now rotting in a single grave.

And up to that moment, not one of them had exchanged a word with Adna, even the village clerk. And there was a neighbour who had helped them during the harvest and still remembered how Adna had looked after the cows among the spruces, dancing till she was exhausted. And he remembered other things too: how Dr Peduzzi from town had had to attend her in the fields, when her suitor had injured her, flinging a stone at her head, when she had turned him down, and had then shot himself. Adna had already been calling herself Drahošová then. He knew both sides of her coin, her fierceness and her ardency, as he knew the village from house to house, nothing but weavers' poverty. He thought about all this: about Štrof, who had first shot himself and then married a girl from Rychnov; about Drahoš, God knows what sort of person he was! . . . and why was the coffin with the dead body not in the room? That is what he was thinking when he frowned, seeing her going back and forth with the jug from the glassworks.

The clock started ticking again! The men at the tables and the women by the stove looked up – it was Francek: her only son, strong, nineteen years old and sunburnt, was standing in the doorway as if unsure why he was alive at all. But he was here – and everyone had the same thought: he was the living image of the stable boy, not the son of his father! And the women, precisely the women, again looked askance at Adna for what had happened long ago and about which everyone knew – including the tailor's wife, the woman who had looked the wife of her lover in the eye at the christening of her last child, and had literally said over the eiderdown, 'This child is the godfather's!'

'I'm always telling you that you have to greet people, but you don't listen!' shouted Adna angrily at her son. He often resisted her, his own mother, not wanting to seem a weakling. She had liked – preferred – her elder son Pepík, who had been knifed to death by bad folk. 'Get on with it!' she quietly ordered her son, with white lips.

Francek obeyed. His father was now at eternal rest, and she was the sole head of the household on earth. In clothes of striped velvet, and taking his hat off and holding it in his hand, he sauntered out of the door and back in again, and tried to take her hand in reconciliation.

'Don't feel sorry for yourself!' and she pushed him off with her black velvet arm.

For the first time now the clerk raised his head as heavy as if of stone, with eyes, covered with a film, which had no longer been capable of sight.

'Adna, where have you put the coffin?'

'In the shed.'

'In the shed!' And there was silence – none of them knew what to say. She had been vigorous over the invalid and was still lively, taking her vengeance over the dead man: even his last covering, nailed together from six planks of linden, was not allowed admission to the room. It was not spite, but rather apathy and inertia, like an accumulation of great, mute fear, that stared out of the eyes of those who had been struggling with heaven and earth from January to December for a scrap of miserable living.

And as if in derision, at that very moment an old lady came in, the octogenarian Bálková, who collected eggs in the villages for the Jew, and was so poor that she often lacked even salt for her bread. And, the sole one to speak, she stepped in to the widow's house barefoot – since the pilgrimage to Chlumek she had had no shoes – and said, 'May the merciful Lord show you his favour today, widow! For you have been spending very little time in his company!' And more quickly and lightly still, as if she were ashamed to her very core, lest the poorest should be in the bad books of the richest, she pressed herself, a bundle of old rags and bones, between the other women beside the green tiled stove.

The singing should have begun, but not a living soul dared to start – it was as silent as if they were under a spell. Had something happened? Would something happen? The women's faces were completely flushed, and the men were smoking in silence at tables piled with earthenware, oval wooden stands, loaves of bread, and hats. And thick, yellow, suffocating smoke gradually crept over the heads of everyone. It stretched out and swirled, and seemed like the upper covering of an evil spirit. The village clerk, his head in his hands and his pale old eyes fixed on the smoke, was continually thinking just one thing, as children and the old do, as fools and the wise do. Was Joseph a prodigal or not? He remembered one thing: how, before he got married, he used to stop dancing halfway through a tune, so as to avoid having to pay the musicians . . . Had he been miserly or not? And the old man was completely lost in thought. The fog between his fading eyes was becoming thicker and thicker, and yet his bad eyes were looking out for someone who could answer his question, whether the legs stretched out in the coffin would dance without payment or not? And as if it mattered. Close to him at the foot of the table, Marjána was dozing with her arms folded under her generous breasts, but when she awoke from her doze, each time there came to her mind Adna's old words about her husband, which she had not been able to banish from her mind for two days and two nights, 'But if he were to die! I'd have to get a big stone and make it rattle over him in his coffin!'

Finally there emerged from a corner a tiny little person in a close-fitting coat, who was both a Calvinist and a Catholic cantor, with a crown of eczema around his bald head, an evil spirit. Small square panes were glistening like mica in the windows of the cottages, but even the sun was extinguished; it was even duller than it had been in the morning, or indeed an hour earlier. Only eyes could be seen, gleaming in the smoke, as all of them began a sacred song uncertainly after the Calvinist, in the name of the deceased, in heavy, drunken voices:

O God, thy will is done,
thou hast saved me from my sickness,
thou hast delivered me from pain,
from all the vanities of the world,
now I go to thee, God of heaven . . . God of heaven!

The widow was sitting close beside Svoboda, shoulder to shoulder. Good friends of his in bargains struck over drink and at markets nicknamed him one of the stubborn, raging breed. Adna had not yet spoken five words to him alone, though he had been turning his head and eyeing her from a table to the bar for a month now. When his brother wanted to cheat him, when his friend wanted to injure him, he stood his ground – that was Jan Svoboda, from the chapelry in the next village. Now Adna proposed a toast from his glass, puckering up her blood-red lips like the youngest of the young, still with the joy of the world before her. At that moment she was not thinking with anger about either the living or the dead, simply staying quietly beside Svoboda, and she settled down like a cat warming itself by the stove.

'So then, Anička,' he said, 'Mother of God, are you a widow, then?' and under her apron he took her hand in his own bony one. And Adna went entirely rigid with pleasure.

'But Anička, you've been a widow even with your husband for a very long time!' and with a roguish smile he moved so close to her cheeks that he could see the golden down on them.

'Now then, now then!' whispered Adna helplessly, clenching her teeth to suppress her laughter. The filthy smoke in the room was spreading only murkiness and spiritual delusion, and as if from some other place, from an unreal world, the drunken voices sang on:

Show me thy mercy, O Jesus!
Turn sorrow into eternal joy,
bear me up to the holy angels,
to the heavenly ones, to thy Mother, O Jesus!

Now for the last time I bid you farewell,
I give you my thanks and pray you
to remember me, and to render
all thanks to our heavenly Father!

Suddenly there was light at the door – the priest was standing there, his red hands clasped on his breast in humility, dressed in a lace rochet and a black and yellow chasuble. Behind him, from the fresh air through the opened door, the funeral knell was ringing, clearly and at length. Adna winced, as though she had been awakened to life from a dream; she dropped to her knees, waved her black hands furiously until she touched the floor, unaware of the world around her, and with only one thing in her mind she spat out, one word after another, the first things that her passion brought into her head:

'Delilah . . . Delilah with the plaits and the teeth! that is what you called me, husband of mine! What's become of you? Do I know why you aren't here and never will be again? You won't be groaning, you won't be shouting, you can't do anything now. Now, if only you could say something once more, if you'd know who it was who said to you, "Stop drinking . . . you'll live longer! . . ." Who was that? But you used to have the same answer the whole year round: "I'll stay alive only as long as the good Lord wants me to!"' Everything that had been repressed suddenly gushed forth in a flood, and Adna went on speaking, struggling faster for words and breath. 'And now at least you can see that he, the Lord, our gracious Lord, did not want you to be with me in one cottage. For I too, sinner as I am, brought oil as well as butter from the heifer to light the lamp to Our Lady. And didn't you say "Leave this house!" to me, calling me names into the bargain – when the cottage belonged to me. And you tried to bite my thumb off! And it was to Marjána, not me, that you later confessed that I had only kept my little finger because you had gone through to the bone . . . An animal suffers like a human being when it feels pain, but you wounded me right to the heart . . .'

The women surrounded Adna, screaming and throwing their arms about violently, in a semicircle, while she was settling her accounts with her dead husband. Drunk and confused, they were all at one with her, because (as they claimed) they thought she was grieving for her husband, that she was mourning him. Two of them, Čejka, the tiny wife of the village clerk, with a face like a crumpled cloth, and the pregnant girl, took her out of the cottage. On the grass, surrounded by the posts that protected the linen from the geese, the yellow coffin was already standing on a bier, and the priest in front of it had his book ready. And because those women had gone out, the rest of the men and women went after them without thought, without will, merely as if in a trance. Further off, under an ash tree, Francek was holding horses in harness, two dapple-greys from the regiment, one handsome as if with a scattering of apples and the other yellowish-white, the colour of old hair. A statue of the Virgin Mary in a short blue robe was strapped to the coffin, and little flames were flaring in four lanterns held in trembling male hands. And again the womenfolk were lifting white scarves to their eyes. Adna was the only one of them who was not weeping, staring fixedly at the coffin as if devouring it, unable to get her fill of seeing it. Quickly they sang it out, and now only the road to the cemetery in the next village remained to be traversed. It was winding, reddish, a single stain between the cottages, through sun, shadow and fallen leaves. All at once the widow seized the wood above the bars on the side of the hay wagon with both hands, swung herself up and sat astride the coffin as if on a horse, behind the statue. 'Down with her!' cried the priest, the only sane person present, but no one moved even a finger. They stared at her with deferential fear, as if they were seeing a powerful, malevolent bird of prey on the coffin, with blazing eyes, in possession of something that could not be wrested away from it. Francek nudged the manes of the horses lightly, and Adna crouched on the coffin as if trying to crush the dead man still further with the solid weight of her body.

Berries like heavy red coral were hanging on the old rowan trees, and in the branches, spreading over the roofs, light yellow and red leaves were shining, which turned over as the wind caught them. At the head of the procession, a young boy, burnt brown, carried an abraded cross with a fluttering ribbon, and immediately behind the vehicle walked the singers, the first being the pregnant girl, all laced up, whose hair and eyelashes were almost white. Children had mounted the rough fences of moss and large stones, and women in blue and red skirts, leaning against the white cottages, stared in amazement at the procession, which drew on mutely, without singing, through the village, so that it merely made the earth tremble under the heavy footsteps. Beyond the bell-tower, a goat broke free from its rough rope, and ran into the procession, and an ugly woman with a child in her arms chased it with angry haste into a doorway, merely to keep it from escaping. And again the procession continued onwards. In the plains, the wind drove two clouds together over one another; the spindly two-year-old saplings planted by the cross huddled against each other, or coalesced, with both their foliage and branches, so that the sun was peering out through them only as if from a blind eye. A flock of birds, congregating together, shot out near the fishpond, and flashed out, black and white, across the sky, their wings beating in the distance. The little pond itself had dried up over the summer, so that the tracks left by bicycles, horses and carts could barely be recognized in the mud at its edge, and the reflection of the widow on her husband's coffin among the bars of the wagon could be seen only in the muddy pool at its centre.

The cripple Marjána was waiting eagerly for the procession by the crucifix at the crossroads, leaning against a blue fence, as she had been unable to undertake the long journey. On the ground, with her hands, bruised and blistered like feet, on her lap over her apron, she cried out in terror, 'God be with us! God be with us! God be with us!', but she did not take her wide eyes off the funeral procession winding along the rocky country road towards the place on the horizon where the church tower met the grey sky and the blue hills. They had passed her by a step when the liquor threw the village clerk, who could take little of it in his old age, on to a rock with his mouth to the ground, so that a tuft of his ancient hair was dyed red. And when Marjána pulled the shawl away from her ears, she heard Čejka murmur, 'You'll say at home that it was robbers who did this to my son!', and the whole crowd of mourners started laughing. 'But he drank an ocean or two of it!' cried Moučka, jumping over the blood-bespattered rock, as lightly as a schoolboy. And as long as she could see the wagon slowly moving, and the crowd of people behind it, just as long could she hear the shouts, the words and the ceaseless crazy laughter that stretched across the plain like the reek of the smoke from the nearby fire of the children to the blue hills, to the place where the earth was already enclosing Drahoš's body.

III

'I'll have six thousand to live on now! *Six thousand*!' exclaimed Adna once on the doorstep to Marjána, with only her plaid shirt folded across her ample breasts. In the mornings the brown turds of manure around in the yard were usually already frozen, her bare feet were violet with cold in her wooden clogs, the air among the branches above the roof was clear and golden – summer was now past, and the court inventory had been drawn up.

'But Jesus, Jesus, Adna! you won't be able to think of dying! Just to be like you for a week before dying . . . but yes, like this – close at hand! I'm so miserable!' With a clenched fist she punched her own head and with the tip of her scarf carefully wiped off pus, rather than a tear, from the corner of her eye. 'In town? they give you carrots. Around the cottages, bread and potatoes . . . all sorts of people will buy the potatoes, when they're unpeeled, but the bread that comes from my hands is only fit for hens . . . but say, aren't you sick of my rudeness?'

That the crippled beggar should not hate the rich woman who was her mistress, indeed no woman apart from her mistress who was moreover the owner of two plots of land, how could things be otherwise between people? In summer all was well – but Marjána feared the snow, when it drifted in the village up to the fences, the treetops would poke out from it like bushes, it would lie on the road, it would lie under the windows, the roof would be filled with it, until she was afraid it would annihilate her, and a white death was lurking everywhere.

As long as it had not fallen, Marjána was able to get to Lojza and find something warm to drink with the milking. 'Auntie!' complained the orphan to the cripple, 'I'm nothing but a slave here!' 'Be quiet!' Marjána told her, 'and what could you say about that, in any case? If I had the body for it, I'd do it myself. But preserve me from someone who shouts and won't shut up even to the deaf!'

The whole village lay naked against the cold in the plain when the first winds blew its trees bare of leaves. Everything was scarce – potatoes, cabbage – and living was hard when housewives had more poverty than flour in their quarters. Though it is written in the scriptures that man should not live by bread but by the kingdom of God – when the village clerk thought of those words, he put his head in his hands and then said, 'That's true of Palestine, where there are two harvests each year. But, brethren, what good comes of want?' And he spoke further to them on this subject. 'Want and ignorance are two blood sisters. And what good has ever come of ignorance? Though there are wise people who do not even wish to send their children to school so that they do not fall into sin, they end up crushed beneath the wheel of slavery. So – my God! – a woman goes to market to buy some rags . . . some clothes for herself, with no idea how much they will cost nor what change she will receive . . . isn't she a slave? Spiritual want is ignorance, and out of every kind of want there emerges only the vice that belongs with it.' And those to whom he said this were so destitute that they ate only one meal a day in bad years, so as to survive from one harvest to the next – they were the true destitute. But at Martinmas even they would shout, celebrate, eat and drink as if no tomorrow was to follow that night, they would fry dumplings and bake rabbits and goats, and liquor would flow freely – that single feast each year was obliged to balance out their entire miserable lives.

For twenty years, Adna had been the only woman in the whole village who had not experienced want except at second hand with her neighbour. And for all those years, she had been a model housewife in spite of her husband's unpleasantness. But now, as if her husband's death had meant only the beginning of real life for her, she grew plump and proud, more attractive and stronger, and the more she did so, the less she bothered about good order in the house. And she yearned – not for red scarves with pink roses, nor for prunes from the market – but for what at her age was otherwise now scarce, earthly love. And the old women gossiped about her: she was always like a mermaid, half woman, half fish – Adna was a woman half white, half black, she ground her teeth during the day, she had thrashed a Gypsy man, and she would die without God, with her face to the wall. Instead of all from the funeral, which those who had attended avoided speaking about, Svoboda came every day, as he said, to keep an eye on the building – the building without a master.

The fact that Francek and Svoboda had not yet shaken hands with one another was noticed first by the mocking eyes of Lojza, who was now only two weeks short of turning fifteen.

'But look at him!' remarked Svoboda to Adna only once, when Francek passed him twice in the courtyard without a word, pulling his braces up over his shoulders – 'Lord High and Mighty has ignored the tradesman again!'

'And what would you like him to do? Must he bend down and kiss your big toe?'

'Nothing,' he said slowly. 'Nothing. But in any case he doesn't do much more than that!'

'He's not like his Dad. Let's leave him – leave him, let's kill him – kill him!'

And it was surprising. In Adna's mind, the dead man and no one else was the father of her wretched son. Perhaps . . . both of them had stood in her way. But Adna was not thinking of what had been and now was past – she was alive only to the world and to pleasure! Carriers, weavers, bricklayers, stonemasons, day labourers, artisans, everyone who went from the fields and into the fields, from town, or who for work turned past her windows towards the long, low ridge of blue hills on the horizon – with all of them she made merry with her scarlet, avid lips. She treated them with liquor flavoured with aniseed to tempt them to come again, so that it should be noisy and cheerful, and so that the bar should be full of people! And people who had been treated only once would certainly return a second time. And when more of them came, she would wipe the chalked debts off the door with her wet palm, simply to increase the joviality. After that, the loud laughter, shouted jokes, whoops and drunken rowdyism would carry into the night from the smoke-filled bar over the poor, lost village, as if hell itself were laughing in the lighted lamps in the windows, red and twinkling, which hung from string tied above the looms. Moučka, the father of five children, did a juggling act barefoot, his soles half dancing from table to table, and did not slip. The 'grenadier' famous halfway round the world recounted his best escapade: how he had bought a substandard cow from a merchant for a hundred and thirty, and in the murk at the market a day later had sold it back to the same merchant for a hundred and forty, also agreeing a further five litres of red wine into the bargain over drinks. 'Bloody hell!' shouted Moučka, and a hoarse chorus followed him.

Even in her husband's time, Adna had come down hard on two of the grooms, who had divided the money they had discovered in a green stocking of hers under the straw in the bed, fairly into two halves. She herself took no care of the money she had in her hands, and began buying sweet rosoglio, fancy sausage and packets of cigarettes as treats. In the briefest of words – 'Woman, sin not!' – she was admonished by the village clerk, Francek's guardian, who despite his failing eyesight was still weaving with his thrifty son out of consideration. But his words were merely water off a duck's back – almost as when he had asked the parish priest for permission to dig a grave for himself in his garden, so that his children would remember him better when they had him in front of their eyes the entire day. And in everything Adna had the upper hand. When Svoboda had suddenly caught a youth with his arm around her waist, she weighed in against him, 'What then, are the two of us married, that you do this to me?' – and as if she had been wronged, she seethed and blazed in anger. As a warning, Svoboda slowly raised a heavy, sinewy hand, on which the little finger was useless, so limp from an injury that it looked like a claw, and said, 'I'd show you!', and the flirtatious youth was already feeling the claw on his throat and the spirit on his tongue. Svoboda, father of a son and two married daughters, was violent, but immediately afterwards good-humoured as if shaking hands. But he had never once yet beaten Adna. Even though she was stronger, more buxom and larger than the women who were underdeveloped and already worn out, she seemed a weakling in comparison to him. And he might have married her in church, buxom Adna with her two plots of land – if she had been worth the ring for her finger.

There was seldom any need for extra help in the household. Francek helped his mother and Lojza too, but told tales to his mother about Lojza's laziness and to Lojza about his mother's wastefulness and . . . also about a third party. What Adna disliked most about him was that he never looked her in the eye – that he was sly. Who can see into a person like that? And indeed Francek did not ask her whether she would marry Svoboda . . . he was merely prying, stealthily, barefoot, at twilight and at dawn, in the barn, in the shed, behind the piles of timber, in every place where he spied two people or two shadows together with their heads inclined towards one another. But mother and son did not clash until once in early spring. Her son cried out, 'Mama!' – and that was all. But that single word, as he said it, was the same as though he had raised his fist against her.

'I'll drive this rake into your eyes! You're the worst troublemaker the world has ever seen!' screamed Adna at the one tracking her footfall. And Francek was as quiet as a mouse; he only rushed diffidently to open his heart to the village clerk, who, with thick glasses to his eyes, was throwing the shuttle with the thread by the window, opened for better light.

'And what am I to do with her, with my own mother?'

'Aren't you a good boy, obeying all the commandments like that!' said the old man in mocking praise of his ward, continuing to throw the shuttle.

And it occurred to Adna that day for the first time, why bother with her son when she could live for herself? She only needed still to marry him off.

And now Drahoš had been rotting for two long (and also short!) years under the earth in the next village, next to the midwife, under a golden lily. In those two years, the property had shrunk, since his widow had been tottering from pleasure to pleasure like a drunken woman, and she had still been giving things away, proud that she had them and could do so. Old Bálková had begged snow boots from her humbly, like a lesser creature, half-crazy Anyčka a multicoloured floral blouse, and one after another, the poor had been benefitting at the expense of the rich woman. And from the pride of giving itself, she was refusing even the traditional slice of bread with salt when she entered someone's house – 'I have it at home!' And so there was no increase.

White mists rose in the autumn, and then it was Advent. The villagers had no chapel of their own, and they were not very assiduous about attending Mass elsewhere; when they did nevertheless go to church, it was so that the entire village should not be seen as a disgrace in the eyes of others. Ah, it was not worth those aspersions of people! The clerk said, 'I like praying at home on my own bench best.' And everyone took heed of that, Catholics, Protestants as well as those who held a secret faith, because, having various beliefs in mind, he said, 'What does it matter where I live, whether in Kladno or in Hlinsko, just provided I bring a fine report to the judgment seat of God! For –' and he said of the Catholic priests – 'a man only preaches because it is his calling and because he's paid for it . . . but if it were without payment . . . ! They seem gentle for a while in church, but the moment they go out through the cemetery gate, they have no idea!' But the womenfolk went on pilgrimage, to the Advent Rorate celebrations, through snowbound fields, and Adna with them.[2] And winter in the mountains was usually so bad that the poorest took their goat or cow with them into their room so that both of them could keep warm together.

Once, it was at four o'clock in the morning, with no trace of darkness: everywhere was white with snow, and the moon shone on the patch as if it were day.

'Ma'am . . . get up for Rorate!' said Lojza quietly to waken Adna. Her young eyes were still continually laughing, though since the summer she had become more subservient than mocking towards her mistress.

'It seems to be coming down outside!' said Adna – and with that she noticed the girl. 'So, young lady, you've been putting on weight recently?'

'That's what peasant boys are able to do' – and she faltered out – 'and this is what peasant girls can do!'

And Adna struck Lojza in the face so that she cowered down to the ground, white as a sheet with fury and fear. And she was ejected from the building, just as she was, in a single light skirt, but only after she had done the cleaning and milking. She went out through the door, and Francek was whistling there, but she broke off halfway. Where should she go? She went to Auntie Marjána, who spent the snowy months with a needle hemming the blanket of the dressmaker for a crust of bread. That was the woman who kept a lover as well as her husband, and had quite enough work on her hands making fourteen shirts for her seven children. Lojza could not tell her aunt anything more than that he must have been able to enchant her or give her a love potion – and only one thing was clear, as clear as the

2 'Rorate' masses, votive masses in honour of the Virgin Mary, with accompanying devotions, were celebrated daily before sunrise in Bohemia in Advent. Their name comes from the first word of the introit to the Mass, 'Rorate caeli desuper et nubes pluant justum', 'You heavens, drop dew down from above, and may the clouds rain down righteousness'.

facts that summer is hot and winter is cold: a penniless orphan was not the equivalent to a bride with a big dowry! Experienced advice was given, and Lojza went off to the big city. It was only after the snow was gone from the ground, and remained lying, dirty and yellow, in the furrows of the field, in ditches by the road and in the ruts of the carriers, that Marjána was able to go to Adna. Nervous, fearful, red-faced as on the first day, her restless eyes flitting from the muddy planks up to the gloomy holy pictures, she said:

'So, Adna! I have a candle from your own hand, set aside for when I die, and three scarves . . . and I always weep over these, not with sorrow but with joy . . . what happiness I have, in winter as in summer? What have I ever received? But you, a widow, need not have done this to an orphan; at least you could have kept the girl!'

So in fact the blessed orphan was the reason that Adna suddenly set up Francek's wedding, with the help of the 'grenadier'. Francek was amenable to it all: to his bride, who had a clear thousand, but no figure as a woman; and even to the deal struck by his mother, who wanted to be on her own. But he did not look her in the eye, he denied Lojza, and on the quiet he continued to boast to the boys and his comrades, when they teased him about the girl, about his mother and about Svoboda, 'But it's better that they aren't married! At least no one is there to order anyone about! So when I step into the room, I'm more of a master than he is!' But he kept absolute silence in front of his mother, even when he was obliged to pay another three hundred for sausage before the wedding. And there was little that Adna did not stipulate in front of the notary apart from her own dwelling: twenty hundredweight of fodder, twenty hundredweight of corn, seven hundredweight of hard corn and five of oats, two clover beds which she wanted in spring, 120 eggs, a room to repair the stove and also twelve gulden for timber.

The entire poverty-stricken village scratched its head. 'How can one woman consume all that? She might have saved it . . .'

'Might!' – said the village clerk – 'but you'd have had to extract blood from her body and transfuse it into someone else's veins!'

IV

'Anička! Anička!' – and he clasped his hands as if in prayer – 'give me some milk!'

'And where am I going to get it from?'

'I'm going down the lane to pick cherries. When I've picked them . . . I'll give it back!'

She burst out laughing violently, with great golden sparks flashing in her eyes. Then she brought out a mug of curdled milk by the handle from the building, with a red scarf over a yellow one on her head.

'And so, Ančulina!' he said, quickly drinking up, 'when I buy it, I'll give you . . . that cherry-tree!'

It was Kaplan, from Humberk, who was returning from the harvest in the area, having drunk away all his clothes and his scythe as well, and he was left only with a sharp tongue and a black moustache below his nose, all those things that appealed to the women. He had been married to the daughter of a ropemaker, but she had wasted away and died by the side of her jovial husband. It was said that the brute had treated her badly – so badly that she had longed for death from her first hour with him; it was said that he had twice set fire to the thatch of the two greatest beggars in revenge; it was said that he had struck an officer in the army with a stone and had given a comrade money to take the blame; but they nevertheless thought him more crazy than evil. They could not help laughing at his antics, when, a grown adult, he had tied a wooden sabre to his side; or when he had made a foal panic in a green meadow; or when he had dashed alongside a horse by a carriage in leaps and bounds until he overtook it. But everyone knew that the prankster had sown more evil than good in the world in his thirty years.

He stayed at home very little; he broke stones, worked on building sites, in turnip fields, every kind of seasonal work – and so he had never yet set eyes on Adna at her dower house. It had not entered his head . . . why had she gone for the milk? After all, she still had all her front teeth and her hair had not yet turned grey, even if she threw a coloured scarf over it. Why? He rolled his eyes and threw up his hands in wonder at everything, in ridiculous amazement at the tree-stumps that lay around in the place where a courtyard should have been, if the lady of the house had cared about a wicker fence or stone wall – at the house with two windows clinging to the green hillside overgrown with lush vegetation – but most of all at the enormous tree-stumps, on which the serpentine roots twisted wildly, grey and white, so that they looked like the shaggy heads of monsters – a tribute to the fact that Svoboda was with her.

'So I have a man with me who can dig them out of the earth himself with his fingers . . . he is *that* strong!' said Adna, proudly.

Kaplan squinted up at the peak of his cap, and whistled a little.

'Well, he's a guest; what else would he be?' said Adna in response. 'Only . . . I can't get rid of him!'

Kaplan eyed her intently with his piercing eyes, eyes without lashes, and then twirled his moustache, black as a raven's feather.

'And so then, Anička! Could I come on Sunday as I used to do?'

'Why not . . . but during the day. No one is here overnight!'

And still her white teeth were gleaming between her red lips, as that same day she had been cheerful about her fate.

'Now then, hang on, you crazy woman, so that you can at least laugh for laughing's sake! The other day . . . it was in winter, I cut rods from the bushes and took them to town as roses. And in spring the gentlemen were annoyed. What for? . . . I said to them, how am I supposed to know they wouldn't like flowers that don't smell sweet? My wife doesn't smell sweet either . . . So what? Shall I come? Shall I not come? What must I do, my pretty one?'

And, with his hands in the pockets of his army trousers with their very narrow red seams, from which his dusty bare feet protruded, he marched away from her into the shade of two old chestnut trees, from which hung extensive foliage, wilted with the sultry weather. The whole day had been so hot, with no wind or cloud, nothing but blue and gold, with a blazing sun high in the sky. It was late harvest in the mountains, and the village was empty. Here and there little bodies with distended bellies, burnt bronze, could be seen on doorsteps in white shirts, dogs on chains were asleep, and on a stone opposite, by the wooden bell-tower, an old lady in a fur coat was sitting cross-legged, munching something, the red spots on her lemon-coloured cheeks in constant motion, but (the Lord knows) with nothing passing through her mind. From above, from the top of the chestnut tree, came the sound, cuckoo! . . . cuckoo! . . . cuckoo! . . . and once more, cuckoo! and the window creaked behind Adna. A grey tomcat leapt out of it in a long bound, with a strong scent of musk under his paws, and was followed by the menacing head of Svoboda above his veined neck, flushed, in a blaze of greying hair and whitish stubble of beard.

'I'm coming through the window for you,' he said, quietly, and deeply. 'I'll kill both of you, both of you – kill you!'

His shirt was open over his sunburnt chest, and his upper body was swaying back and forth as if he was unsure which of the two he should begin with. Once more, his threat was echoed by a cuckoo!

'Kaplan!' he yelled suddenly, in a strange, wheezing voice, 'if you don't come out of there, they will be carrying you out in a winding-sheet!'

Adna laughed in the direction of the chestnut tree, then went into the building, and Svoboda smashed the window. The room was a small one, with an unwashed bench around it, with one table and one bed, whitewashed, but untidy.

'Ah, won't you give me something to drink?' he asked, suddenly tame, to explain his arrival.

'I can indeed render you that service!' she replied, in derisive readiness.

'It's so hot . . . I'm burning up!'

'Why so? On account of that Kaplan?'

She was laughing, and could not stop. He said nothing. She found it very amusing that one guest should be raging furiously indoors while another was making cuckoo-calls in the chestnut tree under the window. The spring corn had been sown when Francek had his celebration, and from that time Adna had been together with Svoboda. He had only to take his cap off the nail for her to know that he was going where she would rather not set foot herself, into the bar, where Francek's unattractive, sullen wife was standing, and Francek himself was going about the yard and about his work in silence, with his hands in his pockets, like a ghost. The day after Francek's wedding, Svoboda had moved in with Adna with his wheelbarrow. She had the upper hand over him in everything, and everything was done according to her preferences. He brought kindling and roots for her in his barrow from the spruce grove, he milked the dun cow twice daily for her, a woman who had grown used to doing nothing, and he even tied the sash of her skirt around her waist when her arm was hurting, but he relied for his living on her grain, as she reminded him every time they had a tiff. It irked her that he collected his peasant's pension from the children to the last penny only for his own use and expenses, until she sued him, and with the authorities in town. The people in the fields digging up potatoes only saw them walking there and back together along the long avenue of rowan trees.

Towards evening the first wagons began to return. Sweaty, spotted cows drew them laboriously, heavy with grain, held by a rope with a top-beam, thin women wearing shirts and red skirts pushed them at the rear and from the sides with dry, raised hands, and with long, large, free steps the men followed the women and the cows with whips in their hands instead of sticks. And all at once, the whole village erupted in shouting.

Almost as if she were her equal, Marjána, the beggar, came in a white blouse to visit Adna, the owner of property. 'My soul!' she said, and a lad in rags, a step away from them, sounded the evening bell in a wooden three-legged belfry. Both Marjána and Adna crossed themselves with their thumbs, and then the former continued with her explanation to the latter. 'You see . . . the Lord God will not forsake his poor ones . . . today has brought me great joy. For the first time in my life I have received a letter in the post . . . and I've tucked it away among my papers for my prayers. And isn't Lojza lucky? Her child died of convulsions a week ago!'

Adna smiled strangely, but not at what she had said.

'You have an easy laugh! And what do you know about all this? With my legs, am I not a cripple . . . and unhappy? I am never well, out of spite, even when I am well . . . on Thursday I wonder what Friday will bring, and on Friday again I wonder about Saturday . . . And I am always thinking, who knows what suffering lies behind me!'

'Hey, Kaplan was here, Marjána!' and Marjána had never before seen such eyes. Were they greedy? eager? blissful? – she did not know.

So evening drew on, but it did not cool down in the close valley. It grew dark under the chestnuts over a huddle of children; full wagons were creaking, empty ones rattling; voices were shouting over the fence, over the road, from little window to little window; dogs were chasing poultry; cattle returning with the cowherds were lowing in the distance, and from all sides something was making itself heard, animal or human. Long ago, and now again, Marjána was telling the shoemaker on a doorstep somewhere else about her letter, between the pictures in her prayers. And again, suddenly, everything grew silent and calm, until lights appeared in the windows. A pale, round, full moon sailed peacefully across the sky above the roofs and the black treetops, and now the light shadows of cottages, fences, trees and forked roots lay completely quiet in its blue light.

'Cuckoo!' came a call from the chestnut tree as it had during the day – the Cock of the Woods was putting on his love show. Adna smiled only fleetingly, because a person laughs more quietly at night and weeps more loudly. But Adna had wept only once in her life, when they had brought her firstborn son in through the door on a spruce plank, with eyes dimmed, like a slaughtered beast.

'Ančulina!' – and he was with her. Two dark shadows met and disappeared into the cottage.

On the hill above the slope, Svoboda was returning slowly from the bar, alone and uncomfortable. He had been sitting for a couple of long hours before dusk and after dusk, from defiance, in the bar. In a corner behind a table he had been listening to the village clerk, who kept his gaze fixed in a single place, explaining in a whisper, more to himself than to him, how useless a man must be when he has completely lost his sight, how unpleasant the world must be . . . but that it was bad even for one with money, because he was forced to believe everything anyone tells him – let alone for a poor man! Svoboda was sorry for him, since he had sight good enough to see the statue between the two linden trees in front of the church at Proseč, but the other thing that he had told him about Kaplan of Humberk was etched into his mind. Once, perhaps a year before, he had reputedly tapped the clerk lightly on the shoulder with one finger, saying with a laugh, 'Bureš, I'm able to do everything – don't you believe me?' and the old man had trembled. Everything! Hmm . . . And just as Svoboda's eyesight was excellent, so was his hearing. He had gone only ten steps under the trees when he heard a well-known laugh in the depths below him; the blood rushed from his heart to his head, and furious, fiery wheels were whirling before his eyes.

He broke into a run, downhill, home – the door was latched. He shook the door, and behind it, behind the closed door he could not open, he heard a laugh, and then Adna, saying:

'You have to get out now!'

'Aha! Not until I choose to!'

He put his knee to the door, which was made only of a flimsy weathered plank, once, twice, but it did not give. In his powerlessness he did not utter words, but only a roar. Again he rushed, again he grasped it with iron fists, so that it creaked, and all at once he wrenched it off the doorpost. And beside him he saw them crouching on the bench, pale in the moonlight, Adna and Kaplan. From the doorway it seemed to him that they were laughing, that they were mocking him, but in truth neither of the two was now laughing.

'Let me through to my old woman!' ejaculated Svoboda, and leapt at them; it was horrible. Before the other man was able to resist Svoboda's hands with his youthful strength, Svoboda had grasped his throat and flung him down violently beneath him on the black floor, of nothing but compacted clay, like a hammer. Adna did not cry out at all, but merely sat on the edge of the bed, as silent as the enchanted streak of moonlight that slid through the window from the bench on to the floor and on to Kaplan; Svoboda saw only his eyes, the wilful eyes, without lashes, of a prankster, and continued to squeeze his throat as if he had a strong vice instead of hands, and to pin him to the ground with his knees. Kaplan struggled for breath vainly several times, as if in a dream, and clutched at something, fidgeting with his hands, and then ceased – the black pupils of his brown eyes dilated enormously and then contracted into tiny sharp points, but it was only when the whites, shot through with veins, began to cloud that Svoboda let his hands go. Weakly, but very bizarrely, Kaplan's head struck the floor, as if claiming brotherhood with it. Dumbfounded, Svoboda plunged his hand into his hair, did not look back, and walked out past the smashed door, beyond which was a silent night and a wide world. Only when his footsteps had died away did Adna call out, 'Kaplan! Kaplan!', twice, but she did not move from the edge of the bed. She waited for an answer – she waited until after this surge of strength she fell fast asleep.

The dawn was gloomy and grey behind the cobbler's gardenless cottage opposite when Adna opened her eyes. Kaplan was lying on the floor with outstretched hands in the morning as he had the previous night. She got up, took his hand, and streaks trailed up the rolled-up sleeve of her shirt, barely visible, thin, bluish-violet. 'Get up, Kaplan! . . . Get up!' said Adna, like a wilful child, and played with his cold fingers. Then, without her scarf, she crouched beside him on the floor, and it was thus that the village clerk found her.

'He has given himself up, that old man of yours!' said the clerk in the doorway. It was with difficulty that he coped with fulfilling his work, as he could see very little. 'And Francek asked him, how did you do it? Show me, old master! And again he took hold of him, and I had to get him away just in time, for he was turning blue under his fingers.'

'Bureš, go and get some liquor for me!' was Adna's reply to everything, and she was already getting the money out of a little pot.

'Woman, woman! what are you thinking of? The police will be here, and I'd also be punished myself in the end.'

And Adna suddenly wept, both about the liquor and about what had been denied her. She did not screw up her eyes, nor her blood-red lips, but as if from a stone statue, tears fell slowly from her eyes and trickled down on to her body behind her coarse, tightly laced blouse. Well as he knew her, he was made uneasy by her, by an Adna dumb with weeping. It seemed as though she did not know why she was weeping, or what had happened, and – it was precisely that which was so terrible about her weeping.

It was the middle of the harvest, with thin rows scattered over the fields of grain of grain reaped but not gathered in; the district was the poorest of the poor; yet no one was at work that day. Heavy, like an evil, destructive cloud, lay murder . . . a killing . . . over the village, between it and heaven. The door of the cottage, wrenched from the doorpost, like a mouth open in horror, was crying out to all the people: the sun is shining on the roof, but below it, below the roof, lay one who had been killed. It was true, and was also said about Kaplan, that he had had wicked dealings even with the lowest of the low . . . but a man had killed another man! At other times, in case of an accident, or when someone had passed away unexpectedly, not of his own accord, folk would came to see and to pity – both of those . . . but now a nose or a face might flash white at the glass and immediately turn away again. And each person in fact would only see some single thing . . . the eyes that had not yet been closed . . . Adna, curled up on the floor without her scarf . . . or the old man smoking at the table . . . no one saw everything. And in the evening, even when the police had removed the dead body to a wagon, groups of people remained standing in the village, whispering and discussing, until night once more covered with darkness what she had herself brought.

V

'God be with you, and all the saints!' Svoboda greeted the village clerk in front of his house, where, with a faded rug over his back to keep off the rain, he was rocking his son's baby to sleep, all wrapped up in blankets and crying, in a cradle suspended on a string. It was early morning, and both cold and windy, as it was everywhere in the mountains.

'Who's that?' asked the clerk at the voice – he was now completely blind.

'I'm just coming home out of prison!'

'You ought to know, brother . . . I was arrested straight away with you! And from March, for the second year I've done nothing but rock this child, nothing but rock it!' And the poor old man at these words dropped the string and stretched out his hands in both directions as if crucified. Poverty had crushed him, he had lost his spirit, and he grumbled whenever he had a listener. 'Look,' he said, 'even my wife would not wait for me. And you know my son, how considerate he is? I can't wash myself and so I have nothing but filth all over my body. What will happen to me when the baby runs away?' he said, when the human youngster whimpered out of the bundle of rags, and his cloudy, blind eyes peered out, as all blind eyes do, as if seeking help from above.

'What about . . . Adna?'

'What indeed! I haven't seen her face – they say she's doing nothing but drink. Even if there's someone in the world who hasn't died, not everyone is equally well or equally happy. Last Christmas I said to my sister, the miller's widow, "Sister, beg death to come for me!" But how is a man to die when he cannot?'

Svoboda paid no more attention to his wretched voice and went down to the bell-tower. People turned from their work inquisitively and searchingly to look at him, they called him by name, but he went on and paid no attention. And so, as at other times it had stood before him, so again there stood before him Adna's hovel – the derelict cottage. The windows were loose in their frames, shabby and grey with weathering, the broken panes were covered with newspaper, and against the wall there still lay two tree-stumps that he had dug up himself in the clearing before the hailstorm. He called out, and no one answered.

'What kind of fool am I, then?' he said to himself quickly before entering. In a corner of the empty, disordered, dirty room, lay Adna in bed like a pile of rags, a pillow under her head on the scattered straw; she was now grey, an old woman, but still like a red rose. There was rubbish, mixed with feathers and straw, in her dishevelled hair, and a grey tomcat bristled on her shoulder. He looked at her for a long while, then sat down beside her on the edge of the bed, placed his hat on his knee, took her by the hand, and spoke, with a smile:

'Mama, old mama, don't you recognise me?'

But Adna did not even stir from her sleep.

'Mama, what are you up to now? Are you doing the housework?' he asked good-naturedly, in jest, without any reproach, as if they had parted in good accord only the previous evening. He blamed her for nothing, as a child without understanding; he blamed only Kaplan, and he was . . . in God's truth, by his own hand. Had he killed him? So misfortune had befallen him, Svoboda, in a fateful, unfortunate moment. Once, in the sultry heat after work, he had slept with Adna in the muck on the floor in the cottage higher up, when he had heard a thief over his head, but it had then been lucky that she cried out, or something might have happened. A few times in the prison courtyard, when he had seen a tiny square of sky above him, something had nagged in his breast, but he had then reflected that it was well and good that Kaplan was where he was, a gardener who planted nothing but noxious, poisonous herbs in the earth rather than useful ones. And besides . . . he was not the one who had provoked Kaplan, but it was Kaplan who had provoked him.

Adna slept soundly on the bed. A glass-maker passed in front of the window, unsteadily carrying on his head a basket full of glittering trinkets and blue glasses, and rudely stared in at them. A boy had arrived to meet a girl in front of the shoemaker's door opposite, and a child was crying bitterly in the dim distance.

'Look, mama!' said Svoboda again to Adna, as when one half chides and half coaxes a child, meanwhile being pleased that it is the way it is, 'everything is as it should be with me, everything is in order with me, when I drink it is always just enough, and I can chop wood without cutting myself. Did Francek really not chop any for you?' and just as it had occurred to him, he took his hat off his knee and went to chop some wood for her before she awoke.

Two years had passed since they had taken one man away on a wooden wagon and had led a second man away in irons, and since Adna had said, 'I must drink so that I can fall asleep!' And since that evil day she had been different and yet the same – after all, what is a human being? – just as when a cloud crosses in front of the sun, casts a shadow on a field and is immediately gone once more. Formerly, she had been feasting and spending; now she was drinking. When the village clerk brought her the news that Svoboda had been sentenced to two years, and when the old bearer of news added, 'I wouldn't have been able to be the judge:

I would not have sentenced him. How is it with a thief? He always sees the gallows before him, and yet he steals. To me, myself, now that I'm at the end of my life, it seems that no one was to blame – that he has inborn passion in himself.' Adna nodded, but had she understood? Otherwise she never spoke to Marjána, who would have come to know it, about either Kaplan or Svoboda, as if they were deadly quicksands, which had to be avoided if one did not wish to be sucked into them spiritually and drown. Good house-keepers in the village, both men and women, prophesied a bad end for Adna, because she had not had either windows or door repaired, and the cow in the byre was giving her poor service. When the sun smiled upon the people, she would sit in the doorway and make conversation with the passers-by, but otherwise she drank – but so much that she would be lying prostrate on her bed, as if dead, for half the next day. She was still alive, but immobile. Once, the Čápeks robbed her of the grain stored in the attic: she heard furtive footsteps above her head, and saw round heads flash by the window; in the morning, she spoke about it at length, shouting between her cottage and the shoemaker's, but she was no longer on guard over her property. Francek, the true son of his father and mother, was playing the master, mismanaging his debts, and squabbling with his wife. Adna did not go to him, and avoided mentioning even a penny of money. When she did not receive any, she would borrow from the schoolmistress, but immediately, as soon as the hen had laid an egg, repay her. She talked most of all to Marjána, who was not getting any sweeter the older she became, cursing anyone who did not give her alms. And Adna spoke often to her about her husband, who seemed not to have died in his bed, but to have been burnt up in the barn at the back together with ten buckets of grain . . . and she believed this as devoutly as the tangled tale about her son, the cards, the wagon and the silver chain.

Yet Svoboda woke Adna from her slumbers by his axe-strokes into the timber and on the chopping-block. She might perhaps not have remembered it when she saw him through the window, if he had not immediately spoken, when she turned away to avoid him at the window:

'Mama!' – and he held out his hand to her at the window-sill – 'don't regard me as to blame!'

'Oh, I know well that you were not guilty . . . it was just destiny – you criminal!'

Svoboda hurled the axe violently at the pile of chopped wood – and then he smiled, and with his hand he touched Adna's throat in the place where menfolk have their Adam's apple, and he said, still as if in jest:

'Just wait, I'll show you what criminals can do!'

'You criminal, you criminal!' cried Adna, as if she could only see and only say one single thing, 'but you've maimed me!'

'Mama!' said Svoboda quietly and firmly – 'I'll do it with the axe!' And now Adna no longer remained as she had been. Timidly and fearfully she fixed her eyes on the shining axe as if on a scourge, and Svoboda himself saw that they were different from what they had been, and now rigid and glazed.

'Get out of my house!' she said again, so as not to give in to him at once, but she no longer had the strength for that.

'Anička . . . just remember the Lord God is above watching you!'

'The Lord God?' asked Adna, as if this were some kind of terror of which she understood only that it had power over her.

'And what, aren't you leaving me my wood?' she said. 'Come into the room, Marjána is looking at you – she shouldn't be seeing you!'

In the place where a boy and a girl had been arguing in the morning, Marjána was now sitting, opposite two of

Adna's windows, like a hungry dog waiting for a morsel. No-where could be seen from the hollow, and they had eaten in all the cottages; but she waited steadily. The sun stood high and warmed both young blood and old bones with its blaze, when a pair of people came out of the cottage, Adna with a bundle of scarves on her back and Svoboda with a hoe in his hand. 'They're a couple of kittens!' she said, for she did not understand, and knew nothing; she only saw an old lady with her old suitor going over somewhere into the fields, with a blue sky and a few more years of life before them.

A ROSE FOR UNCLE: AN UNSERIOUS TALE
OF A VERY YOUNG COQUETTE, WITH A MORAL

ANNA MARIA TILSCHOVÁ

Once upon a time there was a little girl – very pretty, very young, with long hair and short skirts, and she was – very coquettish. When she counted up all – all! her boyfriends, were there five? . . . only . . . five? There was Jenda, the brother of her girlfriend Karla, ten years old, who had long eyelashes, told lies, and looked for beetles and flowers for her . . . there was the atheist medical student . . . there was the poet who wrote ironic love poems in the style of J. S. Machar[1] on sheets of white cardboard with gold edging and sometimes pushed them under her fan and sometimes into one of her gloves . . . and who was unfortunately not here over the summer . . . there was the officer of the 28th Regiment who rattled his sabre . . . and the ridiculous clerk – so ridiculous! – who had serious intentions . . . so were there really – just five of them? She couldn't count Uncle among them? Or . . . could she? Probably better not. For one thing, he was Uncle, and for another, he wasn't in love with her. How could be be, anyway, being so old, so old, and he had a goatee beard! Really! But he wasn't her real uncle, but he was forty-five years old, and it was just . . . as if he were. A pity . . . counting him there'd be . . . six – half a dozen . . . Besides, who knows?

Besides . . . wasn't she pretty? very pretty? weren't those two eyes, looking at her out of the mirror, not too big, but unusual, green, glowing like a cat's eyes? and didn't Hynek sing, 'Love is no respecter of age' . . . no respecter of age . . . in *Eugene Onegin*?[2] and besides, when she ran out into the meadow and ran back again into the road clutching an

1 Josef Svatopluk Machar (1864–1942), Realist poet and essayist.

2 Prince Gremin's aria from Act III of Tchaikovsky's opera *Eugene Onegin* (first performed 1879).

armful of flowers, she didn't give any to the medical student, nor to the mournful clerk, gazing at her so stupidly . . . only to Uncle, she herself, with her tiny, playful fingers, stuck a yellow arnica flower into his buttonhole, and said, 'I'm giving it to you, Uncle, because you're nice and because I love you . . .', didn't Uncle look at her little fingers and didn't he say, 'But what strange little fingers you have . . . so tiny . . .', and didn't he look as if he wanted to eat them, shaking his goatee, him, old Uncle . . . after all, who knows! Ah, she was . . . very, very coquettish . . .

She shook her head and ran off immediately. She ran lightly with tousled hair and rosy cheeks. She tweaked the lining of Uncle's coat with her hand, and said, 'Uncle, uncle, I'm asking you to do something for me, something big – will you do it?' And she gazed at him with her green eyes.

'But I don't know what it's to be . . .'

'But it's very little, really nothing . . . just to tell me the truth, the real truth – do you understand?'

'Why not! So then, what is it?'

'Look me in the eye, look at me properly . . . Look, the medical student, you know the one, he says I've grown as tall as a beanpole and he's got an eye for me, and that one, actually another one, would propose marriage to me, imagine, he'd marry me . . . and the officer . . . and Jenda . . . each one of them says something different, Uncle! Is it true that I'm pretty?'

'Oh yes, you're pretty . . . actually very pretty. Come here, your hair is all over the place . . . perhaps I could plait it for you!' And old Uncle with the goatee beard plaited the hair of the coquettish little girl.

Her hair was long – he spent a long time plaiting it.

'Doesn't it bore you, plaiting my hair?' asked the little girl.

'Oh no, it doesn't bore me, it doesn't bore me at all,' said Uncle, meanwhile looking at her with eyes that were strange . . . they were shining and seemed almost damp as Uncle's freckled hands touched her hair . . .

Her hair shone in the sun, flew in the breeze, and twisted and turned in a dance, as madly as the coquettish little girl herself. The coquettish little girl enjoyed being pretty, enjoyed being happy, and wanted to please. It did not matter to the little girl whom she would please – she only wanted to please, just as she wanted to dance, just as she wanted to sing . . . to chase on her little feet, to laugh with her pretty little teeth, and to show off her cat-like eyes . . . that coquettish, frivolous, little girl. And afterwards, when she danced, in her linen blouse, with a ribbon tied at her throat and with a rose on her bodice, the medical student said, 'If you only knew how your hair curls at the back of your neck . . . it's so awfully pretty! But don't keep laughing all the time! Showing me that all your teeth are there! I wouldn't move a finger if you were to bite me . . .' But the little girl, instead of biting him, laughed at him, and the medical student thought he would have preferred a bite to the laugh. 'I so much want to say something to you,' – whispered the clerk – 'to you and you alone . . .' 'What? Now?' asked the little girl, 'I haven't got time now,' and she rushed off, simply flew off.

'Wouldn't you give me that rose?' – begged the officer, rattling his sabre seductively. 'But I can't, I really can't, I was given it – by Jenda . . .' 'So may I have the third quadrille with you?' – 'Why a quadrille, and why the third one? It's so very serious . . . and anyway we should dance with the people we like, so I ought to dance it with Uncle, see, Uncle!' But Uncle went off without looking at her, hands behind his back and goatee beard over his chest. Of course, Uncle was a serious old man who played skittles with Papa and played whist with Mama, who only read the personal announcements in the newspapers, who had a goatee beard, a bald patch and freckled hands, and who was nice to her. Perhaps he really liked her? Hadn't he brought sweets for her the other day? A cornet of sweets for the theatre, and he was looking at her as he did so. Oddly . . . not like the medical student, and not like the poet . . . Somehow differently . . . In fact it wasn't exactly nice . . . but it was kind, as an uncle is, and not – as someone in love is. When she was hot after dancing or running, he immediately put a shawl on her shoulders. That was nice, and it also wasn't nice. It was nice that he was caring for her, and it wasn't nice that he was touching her shoulders as he did so with his hands – those freckled hands. But it would be awfully amusing if an old man like that should fall in love with her! The other day she had drunk some wine – it had been lovely red wine and she had slowly poured it down her throat from the glass. – It had been awfully good. – 'Did you hear about Filipina Welserová?' said Uncle as she was doing so. 'Her skin was so tender that when she was drinking red wine you could see it through her throat . . . Do you think anyone would see right through you too?' . . .

'Go on with you!' – said the little girl coquettishly, and she did not know what to say and what to think. And for that reason she laughed. Wasn't it better to run with Jenda in the grass of the meadow, pick flowers, and then sit down in the hay, sort herbs in a bag and look at insects preserved in alcohol, and pay no attention to the medical student, or the clerk, or the officer or . . . Uncle? And enjoy the way it annoyed them? Rather than sit at table between Mother and Uncle and listen to Uncle's strange talk, which . . . one couldn't make head or tail of. Wine shining through your throat – that isn't possible, after all. Was he making fun of her? Or did he think she had a pretty white throat? He was making fun of her instead of liking her. And the coquettish, pretty, vivacious, laughing girl frowned. And later, when she was walking with everyone else on a path sprinkled with sand and supported by wooden planks, she ran ahead and walked alone beside the atheistic medical student; and she did not look back at Uncle nor smile at him, and she did not offer him a flower, that angry, frowning girl-kitten.

'Is it true,' – she said – 'what pan Král said about you, that you don't believe in God?'

'Yes, of course,' – said the medical student, stroking his whiskers.

'But that simply isn't possible . . . But surely you can't deny that God exists?'

'Yes, I can,' – said the medical student again, rather embarrassed. 'He doesn't exist.'

'Doesn't he?' said the little girl in astonished surprise. 'I don't believe you. Look,' – she said – 'I'll give you this rose if you admit you believe . . . do you want it?' and the little girl laughed, showing her teeth, and with sparkling eyes.

She wanted to seem serious – she spoke about God, and tried to seem kind to the medical student – she gave him the rose, because she could hear Uncle's footsteps behind her . . . that coquettish little girl.

'And don't I get anything?' said Uncle behind her.

'Nothing!' – and, playful rather than angry, she flashed her green eyes at him. And Uncle walked behind them, saying nothing; he had his goatee beard over his chest and red veins in his brimming eyes.

The coquettish little girl was not evil – she was not good; she was not clever – she was not stupid; she was coquettish. But she did not know how to cope with Uncle. She smiled at Jenda – Uncle frowned; she dipped her little hand in the stream and asked Uncle to dry it. And Uncle dried her hand and looked at the little girl with strange, unpleasantly damp eyes. People in love don't look at one in that way . . . neither the poet nor the medical student had looked at her like that.

Once, when they were walking ahead in front of the others, on a path pale green with moss, Uncle was gazing at her, at the coquettish little girl.

'Why are you looking at me? In that way?' she said.

'Do you remember your history lessons at school – the French Revolution? After the Revolution, a lady lived there, a beautiful lady – and she was called Mme Tallien. She used to wear antique robes of translucent fabrics, and the left-hand side was open, cut away, from her side down to her ankle. You would look lovely in that . . .'

'Me . . .' said the little girl in confusion. 'Me?' she said in astonishment, imagining herself in a translucent robe, and she felt Uncle's eyes fastened on her.

'Where's Jenda?' she said, looking round.

'Do you want to ask him about it?' asked Uncle, mockingly. 'Sit down here at the edge of the forest, they'll catch us up – they're not even in sight yet.'

The little girl sat down, and Uncle sat down, close to her . . . and suddenly laid his head with its goatee beard on the shoulder of the little girl, and half-closed his eyes.

'It would be good to go to sleep like this,' he said again.

The little girl moved her little shoulders and tried to shake his head off.

'Wouldn't you like to give me a kiss . . .' said Uncle again – 'as your Uncle . . .'

The little girl said nothing, could not say anything; she was altogether frightened and confused in her little soul, which was neither evil nor good, but coquettish. She jumped up, ran into the middle of the path, and cried out, 'There they are, there they are!' . . . and only afterwards added, 'No, I wouldn't! . . .' and . . . and . . . then stopped laughing.

*   *

Little girls, be pretty, but don't be coquettish.

THEORIES

BOŽENA BENEŠOVÁ

Two women aged between thirty and forty were chatting over tea.

Beside the tea-kettle, a paraffin lamp was flickering softly, and lighting up the bay window with a mellow, homely light.

Erika had light brown hair full of bronze highlights, and her white brow, soft as if modelled in cotton-wool, was bathed in the shadow of these metallic waves. But though she felt that her blonde, now slightly fading, beauty was shown to best advantage in this way, she was nevertheless gloomy, and was looking at her friend with melancholy eyes. Her over-ripe lips were continually trembling slightly, but she remained silent for a long time.

Her companion, Marta Horanová, slightly younger in years, slightly older in appearance, with a face showing the traces of much thought, and with eyes that were over-serious – almost severe – spoke on the contrary a great deal. Her sentences always tumbled out over one another or merged excitedly, and were at one moment overloaded with strange images, at another moment boldly sarcastic, at another again dryly descriptive.

She was familiar with a multitude of women's destinies, and well able to talk about them. She explained that paní Klárová would have to divorce her husband in the very near future because she had finally lost patience; she knew in detail the feelings of Miss Nová, whose fiancé had dropped her when a cabaret singer had compromised her with a bawdy music-hall song; she had even analysed the feelings and future fate of some Englishwoman with whom she had travelled in a train recently for barely two hours. She spoke at length, and kept conjuring up new figures before her deep, dark eyes, and it seemed to her that she would be wronging them if she did not speak about them as well.

'However do you know all this?' asked Erika finally, not without surprise. 'After all, you live almost like a hermit, and all at once not only do you know all these people, but it seems that you also divine the reasons for what they do, and even their thoughts.'

'It's only something recent, only something recent,' replied Marta seriously. 'But now I have really found out how to classify women. I've learnt to understand many things from the slightest hints, I then think them through thoroughly, and finally I classify them according to my own system. It's my passion now. If I had devoted myself to it in my youth, I'd have been able today to have a lot of material on the psychology of the modern woman. Alas, though, my youth was very misspent, and even worse, also very foolish. Oh, youth so loves unnecessary suffering! It casts pearls so passionately into vinegar . . . and is then surprised, so awfully surprised, when it loses them. People also always make experiments in their youth, but only on their own account, and that is so painful. It's only later that they examine and dissect the souls of others rather than their own . . . Of course I am speaking only about women. Men are much simpler and more naïve . . .'

She stopped speaking, but only for a moment, and poured Erika another cup of tea.

'I'm very glad that I'm no longer young,' she said meanwhile, and a fleeting smile brightened her stern eyes for a moment.

'Don't talk about being young,' replied Erika hurriedly, 'it's not the time for that. Yesterday was All Souls, and the first snow has fallen today. Time flies so dreadfully fast . . . And perhaps it doesn't fly, perhaps it drags. One can't know even as simple a thing as that. Sometimes it seems to me that it has stopped and that I'm fifteen years old. But yesterday when I was standing by my husband's grave, I could not, could not, grasp that he's now been dead for six months. He's more remote to me than the hero of the novel I read without my Mama's knowledge twenty years ago . . . If only he could come and haunt me occasionally! But he doesn't – he's dead, completely dead . . . Or if only one's youth would at least die as suddenly and as definitely as a person dies. But God knows when one's youth actually dies . . . You don't even know whether it's dead and haunting one, or whether it's still alive. And then the whole of life is so feeble . . . Tell me, please, about your psychological material – it interests me a lot. You've got such good theories about everything. And there might be certainty in theory. I think it's certainty in opinion. Or is something completely different possible? I really don't know. I don't even know anything about myself, let alone anyone else. I'm in a rush, really in a rush, but tell me at least something else, please tell me plainly!'

Marta looked at her red lips, very nervous as they were, and at her childishly shining eyes, considered for a moment, and then said seriously:

'If you had had a more honest husband, Erika, you would have known infinitely more about yourself and about others by now. When I think that the woman of today, for whom all traditions have been subverted, and all laws changed, understands definite feelings only when some naïve soul, some stable disposition, speaks to her about them in simple language, it is immediately clear to me that the starting point for my securest knowledge is in fact Pavel Horan. Without my husband I might never have understood how few components one's emotional life actually has, and how easily it can be summarized and categorized . . .'

'Your husband may have a naïve heart,' replied Erika slowly, 'but he absolutely hates all systems and all theories. I know your interpretations would never have emerged if he had been sitting here with us today.'

'They certainly wouldn't,' agreed Marta willingly. 'And Pavel definitely hates theories and systems, you're quite right in that too. But I would never have come by my own theories without him. He was the one who first taught me to understand the confusions of the present day. He always speaks frankly to me, because he is very open and very faithful. And most often about women, for he has an excellent understanding of them. Provided they are not too refined and too clever, he immediately arrives at an estimate of them. And of course his estimate is a masculine one – basically an erotic one. And I've already told you, I understand the slightest hint . . .'

'So that's your understanding,' said Erika quietly, curling up in her chair.

Marta had always regarded her as a sweet, foolish child. But she liked her, she loved her graceful movements, her shy eyes, and the slope of their lids like velvet flowers. And now she gazed for a long time as those transparent eyelids sank lower and lower, until they hardly let out even a suspicion of a glow from those shining eyes.

'Pavel has something in common with you,' she said thoughtfully after a moment. 'He sometimes says something brief, as you've just done, and I think to myself, that must have been ironic. But all I have to do is look at his guileless face to know straight away that irony had never come into his mind . . . just as it is with you . . . But this isn't in your nature: it depends on the fact that he too is able to bury his dead so deep that they don't come haunting him.'

Erika became very uneasy; she suddenly raised her delicate eyelids, and her beautiful eyes darted from her friend to the clock, from the clock to the door, and back to Marta. Her anxious heart was pounding with quick short beats.

'If only a mere glance into your face should also be enough for me to know that you are not thinking of irony!' – she would almost have screamed. But she bit her lip in time, and though it seemed to her that she could no longer look at Marta at all, she turned to her again and again with a restless, injured look.

'Actually, you are – also beautiful,' she said after a moment, and she may not have realized that this time she was actually thinking aloud.

But Marta did not notice. She was burrowing deeper and deeper into her thoughts, and the shadows of complex cogitation flitted across her pale face.

'Men control us most securely with the suffering they cause us, or that which we cause ourselves under their influence,' she said, when she had finally managed to find words for her ideas. 'And to escape from unnecessary suffering is the real essence of the modern women's question. It's not easy, at least for the superior among us, for the seeking and for the unsatisfied. For resistance, and the criticism of the greatest of women's sorrows, is not what we enjoy. Our mothers did not criticize their husbands, because they never understood them. We understand ours, we judge them, and we suffer much. It's only when it becomes clear to us that we are enslaving ourselves to this suffering that we become able to face it. We cease judging individuals and we take in the whole of the theatre that surrounds us. Except that this then requires classification and theories. Do you understand?'

'I don't understand, because you are talking about some strange lifelong suffering,' interrupted Erika tartly. 'But in love there is only one real type of suffering, and no classification and no theory is enough to understand it.'

'What, for example?' asked Marta, somewhat haughtily.

'Jealousy,' replied Erika, and now she was even paler than her inquisitive friend.

Marta smiled dismissively and indulgently.

'Jealousy can never represent suffering for a mature woman, Erika! Never. Consciousness of one's own shortcomings may perhaps evoke some kind of envious longing, grief from the loss of possession may lead a person into selfish bitterness, but . . .'

'I'm not speaking about that!' Erika almost screamed. 'Those are just cool thoughts. But jealousy is frightfully real, and arouses frightful pain . . . Another woman beside a beloved husband . . . A third party, alive as you are, with longings like yours. Someone who might even kill you, or whom you yourself might kill . . .'

'How upset you are, my God, how upset you are!' said Marta, soothing her condescendingly. 'And, excuse me, I'm not going even to give this an answer. I don't recognize jealousy; I only know a legend about it from the times when all women were hot-blooded, spoilt children like you . . . Perhaps I was once like that, I don't know, I try to forget about those days. But this I know, that I haven't felt jealousy since the time when I first learnt to consider and classify – since the time I first had my so-called theories. Later you'll understand so many complex things that you'll find it impossible to occupy yourself with such childish objections as these of yours.'

'Might you also have theories about jealousy?' asked Erika quietly.

'Unshakable ones. You admit, after all, that only two types of jealousy are possible, justified or unjustified.'

And on Marta's face there appeared real satisfaction at these precise words.

'Of course,' sighed Erika, moving her head deeper into the shadows.

But Marta said, with her face fully illumined:

'Right, jealousy is justified in the event that your beloved husband is genuinely in love with another woman. But then you recognize that all self-torture is in vain; that it cannot return your lover to you alive, just as prayer cannot return a corpse to you. And jealousy is unjustified if your husband is not in love with that other woman. But anything more than childish nervousness is evidence of lingering self-humiliation, and basically something as ridiculous as a false hump.'

Marta's joke may have been somewhat lame, but Erika laughed at it just the same. She had a very beautiful laugh, musical and bubbly; her sad eyes were burning and her face slightly flushed.

She rose quickly and adjusted her hat with its long widow's veil.

'I must, must leave now – unfortunately I must leave you and this most interesting conversation,' she said rapidly. 'I've been keeping you unforgivably long. But today it seemed as if I really couldn't leave you.'

Her lips, like raspberries, were no longer trembling, and formed an agile, pleasant bow.

'I'm very fond of you, Marta!' she cried warmly, now leaving through the door.

Pavel Horan was waiting outside the house, and as he bent towards Erika's hand, the radiant and sad eyes of an eager man flashed in the gloom.

'Yesterday when you went to the cemetery to your husband's grave, I didn't have to wait so long for you,' he complained acerbically. 'I won't allow you to meet a woman over tea again before a rendezvous.'

'Your wife is very nice,' said Erika thoughtfully.

'Yes.'

'And also wise in many ways.'

'Perhaps.'

'And there are times when she's also really beautiful. Today there were some moments when I couldn't take my eyes off her. She seemed more beautiful to me than any woman I know.'

'Maybe,' agreed Pavel, absent-minded again. 'But why are you praising her so much today?'

'Because I'm no longer jealous of her.'

He dropped her hand and whistled in enormous astonishment.

'I don't understand you,' he said, boyishly.

'Oh, I was really jealous of her! Of her in particular! And it was so painful – you cannot imagine! And none of your caresses and none of your solemn oaths helped. It was lying upon me like a poisonous miasma. Until she herself drove it away from me . . . She has an excellent theory about jealousy.'

And affectionately she slipped her arm once more under Pavel's.

A TALE FROM HELL

MARIE MAJEROVÁ

Dr Beneš's office was furnished more than comfortably – it might even be said, with a degree of artistic taste. The simple lines of the furniture blended with the elegant olive-green wallpaper, and the becoming softness of the carpets and coverings gave the room a comfortable atmosphere. Sumptuous paintings of landscapes bathed in the noonday sun provided cheer from the walls; the bright green of their trees softened the somewhat heavy impression of all their colours and shadows. The broad window was shielded by a light curtain, so that the view of the bleak hospital courtyard was obscured by the delicate lily-of-the-valley on the tulle.

The iron company which had established the hospital for the ironworks and the mines had not had the doctors much in mind; and Dr Beneš may have been the only one to have conjured up such a delightful retreat from his dreary, empty cell.

The hospital was an extensive one; all the wards still bore the signs of novelty. The garden, with its poor lawn and its stunted, leafless trees, did not even attract the watchdog. Furthermore, the gowns of the patients, in their eternal blue and white stripes, flapping along the footpaths like animated blankets, and the tedious uniforms of the nuns who served as nurses, made a stay in the hospital yet more dreary.

And it was no better out in the surrounding country. On all sides there were shafts, stark chimneys and high walls; the slag heap in front of one's eyes was strangely desolate, like a city overwhelmed with lava – like a landscape under a curse, from a fairy-tale.

At night the slag heap springs to life. A small locomotive, spitting sparks like a dragon, pulls a long series of smoking wagons full of hot, liquid slag. One after another they tip out their loads on to the broad sides of the heap. The loads roll like fiery balls down to its foot, or disintegrate with red-hot pieces leaping down in great strides, or break like soft-boiled eggs, spilling their liquid contents down the heap.

And in the daylight there appear the new forms that have been created during the night: here the intact shape of a wagon like an old castle under a curse, there a tower piled up from pieces of slag, here a gate, there an entire multitude of fragments of slag.

A dismal prospect.

And for that reason the doctor preferred to shut himself up inside his four walls and enjoy his books. He read a great deal; he took an interest in literature, and ever since he had become a factory doctor in that place of mines and metalworks, he had regarded it as his duty to take account of the living conditions of the workers.

Somewhat condescendingly, he made the acquaintance of a certain laboratory technician from the Vojtěšská huť, the local Kladno ironworks. The technician, a lanky young man with blue eyes, visited him in the hospital, read his books, and spoke to him about the labouring class. They had frequent altercations, because the technician was one of the subversive elements in society, whereas the doctor was very attached to social order. He was never willing to believe that the conditions of the labourers were as miserable as the technician painted them; he used to say:

'If things were so unbearable, surely the people would speak up! If it were impossible for them to live, they could not still be alive!'

And the simple fact that they were alive, and that it was possible for them to be alive, was enough to salve his conscience.

Today the doctor was pacing around his room gloomily. He was morosely clutching a small blue book in his hand, like a thing one would prefer to throw away but which one feels obliged to take into consideration for some reason.

'Tales from hell!' he grumbled. 'Nonsense! What sort of tales from hell are these! Are metalworks and mines really some kind of hell?'

He paused in front of the window. Old Kalina, a miner, was walking through the courtyard, a thin, bony, nervous little man. His sharp cheekbones cast a deep shadow into his dark eyes, as if they were still being illumined by his Davy safety lamp. He drew himself up slowly and spat. Little black pools remained behind him like footprints. The doctor drew the curtain.

And once more he began pacing around the room. On the wide bookcase there were two bronzes in the style of Constantin Meunier:[1] a Belgian miner with a pick, and a young female coal miner in her working overalls, with her legs defiantly astride and her hands on her hips.

The doctor paused.

'He's a handsome lad,' he thought to himself. 'There aren't many like him here. They are all poor specimens of humanity – thin, withered, scrawny. Nor are the girls here pretty, either, even if there are few of them labouring in the ironworks these days. – It's true, it's not heaven here,' he said quietly, 'but in any case, what is that to me? I won't be the one to help them if they don't help themselves ... It'll be better if I get some sleep now; one is grumpy on the night shift if one doesn't get enough rest.'

He was about to take his jacket off when he noticed the book still in his hand.

'That book again!' He scowled and flung the book on the floor.

---

1 Constantin Meunier (1831–1905), Belgian painter and sculptor, noted for his depictions of industrial workers and miners.

He drew the curtain of heavy drapery, and the room was darkened. He took off his shoes, threw them down by the door, and lay down.

Confused sounds were echoing in the closed room. The shrill sound of a whistle, muffled by the heavy material, was wailing in a minor key, and indefinite cries seemed to be whispering through the curtains.

Scarcely had he fallen asleep when some kind of unpleasant sensation disturbed him, stinging his eyes. He turned his face to the wall, but the sensation did not abate. It seemed to him that someone was watching him, and that he was hearing two voices whispering.

'Today?' whispered a girl's voice.

'Yes, today!' came the muffled reply.

The doctor sprang off the sofa. By the bookcase was standing a coal miner with a lighted Davy lamp. This was the light that had stung the eyes of the doctor and awoken him. Beside the miner stood a young girl in overalls, the engine driver from the slag heap.

'Come with us,' said the miner in a gloomy voice.

'I don't understand . . . What . . .' stammered the doctor, hunting for excuses. It was strange that it did not occur to him to summon help. Nor did he attempt to resist, for he saw a heavy pick in the muscular hand of the miner.

Accordingly he put his jacket on once more, and said simply:

'But I must get some sleep, as I am on the night shift!'

The miner nodded – and pointed at the door.

They went out.

Outside they were greeted by a frosty night; the hospital courtyard lay in darkness.

'Where are you taking me?' the doctor ventured to ask, with chattering teeth, for in his light jacket he was cold.

The miner was stamping vigorously, his long legs encased in his tight trousers, and his naked back gleamed in the night.

The engine driver replied in her clear voice, which quivered with something like irony.

'To hell, sir.'

They passed alleyways, deserted yards, and the porter's lodge of the ironworks. The slag crackled as they crushed it under their feet. Stacks of rails and pipes alternated with the insubstantial buildings of the workshops; they also passed the offices, and now were standing by the blast furnaces.

In a small chamber, virtually a den, was sitting a man with a long iron rod. Innumerable concrete troughs led from the chamber into the blast furnace. It was dark and cold. Inside the furnace, an infernal heat was separating the iron ore into metal and slag, and this little blackened figure was waiting for the moment to strike when, with a thrust at the weak points, he could force the blast furnace to release its precious material. The foot of the blast furnace, covered with clay, was threatening to crush him at every moment. A signal sounded from above.

'Watch out!' shouted the little man, thrusting out his rod.

He struck the aperture coated with clay, and in a small window there appeared a white glow.

'Quick, or it will close up!' he commanded himself, and hammered furiously, enlarging the aperture.

At last, with a roar and a hiss, the glowing, white-hot mass rolled into the trough. The den grew pleasantly warm. Sparks flew from the trough, and tiny globules splashed from the furnace, burning the doctor's jacket.

The more the remarkable mass flowed out, the hotter the den became, and after a short time the heat was so intense that the doctor was bathed in sweat. The blackened furnace attendant, too, was wiping streams of sweat from his brow.

'Can we leave now?' appealed the doctor to the miner.

The latter laughed, and went out.

'I shall certainly catch a dreadful cold today,' mused the doctor, as he emerged into the cold of the night.

The smelting works were full of lively activity. Locomotives were whistling, pulling carriages behind them filled with loads of iron. The iron was still bubbling in the carriages and sparkling like champagne.

They walked along the narrow tracks until they reached an extensive building with a large gate. They were constantly obliged to dodge blackened figures hurrying to their labour.

In the building a remarkable spectacle awaited them. Three giant egg-shaped structures were suspended in the air. A complex network of staircases, scaffolding and flooring surrounded them. With sharper points the giant eggs penetrated the ceiling and opened round mouths to the heavens. From one of them, thick yellow smoke was rolling, and sparks flying. Its contents were bubbling, gurgling and boiling. In this process steel was being manufactured from iron ore.

The second egg, rotating on its axis, was pouring its red-hot contents into a cauldron situated on the locomotive. And around this were running half-naked workers, turning the egg, driving the steam engine in clouds of smoke and steam, and sealing the filled cauldron. The locomotive pulled away with a whistle and a hiss, and the egg spewed a mass of sparks straight into the doctor's face. The naked backs of the workers, full of yellow scars, merely shook like the hides of horses, but the doctor was momentarily blinded.

When he recovered his sight, he saw that he was inside the third egg, which the workers were lining with fire-bricks. It was stifling here; the sulphurous fumes had not yet dissipated. Even the walls were still hot. The doctor had a fit of coughing.

'But this is extremely unhealthy!' responded the physician in him.

The workers were laughing. Their agonized laughter sounded hollow in the confined space.

As they were leaving, the doctor could still hear the voice of the overseer. 'The middle should be ready in an hour's time, and it will blow here!'

'However is this monster to cool within an hour?' the doctor wondered, but he had no further time to think about it. The floor of the workshop which they were now entering was filled with iron bars and blocks; some were warm, others still quite red-hot. It was necessary to proceed with the greatest caution. Inwardly the doctor was alarmed about the bare feet of the miner. But there was no time for such thoughts, nor indeed for walking: the doctor was obliged to jump from one place to another, with a warning 'Look out!' shouted at him from everywhere, with red-hot iron coming from all sides.

Cranes were flying aloft, holding incandescent ingots in the teeth of their arms; the din of hammers rang out from the deep channels where moulds were being formed; a locomotive arrived, with a boiler, and filled all the moulds that were ready. The iron was splashing and disgorging its hot spittle into faces flushed with the heat; at times the mould overflowed and there was a terrifying rush into the channel. Wherever the doctor stood, he was in the way.

He looked imploringly at the miner.

But he was about to leave, with his companion. Her wooden clogs clattered around the door, from which a freezing draught was blowing in.

They met a man wheeling ingots of a hundredweight on an iron barrow. One after another, there was an entire procession of them, like damned souls in hell, each behind his hot load, like an infinite chain of galley slaves.

Now for the first time the doctor noticed the source of the heavy crashes with which the whole building was shaking. Two huge hammers were beating the soft blocks with their untiringly heavy iron fists. And again there were half-naked figures running about with rivulets of sweat on their bronzed backs, forcing nutrient into the insatiable maws of the hammers.

From here, strapping young men were conveying carts, laden with long bars, to the rolling mill.

In the middle of a long hall, machines were set up in line like ideal workers. And to the front and also to the rear rods were spurting out of their rollers, ever smaller and smaller, and bars, ever thinner and thinner. They were twisting like fiery serpents over the packed black clay of the floor, with deadly agility. And between them, like dancers on eggshells, leapt the young men, catching them with tongs and returning them to the untiring rollers, which spun and laboured unceasingly from one morning to the next – like ideal workers.

The doctor was forced to jump over the hurdles like a racehorse. In mortal terror he leapt after the long legs of the miner, expecting every moment that he would be caught and burnt by a rod appearing from nowhere, or that he would be entangled by a serpentine wire in a treacherous snare.

'They only employ unmarried men here,' remarked the miner in passing.

When they left the rolling mill, the doctor collapsed on the rail track. Sweat was glistening on his brow and his hands, and his eyes were obscured with a milky veil. He was exhausted.

'They have a pleasant life here, not so?' smiled the engine driver. 'Lovely . . . Let's go now and see what it's like in our realm. We don't have any hot wires . . .'

The doctor sighed, but the sight of the miner's pick prodded him with some encouragement.

Again they went past the workshops, where they saw bronzed figures and glowing iron through the open doors, and past stacks of iron standing there like a rich harvest of all this feverish labour and bustle.

They passed through the silent portico, where the porter was sleeping below a ticking clock.

And then they went down a deserted road to the mine-shaft.

There it stood, its chimneys and scaffolding looming ominously into the night. The white wall that surrounded it seemed like a graveyard wall in the moonlight.

Cheerful women driving the engines shouted to their colleague and laughed at the guide she had on parade.

They passed through the branding room; in silence the miner passed a Davy lamp to the doctor.

A bell sounded.

They entered the cage.

The doctor shuddered as an unaccustomed sensation precipitated him into the bowels of the earth. Droplets of water fell uniformly on to the cage, and a cold draught of air rushed past his ears and disarranged his hair. The miner, with his pick, and the engine driver, were standing close by him, but, surprisingly, the doctor felt not the slightest human warmth in the cold interior of the earth. The miner, and the girl too, were standing like statues of cold stone, seemingly not even breathing. A slight vapour of breath was issuing only from the mouth of the doctor.

The bell rang once more, and the cage came to a halt. They stepped out of it. In the distant blackness, the lights of Davy lamps were flickering like indefinite will-o'-the-wisps. They advanced with difficulty, the doctor with dreadful anxiety in his heart that was overwhelming him in the sepulchral muteness of these tunnels. What a contrast with the smelting works with its feverish life: here the shaft, with the silence of eternity.

They advanced steadily. Thin black streams were trickling through the adits like the River Lethe of forgetfulness. The igneous rock, saturated with water and coal dust, was indistinguishable from the black earth, and lustrous veins of black coal were glittering on the walls. They turned off into side tunnels that became narrower and narrower, and it seemed to the doctor that he would never again emerge from this labyrinth of silence.

The Davy-lamp will-o'-the-wisps disappeared, and they did not encounter a living soul on their whole journey. Faint echoes of miners' blows penetrated through to them, the perpetual boring of miner-worms in this vast treasure-earth.

In the narrow passages it was stifling and warm. Suddenly the clattering of the girl's clogs died away; a small dead-end path came into view. At the end of the path, where the head of a stooping man would already be touching the ceiling, a living creature was moving. At the voices of human beings this creature crawled out and cast the light of a Davy lamp on the newcomer.

His yellow face, shaded black, smiled. The doctor recognized Kalina from the hospital.

'Ah,' said the old miner, 'our doctor has descended to hell . . . Please take this,' he continued, pressing his pick into the doctor's hand.

The doctor was no longer surprised. Not even at the fact that here, below ground, he should find Kalina, now at the point of death, hard at work. Nor was he surprised when he noticed that they had hung the Davy lamp at his side and had disappeared. The shaft had swallowed them up in fathomless darkness.

He began digging. The coal was unyielding – hard black coal. In the faint glow of the lamp its edges were glittering like diamonds; the iron pyrites shone into it with golden rays. He dug. Small pebbles crumbled and fell at his feet, but the coal would not yield. He was hot, and the air was weighing on his chest. He took off his coat, and his shirt as well, damp with sweat.

And again he dug. Furiously, as he had been commanded to do by a mute order. His head became caught in the small aperture made by his pick, which recoiled clumsily and ineffectually in the confined space. His crouching posture became uncomfortable; his back was aching as if it were bearing the weight of the earth above him.

He attempted to climb out and straighten himself in the tunnel.

He turned – and a cry of indescribable horror escaped from his hot lips. Behind him the shaft had closed as it had before him. He was trapped. A shiny black wall had raised its sides, full of corners, in the place where a passage had previously been – – –

*   *

He awoke to the sound of his own voice. In puzzlement he looked around: no, there were no walls here; here is my sofa, my table, my bookcase – and, on the bookcase, horror of horrors! Meunier's couple of miners, cold and dead.

Someone was knocking.

The doctor opened the door, full of joy that he would be seeing a human being and hearing a human voice.

Shyly, the laboratory technician from the smelter entered.

'Good evening – am I disturbing you?'

The doctor stared at him, still quite amazed.

'Friend –' he burst out, delighted at the sound of his own voice, 'listen to what happened to me! . . .'

And he described his dream about his visit to hell.

The blue-eyed technician listened with bated breath; at the end the same words came to his lips:

'Ah, what hell it indeed is!'

'And now,' concluded the doctor, 'take your little blue book about that hell away with you, and those two figures' – he pointed at the bookcase – 'I am giving you as a gift. I shall not be able to set eyes on them again without horror. They have prepared too hot a bath for me. And now farewell, I must do my doctor's round on the ward . . .'

MARRIAGE

MARIE MAJEROVÁ

The stifling, sultry day has been baking the street so fierce-ly that the cobblestones are still glowing with heat after nightfall, and the plaster of the tall houses is cooling only very slowly.

The broad pavement is shining white and yellow in the light of the street lamp, the dry dust in the centre showing the traces of the last pedestrians and the straight tracks of the last carriages. Ten o'clock has struck, the apprentices and the maids have disappeared behind locked doors, the faint footsteps of someone walking out late can be heard in the quiet streets, and the helmet of a policeman is gleaming.

At the corner of the street there are three girls talking quietly, regular nightly adornments of this street. Two of them are young brunettes in flimsy white blouses and tiny, seductive aprons, constantly teasing, giggling and squeal-ing. An occasional word impacts on the policeman's helmet like the crack of a whip, at which he nods indulgently and moves towards the street around the corner.

The third is a stout blonde, a mass of fat crammed into a loose red bodice. Her ash-blonde hair is arranged in some kind of high, over-elaborate coiffure. Like all obese people, she must be very hot, for she is shifting from one short leg to the other, and relieving herself with grunts under her breath.

It is quiet.

All the windows on both sides of the street are standing wide open so that the night air should provide at least a lit-tle relief to the weary residents. The ringing of the electric trams penetrates the heavy atmosphere in a lazy kind of way, and the rattling of the carriages floats across like the buzzing of mosquitoes. The dense air seems to be absorbing all the sounds as if it were choking off the waves of sound at their source. Generally, the street has a very dull and enervating aspect. Only from the third floor of a high, grey house can be heard the sounds of two indignant voices, as yet indistinct, and the faint tinkle of a breaking glass.

A masculine voice evidently belongs to a drunkard, accustomed to spend his time in low taverns; a woman's voice is gasping, weeping and piercing with its sharp tone.

The prostitutes at the corner have pricked up their ears, almost grateful for the slight diversion in this long, dreary night.

'And – I'm not moving an inch! I'm staying sitting right . . . here! You – you are supposed to be looking . . . after me – you! You viper! If you could, you'd be choking me like a she-wolf choking a lamb . . . !'

The drunken bass voice fades into the shrill lament of the woman.

'And I won't have it, I won't, I won't! Children to feed, a husband to feed, a rogue, a drunkard! He won't pay the rent, he won't buy anything to wear, the bastard! And he comes home just to sleep off his hangover and beat me and the little ones! Get out right now, get out this minute! You swine, you . . . !'

The wailing turns into hysterical weeping, and in a sudden paroxysm the woman leans out of the window and screams:

'Police!'

The deserted street suddenly springs to life. The windows are filled with white figures roused from sleep, poking inquisitive heads out. And a shrill voice falters out the cry:

'Police, call the police!'

The policeman on the beat is nearby, and so after a short time there appear not merely two policemen but also the police sergeant, and they proceed up the dark staircase with the helpful caretaker.

'What has happened?' shout acquaintances across the street to one another.

Those who have been asleep are refreshed by the cooling air, their mood lightens, and their jokes criss-cross the street like serpentine bunting.

After a short time, the sergeant emerges from the apartment, with the caretaker lighting his way with a candle.

It appears that the furious, drunken husband has fallen asleep in the indifferent, dull slumber of a drunkard. The wife is sobbing and covering up the little half-naked bodies of her terrified children.

The spectators return to bed one by one, and after a moment the street resumes its tedious, tiresome character. –

Now the policeman is standing at the corner of the street, his helmet twinkling in the flickering flame of the street lamp; beside him stands the stout blonde, legs comfortably astride, and she muses, contemptuously:

'And that is what it's like after a woman gets married . . . Leave me alone! This is a thousand times better to me than marriage . . . !'

A LOYAL WIFE

BOŽENA BENEŠOVÁ

For many years, in a quiet town in the mountains, Jan Holec lived the life of a petty clerk with a well-defined career – a tranquil, not unpleasant life divided between his office hours and his free time. In the office he was esteemed both for his industry and his punctuality, which he never turned into an ironic joke and indeed (unlike his co-workers) posi- tively enjoyed; in the town he was liked for his genial good nature and because his opinions did not diverge from those that were generally held there – but chiefly for the fact that he was a guileless man of ample means, potentially well able to support a wife.

And once his salary had reached a certain level, he did indeed marry the girl who had long been his favourite of all the daughters of the town. Her name was Amalie, and she had lovely, serious eyes, the fresh countenance of a child, and a voice that seemed to warm the air through which it was passing, one that thrilled his ear with pleasure.

They lived quietly, and there were no suspicions either in or about them that they were anything other than hap- py, decent people. Little Amalie had economic virtues that matched her husband's income, and that were adequate to the kind of life that was dictated to people of their status by local and familial constraints. She had grown up without the demands of city bustle or entertainment, and any that may have been dozing in her heart were soon sent off to sleep permanently by her domestic tranquillity. With her simple young heart she believed that her life was good – just as good as her husband's. And she loved the husband who had married her, and was loyal to him not only because loyalty was commanded by divine and human law, but much more profoundly – indeed so profoundly that she never had to call laws and commandments to mind. Whenever she heard of unfaithfulness in some woman, she would flare up for a moment in indignant disapproval, but then immediately smile the cold, caustic smile which utterly irreproachable women turn on the slightest off-colour remark that is passed inadvertently in their presence.

Holec, a large, powerful man with a well-groomed moustache in a bronzed, firmly chiselled, countenance, which had long resisted aging, genuinely deserved a good, serious wife. He was an indulgent husband; he never thought of philandering; he did not care for unnecessary attention. He called the slight roughness of his words and gestures 'civic pride', and admired it in himself. In general he was very self-satisfied; he arrived at this estimate of himself because he was a healthy, good-looking man; and also because he had not buried his ambition at the age of thirty; and indeed also because he had married, without self-interest, a wife whom he liked, and whose voice had enchanted him.

A year later, a child was born to the Holec family, but it died having hardly seen the light of day. Both parents mourned its death. But their grief at their loss evaporated without trace after a time, leaving both of them merely with some sort of unacknowledged bewilderment – a bewilderment that their life could be so incomprehensibly peaceful. They waited in vain for a second child, and when they realized that the quietness in their lives was destined to become permanent, both became slightly nervous about their future. There was a smooth, well-beaten path leading into that future, already known to them in every detail – including the fact that it was to end, without deviations or dangerous corners, in the new town cemetery.

However, Holec, a model clerk, knew how to deal with his time without too much inconvenience. He was ever respectful of the official decrees and circulars that were so numerous, in the department of the great institute which he served, that they had long since failed to fit into their assigned files, and had to be piled up in every corner of the office and the entrance hall. Now he devoted himself to these documents with an absolute passion. He reviewed them once more and carefully read all of them through. He was not in the slightest offended or contemptuous if a second decree were to revoke what a first had prescribed, and a third were then to permit it conditionally; but he sorted them carefully and indeed provided them with ribbons with fancy calligraphic titles. It was impossible to say why he was carrying out this great work, which no one had required of him; but he was convinced that it was praiseworthy and deserving of respect.

'My career is your well-being as well, after all,' he used to tell Amalie seriously and proudly. And he used to sit in the office, working diligently, and indeed overtime, and used to spend less and less time at home.

Some time later, paní Holcová began to pine away, although she was not actually ill. But she was changing for the worse: she had aged somewhat, and both her movements in walking and her speech had become sluggish and listless.

Jan, too, noticed one day that his wife's voice, once so clear, had now lost its freshness, and that her eyes had lost their glow and their childlike sparkle. But he did not think it good to say anything; he took action.

In a long letter to his mother, he explained how much important work he currently had in the office, and how lonely his wife was at home meanwhile. He explained this very touchingly, and concluded by asking his mother, equally touchingly, to move in with them and to become Amalie's companion and helper. He was proud of being able to devise this pleasant solution, in which three souls could jointly find happiness; and the same day on which he had posted the letter, he began sorting yet another dusty volume.

His mother indeed made the move, and, overwhelmed with the realization that there was still someone in the world calling her and in need of her, set about working in the little household. She behaved to her daughter-in-law as if she should be healing her of a real ailment, and took over all her work.

'It's a strange method of cheering me up, very strange,' thought Amalie to herself, but because it was congenial, she soon accustomed herself to it.

Life passed in a smooth and orderly manner; nothing exciting ever happened. The tranquillity of the Holec household was exemplary, but somehow debilitating. If the old lady had not been there, husband and wife might have forgotten to speak to one another. They never quarrelled, but the gap between them widened, and it was now impossible to ignore it. But they never even spoke to each other about it. Besides, they did not know what they would think it meant. Was Jan too hardworking, or had Amalie's voice lost its girlish lustre? Even to think of such accusations was ridiculous. How would it be possible to put them into words? And in this way their silence became a solid, if chilly, shield between them.

Amalie spent entire days with her head bowed over her embroidery, calling it work. This was conscious self-deception, however, for her bedspreads, lace and pillowcases had long been surplus to the apartment's requirements, and were being stored in a trunk in the room. She wielded her needle only out of a kind of inertia in motion, and from her conviction that not to wield it would be a disgrace. And it may have been merely for the same reason that she got dressed each day and, sometimes, even read a book. She knew each uneven cobblestone on the street individually, and she had long tired of counting the steps between her doorstep and the church, or estimating the length of the eternally empty town promenade.

Her husband and his mother might have understood her pain, and might have tried to alleviate it. But in the face of this inaccessible and invincible numbness, at first they stood helpless, then they grew weary of it, and finally they became accustomed to it, because in fact it was not in anyone's way.

Meanwhile, Holec was dreaming up ambitious plans. His exceptional diligence had originally been merely a remedy for boredom for him, but the day came when he realized that it was also capital that could be put to work.

After thousands and thousands of requests, complaints and meetings, the institute for which he worked underwent some sort of reorganization, and the officials who had threaded their way through the confusion of old and new orders received some unexpected recognition. An era of accelerated promotion had dawned for them, when good qualifications combined with an influential word might finally gain them a rosette on their collar. But it was difficult to obtain that influential word here in Back of Beyondsburg.

But Holec did not hesitate, and applied for a transfer. And lo and behold, he did indeed win a position in Prague, in an important auditing department which, with a following wind, might prove to be his point of entry into the central office, that goal of all the ambitious souls of the whole institute.

His mother exulted noisily when the happy letter of appointment arrived. Her joy tempered the brown of her venerable countenance with a rosy blush.

'You'll see, Amalie will soon get well! Ah, the big city, the big city! You can't just cross the road from one side to the other there! You'll have to wait there, maybe for a quarter of an hour, and meanwhile a hundred people or even more will pass before your eyes . . .'

She had once spent a single year in the capital; now it sparkled in her memory, and with her words it continually acquired more lustre. Her pleasures in life, long gone, glittered a little in the sentences with which she described her life at the time. She spoke about promenades, about the theatre, about concerts, about shop-window displays; she spoke in loud intoxication.

Amalie scrutinized her for some moments in astonishment. She lifted her slightly protruding chin slightly, with a tense expression, and listlessly cast a blind eye on her.

'Why does she enjoy talking so much?' she thought. 'What was there in it for her then in those people, in their opulence and in their lives . . . And is there something for me in all that?'

However, she listened patiently for days on end while packing. She bade a listless farewell to her old life and looked forward listlessly to her new one. It was only the half-done embroidered towel rail that she packed with some animation; she calculated how many weeks later the move would take place, and she set a day in advance when she would be ready. In other ways she showed no excitement. When her husband or mother-in-law seemed to expect her to show happiness, she would merely raise her eyebrows in astonishment and gaze at them as if requiring some explanation. And they fell silent at this gaze, understanding that it was hard to pinpoint what she was supposed actually to be looking forward to. In her life this was really something definite, and so unshakable that no change could influence it.

Holec made the move a few days in advance, provided himself with the most vital information, got to know the staff a little in the office, rented an apartment recommended to him by a colleague with whom he had made friends at their first meeting, and, excited by his unprecedented activity as well as his new impressions, he expressed his delight to his wife in an almost youthful eagerness he had long never felt.

But when she arrived later, a single glance at her bored, unhappy face was enough to bring to his mind years on end of undefined suffering. He sighed and tried to dismiss the unpleasant impression as quickly as he could. He took the utmost trouble in tidying the apartment, hanging pictures with a degree of up-to-date taste, and arranging the furniture in the manner that seemed to him the most elegant. And, excited by the physical activity, he became voluble. He had a knack for quick, striking description, and the characters from his new acquaintances came to life in his words. From the burly manager, in charge of the department, with his military bearing and with his contemptuous glance, who spoke of the decisions taken by the central office with Biblical reverence, and spoke of the chief director as if of God, down to the menial servants in the office, little men who were simultaneously obsequious and stubborn, all of them marched vividly through Holec's room while the women were polishing the furniture and filling the cupboards.

His mother listened happily, and Blažová, the new charwoman, laughed appreciatively. She was a very serious, dignified lady, who was chary of demeaning herself in front of her employers, but Holec's skill in narration and in acting took her breath away.

'However did this man come by this crosspatch of his?' she thought, sympathetically. 'That woman seems to have been giving him trouble, and she's still giving him trouble . . .'

Amalie looked really unattractive. Her work was disguised idleness, her external appearance was undisguised indifference. Indeed she may have promised herself a little pleasure, a little refreshment, even if only unintentionally, from this move; and now that she was drawing breath in her new environment, and everything was again so familiar, so horribly familiar, she felt a disappointment that she did not understand. She had bidden farewell to everything without pain, there was nothing that she was missing, but the emptiness that had been indistinguishable from life there, somewhere far off, now rose up menacingly and terrified her.

'What are all these people to us?' she finally asked, in her own most strongly held question to the cheerful chatter of her husband.

Jan frowned fiercely. He wanted simply to talk about a colleague who seemed to him the most interesting of all of them, and he took the interruption as a personal insult. He glared at his wife contemptuously. In the last couple of days he had seen so many attractive women that his demands had risen. This one seemed ten years older than she really was, worn out and infinitely tedious. He sighed involuntarily, but because he was a genuinely good husband, he went over to Amalie and caressed her as an excuse for such thoughts.

'We'll have to do some visiting,' he said as he did so.

'That's unavoidable,' agreed his mother.

'And I'll be inviting people here too,' continued Jan. 'One must think carefully about building a career, and I have a plan all made. Not a day should be lost.'

'I'm not going anywhere, I don't need anyone, and I don't care about anyone,' said Amalie, quietly but decisively.

'We'll see,' he replied sternly, and, offended, he did not speak another word for the entire day.

Amalie slept badly that night, and she was very fatigued in the morning. Suddenly the apartment seemed very constricting, and everyone was getting in her way. She was glad when her husband left for the office and her mother-in-law went off to market. She reached out for the half-done towel rail, but did not touch the work. Her head ached when she imagined herself bending over the embroidery frame.

The spring sunshine cast a broad, swirling beam on the freshly polished floor, and lit up the room with an irritating light. It was already fully furnished, but although Jan had made sure that he had arranged everything in as modern a style as possible, and although he had purchased two new pictures and two antique figurines, nevertheless it appeared exactly as it had appeared for eight years or more.

And Amalie, not thinking, not remembering, not even looking at anything, suddenly sensed how much incomprehensible longing, boredom and emptiness was trapped here in the folds of the curtains, and also in the carving of the furniture, and how much was sewn into the innumerable bedspreads that lay around everywhere like funeral palls.

'O my God, O my God, it seems to me that I have after all just simply not been completely happy,' she whispered, in utter astonishment.

Below, trams were rattling by, carriages and motor buses were passing, and the narrow street was thundering as if thousands of people were going by. And the footsteps of all the pedestrians sounded busy and cheerful. They were hurrying somewhere, for some reason, to someone . . .

Amalie opened the window. All the sounds immediately became louder, the April breeze wafted freshly into the room, ventilated and warmed it, brought in the bustle and spun it around her bowed head.

'But what is there in all this for me, what is in it for me?' she said, over and over again, with her empty heart wrung in agony.

She laid her forehead on the windowsill and wept like a child. She did not know why she was weeping, she did not know what was weighing on her head to bow it down, she was simply sobbing in impotent and nameless passion.

She knelt by the window, a tiny, silent little creature whose life was passing, God only knows how, God only knows why. It made no sense; no one liked it, not even she. And yet no one was offending her, and she was offending no one. She loved Jan, she had always thought well of her parents, she would have cared for all her children if there had been ten of them, and even accepted the fact that she had none with equanimity. And Jan was a good man, full of concern for the future . . . ah, where, where was this grief welling up from?

She wept long, she wept bitterly, but her unthinking head grasped only that tears were the sole relief for this entirely unexpected sorrow.

Suddenly she raised her head. She did not know why, but she felt obliged to do so. Some person was standing in the window opposite. She immediately realized that he had been looking at her for a long while, that he had seen and perhaps also heard her weeping. She started up as if a snake had bitten her, and, without drying her eyes, made out the outline of a short male figure. She cried out in confusion and sprang away towards the wall. But the person opposite did not vanish. Now he turned away from the window, and there was no doubt that he was probing the sunlit gloom of her room.

Nothing in the world would have made her look at her own face during this. Humiliation and crimson embarrassment flooded over her as she fled into the next room.

'One's not even allowed to cry,' she thought indignantly. 'This city is awful! Not only am I not going to associate with anyone here, I'm not even going to look at anyone. Because I'm not even allowed to go to my own window.'

She carried her embroidery frame to the window over the courtyard, but she did not even touch the needle. Her hot eyelids were burning, and a gloomy, musty odour emanating from the taut cloth was irritating her nerves to the point of a migraine.

Her husband arrived at noon, smiling at a distance in both defiance and embarrassment.

'I'll conquer your fear of people, I will,' he said in self-satisfaction. 'I've already invited a guest. He's coming to dinner tomorrow.'

Amalie was so horrified that he took pity on her.

'Besides, Herbert knows you already,' he added, to calm her down. 'He said he had seen you a couple of times at the window. And he wanted to pay you a visit by hook or by crook before coming to dinner. But I said to him, "What's the point of unnecessary formality between friends?" It was the first time I'd called him "friend", slipping it in like that, and he understood and just smiled.'

'Who's Herbert?' asked Amalie, in fearful premonition.

'Herbert's a marvellous chap – he's the one I was telling you about yesterday, or trying to tell you about when you interrupted me so rudely. He's the most obliging man in our office. He's been helping me with everything, and he even found this apartment for me. After all, it's not thanks to the fact that it's directly opposite his windows . . .'

'Is he your superior?' asked his mother.

He smiled indulgently, and shook his large head.

'No, no! He's quite a lot younger than I am, and a class lower. But it's better than if he had been my immediate superior. For the chief director is the father-in-law of one of his cousins, and Herbert maintains a personal connection with him – he even goes to visit his family. And if Herbert comes to visit us, it's almost as though the big chief comes to visit us himself. It's a personal contact, you know, a personal contact with the director . . .'

The old lady half-closed her eyes and visualized something very beautiful: a gold collar with her son's head rising above it. She hugged her daughter-in-law.

'I knew straight away that this move would bring great happiness,' she said triumphantly. 'Just invite the man across the way to visit! Perhaps you should invite him every week!'

Amalie wished she could plead that this torture might for God's sake be taken away from her, but both mother and son were already discussing the menu, and no one at all noticed her horror.

'You'll have to take the greatest trouble possible about details,' ordered Jan. 'Herbert is a refined, pampered chap from a rich family, accustomed to comfort and deference. He even comes to the office late every day, and always without repercussions. He says he doesn't want to marry, so he does . . .'

And again he sighed involuntarily, and in remorse caressed his wife as he had the previous day.

She twitched nervously, in embarrassed mortification. After all, she could not explain to her husband the circumstances in which she too had already seen their guest.

'That Peeping Tom, that awful Peeping Tom!' she said of Herbert in all her thoughts, and her eyelids became damp in indignation once more.

That same day there was more bustle in the Holec household than at any time in the highest of festivals. The old lady behaved as if she had the task of preparing a ceremonial banquet, except that at times she half-closed her maternal eyes in a delicious daydream, and her lips whispered, quite audibly:

'Gold collar.'

Each time she engaged in a long conversation about the tableware, and also about the propriety of the lady of the house entrusting the serving at such an important dinner to a servant who had not yet proved herself, rather than undertaking it herself. Finally she summoned Blažová and subjected her to an interrogation as well as an examination in serving.

'Who will the guest be, if so much fuss is going to be made for his sake?' asked Blažová haughtily, once the examination had been satisfactorily completed.

'A very eminent gentleman who is a close acquaintance of my son. He lives opposite this flat.'

The maid straightened up.

'Herbert?'

Both women were surprised.

'Do you know Herbert?'

'Certainly! I worked for him for three years. – But I was obliged to hand in my notice.'

And now Blažová genuinely straightened up with dignity, and turned a look on her audience which only women can understand properly.

'I am decent, my mother was decent, and I intend my daughter to be decent too,' she said, seriously and coldly.

'And is he not decent?' asked Amalie, blushing at the question.

'Good Lord, no! He is the worst of anyone I know! What he does outside his home does not concern me, but in the flat, where I also have to go, I would want proper order! There was hardly a week without some lady coming to visit him – and almost every time a different lady.'

'Ah, there are so many loose women in big cities!' replied the old lady, dejectedly.

'But the point is that it's quality ladies who used to come to him! And all of them used to come in through the back entrance in Vodní Street. He took a flat like that on purpose in a house with a right of way through it. And it's already dark in Vodní Street at five in the afternoon, and if some little madam is making her evil way there, she doesn't even need a veil . . .'

Blažová went out, and the old lady lost some of her enthusiasm in her preparations.

Amalie now left everything untouched, walked through the dining room and heaved a sigh from her constricted heart.

But strangely, despite all her sighs, she felt a kind of mellowness now. For the first time in her life, she became aware of her own firm loyalty, and for the first time she valued it with self-conscious excitement.

'My God, praise be, me, I am entirely innocent!' seemed to be the words spoken by each tiny step she took, ever more emphatically and with ever more self-confidence.

It was only when she glanced at the window at which she had been weeping that morning that some anxious embarrassment disturbed the confident rhythm of her steps, and if she noticed the window opposite, it increased her embarrassment to the point of agitation.

But even though this window reminded her of so many unpleasant things, she did not move away from it, and when the time came for her husband to come back from the office, she even stood behind the embroidered curtain and peeped out into the street.

There was Jan, walking together with Herbert, and keeping him company up to the house opposite. She could see him now much better than she had in the morning, but still not entirely clearly. She noticed that he was markedly slimmer and more graceful than Jan, but that he nevertheless appeared the older of the two. He was pale and clean-shaven, and when he raised his hat it was clear that his short dark hair did not cover his skull completely. He and Jan took time bidding each other farewell, and Jan bowed to him as politely as he could. It was obvious that he was pleased; as he turned away, the reflection of a friendly, promising conversation remained on his face.

And, the whole time in which he was shaking hands with Jan and saying something that was beyond all doubt friendly and encouraging, Herbert did not take his eyes off the window opposite.

'He has no shame – even in front of my husband he has no shame,' thought Amalie to herself behind the curtain, 'he's a really bad man! Ah, tomorrow I'll just teach him how he ought to behave in front of women who are completely irreproachable . . .'

In the hall, Jan's mother was waiting for him.

'We've heard some bad things about Herbert,' she informed him grimly. 'I'm afraid that Amalie may not be polite enough to him tomorrow.'

She told Jan everything that Blažová had said, and also what she herself had deduced from those remarks. Amalie too had come to precisely this conclusion, and her unusually indignant eyes were more eloquent than his mother's words.

Jan listened for a while, anxiously, and then laughed heartily.

'But what is that to us, after all, as my wife herself says?' he said sharply. 'Herbert is a free man – he can enjoy the world however he chooses. He's not tempted by promotion; he's able to avoid working; what would he be doing, if he had no flirtations? And I'm not surprised that women like that. Of course, only superficial women with no conscience . . .'

'Yes, only women like that,' agreed Amalie, sternly.

At these words, all three calmed down – one might say that they cheered up. The personal link with the director was not now threatened, and Jan smiled fondly at both his mother and his wife for the whole evening.

'I've always said that my career is also your happiness,' proclaimed this victorious smile; 'the day will soon dawn when you feel it too.'

At each such smile, Amalie stretched her somewhat gaunt neck and gazed out into space.

'If only he hadn't just seen me crying,' she thought for the whole evening, 'I'd have brought him to heel tomorrow with my first word! But now . . . what will I be able to say to him when I read an intrusive question in his eyes? After all, my God, I don't know myself why I was weeping so ridiculously . . .'

Her night was even more restless than the previous one had been.

'Why has God laid such suffering on me?' she thought with every vague foreboding, but she was unable to decide what sort of suffering it was that God had laid on her. And meanwhile Blažová's verdict was still echoing in her ears, and she continued to be consoled by the thought that she was a profound and conscientious woman.

Finally she fell asleep, and instantly found herself deep in a forest. It was dark; its trees were enormously thick, with black branches reaching down like fringes to their very roots. These roots lay everywhere on the forest floor and were intertwined in strange openwork patterns. For a while she walked through this forest until she found herself by an open cave. Pitch darkness was flowing out of its entrance, and although the whole forest was very dark, this darkness stretched conspicuously into it, like a skein of black wool that needed to be wound into a ball. She wanted to scream, but her voice refused to emerge from her throat; she wanted to flee, but her legs refused to carry her. And now she simply burst into tears, weeping great mute tears. But though all this was terrible, though her legs were shaking with fear, and though her tears did not cease flowing, she felt nevertheless that this terror was not truly a terror, and that there was in fact nothing to be afraid of.

'It's strange, extremely strange,' she thought as she awakened. She had never had such a fantastic dream before.

'Perhaps it's an omen?' occurred to her in the dim light of morning, and this unprecedented idea – that something might happen in life that had been heralded by a premonition – was again strangely foreign to her, and augmented her self-respect.

However, the next morning passed with quiet tedium in the Holec household. They had already completed all their preparations, and there was nothing more to worry about. The tableware had been inspected; the ham, the only hors-d'œuvre they could think of, was set to dry on a platter.

Immediately after their mid-morning coffee, the old lady began getting dressed. She had a well-preserved robe with ermine edging and with mother-of-pearl buttons the size of five-crown pieces, but she also had an old silk dress, and she found it difficult to decide which of these festive garments she should wear.

'And what will you be putting on?' she asked her daughter-in-law.

'I'm staying in the grey blouse I wear in the house,' replied Amalie firmly, 'so that this chap will see at first glance that I'm not flirtatious.'

She was glad to have said it and thus to have blocked the way to a possible change. She had a translucent décolleté blouse with short sleeves edged with puffed lace, she had ornamental hair combs, and she also had a series of attractively styled false curls with which her fashionable hairstyle could be improved. These things had hitherto seemed entirely innocent to her, but since the previous day she had sensed danger in them, and she avoided even thinking about them.

'No,' she thought firmly, 'even his gross vanity must not be allowed to bother me. Let him come to know the differences, let him finally come to know them, and let him be ashamed of himself!'

But she was not quite at peace. Unusually, her heart was pounding intermittently, even under her customary blouse; and each time her heartbeat quickened, the pendulum of the clock slowed, and it invariably took an inordinately long time for a quarter of an hour to pass.

Finally, when it was now beginning to get a little dark, she lit a candle and stood in front of the mirror.

Never before had she been so dissatisfied with herself; never before had she seen such gauntness and pallor in herself.

'But perhaps I look too old, after all?' she pondered, in utter discontent, 'after all, my God, I'm still young . . .' And she quickly picked up a second mirror to examine her profile. It was not the worst. No trace of wrinkles, a pale pink complexion, eyelashes still long. She hesitated a moment, then tucked the pretty false curls into her hair and powdered herself just a tiny bit.

'Everything I'm doing today is being done for my husband's career,' she thought to herself seriously.

The hairstyle was a great success, but now her grey blouse simply did not suit it. There was really nothing for it but to find a different one. When she put it on, it seemed to her that she was a victim.

Then she went to the window. The windows opposite, those mysterious, treacherous windows were dark, and their blinds had been drawn so tightly that it was not even possible to discern whether lights were burning behind them. Ah, no one can ever perceive what is happening in a house with two entrances and curtains like those!

She gazed long, long, at the flat opposite, and all the indignation, all the confusion, and also all the pride, that had traversed her little heart in the past few days, became fused in an attitude of dignified patience.

The lamps had already been lit in the streets, the day had merged with the evening in the enchanting spring twilight, and Amalie was still continually gazing, motionless, at the closed blinds. Without warning, she jumped when she heard her husband's footsteps.

'I'm glad you have put on pretty clothes,' he said, unusually kindly, having barely entered. 'Just overcome your nervousness as a hostess, and everything will go brilliantly. Our guest won't notice a thing.'

'For your sake I'll even overcome my nervousness,' replied Amalie, allowing him to kiss her.

The guest arrived in person very shortly afterwards. Now he was standing in front of Amalie, and she was unsure whether to offer him her hand. She was expecting something very embarrassing, and her legs trembled in sudden weakness.

But Herbert kissed her hand while barely touching it, and so courteously that there could be no doubt about his utter respect for her.

He was a handsome but unassuming man. His clean-shaven lips were attractively set in a constant smile, pleasant and unobtrusive, but his dark eyes were serious and searching.

'My friend Jan must answer for my discourtesy,' he said to the ladies immediately after being introduced. 'He is at fault. He refused to let me pay my respects to you earlier. But it's understandable . . . after a move, the lady of the house has so much work, so many things to care for, before she can make a flat really homely . . .'

In saying the words 'my friend Jan', he set the whole room at ease. In saying 'really homely', the furniture, the lamp, and indeed even all the bedspreads, acquired some alluring importance.

All of them sensed the confident, courteous poise of his conversation, and identified with it as if they were being flattered by it.

Even old Blažová was greeted in almost friendly terms by Herbert.

'Look, my old guardian angel is back with me,' was all he said to her, but somehow pleasantly, so that it seemed to everyone as if he were rewarding her, and Blažová genuinely beamed. Nevertheless, in this single sentence there was not only friendliness, but also utter arrogance – something that instantly set an abyss of difference between the charwoman and the others.

'How can such a woman slander him without feeling ashamed!' thought the old lady at once. 'We'll have to let her know that we simply do not abide that.'

They took their places at table and Jan continued to play the perfect host. Everything had been beautifully ordered, the conversation did not flag; all was to the taste of the guest. Only Amalie was staring absent-mindedly, and although Herbert courteously attempted to elicit more than a monosyllabic answer from her, he did not manage to do so.

'Did he see me weeping at the window, or didn't he?' she thought, hundreds of times, during the evening, and this mystery vastly infuriated her.

But Herbert simply did not seem like a man capable of rude questions, or indeed of any kind of insinuations, about completely irreproachable ladies, and Amalie, who had never hitherto met a man from the wider world, and on whom the eyes of a successful womanizer had never rested, imagined a seducer and debauchee in quite different terms.

She would have liked to give him better answers, but she was unable to. Not even the dignity of a completely irreproachable woman counted for anything against him, for he was not threatening her in any way. And indeed she was becoming more and more confused, and when she felt that Herbert's glance met hers very briefly, even in passing, she became extremely apprehensive.

'It was a very good idea to put on a new blouse; next time I'll wear a pearl necklace too,' was the only completely coherent thought that occurred to her the whole evening.

They talked exclusively about the Holec family: Herbert prevented other subjects from being raised. He was familiar with all the relationships in the office and also in the city, and was able to give advice so trenchantly and at the same time so tactfully that he forestalled any gratitude. He also alluded to the chief director in an appropriate way, and, as if he had not noticed Jan's tense face, remarked as if to no one in particular that this powerful, dreaded gentleman was very approachable in a family setting, and an obliging man.

Jan reddened a little more, and tried to control the joyous trembling of his nostrils.

'If only my wife would show more tact to Herbert,' he thought indignantly, 'but she's ruined every stroke of good fortune of mine in my life . . . And now she's ruining this one too . . .'

However, the old lady unbent completely. For forty years no one had devoted so much attention to her as had this unknown man, who she imagined would desire her entirely for himself.

'We have wronged him,' she conceded guiltily, 'but I'm trying to make amends for my mistake with humility, while Amalie is really behaving rudely.'

'At least say something pleasant,' she scolded her in a whisper.

But Amalie could not. With horror she was noticing, ever more clearly, that whatever she did, whether she remained more glumly silent or stared more intently at the lamp or at the embroidered tablecloth, an incomprehensible affinity was emerging between her and her guest.

It seemed to her that his watchful eyes were being fixed on her, and that every dulcet phrase had some specific meaning which she did not understand but which was of particular importance and was directed wholly at her alone.

And Herbert sat opposite her, tilting his fetching, slightly balding head back a little, and his practised eye was reading her simple face. He liked women who were easily won and easily discarded; he liked naïve women; he liked those who were treading the primrose path for the first time; and without being in the slightest degree captivated by her, he was sensing the pleasant joy of an easy conquest, which now that the first flush of buoyant youth had passed, was for him the best of all loves.

Opening the second bottle of wine, Jan proposed a toast to their honoured guest, and the old lady gazed at him with eyes sparkling with affability. A moment later, those eyes were already motherly.

'Why don't you get married, Herbert?' she asked demurely, 'you, who seem made for family life?'

Here, for the first time in the whole evening, a sorrowful expression appeared on their guest's face. His eyes turned serious, and his lips quivered slightly.

'It's my destiny,' he said quietly, and for a moment he bowed his head as calculatedly and languidly as he could. 'There are times when I'm really overcome with longing. There are moments in life when longing and emptiness descend on one like a lead weight. There are moments when ladies weep passionately and lament their fate with hot tears. But we men do not have even that relief . . .'

Amalie went very pale. There could be no doubt that Herbert had seen her very clearly. But this thought, which till now had seemed so terrible to her, which had frightened, depressed and disturbed her, suddenly lost its terror. Ah, she was hearing so much tenderness in his voice; she was sensing so much sympathy in the warmth of his words!

'Yes, ah, yes, longing and emptiness descend on one like a lead weight,' her heart repeated after him, trembling in tune with his seductive voice.

And Amalie, tiny, desiccated, and reserved as she was, became convinced at this moment that her woes in life were not only difficult but also complex and inaccessible to the understanding of ordinary folk like Jan and his mother. In a flash she came to believe that she had been suffering all her life; she came to believe that blamelessly, she had been bearing a heavy burden that had been destroying her strength, her freedom, and her heart. And no one had seen this before this lovely, wonderful man, who had grasped her in a single moment, who had articulated her exceptional nature in a few words, and had spoken to her so profoundly and intimately, while Jan was opening a third bottle and his mother was listening with a foolish smile . . . Ah yes, a great abyss of a gulf was opening up with Herbert's words, but this time it was marking the division between two melancholy, exalted beings and two mundane creatures.

Herbert's depression lasted only for a moment. At first Amalie seemed to feel how he was overcoming it with great willpower so as not to reveal it also to the two uninitiated. She was looking at his lips, which were now unsmiling but trembling slightly with some intimate sorrow.

'I'd get married straight away,' he said slowly, 'if I could find a wife I could love and who would love me. A simple, faithful wife. For it is only for one like that that my heart is searching.'

'You'll find her,' promised the old lady, in a motherly voice. 'You'll certainly find her. There are still women like that.'

'Ah, yes,' thought Amalie, ardently, 'there are still women like that!'

She did not doubt now that she understood Herbert's entire life, and the gloomy destiny of his ever-searching, ever-disappointed heart. For how few women there are who are utterly loyal and irreproachable!

The old lady repeated her assurance, 'You'll find her, you'll find her,' and Jan, who had softened the whole evening to the same conviction, nodded no less vigorously.

'I have not stopped searching, and I have not stopped hoping, after all my great disappointments,' replied their guest slowly.

The flame of his glance swept over Amalie's face at this moment. It provoked no blush; it sank in much more deeply.

She felt all her blood rush to her heart in bliss she had never felt before.

Even now, she did not speak; she had not spoken the whole evening; but now her eyes no longer avoided Herbert's gaze. And when they made their farewells, her hand was as cold as ice, and his lips touched it as the seal of an eternal covenant.

Jan accompanied their guest to the door of his house, and when he returned, he was so pleasantly excited that he had no thought of sleep. He walked up and down the room for a long while, sipping wine, with a satisfied and pensive face.

'If Herbert has a word with the director before long, I could be promoted in six months,' he said after all his cogitation.

Amalie did not reply. There was a vision rising before her half-closed eyes: she was scrutinizing all the details of the gloom of Vodní Street, where hardly anyone passed in the evening; she made out a room whose blinds were closed so firmly that they did not admit the smallest ray of light . . .

'Did you hear me?' repeated Jan impatiently. 'In six months! Isn't that wonderful?'

'Wonderful,' agreed Amalie from her reverie, but in that single word her voice had regained all the enchantment it used to have in her early youth.

And then Jan was genuinely stirred by her sympathy, and in reward he caressed her for the third time.

SOLITUDE

ANNA LAUERMANNOVÁ-MIKSCHOVÁ

From time to time, the rocking chair was slowly swinging, and the sand below it softly gritting. Paní Teza Uvarová pulled a ball of fine wool towards her, which had rolled to the edge of the lawn. She was knitting a child's stocking, her needles flashing in the lazy movements of her fingers, with her eyelashes sometimes remaining lowered over a dropped stitch in her knitting. It was at a moment like this that she was listening, though only absent-mindedly, to the words of her guest – her neighbour, Peklín.

He pushed her chair with his foot, making it swing more violently. 'Dear lady, how many stockings is it that you have been knitting?'

'This is the twentieth, dear friend. Don't you think that good?'

'No, a hundred times, no!'

'Don't you like women's handiwork?'

'Why would I not like it? Having all one's buttons sewn on counts as one of the greatest pleasures of life. But this stocking of yours is offending me: you are giving it the attention you're robbing me of having. Your knitting is getting in the way of your conversation. Besides, that stocking doesn't suit you.'

He was speaking in jest, in a full, well-modulated voice, which was tickling her ear pleasantly.

'The stocking doesn't suit me. What else should I be doing, then?' The slightly animated gaze of her pretty brown eyes twinkled questioningly in his face.

'Nothing! Laying your head on this lazy old chair, and waving a rose in bloom in your hand, perhaps. You have such beautiful hands – it is a shame to use them for that hideous knitting.'

'I am no longer young enough for coquetry with a rose,' she sighed, smiled, laid the stocking down on her lap, and folded her hands over it – hands genuinely very beautiful, and adorned with glittering rings. She looked at her neighbour with that keen interest that prevails in women when they begin to sense courtesy in a man.

The two had long known each other, sitting in the homely garden that stretched around the summer house, whose name, 'Solitude', was engraved in golden letters on its gable.

In front of the garden, meadows extended into the distance, with golden rectangles of waving grain stretching as far as the foot of the forest-clad mountains. Here and there, down below the mountains, were scattered tiny, modest hamlets with church steeples, as if assembled out of the toy box of the child of a giant. Closer by, Peklín Castle shone white, with its proud row of windows glittering in the west like a row of rubies set in silver. All this was spread out in the distance below the mountains. 'Solitude' was genuinely isolated: there were no buildings around it, and there was no human activity, except for the cow-girl repeatedly sounding her horn at the cattle grazing in the fields after the haymaking. Otherwise, there was complete silence here. There was only a stream gurgling through the meadows, and, spreading out behind 'Solitude', murmuring a little louder as it skipped over the large accumulated stones of its bed, and then running loose down the slope, hurrying to do its work. An old mill was hidden in the forest, its wheels turned by the stream. The mill could not be seen from 'Solitude'; only occasionally did the wind carry its knocking into the quiet garden.

Paní Teza had known this landscape from her childhood years. She had spent many lovely holidays there with her friend, the sister of the current landowner. Peklín had been instrumental in the purchase of her beloved 'Solitude'.

'No, I am no longer young enough,' she repeated, more emphatically, at his courteously incredulous smile. 'I have joined a philanthropic society. I have taken on this work, and it must be completed.'

'Are you an enthusiast for philanthropy, dear lady?'

'Not at all – I have no enthusiasm for it at all. There is a double shame involved in it – for the person who receives it as well as for the person who gives it, if the former is slightly tainted with pride and the latter with something of oppression.'

She sighed again, and rocked in her chair.

'If I had been a man, I think I would have undertaken work in the field of social improvement, which might have rendered all philanthropic activity redundant. But as a woman . . . What is left for us to do? The areas of activity which you men have left for us are so few.'

He listened with a haughty, condescending smile on his lips.

'Dear friend, you are becoming bored.'

'What makes you think so?'

'You are thinking about the limitations on the rights of women. There are only two kinds of women who ponder this subject: those who lead miserable lives, and those who are bored to death.'

'You are forgetting the third kind.'

'And what might that be?'

'Those who stand at the dark threshold of old age. Before that, there are rights – though no lawgiver provides them, a woman can usurp them through her youth, her beauty, and her loveliness . . . After that, after that terrible threshold of old age, there is a fearfully large amount of unpleasantness. Consider how awful it is to be aware that one is losing one's value. It is easy to be worthy of love if one is loved. But if one is no longer loved – You see why it is that I am turning into a philanthropist; in this world, one must have some purpose.'

She laughed, half bitterly, half merrily, exposing a row of little teeth.

'She's using her old age to flirt,' he thought to himself, and said, 'My dear, you are speaking with endearing humour about things that will not come to pass for a long time yet.'

'I am fully thirty-five years old. I am standing before that threshold: before the most difficult test in a woman's life, how to grow old gracefully. I have given the matter deep thought, and I have come to the conclusion that goodness is the grace of old age. You see, my philanthropic inclinations stem from this.'

In the air she waved a stocking that she had been knitting for poor children. She swung her left leg over her right, and, rocking, looked intently at the toe of her little slipper. She had tiny, exquisitely shaped feet, and though she was very wise in recognizing that she was approaching the threshold of old age, she could not abandon the bad habit of eighteen-year-olds of calling anyone's attention to this attractive feature, which had not withered with age.

And Peklín, too, was looking at her slipper.

'You have always been good,' he said warmly.

'Perhaps, but without being aware of it; now I intend to be consciously so. Out of love for my neighbour and also out of love for myself. There is some selfishness in it too.'

They were both silent for a moment; it was pleasant to keep silent, to look one another in the face slightly inquisitively and questioningly, and meanwhile to listen to the buzzing of the insects in the summer air.

'Thirty-five years – she was really not lying.' He was calculating rapidly in his mind; the dates matched. 'A pity; she could have been a little younger, although no one would have guessed her to be that age.' And a quotation from Mantegazza came involuntarily into his mind, 'If you wish to love, love a young girl, but be loved by a mature woman who understands how to love tenderly, gratefully, and with the entire charm of the evening twilight.'[1]

Teza Uvarová was a widow of ten years; God knows why she had not remarried.

Peklín was forty years old, and as yet unmarried. He had long abandoned the sweet melodies of amorous affairs. A rumour was current about him that he was well versed in hunting for his game in foreign fields, and plucking fruit in other men's orchards. He could never be caught in the act; his reputation remained intact. He was now a deputy of the Empire, spending the winters in his home town, and he was aware of his unavoidable need to get married. He was ambitious, hoping for promotion; he wanted someone to be in charge of his household. Although he would have been welcomed by many a young girl, he was wary of joining his fate with the immodesty of youth, full as it would be of vexing demands.

His poaching in foreign fields had provided him with some valuable experiences, among which the one that stood out was that of an older man playing a grievous role, either a little ridiculous or superhumanly uncomfortable, at the side of a young woman, in which he must be either a slave or a tyrant, and almost never what he should be.

Teza Uvarová was still beautiful; she was intelligent and rich, and he judged that she would be able to run his household better than any young girl would.

1 Paolo Mantegazza's theory of love was widely read at this period. The actual text of the passage here ironically quoted is: 'If I may be permitted to express a bold desire, I would like to love a young girl and be loved by a mature woman who has begun to require evening twilight and dimly lit lamps' ('Se a me fosse lecito esprimere un desiderio audace, vorrei amare una giovinetta ed essere amato da una donna matura, che incominciasse ad aver bisogno dei crepuscoli della sera e delle lucerne poco abbaglianti': Paolo Mantegazza, *Fisiologia dell'amore* (Milan: Presso Giuseppe Bernardoni tipografo e la Libreria Brigola, 1873): 241.)

Ever since she had been spending the summer months at 'Solitude', he had been seriously entertaining the thought of attaching her fate to his own. He had reasoned, he had thought it over, and he was waiting until she should give him an irrevocable sign of her favour; nor was he particularly impatient in his waiting.

In the ten years of paní Teza's widowhood, the death of her husband had freed her from many of the hardships of an unhappy marriage. Widowhood had enveloped her in a feeling of exultant liberty.

Up to the age of thirty, she had lived in cheerful independence. She had turned men's heads, she had distributed her favours, and she had not troubled herself on account of the rumours circulating about the freedom of her life. She had been thinking how passionately she loved her solitude – a solitude filled, of course, with the serenading madrigals of the male sex in adoration of her.

In her thirtieth year she had meditated deeply on the notion of a solitude impoverished by the sound of those madrigals. And now she was paying closer attention to the enemies threatening her own face. As yet no wrinkles had appeared, but a kind of wistfulness had taken hold of her. She was laying her head down frequently, as if seeking some kind of support for it, and yearning, but not knowing for what object. In the dreams of her yearning, not one single male face appeared, but a few little heads of angelically beautiful children. What could she do? It would be impossible to achieve the latter without the former, but it was more difficult to find the cause than to find its consequence.

She was not one of those piously naïve little souls, one of those happy little female creatures, who never cease dreaming of the Promised Land of noble manhood until they take the plunge into marriage. Like many clever and sensible women of thirty, she had become a specialist in male psychology. And the psychologist in her was gradually turning into a sceptic. She knew many, many married men, exemplary husbands, loving fathers, but she did not know a single older bachelor who was not tainted with deceitful selfishness. The privileged position of men had led them to this selfishness, to a selfishness that was so repulsive to her. And she did not have enough feminine humility to tolerate them in patience.

Between thirty and thirty-five, she was still distributing favours here and there, more and more devoutly. Anxiously and gratefully, she was sparing the feelings of those who gave her the opportunity for that distribution, and adding to each favour a morsel of the slightly bitter herb of her own resignation.

Then she was continuing to meditate in her 'Solitude', which she loved so much, because it gave her so many opportunities for meditation.

The years of indulgence now past, it was necessary for her to prepare herself for the years of reason and discretion. She was astonished, realizing for the first time that there is a very large space reserved in life for the rights of a woman's heart, but almost none for the rights of a woman's intellect. And yet a woman, too, is obliged to live a good half of her life with heart and brain in equilibrium. But how? She longed for useful activity. She thought it over, – the choice was meagre and difficult. Finally, she inscribed the title 'Philanthropy' on the door-post of her new activity.

She ceased dreaming in her rocking chair, waving a rose or a lilac blossom in her hand. Grey stockings and piles of coats and bodices for the children of the poor filled her house and her mind with some degree of satisfaction.

But a mysterious, evil Fate does not grant people such satisfaction in the vale of tears and storms of this life. Paní Teza was therefore destined to experience certain events which would rouse her from her tranquillity.

At the beginning of the holidays that year, her nephew came to her 'Solitude', bringing a friend of his with him, a good-looking young lad, who was somewhat taciturn. Her nephew left two days later, but his friend stayed on at her invitation. 'Solitude' provided quite enough space for this sickly human fledgling. Even her old aunt, with whom she had lived amicably for many years, interceded for the young redhead, who was the son of her closest friend.

The redhead set about curing his persistent cough in the resin-laden air of 'Solitude'.

When he arrived, he was croaking very hoarsely; after some conversations with paní Teza, in which he confided to her all the anguish of his love to some heartless coquette of a girl, he stopped croaking. Paní Teza seemed to have been able to pour balm on his wounded heart – and also his wounded lungs. Gradually he began to find a healing enchantment in talking to her. His voice became youthfully clear, and behind its sound, hopeful horizons of life began to unfold before Teza's eyes. She did not interrupt him, but merely slipped into his feverish solo occasional pieces of advice, interests, and her own more mature experiences of life. On the second occasion, she turned him into gold merely with a glance of her light brown, luminous eyes. She was knitting no grey stockings while talking to him, but toying with some flower or twig as she listened.

On one occasion she plucked a sprig of an otherwise carefully tended laurel bush, occasionally chewing on it during a lively conversation. When she got up, she threw the twig away carelessly. Reaching the corner of the house, however, she noticed that the redhead had picked it up, had kissed it, and had put it away in his breast pocket. The Lord knows how she could have seen this around the corner of the house, but it is well-known that women can see around corners if they wish to see something that pleases them.

So began a fortnight of lovely days, brightened by the sun in the summer sky as well as that other sun in her heart, proclaiming in their warm rays their treacherous awareness, 'I am loved; what enchantment there is in such a surrendering, delirious – and above all, respectful – young love!' –

Her old aunt was amazed that paní Teza was now playing Chopin so often; she was amazed that she was wearing freshly ironed white dresses which she never put on at other times; she was amazed that she, never a lover of great exercise, was undertaking long walks in the neighbourhood; she was amazed that she was bringing to the table certain dishes that were not otherwise eaten.

Paní Teza had someone for whom to play, to dress, to cook, and to tire herself with long excursions. Paní Teza was complying with one of the principal needs of a woman's heart: she had someone whom she could pamper.

And the woods around 'Solitude' were breathing out their resin more fragrantly, the stream in the meadows was singing more mysteriously, and the marsh marigolds in the fields were glowing as if sown with gold.

When the redhead left, the scenery changed. A desert spread out around 'Solitude'. Paní Teza was dejected; she no longer dressed up, but went around in her old dressing-gown. It was as though she had only now made that staggering leap from the meadows of indulgence and warm tenderness into a rational and empty old age. With that leap there were two things she had not lost – her comfortable old dressing-gown and her virtue. Even with the redhead, she had never deviated from the precise limits of the permissible.

Soon afterwards, Peklín returned from Vienna. She received him cordially and affably. He did not interrupt her in her new philanthropic endeavours, nor in her knitting of grey stockings, but he brightened up her life with his ideas. He told her about the Reichstag, about politics, and about social and national affairs. She read the newspapers and books that he brought, and followed him in his interests and activities attentively and a little jealously. How many interests there were in the life of a man, compared to the life of a woman! His ideas were enough for her; she was almost surprised when he began to supplement them with devoted glances. – –

Peklín now discarded his half-smoked cigar, coughed, and smoothed his luxuriant moustache with his handker-chief.

'Dear lady!'

It sounded like the salutation of an official letter. She looked up intently.

'You speak so often and so readily about your age! I must finally believe, what your face does not betray, that you are no more than twenty years old.'

'To what do I owe this ceremonious introduction, dear friend?'

'You must not laugh; let me finish! Dear lady, dear friend, I intend to speak about myself. Look, it has become neces-sary for me to sit here opposite you to exchange my views with you. But I long to continue.' He cast her an indulgent glance. 'If you still permit it, I shall count you as a comrade in age. To express myself somewhat figuratively, we are both standing at the summit of the mountain of life; we shall be standing there for a while, perhaps; then we shall slowly undertake the pilgrimage down from the heights. The journey will be long, perhaps – but we cannot deny that it will be one down from the heights. – Have you ever noticed that two who lean on one another descend from the heights better than one? What would you say if I were to offer you companionship in that journey – if I were to offer you my shoulder in the rest of life's pilgrimage . . .'

Her countenance was flooded in blushes; she set her fingers quickly to run through the grey wool of her handiwork. She sensed that he was speaking in exactly the kind of formal language that he customarily used in Parliament – a language that flowed so gracefully because his heart was not pounding anxiously. She sighed, and laid her hands on both arms of her chair; and at this Peklín leant over them and whispered, more warmly:

'I should like to entrust my happiness to this little hand, this tiny, tender, little hand!'

He remained bent over her hand, playing flatteringly with the jewels on her rings. And paní Teza remembered. – The redhead had sat, bent over her hand, in just the same way at the moment of their parting. He had been unable to speak, and had bent over to hide the tears welling up in his eyes. And it had cost her a short but rather painful struggle not to bend over his head and press her lips into his luxuriant curls. She carefully examined Peklín's thinning scalp, bowed over her hand, but felt no urge to press her lips against it.

'If you wish to be loved, choose an older woman who loves gratefully, tremblingly, with the entire charm of twilight.' Mantegazza had omitted to add, '. . . who loves you gratefully, tremblingly, if you possess the entire charm of your devoted, passionate youth.'

'My dear, dear friend, thank you for your trust.' She paused, but pressed his hand warmly. 'But I require some time to decide. A very, very short time.'

Peklín looked up, in disappointed surprise.

'Is there something or someone standing in the way of your decision?'

She laughed. 'The bad habit of my solitude is standing in the way a little.'

Half an hour later, they were riding off together in Peklín's carriage. At paní Teza's request, they were intending to drive to a distant estate belonging to Peklín, situated high in the mountains.

The carriage carried them well, the fresher breeze of the air disturbed by its motion refreshing their faces. Each of them was huddled in one corner, and they spoke little; but occasionally they looked at one another with a pleasant smile that said, 'Life is good, and who knows what surprises it may still have in store for us!' The countryfolk going on foot along the road bowed respectfully before the lord of the manor, and both of them sensed the charm of the almost unconscious hauteur felt by those who ride towards those who walk. They met the carriage of a neighbouring landowner, whose family turned to cast appraising glances at paní Teza.

Peklín smiled carelessly; he flashed a sidelong look at her figure. He had nothing to be ashamed of; in his carriage she seemed a queen.

He smoothed the blanket at her feet, and with her hand she brushed the dust off his velvet collar. It was the first gesture of a more intimate nature she had made towards him. He took her hand and held it in his own for a long time.

They drove straight along the road that stretched to the foot of the mountains; the scent of the mown hay from the meadows wafted over to them, and both of them had the same thought, 'So it seems now to have been decided.'

'It will be good, and there was urgent need of it,' added Peklín to this feeling in his thoughts. 'She is lovely and sensible. She will never shock by suddenly erupting with a shout of "Jesus, Mary!" She has none of the false enthusiasm or the false sentimentality of hysterical women, nor does she have the didacticism in which intelligent women imagine salvation must be found. She has feeling and also a mature, self-made intelligence. But will she be flexible enough with this mature, self-made intelligence of hers? We shall see – '

Peklín had full confidence in his capacity for mental arithmetic, which he used to keep his entire environment in measurable bounds. He quickly calculated the approximate value of her fortune.

'She will want to keep independent control of it, at least at first,' he thought. But he remembered that it would be advantageous to pay off the small debt remaining on the estate. A property can be managed better when the estate is free from all debts.

'You have a lovely little ear, as pink as a seashell,' he whispered quietly to her, so that the coachman would not hear, and looked lovingly at her.

'I am beginning to be in love! Hallo, I am really beginning to do so!' He felt great satisfaction in this revelation.

'Would you mind my smoking a cigar?'

'Not at all, dear friend.'

She pressed herself deep into the cushions.

'I shall wean you off that, my dear; smoking is not pleasant, even on a journey, and it is not healthy, either,' she thought to herself, but at this moment she too had resolved to marry Peklín.

Little clouds of smoke from his cigar were circling in the air; she followed them with her eyes, then wished for more of them. The setting sun irradiated a whole flock of these tiny clouds with a rosy blush, and tiny, indistinct children's heads were once more appearing in them.

Her long eyelashes were almost pressed to her cheeks; an extremely strange confusion of anxiety and hope was circling in her head.

The road began to climb; from the elevated viewpoint, the landscape was stretching yet further into the distance.

Both of them gazed at the rectangular fields in the valley below, and at the mansions of neighbouring landowners enthroned above groups of huddled cottages.

The sharp points of the church spires were projecting like black needles into the misty, silvery fabric of the air. The fields along the road began to thin out, reddened with thickly growing poppies; the slope fell away to the other side of the road, besprinkled here and there with young spruce trees and grey with moss-covered rocks. Then the greenish darkness of a spruce forest drew breath in them, in which a stray, abandoned, as it were fearful birch tree stood out in white beside the cold, bluish pallor of the old larches.

When they emerged from the forest, the landscape had assumed an entirely different, mountainous character. The fields had almost disappeared, and blackened woods alternated with the green of the meadows of the hilly tracts. The mountains closed off the horizon like the petrified waves of a dark sea, over which lay the horizon, red like a bloodstained table. An old sawmill sang its acerbic, mournful song, in which the tall tree-trunks were wailing.

A chill was blowing from the whole landscape – a chill in the colours and in the air.

'It is a mournful region – does Fanynka not find it depressing?' asked paní Uvarová.

'She has a husband and children – it is not open to her to find it depressing,' replied Peklín carelessly.

Paní Teza had her own particular purpose in expressing her wish to come up here into the mountains. She had an interest in seeing Fanynka, the wife of the farm manager at the Nemodlin estate.

She was bound to the memory of this Fanynka by her recollection of a lovely little romance from Peklín's youth.

Fanynka was the orphaned daughter of a teacher; she had no relatives, and the lady of the castle, Peklín's mother, took her into service as a runner of errands, who brought all that was needful from the town whenever the horses of the estate were being rested.

When she grew up, she advanced to being a parlour-maid, and at that time the young Peklín discovered in her every kind of talent, and a fine instinct for many of the arts. He took care to educate her, lent her books, and taught her to sing to an old-fashioned guitar, an instrument he had found in the attic of the castle and which he had restrung. Fanynka read, sang, listened attentively to the improving lectures of the young master, and sometimes burst out weeping bitterly for no reason. When she was asked why she was weeping, she accounted for it by saying it was merely because she could never become a teacher. To be a teacher seemed to be the one single dream of her life.

The young ladies of the castle complained that their dresses were being badly ironed, and laughed at the poetic efforts of the sentimental parlourmaid. Peklín stood up for her everywhere and in everything, and this gave rise to some fears on the part of his mother, but he immediately countered these by saying firmly that Fanynka's education was his favourite holiday amusement – that, and nothing more. –

Not far from the sawmill, a chapel nestled in the embrace of a churchyard, both of them modest and enveloped in the poverty of the mountain region. The chapel seemed sick, from the perpetual dampness of its walls. To its right was the Nemodlin house, a small building with tear-stained windows squeezed under a bulky roof.

The gate of the courtyard opened as if on command before the horses of the master. The farm manager bowed to his employer. He was a tall, thin man with a round back and a narrow chest, with pale yellow hair protruding like thatch over his low, freckled forehead.

No sooner had the master's carriage entered the courtyard than there was barking, changing into joyful yelping. A brown hunting hound, chained to a kennel near a dunghill, was vainly straining to free herself from the chain.

'Isn't that your old Diana?' asked paní Teza, stepping on to the running-board of the carriage.

Peklín nodded, adding that she was no longer needed for hunting, and that he did not have the heart to shoot her.

'And she is tied up,' exclaimed paní Teza.

'Dear lady, if I were to untie her, something untoward would immediately happen. Either she would get her teeth into one of the chickens, or she would run into the house. She is nothing but trouble – she must not be allowed to forget that she was with the gentry.'

'Quiet, bitch!' The manager picked up a stone.

Peklín quickly untied Diana and stroked her. Soon she was leaping up on him, up to his face, and then again whining and meekly crawling to his feet.

Fanynka came out on the doorstep and approached the carriage with the shyness of a little girl. Fervently, she kissed the hand offered to her by paní Teza, and at the sight of the lady's face, her eyes filled with tears as if looking back, in wistful remembrance, to better times gone by. After all these years, she was little altered; her regular face was very slightly yellowed, and her straight nose, as if suspended on her two dark, horizontal eyebrows, somewhat more prominent.

'Her Egyptian profile has not changed,' thought paní Teza to herself. But a more painful line was etched around her lips, and her dark eyes, once set in their white sockets like glittering agates, were somewhat sunken, as if marked by a shadow of renunciation.

A number of tiny children suddenly appeared, as if springing out of the earth.

'Are these all yours?' asked paní Teza, placing her hand on one of the children's heads.

'All of them, my lady. There are too many of them,' said Fanynka, shyly, wiping the little nose of one of them with her apron, and pushing them aside; then she brought the largest one to the front.

'This is the eldest, Stáňa, my lady.'

She seemed to be expecting some kind of praise for her firstborn son from the lady's lips.

Stáňa, whose baptismal name was that of the landowner, was slimmer than the rest; he was the only one wearing shoes, and he differed from his fair-haired siblings in his dark head of curls.

At the invitation of the farm manager's wife, paní Teza entered her house. The passage through the building was dark and paved with red brick, and saturated with the warm breath of the cowshed adjoining it on one side.

The farm manager's sitting room, as if tucked away from the large barn, was beautifully ordered. There were impatiens flowers blooming in the windows; beside the two beds covered with pink eiderdowns stood an old sofa from the big house, and over it there hung, on the wall of white plaster, some photographs, reproductions of old Italian masters. These were mementoes from Peklín's travels. A shelf with a few books provided paní Teza with the opportunity to ask whether Fanynka was still reading as diligently as ever.

The manager's wife smiled wanly, and, wiping a chair with her apron, invited the lady to be seated.

'Oh no, I have got out of the way of that,' she replied. 'People here are not accustomed to see someone with a book in their hands; it is not as it used to be in the castle. O God, O God, my lady.'

'But are you happy and contented? Don't you find it depressing here, Fanynka?'

'I have these children – I have no time to find things depressing. – At first I thought I would not be able to bear it at all. As soon as I could, I escaped down out of the mountains. But my husband would not allow it. A countryman of his sort does not understand finding things depressing.'

'But is he a good man?' asked paní Teza, with the blunt audacity that masters customarily adopt towards their servants.

'He is good – at least, he does not drink. He is good and hardworking; the master is pleased with him. What more can be expected of a countryman like him?' A mercilessly aristocratic line was fixed around her lips at these words. – 'He understands his own affairs – otherwise – you should know, there is not much conversation with him. – At first I used to think I should go mad here, but now I have got used to it. – One day here is much like another, and one worry like another. I have been married for eight years now, and yet it seems like yesterday that I left the castle. That is because things are always the same here.' –

The manager's wife spoke at length, with a certain ravenousness. She asked questions and recalled old times. Some of the words she chose fitted ill with her surroundings, but she used them with a certain deliberateness; she obviously wished to make it clear that she had not forgotten aristocratic manners of speech. Her interests remained fixed somewhere down at the foot of the mountains. With particular emphasis she uttered the words that her spirit had been put to death since her migration into the mountains.

'And why did you marry the farm manager?' asked paní Teza, with her interest deeply aroused.

For a while, Fanynka gave no answer, as she was straightening the cushions of her youngest daughter, who had just woken up. Her self-conscious, questioning look struck the eye of paní Teza as she said, 'The master wanted it to happen, and gave us this place –'

She was trying to put a piece of bread into the baby's hand. As she bent over the child, her cheeks went red with a furious blush.

To paní Teza it seemed that there were no further topics for questions; a flood of impressions was swirling in her brain. The freckled face of the farm manager flickered past the window; he was evidently just going to do his master's bidding.

Peklín came in rather noisily, and Diana pushed in through the door behind him. Stáňa also slipped past, stood by the stove, and spread his fingers in his trouser pockets, looking expectantly at the master.

Peklín sat down, an embarrassed smile curling in his face. Uncertainly, his gaze flickered over the faces of the two women.

'Why have we come here? Ah yes, "because I am a lady who wanted to".' Paní Teza felt a little nauseous, as one might feel when arriving unwittingly on the trail of some delicate secret.

'So you have a new kitten?' asked Peklín, avoiding the eye of the manager's wife.

'Yes, the children brought it here!'

'What a pastoral idyll it is here – you will have noticed the mother hen sitting in the coop behind the stove. Those will be young turkeys; they are very delicate, but the manager's wife knows how to raise them. She has the task of delivering poultry to the master's table. – How are your poultry this year – how many have you delivered so far?' He was trying to supplement his voice with a lordly accent.

The manager's wife mumbled an answer. She could not bring herself to invest it with the utter servility which the question had required. 'But we used to speak to one another in a different way, once upon a time,' was written all over her face, and something unspoken and unresolved was floating through the air of the small space.

Peklín bowed his head and began to scratch semicircles on the floor with his stick; the little kitten jumped down from the stove and began catching the stick with its claws. The master was completely absorbed in its playfulness, as if unaware of the two gazing fixedly at one another.

Diana, whose tear-filled eyes were bearing witness to the hardships of a dog's life, looked anxiously at her master. At times her eyes flashed green, and this happened here when she brushed contemptuously against the kitten; it seemed that only the old fear of the master's whip was restraining her appetite for biting it in the back of the neck.

Fanynka's eyes wandered from her master's face to that of paní Teza.

'And will my lady be staying long at the villa this year?' she asked, finally, as if she were trying to revive the flow of conversation once more.

'We are hoping that my lady will remain here for a long time,' replied Peklín for Teza, with a hard, imperious look, which struck a blow in the face of the manager's wife, and then strayed, picking up an understanding smile on its way, to paní Teza. Fanynka grasped the meaning of that look; the burning light of excitement faded from her face.

And again there was silence – a silence which was interrupted by Peklín, as if in increasing boldness, by the spoken question:

'And you, my boy, what are you gaping at? Are you waiting for something?' He reached into his pocket and pressed a small coin into Stáňa's palm. 'Now then, how are you learning? Are you learning well? I'll have Stáňa educated. If he learns well, I'll put him to study myself.' He lifted Stáňa high above his head; the boy's eyes were laughing with pride. They were Peklín's own steel-blue eyes.

The lord of the manor smiled with self-satisfaction, placing the boy back on the floor.

Paní Teza felt that he was attempting with his promise to apply a plaster to the wound of the manager's wife. But she found his self-satisfied, domineering smile repulsive. In some degree of confusion, in which she felt herself humiliated, she drew a final, definite line under her conjecture.

'Even my far-sightedness does not make him afraid – and he reckons me older and wiser than I am.'

She would have forgiven him every indiscretion of youth, but she felt herself unusually affected by the practical state of affairs at the Nemodlin estate.

When they entered the carriage, the manager's wife kissed her hand less warmly than on her arrival, but a long, uninhibited look in the dark eyes of the young woman was resting on the master, as he wrapped a warm blanket around the feet of his new queen.

'It will be cold; fasten your cloak. Here in the mountains the mist falls early.' His voice bore the unmistakable sound of tender care.

Fanynka was standing by the carriage in a light dress, her limbs as if crippled by the cold, and suddenly there was something extinct in her eyes.

Diana, tied up once again, to prevent her running after the master's carriage, began howling in agony; in her canine voice there was something of human despair.

The coachman spurred on the horses, and they rode out of the courtyard.

Alongside the chapel and the sawmill, and up to the forest, they were accompanied by Diana's howling.

Twilight pressed down on the landscape. The sky was yawning in pale helplessness; it lacked the strength to cast streams of light on to the earth, although the last gleam of the sun was yellow and phosphorescent in the west. Mist began to creep over the dark waves of the hills; a damp chill from the forest was breathing over them. When they drove into the forest road, Diana's howling could no longer be heard – they missed it.

'She has bad manners, old Diana.'

'Why then did you not shoot her?'

'I cannot shoot any of my hunting hounds. It would make me feel awkward. I am tender-hearted.'

'Is that so?' – it sounded a little mocking.

The forest grew dark, and seemed to demand silence. Teza pressed herself deep into the corner of the carriage, and even Peklín had no appetite to continue the conversation.

Dark nocturnal shadows wound their way into the forest; both of them felt the need to spin the thread of their thoughts in that utter silence, broken only by the monotonous trotting of the horses. The wheels dug into the soft forest road as if they were driving on moss.

Once, paní Teza drew herself up, and looked back.

'I was dreaming that someone was running after our carriage.'

'That is what one dreams, driving through the forest in the darkness.'

'Did she notice, or did she not?' The question went back and forth in his mind, as when grain that is too dense is tossed from one sieve to another. 'If she did notice, what of it? She is sensible enough not to have prejudices. Or do women always have prejudices in these matters? They do indeed, but a woman's prejudice always condemns only another woman. It justifies the man . . .' But some uncertainty was still oppressing him. He reached out to the seat of the carriage, in case he should find her hand there as he had done on the way to Nemodlin. It was not there. She was clasping her cloak to her breast with both hands. And then the image of the dark eyes of the farm manager's wife floated into the darkness of the forest. 'That woman loved me, slavishly, devotedly, as only simple female beings are capable of loving.' He saw her lost, uninhibited gaze at him. The memory of the past lulled him into a pleasant state of inactive half-sleep, similar to the state he usually experienced in pleasant digestion after a good meal.

'He is well versed in putting out of his way things he no longer needs, and how skilfully he does it. Diana on a chain, Fanynka passed on to the farm manager. He would have felt awkward if he had shot the former and simply left the latter. What an artist of life he is! And he is able to summon up whatever is necessary.' – She was now perfectly clear about her necessity in his life, but she was not flattered by it. A woman does not wish to be merely needed; she wishes to be loved, even when she does not herself love. To be needed – for that, her charitable intentions were enough.

With a quick sidelong glance she searched for his face in the semi-darkness. A smile was meandering through the thick network of wrinkles around his eyes. She guessed well that he was remembering Fanynka's devoted love.

Playing the coquette with him, stirring him up to passion and then kicking him away and planting her foot in the back of his head – and Fanynka would be avenged. Like lightning this thought flashed through her mind, and her heart was thumping a little. But the lightning was extinguished as quickly as it had appeared. – 'For what purpose?' Playing the coquette – who knows, perhaps it would bring her disappointment. It would fatigue her and disturb her tranquillity, and she was already protecting herself from all weariness. And for what purpose, again, would one want to persuade oneself of the bluntness of one's weapons? And behind all these conscious thoughts there lurked in her a single feeling, an almost unconscious one. It was not worth her while; all that drew her to it was deliberation, and none of it was pleasure.

Poor Fanynka! There is a considerable degree of folly in a woman's love that is as submissive as that; perhaps a little happiness as well. – She made a long pause in her thoughts. The forest was breathing sadly upon her – how did this happen, all of a sudden? She seemed to sense her loss of the wise, of the cool – her loss of those who cannot lose anything themselves.

They drove downhill out of the forest. The wheels of the carriage were creaking slightly, and this was pleasant to both of them, providing a suitable excuse for further silence.

The mist was gathering over the countryside lying below them in the valley. Its tattered threads lay in the alders by the stream, on the foot of the hill, and further down the valley it lay like a great, thick, grey shroud covering the contours of the landscape.

After a while, some lighted window in the landscape glowed, as if under a veil.

'And the housekeeper in the castle has lit the lamps in the dining room. I had almost forgotten that I have invited the parish priest, and also the revenue officer, for the evening.'

'Will you not be arriving late?'

'By no means. Drive faster, Kapka!' he ordered the coachman. 'It is my custom to play cards in the evening – failing anyone else, the housekeeper is obliged to play with me.'

She smiled in silence. 'It is my custom to play Grieg in the evening,' she thought to herself. 'Ah, these long-established customs of ours may well clash with one another.'

'And where then is "Solitude"?'

'There.' He waved his hand towards the far end of the valley.

There, far away, a light glimmered in the mist like a jewel buried in the dust.

'Solitude, solitude, my freedom!' – Something within her was exulting at the sight of this solitary light, which they had kindled to welcome her.

The wheels were no longer creaking. They had come down, and were going straight ahead. They were speaking indifferently and politely to each other.

'Whatever happened to that pleasant feeling of growing love, or something like that!' – With some ill humour, he announced that it had now melted into the mist.

'Surely it will return.' For the present, he was looking forward only to a good dinner and later to a pleasant round of Tarot.

The carriage came to a halt.

'I am home.' Her voice sounded impolitely cheerful.

She jumped out of the carriage and shook his right hand. The door of 'Solitude' slammed shut behind her.

He rode back to the castle.

'She is very private. Perhaps she is too sensible.'

A mist of doubt enveloped him, and through it the mournful farewell howling of Diana seemed to be crying in his ears.

The lawyer and the painter

'Dr Zima!'

'Ah, hello, dear friend!'

'I'm so glad to see you. I've just arrived back from my study trip – and you're the first person I've met now I'm back home. And it's important to pay careful attention to the person one meets first after getting back from abroad. He gives a certain tone to one's confused, volatile feelings – one might say, often even to one's destiny –'

'You were always a dreamer, Horáček! Where have you actually come from? Italy?'

'Yes, of course! Italy – though you haven't asked me, my dear, cold, reserved doctor – Italy is a country entirely different from what people usually say and write about it. But I'm not going to tell you what it's like, because if I told you about it – it would have changed again.'

'Oh yes, you've always enjoyed making jokes. I'm glad to see you – youth, cheerfulness, liveliness personified. Will you be staying in Prague now?'

'Today? Today, certainly. – I haven't yet thought about tomorrow.'

'That's never been your custom.'

'Were you asking me about the future, perhaps? What I'm going to do with my life, as they say?'

'No, not literally. In any case I'm satisfied that you're here today. Surely you won't refuse the invitation of an old friend, your cold, reserved patron, who would be glad to spend time warming his chilly lawyer's heart at the sacred fire of art, youth and –'

'No, I won't refuse, for God's sake, I won't refuse!'

'Wait a moment. You don't know yet where or why I'm inviting you –'

'Where or why! What a pedant you are, doctor. All I need is a kind word, a hint, from you – I'd follow you to my doom!'

'We won't go there. But we'll go and have a good dinner and some wine, and we'll sit and talk. Something strange and interesting has happened to me; it's almost an adventure . . .'

'Let's hear it!'

'It's almost a novel . . . and so I'd like to sit and talk. If you remember, I always used to find it very pleasant to sit and talk to a friend in the evening.'

'I do remember – indeed I have rather unpleasant memories of this predilection of yours. Forgive a simple chap his frankness, doctor, but you used to be intolerable sometimes, when we were sitting in the evenings . . . one's blood used to run cold in one's veins from your wisdom and precision in word and deed – '

'I've become unused to all that, one could say, so have no fear on my account. All that wisdom and precision in word and deed has entirely gone – I'm quite sure of that!'

'You're piquing my curiosity – you're piquing it far too much. So what is it – have you got married, my friend?'

'No, God forbid, in fact . . . but why should God forbid it, that's really not what I wanted to say! You can see, my dear Horáček, where my famous precision has gone. I'm not married, though I don't know whether I should say "not yet" or "almost"–'

'Aha! It seems to me that I'm on the verge of understanding your adventure. – "On the verge of an evil deed," would you say?'

'I'll tell you all about it this evening – this evening! But now, dear friend, we must part, unfortunately; I'm on the way to the office. – But excuse my rudeness! How are you . . . how is your art progressing . . . you must be exhibiting something this year –'

'My dear doctor, you oughtn't to be saying that – no, you definitely oughtn't to be saying that!'

'What do you mean?'

'That polite affectation. For you don't care the least bit, not at all, how I am and what I'm painting! For you have your own delightful adventure, and you have no interest in anything else at all. But that doesn't matter. On the contrary. Now goodbye till this evening . . . where shall we meet tonight, then?'

*   *

She. (Pages 1 to 3 from her diary.)

– Yesterday I said goodbye to school, and to my first, blissful, carefree youth. This time for good. I'll only be going to piano and French lessons for another year or so. I'm eighteen years old. I've taken five classes at the Girls' High School, one advanced class in Vinohrady, one class at the Minerva girls' gymnasium . . . no, two classes, the 'prima' and 'secunda', because we also had Greek for the second half of the year; the boys need two years for that! Women grow up faster.

I wanted to do some serious work – study. I realized that I wasn't suited to it by nature. That was something painful to realize, and I suffered a good deal on that account, but I must calm down and look somewhere else for my métier.

Where's my métier?

Obviously in marriage. Not in art. I play the piano very badly, I could sing but I don't have a voice, and I used to be only moderately good at drawing and writing.

Marriage, then.

I'm writing this big, but scribbled, word here on the first page of my diary, and not without emotion. Though I'm writing only for myself, who knows, maybe when I'm dead it'll be printed as an interesting document for understanding women's psychology. So then, I'd better take care about every word.

I'm not afraid of being laughed at if I say that marriage is a serious thing. Most women get married when they get a suitable – maybe sometimes unsuitable – opportunity. Just for the sake of getting married.

Now that isn't right.

First I need to set up my ideal of a husband – a kind of model. Then to look for the real thing according to that model – and to make no concessions to its requirements, not in the slightest detail! –

A summary of the model for my husband would look something like this:

Tall, healthy, dark. All his teeth, and all of them in good shape. All his hair, and all of it black. Excellent eyesight – the colour of his eyes doesn't matter, but I prefer dark. That's his outward appearance. I'll describe that first, though naturally I think his mental ability is more important, but I won't go any further about either of them.

His mind. What ought a husband's mind to be like? Of course, at the same level as his wife's. God forbid I should get married to a man who is more stupid or more clever than I am myself. Either would be a mistake in a perfect marriage, as all noble spirits imagine it.

I won't allow my husband to have left school with a distinction, because I didn't finish my studies with a distinction either. It would be best if he didn't have a school-leaving certificate at all. They've become sick of them – they don't even want them at the magistrate's office any more. So I'll allow a school-leaving certificate – at most, a law degree. But he mustn't be able to play the piano better than I do, or to know French, German, drawing, etc. But he must be able to give the impression of being an intelligent, profound, modern person just as I can. In short, he's got to understand and know everything, but not to be annoying with it. I can't give more explanation or a more detailed analysis; I'll leave that to his wit.

Then of course he's got to love me dearly. After all, that is the first condition, for I'm certainly not getting married without love. I want him to be gentle as well as strong, for him to know how to command me as well as go down on his knee to me, all in the right measure, especially as far as the commanding is concerned! And he must love me with an amazing love . . . ah, I think I'm already in love with him too, if only there is one like that in the world, as I've described him here!

Have I forgotten anything?

Status? Of course he should have a decent enough position to be able to support me – so that my trousseau can somehow be kept intact and not touched. One ought to think of the future. Children, etc. Children . . . that's another important question, and ought to be discussed further, but one needs one's actual husband to talk about that. About their education, and how many of them. I think my Mama is right on this point, a woman of the old school, when she says, one child is enough, or at most two – for pleasure and also for taking care.

Those women of the old school sometimes had sensible ideas.

(Page 4:)

– Perhaps that was the one?!

(The rest of the page deleted. Then ten pages torn out. Page 25:)

– Really, if I hadn't been brought up too well, and if I hadn't believed in ideals, I'd have despaired by now.

Every man is either a cheat or a cad. As for me, quant à moi, I'd pick a cheat sooner than a cad. To hell with it, he doesn't have to have all the points I set out in my model! But he shouldn't show the deficit in such a stupid way!

After all, I'm not perfect either, but I do know how to seem so. And life is nothing but appearances. Everything is an illusion, a deception. To hell with it all – but let there be at least a bit of skill in it!

(15 pages missing.

Page 56:)

– No, I don't despair. I'm determined to go on searching, always to be searching, wherever I go. If I must descend into the depths for a man, I'll descend! If I must ascend, I'll ascend!

It's going to be hard to justify these excursions at home. Papa and Mama are of the old school, and would be horrified. I'm going to have to visit my girlfriend more often and linger more at piano lessons, French lessons etc. The world wants to be deceived – I can't help that. When I have children I won't forbid them a single thing. I'll give them complete freedom – they'll get used to it, there'll be no forbidden fruit to tempt them, they'll be model, virtuous children, I'm looking forward to them! If only I had a father for them by now!

(A few pages torn out again. Then the diary ends, in irregular, agitated handwriting:)

One of them is a painter; the other a lawyer. Neither of them is dark, but they aren't ugly either. The painter is a kind of lovely savage, uncouth. First he begs sweetly for a single kiss, and then, without asking permission, kisses me like a lunatic – it's a wonder he doesn't suffocate me. These days I'm visiting Emilka Svátková very often indeed. Mama is surprised how much she loves me all of a sudden. I'm not surprised, haha! The lawyer is rather comical, but after all he's a lawyer and I think he has a fortune.

I'm in a difficult situation. Both of them love me – one ecstatically, the other seriously. Serious love usually lasts longer. I shouldn't care about their positions, either: after all, I don't need that. Besides, the painter is beginning to make a name – he's winning prizes and bursaries. He's just come back from Italy. I'm going to see him tomorrow. I've promised him that . . . *(Heavily crossed out.)*

* * *

All three of them.

In the studio of Horáček, the painter.

Dr Zima has arrived to tell his friend some happy news. His lovely adventure has ended with his engagement. The mysterious beauty, whom he met at a society masked ball, and about whom he told his friend the other evening, – is the daughter of a rich, decent family, a naïve, romantic creature as women usually are; her dream – that's the way these creatures talk – has apparently always been to meet a man in some unusual way. For example, at a fancy-dress ball, where she might be able to pose as a seamstress, or as an artist's model, to win a man's love in this way, and then to surprise him pleasantly by announcing, 'I'm an honourable girl and I have fifty thousand!'

'"This has been my motto," she said to me: "If I must descend into the depths for a man, eh bien, I'll descend into the depths for him! And I descended as far as being a model!" She didn't remember, poor thing, that models don't attend society balls – though on the other hand I must admit she played it quite skilfully. Ah well. She's lovely and she has fifty thousand.'

Those were the words of Dr Zima, the lawyer. The rosy countenance of his slight, fair figure glowed with astuteness and bliss.

Horáček, the painter, congratulated him sincerely. One sentence in his friend's account had given him a little pause. But he said nothing.

The lawyer wandered across the studio, making his way through a pile of junk, tripping over the carpet, grey and stiff with dust, knocking into chairs and tables on which cigarette butts were lying besides the remains of food, empty bottles, unwashed beer mugs and teapots; there were two spoons as well. And, absent-mindedly, he looked at the pictures hanging on the walls and strewn around on the floor.

Suddenly he paused.

The painter had been following him on his pilgrimage. A smile was playing in his eyes.

'Who's this, Horáček? This woman?'

Dr Zima was pointing at a fresh, rosy, exuberantly laughing picture. Such a pretty, young, warm, life-affirming figure of a girl . . . on which everything was glittering with mysterious mockery. Even her hands, covering her face, even her little legs, with their pink, ridiculously tiny knees, indeed, even every invisible, unpainted, but surely exquisite, blue vein of this little body, all were laughing, laughing! The devil with those veins! If only the little girl were not covering her face . . . though the same surreptitious, exuberant laughter was shining through her slender little fingers, her likeness, her likeness could not be made out. And Dr Zima would have paid a hundred to know who it was.

'Who is that?'

Horáček stretched out his long legs, rocked, and stared with a peculiar expression. There was laughter in his eyes similar to that of the girl in the picture, but more repellent. He replied, slowly:

'It's The Naïve Girl.'

'What's her name? –'

'The picture's called "The Naïve Girl". I don't know what the model's name is.'

'Is it a model?'

'Yes, an artist's model. What is there in her that can't be seen?' –

'Hm . . . That laugh . . . An amazing likeness.'

'She was a good girl. A naïve, romantic creature – as women usually are. She also had her own dreams! Women of every social class usually have them. This one said: "If I must rise up for a man, I'll gladly rise up! Ça ne gène pas."'

'Did she really know French too?'

'No. I made that bit up.'

'Oh, is that so? Well, well, likenesses are sometimes – astonishing!'

'Oh yes, definitely – among women.'

'Ha, ha! You're mischievous. But I'd almost forgotten. I actually came to you with a request. Would you mind making me a wedding announcement? Something simple, you know, nice paper . . . an unusual font – it's all the rage just now, and my bride understands these things. You will do it, won't you? Goodbye!'

'With the greatest pleasure! Goodbye!'

'Oh, pardon – for I haven't told you her name! How would you be able to draft an announcement without knowing her name?'

RŮŽENA SVOBODOVÁ

He trusted the wind to guard the flame in the lamp
and the fragrance of the flowers in the gardens.

I

Filip, the huntsman, paid court to her faithfully for three years, and it was only at the end of the third year that he dared to say to her:

'Anča, I'd like to be the one taking care of you.'

And he could not manage anything else for another whole year.

He was not particular in his choice of words, and his simple, ardent emotions, without subtle shaping, lay like a lead weight on his breast.

He did not know how to say anything else, and in any case he did not dare to.

The notorious case of Žofka from Plavá Hůrka was too well known in the area, and fathers were assiduously guarding their daughters.

Anča was a beauty who had been carefully brought up, with dark brown wavy hair, an ardent face, and with eyes that were at times sweetly alluring and at other times dully bored. On her face, low under her left eye, she had two brown beauty spots, attractive small moles, which suited her and augmented the coquetry of her sweet face.

Her mother espoused the tradition of eighteenth-century women – the tradition of faithful beauties.

Her husband never set eyes on her unless she was carefully groomed, powdered, and spotless in a white apron – always full of smiles, hiding all the unpleasant domestic chores from him and putting on show only clean, polished rooms full of fresh air and flowers in bloom. She had taught her daughter from childhood to believe in the divinity and infallibility of her husband, and soon inculcated in her all the mysteries and precepts that would enable her to charm her own husband into old age, so that he would never be estranged from her and would not cease regarding her as a delightful woman beyond compare.

Her daughter readily believed her, because her mother's marriage was genuinely happy and good, and because her mother was truly adored by her aging husband, wearied by his office-work.

Her mother wished her daughter to enjoy herself, did not push her towards marriage, had her driven to entertainments, and made the final moments of her freedom delightful before her marriage, which would initiate a long gamble for an artificial eternity of fading emotions.

She had her driven to harvest celebrations and excursions without consulting Filip, the huntsman, who suffered in furious anger.

She took her on an excursion on a day when the huntsman was obliged to be at a meeting in town, and when he could not accompany them.

Anča was dancing in a hall with some good-natured boys, who were good dancers: she had engaged herself for the whole afternoon, not thinking about anything other than waltzes.

A carriage rattled along the road; it stopped right outside the garden hall, and Filip, the huntsman, alighted from it.

Anča's companions were alarmed.

'Anča, Filip has arrived!' they announced to her, excited by the fact that something was amiss, and curious to see what would happen.

Filip, the huntsman, came into the little village hall, stood on the threshold, his eyes darting hurriedly and irritably among the dancing couples.

Anča was dancing and laughing with her hair flowing loose, drunk with the rhythm of the waltz; she seemed not to have seen her admirer.

Filip waited for her to pass by.

He asked her for a dance.

She bent her dark head down towards his shoulder and said, with a fond smile:

'I'm engaged for it.'

'The next dance, then!'

'I'm engaged for that one too.'

Filip, the huntsman, had a simple heart, and was capable of producing results with straightforward means.

He stamped his foot, swore, and said, passionately, full-throatedly, in a voice full of wicked, youthful magic:

'You come with me right now, or else I shall leave and I won't come back!'

It was effective.

Startled, the sorceress Anča let go of her partner, looked reproachfully at Filip, and danced the rest of the waltz with him.

After the dance, the huntsman took his sweetheart out into the garden.

He had something to say to her.

He would not leave her in the arms of strange men. All that must come to an end.

They walked along the riverbank, under the shadow of flowering, fragrant lime trees and branches of oak trees, with their sharply outlined foliage, under the shadow of ancient trees bowed over the river in deep shade.

Their outgrowth and the leaves of the lilies were soaking in its quietly flowing waters. Tiny, agile dragonflies and butterflies were resting on the river plants.

Filip was breathing heavily, walking with great strides, and dragging little Anča behind him.

'Where are we going?' she asked him, in quiet terror.

He did not reply, but took her in his arms like a doll, and carried her through the garden without a word, as if he wished to take her where the river was deepest, and fling her in, so that she should not trouble him any further.

She did not know what would happen to her; she was afraid to say a word, and resigned herself as if decorously and defiantly to death or life, but her heart was pounding in alarm. They arrived at the end of the garden – at the wall that abutted the river.

'It is deep there,' thought Anča. 'I shan't be able to get out from there! O God, may all my sins be forgiven!'

The huntsman lifted her lightly, set her up on the high wall, holding her in his arms, scarcely touching her, and leaving her not much certainty or hope of living much longer.

'I have had enough of all this!' he said, with fierce vehemence, with the charm of a brutal abductor by whom it is sweet to be possessed. 'Either you tell me you love me, or I'll throw you off this wall! I'm not going to share you with anyone else. Either you'll be mine or you won't be anyone's!'

It was not out of fear that Anča told the huntsman that she loved him and no one else. No, she had genuinely loved him for a long time already, and she could not wait for the moment when he would ask her for her love, and she could not wait for his sweet, passionate kisses, for his lips scented with the blossom of the lime trees.

With the wall she had gained access to his stubborn, proud heart, and in the ecstasy of surrender she promised him all the eternities and unchangeabilities of love that he was demanding of her. Without realizing what she was actually promising, she vowed never to look into another man's eyes again, to shut herself off from the world – that is, from waltzes, music, suitors, everything and everyone. She thought of ten times more vows than he was demanding, and voluntarily, between their kisses, and merely for the pleasure of promising, pledged a fidelity that can be kept only by the dead, forever asleep deep beneath the earth.

II

Anča and Filip were married within six months, with great, deeply rooted, illusions about the eternity of their emotions, and about a love that would persist beyond the grave.

Anča never grieved her husband in any way. She had inherited all her mother's enchantment. She bade him farewell with a smile and greeted him with a smile. She was never irritable, she concealed everything unpleasant from her husband, and she had the kindest of words and the tenderest of care for him. She dressed in order to please him; she was always well turned out, delightful and tasteful. Before he came, she would comb her hair, powder herself and put on a clean white blouse. He never saw her dishevelled, and never ill-tempered or complaining. Indeed she was constantly smiling, always willingly adjusting her beautifully coifed little head to his orders, as if she wished to understand everything from the very first word he spoke and to obey as meticulously as she possibly could.

To her husband, everything she was conjuring around him became a pleasant custom, and later an obligatory commonplace; he accepted all of it without gratitude, and almost wearily. And Anča's smile faded on her sweet lips, and her movements in listening to him became mechanical. She seemed to be listening, even though her thoughts were already lost and wandering elsewhere. She was not discontented; she did not fret while she was ordering everything in the household so as to give him pleasure; she denied herself and exercised restraint, and he let everything pass without comment. She did not fret at all, even when he failed to respond to a single one of her thousands of small and great kindnesses. She knew he had neither time nor peace of mind, that he was always occupied with nurseries, labourers, gamekeepers, fillers, poachers and vermin, and she compared him, not to his disadvantage, with her father, who was attentive and grateful in spite of all the greyness and toil of his life.

But there is no actress in the world who would want to play the loveliest Shakespearean female role every day for years in front of an empty, dark auditorium, to dress in a beautiful robe and distribute the choicest flowers, to rant, to rejoice or to die, never seen by anyone. If she were compelled to do this by some ordinance or some vow, how might she be playing after six months, how after a year?

For that reason, the smile was fading on Anča's kind lips; for that reason, her obedient movements were becoming mere habit, and her dark eyes were growing dull with boredom.

After twelve months a daughter was born to her, who died at six weeks.

Grief may also sometimes become a comforting occupation.

Anča was still a delightful woman, but all her charms came to resemble a well-played game, and day by day her inner joy was evaporating.

This is how she and her husband were living: she was always speaking about him, and he was always speaking about himself.

Something in her soul had died, and the whole field of her past life, when she had been cherished and loved, was lying fallow.

Because she was always accustomed to speak about his interests with the utmost attention, he was absolutely sure that there was not the slightest place in her soul that did not belong to him, and he had no concern on her account.

They spent three uneventful years in contented marriage.

He never spoke to her about love and never alluded to tenderness. He felt that being faithful as a husband was enough to compensate for all the confessions and sweet words with which he had never become familiar. If at times he became angry, pounding the table or knocking chairs over, because the gamekeepers had done something untoward, and he therefore felt obliged to find fault unnecessarily with things at home, he knew that Anča would maintain the same sweet smile through all of it and that she would not even notice it.

He was a good man. He made no great claims on happiness; a faithful wife was enough for him, and it was not his fault that he had achieved a life with her that would have sufficed for the most sensitive and most eager of men, and which had come to him with superfluous elegance.

III

A late spring came, after a long, dreary winter, at the Lichnov hunting-lodge.

During the winter, Anča had spent entire evenings reading books, and used to look forward to that the whole day during her housework.

Snow was still lying at the hunting-lodge in April; the forests were raw and the lodge damp. But suddenly the sun came out, the snow thawed, the springs were brimming with water and the undergrowth burst into blossom. Anča's husband used often to go into the village to drink with the gentry and play Tarot.

She used to sleep with a loaded handgun over the bed, but did not usually fall asleep until morning, when her husband returned.

Spring finally came.

She thought she had never longed for it so much.

She walked through the liberated land, and said to herself:

'Youth, youth, the glory of life!'

She felt that she was stretching out her hands over it as if over the unstoppable current of a river, thinking that she would catch it in her fingers, whereas it was passing between them irrevocably, like water.

She saw her sister, a sweet little girl, with a handsome lad. They were in love with each other without being betrothed. Everything lay before them as a question that was entirely unanswerable. They loved each other as if they were themselves unaware of their love, and they were not spending their youth in consciousness of happy moments. They were squandering their happiness, the only happiness worth living for, as if they had recklessly denuded an entire garden by picking its roses.

The sun pierced intermittently through a breathless spring sky, sympathetically touching the beautiful young faces of the two lovers.

But they did not notice it, for they had no need even of the sun.

Anča said to them:

'Children, children!' – and, looking at them, she realized how remote she had become from her own youth.

'Life does not return,' she said to herself, 'and I have reached the end of my youth!'

She remembered driving along a distant road with drifting snow, through oak forests, with foliage like shrivelled silk, under a spring sky, young as if just awakened from sleep.

Something was lulling her to sleep and intoxicating her.

Her soul seemed to have been poured out all over the whole landscape.

But when she returned home, she was overcome with an incomprehensible, ravenous sensation of happiness and joy.

Something was impelling her to utter a cry of shattering despair, enough to awaken a God who was slumbering in boredom over the monotony of the world, and she would have been glad to press her lips to the cheek of someone dear, someone anonymous, someone unknown.

'If only someone strong, handsome, commanding, would embrace me now in this sunshine, in the glory of these fleeting sunny days, and drink my soul dry!' she prayed.

With eyes wide open she gazed around.

There was no one who would have kissed her, no one for whom she might been ardent. There was no one but the sun, which to her passionate longing itself seemed cold and faded.

In the evening she returned to her little room, with its back to the forests and its small windows facing the valley.

The windows had been open since morning.

She realized that, from the great silence that had descended from the unlit plain.

It was a bold, challenging silence of great distances.

Longings were fleeting through it and stirring her delicate, untouchable heart.

She leant out of the window. Her hair was brushing her cheeks, her lips quivering in anticipation.

She was not thinking of anything definite, she had no firmly delineated wishes and dreams; she was feeling only an all-embracing desire, ubiquitous in origin, resembling the waters of spring in its richness. She closed the window, lay down and slept. And the whole night long she dreamt a dream of defenceless danger, that she was kissing a most precious, intimate, beloved face, that she was covering it with her tears, and that she was pressing her own voracious cheeks to it. But she had never seen its features before; it was an unknown face, of someone never before seen, who was entering her dreams before entering her life.

IV

Her sister had become engaged. Her sister's bridegroom arranged a pre-wedding ball.

Filip and Anča were invited, and did not refuse.

The groom was clerk to a Jew, a millionaire, who owned an enormous forest estate that bordered on a princely estate.

The Jew was a worldly man with high connections in the circles of the nobility; he had a mansion in Vienna, and a villa in an old park outside the city. If he deigned to appear in the society of his officials, they imagined it as if he were descending to them from heaven.

Anča's future brother-in-law took courage and invited him, not of course expecting that he would come.

Whether from a whim, or by a chance that had prevented him making his intended journey to Vienna, or because he did not have enough to occupy him, Frank did attend.

The company stiffened, somehow, and fell silent after his entry. It was only those who were dancing who continued to enjoy themselves under the power of the music.

Frank stood at the door of the hall, and half-closing one eye, surveyed the youthful dancers indulgently and wearily. He was accompanied by one of his clerks.

Suddenly Frank's attention became focused.

'Who is that beautiful woman in the brown dress who has just been dancing in front of the mirror?' he asked, animatedly.

'It is the wife of Filip, the prince's gamekeeper,' answered the clerk.

'Introduce us to each other!' demanded Frank, curtly.

V

Half an hour later Anča and Frank were sitting and conversing on a bench among the flowers.

He was favouring her with admiring glances that were humble and at the same time insolent.

He managed to speak with both confidence and tact about her complexion of golden marble and about her seductively melting eyes. He was reading her face as a fortune-teller reads her cards. He was speaking with the assurance of men accustomed to make conquests by firm words, to impose their will by issuing orders:

'I'd like to see you on Friday. I'm leaving tomorrow and returning on Friday morning. Shall we meet on Friday?'

His words were so direct that she doubted whether they could be the words of a seducer, and afraid to enquire into what lay behind the sound of his words, she replied evasively:

'I have a great deal of work to do. I am usually very busy on Fridays!'

'I'll come to you on Friday!' he told her, inexorably gazing with his deep grey eyes at her cheeks, which were pale with astonishment.

She was breathing heavily.

'I'll introduce you to my sister! She's here at the ball – I'll call her. Allow me! She's eighteen years old. Pretty. Lively. She'll entertain you. I don't know what to say to you. I've only come here out of the forests so that I can see other people once again.'

'Young girls do not interest me. No young girl knows how to make love. The only woman who exists for me is a married woman.'

'I'll introduce you to my sister – I'll go and fetch her. She is fiery.'

He held her back.

'Why are you so restless?' he asked, devouring her with an experienced glance. 'Why are your hands trembling? Why do you claim that your sister is fiery? I'll tell you something. You are a hundred times more passionate than your sister – than that young girl. Confess it! You're blushing like a little thirteen-year-old girl! Have I guessed it? I have guessed it!'

'No, absolutely not – you are mistaken!' replied the virtuous woman in her.

'Ah, dear lady, beautiful lady, you will not deceive me. I understand people – I understand women. How many of them have passed through my hands – though I do not say through my heart! But I have acquired a kind of skill in making spiritual diagnoses about them. You sit before me, and you are thinking God knows what secrets to yourself. And meantime I am reading, from your unkissed lips, from your unadorned complexion, from your trembling fingers, from your insatiable eyes, that you are sitting here aflame, completely scorched by your own heat, that you merely lack the courage of your passion, that you are concealing everything with your smiling demeanour. And if I were now to tell you of great passion, of ardent lovers, of a world in which there is neither labour nor tedium, where there is only delight and intoxication, I know you would listen and devour my words, and ponder them for nights on end!

'Tiny kisses are trembling on your lips, kisses that you are not permitted, and do not wish, to give to anyone else, and when you return home, you will bestow a wreath of kisses on your sister, all around her face, with the tiny, promising, thirst-inducing kisses which you were longing to have been given yourself; you will touch her skin, not with the palm of your hand, not with your fingertips, but where the skin is most sensitive, with an upturned hand unused to the sensations that you would have wished, so that someone will caress you. I know you are listening greedily, and burning to your fingertips! At least admit that I have guessed correctly!'

'Not in the very least!' replied Anča, as forcefully as she could, with a suppressed laugh of embarrassment. Her mouth was uttering the words in all seriousness, a defensive, clear 'no', but immediately behind them, perhaps even at the same time, every inch of her flushed face was laughing, and her tender voice was ringing with laughter too. She hid her face in her handkerchief.

'Then why are you blushing?' repeated Frank, noticing how another blush was flooding over her countenance, how it was emerging even in the small uncovered places on her cheeks just where her newly grown brown hair was gently curling into two tiny ringlets.

He moved closer to her.

He did so without her noticing.

She moved away and rose from the bench.

'Why are you getting up?'

'There is not enough room for me.'

'Why? Why are you getting up?' he said brightly.

'I need more space!' she repeated.

'Ah, I know you are a decent lady – sit down! I shall be mannerly,' he said, suddenly sober, and he sat down.

They spoke about the ball, about the forests, about the wild game, and Anča told him about Andělka, the forester's wife, a woman punished for twofold infidelity, and beaten out of jealousy, about her hard-hearted husband who had taken vengeance on their innocent child, about their having barely held him back from suicide. They spoke about inconsequential people and matters, and both of them knew that nothing had been concluded – that presently they would return to the earlier conversation, indeed, that both of them were anxiously trembling, impatient to return to it. If all in this conversation had ended with talk of hunts, banquets, the kitchen staff of the nobility and the abused woman, with what desolation she would have returned to the wasteland that was her home!

Her face, animated with sin – with an indefinite longing for sin –, and her trembling fingers, gripping the back of the bench, spoke for her, and betrayed that she was not thinking about what the handsome Jew was asking her, about the guests whom the prince was inviting to the hunt, but about the trembling confusion of her dissatisfied inner being.

She answered him as precisely as she would have answered a teacher, or indeed the prince himself.

His swarthy, narrow, bold face and his fine nostrils were quivering with the expressive confidence of a handsome, mature, dark-haired man, aware of the power of his good looks, enchanting women at first glance with his combination of assurance and arrogance. His insolent eyes glowed with all the untamed aristocratic fire of the ardent southern race, to whom love is one of the most important, supreme, occupations of life, as honour, money, power and the other ambitions and vanities of life are to northerners.

To entertain her, Frank said:

'In an old tale about a Muslim who converted to Christianity, it is said: And the minister spoke to his king: "Fear not, we shall baptize that prince of Arabia. The Arabs are passionate worshippers of women, and love will accomplish more with them than if we were to pledge him power and wealth. I have a beautiful daughter, who will certainly incline him towards Christianity!" The minister was not mistaken. The Arab prince became a Christian.'

The young millionaire leant over towards Anča.

'That is what we Orientals are like! – Shall I see you on Friday?' he said, after a short pause, ardently, close up to her face.

She could smell the scent of his warm breath, the scent of a fine cigar, and a man's perfume that was somehow expressive and powerful.

His manicured fingers touched her wrist.

She heard footsteps. A couple from the town passed by, but he did not see them.

'I am going back into the hall. What will they think about me! Leave go of me – they are looking at us. My God!' said Anča, startled.

'So that is what you care about. That is what you care about, my pretty one! You only care about other people!' said Frank, delighted. 'Ah, I see now, we shall have something pleasant to enjoy together! I shall come to you on Friday. If you are the woman I think you are, the woman I am longing for, you will be at home on your own. And I shall come.'

Anča did not reply, nor did she look back, as we went into the hall.

Frank gazed after her, devouring her agile figure, filled with life, and her shoulders, pale as if of ivory, adorned with a shawl of autumnal gold; and from their slight, scarcely perceptible, but intoxicated, quiver, he knew that he would be permitted to come on Friday and that he would find her entirely alone.

VI

' . . . And music will be playing outside your windows every day, a fountain will be murmuring outside them at night, and I shall fill your chambers with the roses you love, the souvenir de la Malmaison . . .' promised Frank. 'You will never be upset – I shall never make you sad. You will not suffer coldness and boredom; my love is not like Christian love. My love is bright, sparkling and new every day. I would be ashamed to repeat today that I love you in the same words I used yesterday, and I could not offend you with silence. You do not wish to go with me – you are reluctant – but I know that you have been thinking about me the whole night; that you have been repeating every word of mine; that you are intoxicated with them!'

Anča was sitting delicately poised in one corner of the sofa in her living room, in a dress with light grey stripes, with her eyes fixed on her leg, which was swinging nervously.

A velvety shadow lay over her skin, and her moist dark eyes were tensely concentrating on what was unfolding deep within her. She raised a pale hand to her face, laying it down on the sofa in a motion that betrayed the pace of her thoughts.

'Dear one, pretty one,' said Frank to her, 'you have not yet lived; they have buried your grace and your beauty in this deaf, devouring solitude. I will show you the world, and I will show you to the world. I will not lock you away – I will boast of you! I will array you in the clothes of a queen – I will adorn your head and your neck with the most beautiful jewels . . .'

'And music will be playing outside my windows every day . . .' repeated Anča dreamily, and a sad, rueful smile passed over her lips. 'I have been listening to you quite long enough,' she said, 'but now you should go, pan Frank. I have no reply to you other than No, No, No, No, No! I shall remain where I have been planted. If I fade, I shall not have belonged to this realm. But I shall not defy my destiny!'

Frank smiled.

'And yet you were waiting, alone, for me at home!'

Anča shuddered.

She tried to lie and could not do so.

He regarded her with half-closed eyes and drew a loud breath of delight.

'How red your lips are! That is blood, it is not from mere exertion! – – – And what eyes! They are dark flames! And what little teeth you have! A person would love to be bitten with those!'

He was burning her up with every word.

'Your Christian husbands do not know what love is. They bore every woman with their selfishness. They cannot understand her with all her feelings. A connoisseur of wine is entirely taken up with it. He pours it into a glass, watches it pearl, raises it against the light, cannot have enough of its radiant colours; he never touches the rim of the glass in case he contaminates the fragrant bloom of the wine – its "Blume", flower, as the Germans call it – with anything else; then he tastes it, scarcely touching the rim of the glass with his lips, to cleanse his palate with it. A lover should behave like that too, and that is what lovers who belong to our race are like. Into every sphere of life we bring the ardent temperament of our wandering, spirited race! There are no lovers apart from us! Will you come with me?'

'No, I will not come,' replied Anča, forcefully and indignantly, 'you will not persuade me – I cannot! I will not come! Even if I am to die of boredom here, I will not come! Even if I am to be consumed with burning desire, I will not come. Even if I have to be burnt up with desire for kisses and for love! You have understood me well! Ah, if our husbands were able to notice how bored we are, they might either take infinitely more care of us or love us infinitely more! And now I have said more to you than I ever wanted to betray. So go away! Go! Go!'

Frank breathed out in intoxication.

Anča rose.

He held his hands out to her. She moved away to the window.

'My husband is returning. I can see him coming in the distance!' she said, with a victorious, embarrassed smile. 'So go, go!'

'When may I come again – when shall I see you?' he asked, almost in desperation. 'I must see you again!'

He stared at her with pleading eyes, and went out towards the door.

His delicate nostrils were quivering, and his entire ardent being was aflame over the space between them.

Their eyes, tortured with passion, met in a greedy gaze, and could not be separated.

He was already standing close to the door, his back against it.

'When may I come?'

'Never!' replied Anča.

Tenderly and sadly he opened his arms, and pleaded:

'At least then to say farewell!'

Anča threw her proud, dark head back, half-closed her eyes, dashed across the room, flung her arms around Frank's neck and kissed his fragrant lips – and also suddenly, in a moment, bit them. She let him go, turned away, and crossed the room, with her head deeply bowed.

Frank went out.

In the entrance hall he met Filip, the gamekeeper.

He was sure that the gamekeeper would not fail to see the bloodstained mark on his lip left by the teeth of his beautiful wife.

He hinted to Filip that he had been looking for him; and because he was in a hurry, and could not return, the gamekeeper hung up his gun and accompanied him to the carriage that was awaiting him below the mountain.

As they walked, Frank said:

'Have you never longed for money, for a great fortune?'

'Who wouldn't have! And today I think I shall win! I believe I am winning the first prize!' smiled the gamekeeper.

'You are to be envied for your beautiful wife!' said Frank, after a short pause.

This hurt Filip, but he made no answer.

Frank interpreted this as indifference, and asked, too boldly:

'Do you love her?'

'How should I not do so! After all, she is my wife!' replied the gamekeeper, with the directness and self-evident honesty of good, simple people.

'If I were to offer you a large sum of money, would you accept it?'

'What for, and why?' asked Filip, sullenly and suspiciously, and there was something grieving his naïve heart, something that was making his breast ache. 'Why would I accept money from you?'

'Don't be alarmed,' said Frank, throwing him into confusion. 'I don't want to bribe you to commit a crime, nor to cheat a prince. I shall be discussing it myself with the director. I would like to ask you merely to act as a mediator!'

Frank entered the carriage, carefully spread a cover over his knees, bowed with a smile and rode off.

Filip felt that he had been betrayed, and as he went up to the hunting lodge he thought he heard a cold chuckle behind him.

VII

Anča was smiling when he entered. She was smiling as expansively as ever, and greeted him with kind words in a pleasant voice.

'What was Frank doing here?' cried Filip, instead of greeting her.

'Looking for you!' replied his wife.

'And wasn't he rather looking for you, for you, my lovely wife?' exploded Filip, no longer with suspicion, but with a terrible, knowing sneer.

Anča turned away and said nothing.

Filip, one of the class of men whose love is stimulated by a woman only when they intend to murder her out of jealousy, put his gun to her heart, and said:

'My God, Anča, I'm going to have to kill you! If I find something out about you, I'll put this gun to your breast like this and pull the trigger!'

She stood against him, pale, with glistening eyes, motionless, and, barely moving her lips, said:

'Do so!'

If Filip had guessed what had happened at the ball during his rounds of Tarot, or what had occurred a little earlier in this room; if he had had any inkling of the newly awakened evil longings of his wife; he would have understood how much deep indifference to life, and particularly to life with him in the solitude of the hunting lodge, reposed in her words. But he did not realize this; it seemed to him that it was innocence that was speaking in this way, and he hung up his gun. He was silent and ruminated until the evening.

'My God, Anča, if only you were old enough not to attract anyone! Or I'll disfigure that face of yours!'

And she whispered:

'And music will be playing outside your windows every day . . .'

VIII

To the amazement and envy of all, Jindřich Frank promoted Anča's young brother-in-law and gave him an very expensive gift for his wedding.

He made the acquaintance of Anča's father, became a frequent guest in his house, invited him to visit him, and showered him and his family with gifts.

Through the good offices of her sister he sent Anča fruit and flowers; he sent her jewels hidden among the flowers.

Anča kept the flowers and returned the jewels.

Through her sister he sent her letters, that were daily more passionate and more importunate.

To them Anča replied:

'No, no, no, no!'

She did not move an inch outside the hunting lodge.

He wrote telling her how he was suffering – how he was grieving for her.

She did not reply.

He wrote telling her that he would shoot himself outside her windows.

She wrote to him:

'Please do not make my life difficult. It is not easy.'

A message came for her, sent through her maid, returning from town, that her mother had fallen seriously ill.

It was towards evening; her husband was out somewhere on the estate and not at home.

She veiled her face and went out.

Primroses were in bloom in all the meadows and valleys, and the grass was golden with little dandelions.

The earth was quivering in the pale sunlight of early spring, and all was bright with verdure.

It was twilight in spring.

Anča descended the hillside to the main road leading to her hometown. There was an hour's walk to it through the forest from the crossroads.

She was hurrying so as to get there before sunset.

She had made this journey countless times, joyfully and happily. Today she found it hard and fear-inducing. She was afraid on her mother's account. She knew she would not have been summoned unless the illness were serious.

She usually sang while walking home, but walked silently today.

She entered the forest, and could hear the blood coursing in her veins.

She was afraid, but dared not admit to herself what it was that she was afraid of.

The path, leading under a rocky outcrop and over a slope planted with young birch trees, was so full of bends that it was never possible to see more than thirty paces ahead.

Anča was so anxious that she could not breathe. Beyond the second bend she thought she could see a human being – a dark, motionless figure.

She was startled.

To turn back would be ridiculous and pointless.

She resolved to go on bravely.

She quickened her pace.

The figure was moving.

And what she had most feared, and what at the same time she had most fervently desired, came true.

Frank was waiting for her – handsome, dashing, darling, longed-for Frank.

She tried to avoid him.

He stood in her way, and, fixing her with an ardent, mournful, and gradually all-consuming gaze, he spoke of his great sorrow and his yet greater love for her in a faint, uncertain, tender, pleading voice. He told her that her mother was not ill at all, and that he had taken the liberty of deceiving her and luring her out. The charm of his radiant personality, exalted in love, of his warm, stimulating voice – all the mysterious enchantment that is exercised on human beings by the human voice, capable as it is of communicating the slightest tremor, of conveying pain or intoxication – all its sweet, tantalizing essence enveloped her being, bathing her as if in warm water saturated with intoxicating perfumes.

All that had been struggling within her in the previous weeks – her consciousness of duty, honour and strictness of life, against the terrible longing to forget, to cast everything away and to become drunk on a moment of love, to live, to live, so that life should not pass in vain, to burn in passionate involvement without reflection – all this was now engaged in battle within her once more.

Her greedy curiosity to see what such a life of heightened passion would look like in the world, in celebrations, in beauty, but chiefly in love, in ardent, humble and refined masculine love, drove her into the arms of Frank.

All in which she was rooted – tradition and her upbringing – was persuading her to stay, to utter her final, most definite 'no', to go on living her poor, grey, lonely life, its voluntary imprisonment, and its pointless, stubborn fidelity to someone who spent his time playing Tarot or drinking beer, and gave her neither tenderness nor affection nor loving glances, indeed not even gratitude for that fidelity.

Her fiery longings were enticing her, saying, 'And life will pass, and what will it profit you to have sat in a damp hunting-lodge, to have kept terrified watch the whole night long, ready to shoot poachers or burglars, to have dressed yourself up for the sake of the old fir trees, to have combed your hair and beautified yourself for the pine trees?'

She was thinking, was thinking, and the words of Frank were intoxicating her; now she was no longer listening to what he was saying, aware only of his sweet, flattering, caressing voice, with all her senses engaged. - - - - - - - -

'And music will be playing outside your windows every day!' spoke a voice, through the heavenly spheres.

'For whom are you living in that solitude? For whom are you burning there?' said Frank, with a kind of desperate agitation.

'What are you asking of me?' asked Anča, unable to escape from him. 'What are your intentions? What are you imagining?'

He outlined his proposal.

She should leave her husband, not return to him even that same day, seek a divorce from him so that he should have no rights over her, come with him, with Frank, and should be his wife – as if she were his wife, for such a liaison could not be legalized. He would introduce her to his family as his wife. He would never call her anything else. He would beg his old mother to give them her benediction. He would never love other women, and would never prove unfaithful to her.

Anča might well have had misgivings about what he was promising, but she was unwilling to harbour doubts;

she wanted to believe him, to believe every word many times over, to feed her hungry, lonely soul with all his promises, to satisfy her ravenous longing for life with them, for a beautiful, unknown, intense life that would be more colourful and more erotic every day, for a fiery, attentive, extraordinary lover. She believed him not out of naivety of heart, but because she sensed what a celebration of joy she might have spoiled if she had been unable to give him her complete trust.

IX

In the morning Filip, the gamekeeper, returned from the village tavern, where he had been playing Tarot and drinking. His wife was not at home, and he was told by the maid that she had gone to take care of her seriously ill mother. He had still not seen her at noon; when she was still absent even in the evening, he decided that he would go the next day to fetch her, and he set about doing this.

Among the gardens at the entrance to Anča's home town, he met a clerk he knew, who used to visit his wife's family. He stopped him and enquired about the health of his mother-in-law. Startled, in embarrassment, the clerk blurted out, 'Thank you! She is well!' – and, not expecting any further questions, he hurried off towards the forests.

Filip was unable to decide whether the clerk was insane, or whether misfortune had befallen Anča or her family. He felt that the clerk was not telling the truth, and that something was being concealed behind his timid behaviour.

A few minutes later, he met a uniformed servant from Frank's factories. The servant walked briskly up to him, bowed, gave him a letter, bowed once more, and disappeared around the corner of the street.

Filip thought that his young brother-in-law must be sending him news about events in the family.

He opened the letter, and read:

'When you read this letter, I shall be a hundred miles away from you. I shall never return to you, not on account of any rancour of yours, which you did not show, but on account of my own great selfishness . . .'

The letter was written in a woman's hand. He felt that someone had dealt him an unexpected blow to the heart. In his mind he seemed to be seeing stars.

He glanced at the letter.

'You have frozen every smile in me – all the warmth of life . . .' he read in one line, and 'Forgive me' in another.

An image of Frank loomed up in Filip's mind; he linked it with the image of his wife, and in bitter, poisonous understanding he guessed what had happened. The next moment, he refused to believe it.

He stood at the corner of the street; a young lady was looking at him from a window behind a flowerbed, and it seemed to him that she was laughing at him in foolish embarrassment. In an unpleasant moment of recognition it occurred dully to him that she was the tanner's daughter, 'and I must not remain standing here, for she knows what has happened, and the whole town knows! Even the clerk knew about it, and the maid too!'

He returned to the forests. His legs were heavy, and he lacked the will to command them. But despite the exertion, he tried to go faster and faster; and when he had gone out beyond the town walls and reached the first trees of the forest, he started running along the road, he dashed a few hundred paces, he turned off on to the first forest path, he leapt over a ditch and he fell into the brown leaves of the previous year. He was longing to hide like a wounded deer, not to reveal his grief to anyone, indeed to hide away from himself.

He lay long in the grass, biting into a dry branch to quell his sobbing, but tears were flowing from his eyes, running down his cheeks, and falling into the dry hornbeam leaves.

He wept, swooned, fainted, lost hope.

He remembered that he had not read the letter right through – perhaps he might find some word there of explanation and hope.

He rose. Though he still had his fingers on it, for a long time he could not find it. With trembling hands he took it out and read it.

Anča was asking him, piteously and contritely, for forgiveness. She was begging him not to mourn, and speaking to him in kind words. All this passed by as he quickly read it.

There was one part of the letter that struck him, and he returned to it: 'My joy dried up there. Everything that was an essential part of my being, and therefore my whole self, died. Do you believe that a nun, singing in worship to God in her contralto voice, like a sweet violin, would not fall silent if the heavens were suddenly to fall, and she were to realize *that God did not exist and that he had never been listening to her*? Are you capable of imagining that a human being should sing to someone who has never been listening? And I am convinced that even a creator God would have thrown his work aside, like a game of dominoes, if he had not succeeded in creating beings who could marvel at his perfection. I know that I have sinned, but I have sinned solely out of my great desolation of heart!'

Filip finished reading it, and his heart suddenly turned cold; his burning turned into a weighty bitterness.

Only a short time earlier, Anča had been part of his own self, a being inseparable from him, whom he had absorbed into himself over the years, whom he had loved almost in loving himself. Now he felt that she was an alien, hostile element in him, an illusion of his life, something that he had never absorbed, and that she was a betrayal of his inner self.

She had not been his beloved guest, she had been his enemy; and when she had left him, it had long since been reason, not emotion, that had been struggling in her. Indeed, he had long been harbouring a foreigner with a cold heart in his house, perishing 'up there'; his love, dumb, slight, primitive, but faithful and reliable, had not been enough for her, though it would have lasted, with the same tiny flame, through to old age. She did not want to drink life in tiny sips, but to drink it all in, to become drunk with it, all at once, as if with fine wine. All the forgotten and almost extinct feelings that he had experienced intermittently in his years of adolescence, feelings of burning sorrow, of loneliness and disillusion, reawakened and merged in a single great flame of anguish. He wept because he was feeling as alone as if there were no longer a single person left in the world, as if all humanity had become extinct. He had loved his wife as his inalienable possession, as a great, entirely dependable security, as he had imagined that a wife should be loved, and as his father had loved his mother, as his friends had loved their wives – with a mute, faithful, self-evident love without tender feelings, without confessions, without adornments or much talk – with a love without betrayal. And she had gone off with the Jew, for his millions. One day he will abandon her, cast her off, but he, her husband, will not then accept her back. No, even if she were to beg, and to die on the doorstep of the damp hunting lodge 'up there'.

He was burning at the thought, and yet, for a moment, was hopeful. A part of his brain was asserting that he would never, never accept her, and another was hoping that she might return, and that all should again be as it had been before; the latter possibility exhilarated him and gave him relief in these moments of despair.

He returned to the hunting lodge, but he did not have the courage to pass through her little room; he did not have the courage to enter the bedroom.

He went out into the forest again, wandered through the woods, forgot where he was going or what he wanted, returned home late that night, and lay down hungry on the black wax sofa under the antelope horns in his office.

He fell asleep from fatigue and faintness, with only half of his consciousness; the other half remained awake, meditating as if with rosary beads on the vicious circle of his new misery, his loneliness and his bitterness.

In the morning he awoke, frozen with the definite knowledge that Anča was not there, and in all the succeeding nights he was wakened by the sentences, seared into his memory in horror:

'She has left me! She has abandoned me!'

And all the following days were a seesaw of emotion for him, of the saddest love, of the most unambiguous condemnation, of wistfulness and rejection, of hope that she would return and of despair that she would never return.

He no longer spent time drinking, no longer played cards, and avoided company; but whenever he found he could not avoid meeting people, assured all those who had not asked him that although his wife had left him, this was a better outcome for both of them, indeed a far, far better outcome. But nevertheless he did not cease waiting for her, and when he returned from the forest, he nourished the belief that he would suddenly catch sight of her swaying in her white blouse and apron, with her hair carefully done, smiling and kind; and there were times when he wept before her image, and other times when he cursed her.

A year passed, but the lady did not return; the lady never returned again.

X

On a high terrace planted with clematis, in the shade of ancient trees on a bank of a quiet arm of a river, there stood a small single-storey rococo house with white shutters, with a roof in a somewhat Chinese style, with an external double staircase adorned with an elaborate lattice, and with chaste stucco decoration.

The French pavilion was the centre of a small French garden and a large park that had been left uncultivated for years and was deliberately little tended.

The old orchard was divided by the quiet river, filled with waterlilies, like a water garden, which could be crossed in a small boat; two high arched bridges connected its banks,

It was a lovely property, bought and laid out long, long ago for the mistress of a prince and abandoned for a century, and now it belonged to the millionaire Frank. After a great tour through the cities, spas and mountains of the world, the unmarried Frank husband and wife had returned to this isolated, quiet spot.

Anča could not stop smiling, for of Frank's promises, not a single one remained unfulfilled.

Indeed so: her rooms were filled with the pale 'souvenir de la Malmaison' roses, a fountain was murmuring all night long outside her windows, music was playing every day outside her windows, and she was not yet bored by her surfeit of happiness.

Frank went off to his factory and came back to her, astounded by her as if he was seeing her for the first time.

It was characteristic of his energetic, lively nature, which idolized life.

They spent some days in childish, playful happiness, others engaged in art, others again in thousands of kisses.

They were conscious of their moments of joy and multiplied and prolonged them, savouring them as something transient and irrecoverable.

Their mental worlds seemed to have been created so that one should pose a question and the other reply; that one should smile and the other be delighted; that they should be exchanging joy with one another and enriching one another.

At first, Anča could not call her first, deserted husband to mind without pain. She consoled herself by reflecting that because he had loved her very little, he had lost very little. I have conferred slight grief on him, but great joy on myself, she persuaded herself, and yet some of his gestures haunted her memories. In her mind's eye she saw him fold his arms at table, she seemed to hear the cadence of his rich forester's voice, she imagined her simple whitewashed rooms in the hunting lodge, the long winter and the eternal snow.

But even grief dies, uncultivated, as unwatered flowers do, and after six months Anča had consoled herself with the thought that things were better for him too – that he would be playing Tarot with his friends, that he would be going hunting, or that he would forget her in his work and in the society of his friends.

No word of him arrived from home, and she also avoided asking any questions. Frank never reminded her of him.

There was no past for her: there was only a sweet present, a warm, enhanced life in apartments fitted with Chinese silk of old gold, music, waterlilies, an ancient orchard, flowers in bloom – a beautiful world.

XI

The Franks were expecting a son; both of them believed very firmly that it would be a son.

Anča came home in her gold bonnet, inwardly radiant with her pregnancy; she would saunter through the spring garden in her robe of cambric muslin, and there were moments when she looked like a female saint. She seemed somehow illumined, in deep sunlight, by her life, and by what she was expecting – the enhancement, the multiplication and the deepening of her happiness.

However, there came a moment when they were standing around her bed, and she was no longer able to recognize anyone; when the famous physicians did not know how to keep her alive; when Frank would have sacrificed both his newborn sons for her life.

Anča's lips turned blue, and in some moments of artificially induced consciousness, a pale smile of gratitude and love lit them up like a ray of autumn sunshine, and this did not disappear even when she later passed away completely.

All the windows in the pavilion on the bank of the river of waterlilies were standing wide open.

It was spring once more – the anniversary of the spring that had roused her to life the previous year.

The valleys were full of primroses, and all the ridges were in bloom.

Anča was lying in a golden coffin in her yellow Chinese salon; the light of the candles was flickering over her face with its pale, grateful smile, and Frank knelt by her side all the remaining moments until she was taken out and buried.

XII

Months passed, and days rushed by. Anča's grave had long been adorned with 'souvenir de la Malmaison' roses. Everything in her pavilion remained unchanged as if she were still living and smiling there, the fountain still murmured outside her former greedy windows, and for the whole summer music was playing there every day as if the beautiful lady were living there – exactly as her lover had promised her.

And one evening soon after her death two men met by the gate of her orchard, almost unknown to one another, both in mourning, and they shook hands with one another in silence and now with no further recriminations.

THE DEATH OF OPHELIA

RŮŽENA JESENSKÁ

My son, my prayers have been answered! You are no mere fancy now – you exist, you are coming . . .

To you, my son, I write these lines – to you, my future life, to you, the immense fusion of my love, my passion, my tenderness and strength, to you, now conceived but as yet unborn, long alive in my will and my invincible longing, to you, who will utter aloud all that has remained locked in my soul because I am a woman, to you, who will grow up to the sun out of the twilight of my sweet melancholy; to you I write these lines so that you may be certain that you are hearing me, if I should pass away before I am able to open your heart to persuade you that your existence is necessary – that all I have experienced was only in order that you, you, should live, you whom I have summoned, you for whom Ophelia died.

Do I need to name you? Ah, my head soars to heaven in longing for the sweetest sounds that might be embodied in your name. I shall ponder over which name will be fit for you. But not today. Today I wish only to say to you that Ophelia has died. For the last time, now for the last time, she has adorned herself with flowers and breathed her unhinged sentences . . .

Ophelia has died.

Ah, how I loved art! I devoted almost my whole life to it, all my strength and my creative talent; I gave it my youth, the tempests of my passionate blood, my days and nights, passing unceasingly in struggles and adversity, in triumphs and in exhaustion, in eagerness and in disillusion, in joy and in tears . . .

But I confide to you that I thought of you continually, that I comforted you continually, believed in you, trusting that you would be the final great goal in life for me.

At the time when I was delirious with love for Ivan, I was already becoming aware of you in the fever of my dreams. Everything was for you . . .

In May I played Ophelia for the last time. Officially, I went off on vacation. No one – no one – knew that I was going to meet you, that I was going in pursuit of my *vision*, which I wanted to draw out to my heart from the infinity of dreams through my magic will, and kindle life in it.

I was acting, and the theatre was full. I received neither roses nor laurels, because no one realized that I was leaving. And I left! I bade farewell to the life I had been living, to art, to everything, so that I could proceed to the crossroads at which I was to await you.

No one could have understood where I was going . . .

So that you might know everything, my son: the beginning of beginnings, your origin the most secret!

After the theatre, I returned home. I could still hear the carriage when I was opening the door of the salon. It brought me home from the theatre for the last time. Ivan came out from his room to meet me.

'Ophelia!' he said.

It was in May. I happened to be wearing a thin white dress. And I was carrying some flowers. Red roses. I don't know who sent them to my dressing room.

When I first played Ophelia, years ago, many, many years ago, Ivan gave me red roses and kissed me inordinately . . .

I felt those kisses when I departed in May this year. I felt those kisses in my blood, when I went home for the last time as – Ophelia.

'Ophelia', repeated Ivan.

I offered him my lips and he kissed them.

And then the silent moon sailed through a very distant and gloomy sky, and I lay lonely and pensive, gazing into the empty night . . .

I was searching for you in those lights that appeared as if by a miracle over the pale curtains . . . I created a destiny that night, *your destiny*. I lived that night with great will. May the energy of that night be a beautiful inheritance for you. And I was very lonely.

*   *

'Ophelia died,' I said to Ivan, your father, the next morning, and I went out . . .

I had in mind his smile, with which he kissed me when I went out.

I went off into the roar of the city. Its bustle and its ubiquitous ornament were very striking because the sun was so bright. Even the movements of the people were somehow more provocative and pathetic; their sunshades were bright-coloured and their hats were full of flowers. I went on walking the streets until they had disappeared and I found myself somewhere outside Prague where I had never been before. It seemed to me that it was a great festival.

I was continually thinking of you. Not for a moment did I leave you. You were living in my heart . . .

I remember the date. May . . .

I don't understand and cannot discover the reasons why my husband resisted your arrival so stubbornly.

I refuted all those reasons, repeated a hundredfold . . . My art was supposed to have suffered – through you!

I don't believe that something made profound by you could only be raised to its full avid strength by the application of all knowledge of life. But if it be so, I will abandon art so that I may live *for you and you alone*.

My inner being, supposed to be softened, strange, excited, is not sufficiently insured against the disasters of the physical events that might happen to me for me to bring you into the world.

Are these fairy tales, do you think? Ah, how strong I am! I could lead you through the terrors of hell and of the bewitched regions in the vale of foolish tears that we call life, so that you could discern in yourself the reason for life and the purpose of death.

But I am hoping that I shall not die without bringing you up and giving you the sanctification of a great love.

It was May, and I went out for strength to the sun and to the flowers, because I believed that when I returned home, I could shake your hand . . .

*　　*

I was walking through an unknown avenue of fruit trees. Everything was in bloom. The trees seemed like wedding myrtles. So white, so white, intoxicatingly white. And music could be heard from the city, music both close by and distant. My heart was pounding . . .

*　　*

I returned home. I had never seen myself as clearly as I did that evening in the big mirror in the workroom. I was as beautiful as I had been on the eve of my wedding when I was walking with Ivan along the embankment. How I loved, loved Ivan! How dear he is to me today! . . . But today . . . He it was who gave me you! . . .

Bells were jangling . . . Oh, how the bells were ringing on that May night! I can still hear them. There was more in their song than a call to prayer: there was a call to love in them, to creative power, to the highest ecstasy that is given to human beings so that they may become the greatest according to their powers and their destiny.

In my heart I felt great humility as I sat with Ivan at table. He looked at me and I think he understood me. He saw my passion swell in stormy evenings in the mountains, in sunny days at the seashore, on quiet nights in Prague. He knew, and he merely hesitated.

That evening I said . . . 'I want to suffer, I have the will to suffer, we human beings are full of errors and shadows and we need repentance, we need to suffer. Anyone who only snatches at pleasure and never suffers will experience evil.'

I was afraid I was speaking rather affectedly, but I needed a stratagem to persuade him that your arrival was *necessary* and *inevitable*.

I am persuaded that he will greet you with joy; it is only that he did not wish to grasp your imminent existence. But he will love you unreservedly! He does not know you. And people are not able to love mysteries, chimeras, as they deserve. You are truly still a chimera to him. And I love you now indescribably. I love you with my life.

I said to Ivan that his love did not satisfy me. I confessed that to me out of my great love for you. Truly, it was a crisis. I said that I wanted, I wanted . . . The fatality of my energy – and somehow that is what he called it. He was still raising a hundred compelling objections against you.

But again I am excusing him: *he did not know you.*

I was mesmerized by fear: what if tomorrow, even tomorrow it should be too late and I should not find you in the darkness?

Ivan implored me to abandon my desires, saying it was a gamble with life.

I do not know why he was so concerned, but finally – a gamble with my life, yes, let my life be. After all I want *your life, your life*. And your life will be my life, even after my own life.

I shall bestow on you the best that is in me, every ability of mine will develop into creative force in you; I feel unambiguously that you are needed so that I may have meaning. That which I have created myself is a mere bubble compared to what a man created by me will create! Ivan has a spectral fear of your coming. Is that not pride, fearing his being overshadowed?

I am still continually speaking of that May evening.

We opened the windows to the garden. The night shone with millions of flowers and scents. In the darkness, yellow flames of lanterns trembled like burning tears over the heights and depths of the city.

The water roared.

We kept a strange silence. We lit the lamps, sat down at table, and extinguished them again. Music was heard again from a distance.

Ivan sighed, 'My Ophelia . . . my Ophelia!'

I smiled happily, and said, more quietly than he did, 'Ophelia has died.'

We sat in the darkness. I saw great stars between the curtains . . . and you, you, my son. And in *that glorious, great night, your life was conceived . . .*

*   *

I continued to look at the great stars between the curtains, until they faded, faded, and a white streak of light entered the bedroom . . .

I fell asleep in a prayer filled with faith. I invoked the mystery that surrounds us, that invisibly enters the blood of all creation and vegetation, and even touches stones and clods of earth, I invoked it, sovereign, unpredictable, that it should enter me and breathe into me a part of its miracle. And in that glorious, great night *your life was conceived.*

That is the history of your origin, my son! Now you are no longer a chimera, you exist, you will come. Let Desiderius be your name, you, longed for, you, desired! You were conceived in May, on the day of St Desiderius.

I wanted to shout out my joy to the whole world, and at the same time to hide it from all. Everything that once tormented me, the various trifles that irritated my pride and vanity, the injustices that humbled me, all the events that sparked my anger, all this disappeared. I am becoming a creator, and I am certain that I shall create a beautiful person, even if I contribute nothing to his upbringing – for I am filled with blissful beauty and love. My thoughts are as clear as if it were that day, and that night that followed, in which great stars were shining: I remember the best time of my life, the joy of my work and my art, the dear people whom I encountered; I forgive every evil in quiet forgetfulness, and I experience over and over again my great love for Ivan, who gave you to me.

And I am expecting you. My thoughts, gilded with love and memories, are at the same time expectation.

I love to sit at the window over the gardens, which are filled with songs and perfumes.

It's high summer, but we have stayed in Prague. I don't want to leave the place of expectation. I'm not longing for the wide horizons of the mountains, for my gaze is fixed further, beyond the most exposed regions of the world; I'm not longing for the silence of the forests with the music of trees and streams, for in my soul I have a flood of all delights. I close my eyes and I see everything that is most beautiful; I approach paradise in dreaming of you.

Ivan comes up quietly as if afraid of waking you . . . But your bed is still untouched, though something is already rising above the azure curtain that is moving softly, barely perceptibly, when I touch the white eiderdown . . .

Now Ivan is talking to me about you, and I sense from the tone of his voice that he already loves you.

*   *

The pains and torments that afflict me are beautiful, and I accept them as caresses of great kindness. And they are necessary if life is to maintain equilibrium and an exceptional series of ecstasies of pleasure. It is amazing how gladly I tolerate all the difficulties that are associated with your coming. And how impatient I used to me at the least illness, and irritable to the point of self-indulgence.

And I fear nothing. I would guide you through the abysses of terror and despair, my Desiderius . . .

*　　*

A long time has passed . . .

Ivan is full of worries and anxieties, but I am calm. I gaze into the gardens, which are cold and white, and I see in the blue, sparkling air your beautiful eyes and a smile that kisses me . . . I am amazed that I have lived my whole long life without you, without your significant, beloved presence. It occurs to me that it is only through you that I am becoming a happy, loving woman.

And a good human being . . . It was the beating of your heart that accomplished that. I listen to that strange, intimate, most beautiful music as a dream of immortality, as promises of eternal joy, Desiderius . . .

*　　*

I haven't written to you for a long time . . . Something vanished . . . Did something really *vanish*? I haven't written for a long time . . . I haven't dared to.

It's to you, my son, yes, to you that I write these lines – for I believe in my terrible love that you will hear them even if something has vanished from your presence. My Desiderius . . .

Ah, a day dawned, white, too bright, and suddenly everything went black. The last thing that remained firm before my eyes was the clock – I saw the horizontal black hands on its dial as if they were slicing a contorted white face with their shadow.

With those black hands, everything went black; the room was flooded with shadow, my eyes, my breast, my heart – – – And a terrible pain was choking me. There was a feeling of terrible choking as if the hands of that clock had been tied darkly and relentlessly into a cruel knot and were strangling my life together with yours, Desiderius . . .

But you came, my son, you lived. I heard your cry; I shall not forget your voice. You lived . . . And that is a consolation to me in my sorrow, now that you are dead.

I died with you; I lay cold, motionless and indifferent, like a stone. And finally I again saw the face of the clock; its hands were both raised to heaven like clasped hands . . . Bells were ringing outside.

I pronounced your name . . . And Ivan emerged from the gloom of the bedroom. My dear Ivan! He seized my hand and kissed it . . . And in the warmth of his grief he silently kissed my brow and my hair. I understood that he had felt much pain, and it seemed to me that I could feel those kisses even in the gloom.

I looked at him . . . In his eyes I could discern unease and fear . . .

But I knew you were dead, Desiderius. I realized that in a single moment of grief – when your cry fell silent and was not repeated.

'But he lived, he really lived?' I asked Ivan.

'He lived, indeed he lived,' he repeated tenderly.

'Where is he?' I asked.

'He is buried . . .' And, anxiously, he added, 'But you, you have been kept for me.'

I smiled. I know that I smiled, but he misinterpreted my smile . . .

Tears sprang forth . . . tears so warm and relieving.

Through my tears I looked at Ivan, Desiderius. How Ivan had aged in the few days of that time, your poor father!

Your bed is empty. The blue curtain hangs motionless against the white eiderdown.

For a long time I lay listless. And I have been thinking about your return. But I have not been expressing my hopes . . .

I took hold of your father's hand and observed his pulse, and I thought it was the music of your heart.

You lived, Desiderius, and you will return so that you will live once again.

* *

My fainting departed, pierced by spasms of grief.

'You've returned to me, from halfway to the other world,' said Ivan, when we went to the cemetery for you for the first time.

I know my face is faded, my eyes are sunken, my smile is frozen, my hair has lost its sheen; and I also know I have lost my strength.

'I need to recover – I'm longing for that,' I replied . . .

He did not understand the reason for that wish. He pressed my hand feverishly. The car was filled with flowers – violets, roses, freesias, narcissi, lily of the valley, daffodils, forget-me-nots.

I don't know which you like most. I took all of them.

It's March. It seemed to me that I hadn't been out of doors for a year – that it was a long time since I had seen crowds of people or heard the chatter of the city.

When we alighted from the car, I shivered, leaning on your father's arm. He noticed it. 'We have a son,' I said with a smile, which I wanted to give him as a reward for his love and care.

His face is a mirror of my unhappiness . . .

We arrived at our family tomb, at the future abode of all of us . . . For the first time I read your name engraved in gold on the black marble: *Desiderius*.

Look, my name and also Ivan's name, your parents' names, will be written there too . . .

And years later the name of another too . . . Whose name then?

Ah, why did I conjure up a fairy tale at your grave, my son . . . It was the whole course of a life renewed.

*   *

Ivan has taken me away to the seaside. I have recovered completely. No one understands my longing for you and my love for you as does the sea. I sit on the white sand the whole day and look at the blue shimmer of a distant space. My thoughts escape me, my griefs are lost like the mist that enveloped my soul, and I am left only with a heart with great longing for you.

Sometimes I feel like a tree that rises towards the sun from the ground, so that it may envelop itself in blossom and bear fruit. Ivan approaches and strokes my hands, and everything glows with joy that I am again fresh, bright and at peace.

Today he sat beside me. Fishermen were drying their nets nearby, and white sailing boats were approaching the shore. The sea was the colour of the moss that covers the ground in our forests, where a ray of sunlight seldom falls. And it was as still as a sheet of glass; only its shades of colour were changing.

We stayed silent for a long time.

Finally I said, very quietly, though my voice was trembling:

'If only Desiderius would return!'

'There is no return from there,' said Ivan, shaking his head, and he went on very quickly, virtually gasping.

'He lived a short time, maybe an hour, except that it wasn't even an hour. Today we are mourning his passing, but in a century's time, won't it be immaterial whether he lived a second or for twenty or eighty years? And then – life is grief; comfort yourself with the thought that with his life a chain of sorrows might have been awakened.'

Ah, my husband began to philosophize!

'Don't you think it would be better if humanity were to die out?' I said cheerfully.

'It probably won't happen,' he laughed, and added, seriously, 'But let us accept the size of the sea, breathe in its peace that touches us as if with mysterious invisible wings – and let us become calm forever.'

I said quietly, 'The sea is truly miraculous; it heals wounds, it quietens lamentation – *it restores courage – and it multiplies longings.*'

Laughing children in white and red dresses, with bare knees, ran up to us from the top of the groups of baskets.

'How pretty and happy they are,' I cried.

Ivan took me to supper and was very talkative. I know why he was like that. But in spite of all his sincere efforts, he was unable to purge that longing, that you should return, our son, from my soul.

*　　*

The sea is getting rough and towards evening is very stormy. It suits me. My soul is seething with passions too. My blood is calling for you.

It will not stop until you return. I am walking alone on the beach, calling you aloud.

No one hears me. But I am heard by – the air, the sea, the sun, the mystery . . .

I feel some magical return of youth. And that is you, Desiderius . . . Now you are returning in the mystery of my blood. Ah, swans were flying over my head today. I followed them until they fell. Today a dark young fisherman came ashore, and he had nets full of fish with gold spots. Today I found amber, like a shining teardrop, in the sand. Today

Ivan brought me a tame grey parrot that he had bought in a fisherman's hut. What pleasure it will bring you, Desiderius! Today is so incomprehensibly pleasant, except that you are absent everywhere . . .

Ivan is saddened that this great longing has overwhelmed me. Truly, *overwhelmed* me. Nothing calms it; nothing tames it.

* *

While the sea was raging yesterday evening, I wept with it. Ivan had to clasp me in a firm embrace, or I would have flung myself into the dark abyss of the shrieking waves. O God, I distinctly saw your eyes there, sparkling blue and sad, as if enticing me . . .

And today the sea is again quiet and smooth, like mysterious, gloomy velvet. And I am lying on the sand, tears course at times from my eyes, and again I am calling, I am calling you.

Ivan is alarmed about me. He suffers and laments that he is losing me. But all his logical arguments fall into my soul as if into the bottom of the sea. And above all my burning longing for you remains victorious.

'You're crazy,' said Ivan today. And he kissed me dreadfully.

O God, his will-power and his philosophizing – how in vain it all is.

We proceed . . . But it seems to me that I am ahead of him. The sea is quiet and smooth like mysterious azure velvet . . .

How flatteringly today kissed my body! And when I closed my eyes, it seemed to me it was carrying me to you . . .

* *

I am living days of strange giddiness. I had the definite impression that you escaped from me on the waves into places unreachable by human power, but suddenly you distinctly appeared close to my sight in today's pinkish twilight. I held out my hands to you. Ivan has comprehended the inevitability of your existence. He knelt down. I have never seen him so pale and excited. Your father was weeping, lowering his head into my lap.

*   *

We are back in Bohemia. Nothing is more beautiful than to return from the seaside to our forests, to our pathways and dividing ridges, where we used to meet and love long ago, where we know every forest path in the colours of dawn, every dike covered in bluebells and pinks.

And to have the full spirit of the sea and of its wide horizons, of its passion and of its calm!

Never in my entire life have I been as happy as I am now. Never. My son, you are returning to me! You were conceived by the sea – and you are being made flesh in my blood in the magical chambers of the forests and groves silenced in the stillness of anticipation, through which only the breath of the leaves and of the wings and of the invisible spirits is to be heard.

Never have I imbibed the beauty of the earth and of the horizon as I do now. I walk, and I accept it.

For you I accept the kisses of this beauty. Ivan and I wander through the forests and are seated on the moss. I wait to hear the music of your heart. Your first greeting.

I see you tiny, like a little angel, I surround you with playthings, I see you grown up among your books, meditating on the first mysteries of life, I see you beginning to grieve with the longings of youth and thrilled with love, I paint a tender, blossoming image of a girl beside your image.

The kisses Ivan breathes on my brow multiply in the future into thousands of immortal gifts in your children, Desiderius . . .

It was necessary to return to Prague. The mists were drawn aside like curtains of melancholy. It is pleasant in Prague. Mist, twilight and even nights are filled with lights in the heavens and also on the earth.

And an intimate, most beautiful music calms all my sorrows and raises me from all my fainting, like a dream of immortality, like a promise of eternal bliss: the beating of your heart.

*   *

Yes, there is something I fear: not grief, not struggle, not the terrors of those convulsions – but my face, my own face.

I gaze long into the mirror, and I remember the image of Ophelia. I am not like her now. My countenance has taken on the colour of clay. Something fearful is in my face. My eyes are sunken as if they had looked into some unplumbable abyss. I am not grieving the loss of my beauty, but I am afraid of its image. It is as if someone alien has appeared there in the mirror, someone who desires to harm me.

The doctor is paying regular visits to us, and he is talking about the theatre. Today I told him that Ophelia has died, and you will not summon her back to life. I want to think and speak only of you, and prepare the way into the world for you, Desiderius.

I want to hear advice, and to be faithful to every suggestion, so that you should reach the place to which I am calling you, and become that with which you live in my dreams.

This evening I went outside, veiled, the last time before your arrival. I do not want people to catch sight of me now. I went into church. No one saw me or heard me . . . Only the Unknown. The Mystery.

*   *

O Desiderius. My soul is sorrowful unto death . . . Something dreadful has occurred.

I was lying on the sofa in the bedroom. Ivan came in and said, 'Don't be alarmed, darling. The doctor is here. We'll have a cigarette together and then we'll come through to you.'

'I'm dozing,' I said numbly.

There was no sound. Only the parrot, your grey parrot, laughed intermittently.

I got up. I don't know why I got up and went into the salon . . . Their conversation could be heard from Ivan's room . . .

Oh, why did I go into the salon! I seated myself in the rocking chair . . . I overheard some strange words . . . They were talking about *me*. I strained to hear . . .

Now then, I know Ivan is full of worry about me, but is the doctor too? Yes, really – he is too . . . I was ashamed of everything. From their alarming words, I discovered my fate.

Word after word determined my inevitable end . . . I was mortally tired and I would not survive your birth. I would not live to see your arrival, you longed for, you beloved.

The doctor was speaking like a judge, and I was being condemned. Ivan groaned a few times and was speaking as if he were choking.

I was choking too. My blood ran cold and my heart was pounding, ah, pounding – it was a wonder it did not drown out the sweet speech of your dear heart.

And then – what followed then was worse than everything that had preceded it. I would renounce that happiness – being reunited with you, the joy in seeing your life, your maturing and your development – for the knowledge that you will live as I have desired. O God, for I have survived my own life, and could depart on the threshold of your life. I have fixed my eyes on it from a distance – the sunny perspective of your age has shed clear light on me like the most real, the most acute presence.

O Desiderius . . . But they were saying something about you there. I did not fully understand; my senses had failed me. But they said something about you, that your coming would mean *both your death and mine*.

I don't know, perhaps I misunderstood.

I recovered from my faint. The doctor picked me up. Ivan knelt in front of me.

They placed me on the couch.

I looked at them. I did not tell them what I had heard, but they guessed it. And both of them started speaking strangely, amassing an abundance of hope and joy before me, so as to confuse and adroitly overturn what I had overheard, and to erase the terrible impression. I remained, and remain, silent. I merely gaze into a void where there are neither colours nor stars.

I wanted to go outside once more, but it was now impossible. So I sent for a goldsmith, and sold him all my jewels. Ivan took the money away. He knows poor young men whom it will benefit. With it I am bribing Providence to accede with some generosity to my prayers for your life . . .

Once more I am beginning to believe in your life and I am ceasing to lament my own premature departure. Ivan swore to me that if a single sacrifice were needed, he would sacrifice me for you. Besides, Ivan promises me that all will end well, and the doctor endorses that. But I do not believe them.

I sense that at the moment that you awake, my life will be enveloped in deep darkness. I am departing, Desiderius, but I believe *in your coming, in your life and in its continuation* . . .

I sense that you live, and that you will not cease living until I die. That is infallible and certain. I arrive at this faith through my own will. *I shall give you life.* I rise above pain, I soar above faints, I find strength in weakness, until I rise to mortal combat in the knowledge that I *give you life*.

I see afar off.

O my Desiderius, I am setting my life within your heart; I am giving you the strength of love and the power of beauty as an inheritance. First you will gladden your father, and later the heart that you will choose for yourself. Me, your mother, you have already gladdened before the gates of life . . .

*   *

Epilogue

She gazed with melancholic eyes into the white radiance of the dream that died together with her.

Spectrally beautiful was her passion, which had over-whelmed her with its invincible, destructive force. Her tragedy burned like a yellow wax candle over her extinct dream of the future, not in her death, but in her dreadful longing.

A TRUTHFUL TALE OF A STONE STATUE

RŮŽENA JESENSKÁ

An offshoot of a tiny street, curled as if ready for an embrace – and in its last house, high under a sloping roof, Hippolytus opened the window for the first time. And what he saw, what he saw! Distant, intricate gardens, full of almond blossom and green paths disappearing from view . . . And little houses, palaces as if from fairy tales, and towers. Towers as if carved from turquoise, close by, and beautiful. He closed his eyes and saw everything as if in a dream. And again he looked. That Baroque house opposite – how it sinks in the yellow lights of evening! At one of the windows a pretty girl is examining an alpine violet in a pot; see how she plays the coquette a little, smiles, has lovely blue eyes. She has disappeared again, but has appeared again after a while as if emerging from a cloud. Laughing whimsically, she is feeding pigeons with rounded greenish fantails.

Hippolytus was pleased with his new apartment. Somewhere in the third house there is someone always playing an old, whispering spinet in the evenings, quietly and longingly, and breathing, rather than singing, a song, always the same, forever the same. It begins, 'Twilight promises golden stars . . .'

From the windows opposite, Hippolytus was soon observed, pale, almost as white as chalk, with a long, protruding nose, and dark, searching eyes, with hair as black as Japanese lacquer, with a white parting in the middle. He was standing at the window, as if seeking, desiring, something.

One day, as it was growing dark as if behind thick cypress trees, Hippolytus saw a new, hitherto unseen shadow in a window opposite, in a different apartment again. It twinkled enchantingly near the light and was then lost somewhere in a black stain of darkness as if behind a curtain.

It was something that was excessively beautiful. Hippolytus stood and waited. The next day, the shadow finally became clear: an unknown girl approached the window, with narrow, elongated eyes, and long, flowing hair, braided in plaits of the colour of old gold. Her gaze wandered towards Hippolytus, and remained fixed there.

That single gaze was enough for them to understand that they had long been searching for one another. The clouds raced over the roofs, and the two of them gazed at one another as if enchanted. Hippolytus recovered himself, placed a vase of narcissi at the window, and bowed to the girl opposite as if he were at a ball. She smiled and waved. And so they became acquainted, and conjoined as if on a whim.

She would wear a lovely soft, silken, flowing robe full of pleats and seductive folds, and would look at Hippolytus as if she were calling to him.

Once he met her on the street accompanied by a dignified matron; a gold coach with an archbishop rattled by from the palace to the white castle of the king, and crowds of old women and inquisitive children rippled with the motion of the noble vehicle as if they were its retinue – and there, somewhere under the wrestling giants at the castle gate, she stood, smiling, silent, and close by.

Hippolytus thought how strange it would be if he should say something to her, or if she herself were to say something. Would he survive the touch of her hand? Her lips? He was extremely agitated by her distant gaze, the declaration of love in her eyes. He greeted her courteously and went down to his home – – His dearest, faithful love! What transports of delight she afforded him!

She seated herself in her chair, clung to the heavy Indian upholstery, gazed at him in devotion and offered him her lips. Her lips glistened with blood as if with jewels. Hippolytus sensed their moistness and passion through the blue space of the air.

Something ridiculous occurred to him: to write, on a glass plate, or, better expressed, in the air with his finger, a declaration of his love to her, just words, then, words, which he held in contempt, regarding them as ridiculous and superfluous.

'I have sought you and have found you; I love you, star of the twilight of my life.'

She replied to him in tender, very slow lettering on the glass, 'My chosen one . . .'

He straightened up in immense joy and pressed his hand to his heart.

And he wrote, 'My name is Hippolytus, and what is yours?'

'Irena.'

'Irena!' he whispered, closing his eyes in dizziness, and, with an expression of great bliss, he wrote, 'O enigmatic joy, I touch you, and I accept the radiance of your lips, your eyes, your breasts . . .'

A pause after each word was filled with passionate gestures.

Impassioned, Irena answered, 'I wish to be your eternal light.'

'O Irena, wellspring of my life, my heart is making its confession, and it devotes itself to you.'

'O Hippolytus, I hear its song, and I understand and embrace it.'

'I am joined with you in the bliss of superconscious pleasure.'

'We two are one, mystically inseparable, in life and in death.'

A long silence, filled with ecstasy.

He disappeared from the window, and the girl lay on the chair, half swooning. Her satin dress, grey with pink carnations, lay languidly over the floor, and her hair gleamed like gold.

Once, neighbouring ladies were standing by their windows, watching Hippolytus; elsewhere neighbouring ladies were standing by their windows, watching the beautiful lady. And they were greatly diverted by it. Birds were flying from branches to the window ledges, laughing mischievously; little clouds were sailing by, with a smile on their white wings; the stone maidens on the houses on both sides were exchanging places and attitudes. Their lips were contorted with laughter; their eyes were moving to and fro; and their gestures were very lively.

So Hippolytus and Irena loved each other through the air; they trembled with desire, glowed in ecstasy; it is a wonder that they did not die in convulsions. And they were very happy. He stood by the window and wrote on the glass: he wrote at virtuosic speed and received answers full of ardour. The trees were flowering, and the birds building nests.

Irena wrote, 'I wish only to be with you forever. Nothing else holds my interest any longer. I shall not leave.'

And one fine morning she had her bed moved close to the window; she lay down on it in strange pleasure and now no longer rose from it. The bed was of gold bars and was all lacework, embroidery and ribbons. And there she lay like a female saint in a transport of love.

In increasing fervour, Hippolytus became daily paler and more translucent; he too did not go out, standing at the window, writing in the air, inclining his head, blowing kisses, lighting green, red and blue lamps in the shadow of his room, placing ever new flowers in vases, and kneeling long at the open window as if before an altar. And when he smiled, his thin lips exposed two rows of large white teeth, making him appear like a walking skeleton.

Irena had a pale, sweetly tormented face and a bright smile, full of enchanting promise. She yielded to him passionately, like a cloud to the winds, like a seashell to the boundless sea.

'I am dying', she wrote once at the close of day, with her thin white finger.

'I shall die with you,' answered Hippolytus. He brought red roses and placed them in the window; he kissed them and raised his head once more.

'Yes, I thank you, I sense their fragrance and, with them, your kisses.'

'I desire your lips.'

'Kiss them,' she replied.

He half-closed his eyes and accepted her lips through the distance.

The neighbouring ladies laughed heartily, enjoying themselves as if at a theatre. But though they might have wept in a theatre, they laughed at home, and that was the advantage of their rare enjoyment.

The sparrows were chirping; the sun was entering intrusively into every crevice of the apartments. And the scents of the flowers in the windows on both sides were merging.

The clouds were racing very quickly, carrying the songs of the festivities from the towers.

Hippolytus and Irena saw no one but each other.

A melancholic student, who lived in a garret room high in an attic, saw both of them – Hippolytus in one window, Irena in the other, and he saw many towers, the river, and the bank of flowers.

To himself he said, seriously, 'Every human being should live this way. Whether is it a farce or a drama, always to the full, and without embarrassment, taking no account of windows, doors, dark corners of any type, walls that are dead, in which prying eyes and ears skulk.' He was a very romantic lad.

Day by day, Irena became paler and paler. Occasionally someone obscured the window with curtains, and the fair Irena became invisible, disappearing like the moon in the clouds. But the window was revealed once more, and Hippolytus, waiting faithfully, spied his beloved.

One evening, his lovesick hands stretched out a great distance, but nevertheless they could not reach the windows opposite.

It was night. What a night it was! Even colours became perceptible in its bright whiteness. The castle was shining as if carved from marble; the towers, marked out as if in silver, rose towards the wisdom of Space; scattered lights with extended, flickering rays lingered in the heights and also in the depths of the city.

Irena was again alone in her chamber. Hippolytus looked at her, continually looked at her, as if he were growing into her. Her eyes were open, and she waved her hand as if she wished to bid him farewell. She did not raise her head, and did not smile as she usually did.

Hippolytus leant out of the window towards her, throwing red roses into the translucent darkness.

But Irena remained somehow motionless, fearfully motionless.

A bluish light shone on her head, bringing her open, motionless eyes, resolutely fixed on Hippolytus, close to him – – –

With a cry, Hippolytus fell to the floor in a terrible transport of love. And for a long, long time he did not waken – –

And when he recovered, he saw something unexpected. The chamber opposite was adorned with black draperies, and Irena was lying by the window in a glass coffin, cold and white; large green emeralds were gleaming on her breast, and her golden tresses were glistening, flowing over the satin of her robe.

What breathtaking beauty! She sleeps under the glass lid of the coffin as if in the waves of the ocean!

He leant out of the window and gazed, horror-struck, at his dead lover.

The neighbourhood ladies were also watching, and were greatly amazed.

The air was full of sunlight during the day and full of moonlight during the night.

Hippolytus placed large bunches of passion-flowers in bloom by the window, and lit the yellow candle in the room, that had once burned at the head of his late mother, with a memorial wreath.

Barely audible songs were floating in the air, and they left no echoes. And death-knells were falling like nocturnal butterflies from the nearby towers. And Hippolytus was standing, standing . . . motionless; and he was gazing, horror-struck, at his dead lover.

The moon was shining very brightly.

Pale and cold, in invincible longing, Hippolytus crept out of the window and sat on the wide window-ledge beside the old grey statue which had a hand outstretched towards the house opposite. Ah, how close Hippolytus was to his lover! And how those statues were empathizing with him!

The night chill overcame him, and the silver of the light poured over him. He leant against the grey ledge, stretching his head forward as far as possible so that his closeness to the dead woman might be yet closer . . .

Just so, in that pose of an absolute surrender to the immobility that was personified in the beloved dead Irena in the window opposite, the gloomy youth from his dormer above spied Hippolytus through his window. Astonished, he gazed long, long; he was unable to understand what was beyond the world, and beyond life – until the light changed, and white mists descended like veils on to the grass. The clock struck, and somewhere bells rang briefly and then fell silent . . .

And when grey dawn broke, that student high up realized in amazement that a statue had been added to the garden of the Baroque house, a real statue, as if the grief of love had become embodied in stone. Quickly he went down and examined the new statue – he readily recognized in it the man, that well-known man, who, turned into stone, his hand on his heart, is gazing with an expression of immense love into the open window where his beloved is lying in a glass coffin, surrounded by burning candles . . .

Dawn broke. And the neighbouring ladies also rose from their beds, and neighbouring ladies from the whole street ran – to the lover turned into stone, that lover who had entertained them so much while he was alive. There was much talk and deliberation, but it was certain that pale Hippolytus had turned into stone, and that he sits there to this very day, his hand on his heart, his head stretched out into the void, on the ledge of the old house above the homely almond orchard.

Irena has long been buried under a granite tombstone, on which lily wreaths often wither. And, turned into stone, Hippolytus, her adoring lover, is continually gazing into her inaccessible chamber of love . . . long deserted.

And lovers, who are accustomed to wander below the blossoming branches of the orchard, like to point out the old, welcoming statue, overgrown with moss, with its smile of melancholic happiness.

THE CHILD

LILA BUBELOVÁ

It is silent in the wards, only now and then
a footstep rustles and a dark shadow passes,
as a nursing sister walks quietly in the corridors.
And outside the sun is shining, it is spring,
and birdsong is heard through the windows.
Now fifteen minutes are past, it is the end of visiting,
the doors are closed on the waiting rooms,
where one may linger, who came to encourage.
A human sound was heard among the birdsong –
a doctor whistled, almost like another bird,
hurried upstairs and whistled again,
and went to the 'Spiegel'.[1] In that there were floating
shapeless rags in a pail of blood,
a wad of cotton wool and a piece of human flesh,
and streams of water mixed with blood
were coursing in the centre to the drain.
And at the window – as if a grotesque elf
were hiding in a bottle – so there in the alcohol
is submerged a human embryo –
left after the most recent abortion –
and it grins strangely, perhaps at the bottle
in which permanganate is dissolved in a red liquid,
perhaps at the bottle partly filled with lysol,
and at the sizeable pile of tampons,
and at the boxes with mercury ointment,
or at the garden drenched in sunlight,
or at the song of the birds, if that is preserved in alcohol.
All this the doctor saw in an instant,
he threw his white coat on to the iron table;

1 'Spiegel' ('špígl'), i.e. speculum, not here in the usual sense of a small surgi-
cal instrument used to dilate the vagina for the purposes of examination, but
referring to a specialist section of a gynaecological ward in a hospital.

even his footrest was drenched with blood,
as it ran down over his rubber coat.
Then he shouted into the corridor, 'Sister, bring the little
one here!'
At that shout it was as if something had been torn asunder,
a doorhandle clicked somewhere, and instantly a terrible
shriek
echoed through the building. 'Leave me alone!'
That resounded in the staircases and faded,
and echoed again in the brightly lit room;
and you could hardly understand and discern
that it was a human voice – and a child's voice.
And the sister brought the creature to the 'Spiegel'.
So the child swayed about in her hands,
hardly able to walk; she placed it on the table,
that child, hardly older than six years,
here, on this table on which prostitutes
and pregnant women had been lying, which gave them aid.
And to terrible screams from the child
the doctor treated the many wounds
that now covered the entire tiny, scrawny, little body
so that it was almost broken apart.
Then, fatigued and half unconscious,
the child was carried by the sister to the bed.
Then turning around, she heard a conversation –
somewhere from the room, eyes were gazing,
so appalled, and half inquisitive.
She went over there. 'Sister, is it the Cross,
that it screams so –?' 'No, don't be surprised,
for it's terrible, as you can see!
See, I heard today for the first time
what terrible things actually happened to the child.
One of the visitors came to the ward,
a lady who lives next to her mother.
That mother – do you realize – of that child

sold her, she said this in so many words,
and is said to have received five gulden, can you believe it?
from the guardian of this child,
and is said to have held her mouth shut
when the man raped her. She was six years old.
And that guardian is a syphilitic,
and he has infected the child.
All that was told me by the neighbour,
who said she had heard and seen it too –
what do you say? – and that girl
is a terrible creature – she said, "You whore!",
when I first took her to the doctor!'
O child, child, a terrible reproach,
and horror of horrors – don't you realize that
you must speak respectfully to Sister?

A THORNY QUESTION

MARIE MAJEROVÁ

We were reminiscing on All Souls' Day about all those who had passed on from us that year; we talked for a while about Markéta B., whom he knew better than I did – although I too had been at her funeral as a female acquaintance, and I remember that many things at that time had interested and astonished me. And he told me the story:

'The inflexible appearance of her husband must certainly have struck you. Everyone was speaking about it, and everyone was sorry for him, attributing the stony expression of his face to his immense agony. One speaks of the limit of pain; if anyone had reached it, he was certainly that person, so people judged. He stood above the grave dismissively and sullenly. He spoke to no one; he answered no one, not even responding to the expressions of sympathy flowing from hearts that were certainly sincerely moved. They were not offended, but withdrew silently and respected his great pain. The reality was so terrible and so inexplicable. It was generally known, both through word of mouth and through newspaper reports, that his young wife, an assistant art teacher at a high school, had shot herself for no reason just at the time when he was first on leave in Prague after many months spent in the field.

'A domestic tragedy of this sort usually carries in its wake various secondary stories and amplifications – all kinds of confidential whispered explanations; but there was nothing of the sort here. Neither the most trustworthy of her confidantes, nor any of her (perhaps once rejected) former admirers was able to satisfy the insistently curious with the slightest word. And so it happened that after many conjectures, and much floundering in the dark, all the mourners stood there silently, and, surprisingly, not a little disappointed: the fellow students of the deceased, her office colleagues, her pupils – all in tears, carrying flowers; and then his own friends from the town, and also some men from a marching regiment located by chance in Prague. There were many flowers – as many as can be borne only by sensitive ladies stimulated by romantic circumstances, and captivated by a mysterious tragedy of a young creature of their own gender. Everything was filled with the scent of roses, of tantalizingly sweet late autumn violets, of carnations, and of lilies of the valley grown in hothouses. The flowers were exquisite, but they were wilting, somehow too quickly, in the chilly breeze, and the astringent bath of mist was assuredly failing to revive them. I watched the blooms fall into the yellow clay during the intermittent sobbing and weeping of those who had brought them; all the flowers were from strangers, and none at all from her relatives. He had not brought a single flower himself; the deceased lady had neither mother nor siblings; her aunts were obviously ashamed of her.

'But it would seem that you did not know her domestic circumstances – at least not as well as would be necessary for you to understand what had happened.

'I was in my final year at the training college when she entered it; we spent just a single year under the roof of the college, but I believe I got to know her better than her girlfriend, and perhaps better even than her husband, for if he had seen and valued her as I did, the misfortune would never have happened.

'You will already have guessed that I was in love with her too. If I admit that too, it is a deliberate emphasis on detail, and not a foolish sneer with which I might wish to mock myself in order to seem to have risen above my foolishness at the time. Oh no. There were a few of us; she always had a crowd of admirers – as did all of her classmates – that changed year by year; as at one end they fell off, at the other they increased. Dissatisfied with small successes, they changed very frequently: she was a cheerful companion and an intelligent friend to everyone, but they required a cooing dove. Her most constant admirers numbered two: Verner and me. I loved her familiar smile, her sonorous laugh, her heartfelt conversation, her trustworthiness and her open embrace of life; I contented myself with the joy and freshness of sensation that her presence inspired in me. I never uttered a single word to her about love, and therefore achieved what others were vainly seeking from her: with me, she herself used to initiate conversations about love, of course entirely general, humorous and joking ones. We reached verdicts about everything scornfully and rationally, with the impatience of youth. I soon abandoned all hope, and did not contemplate some turn of fortune, or future happiness, with the slightest sigh; there remained only the constant brightness that poured from her personality, that was always dear and near to me, which cheered and caressed me almost like the affection of a beloved sister.

'It was otherwise with Verner. He imposed himself on her in all the ways that were whispered to him by his passion, his unbridled debauchery, and his great complacency. He was certain in his mind that she could not resist him because he had dark, flattering eyes, the elegance of a wealthy scion, the attitude, and God knows what else; in short, just because he was irresistible. She laughed in his face, but was incapable of being scornful, and was also incapable of hurting him with her laughter. If she ever perceived that she had offended him or pained him, even slightly, she would immediately attempt to put things to rights with affability, and so unwillingly always restore to him the thread he had been holding on to.

'Laughter was her charm, her defence, a gift of God that she did not disdain. Her laughter gained her friends, but – a strange thing – her laughter made enemies for her and damaged her reputation. That is what people are like: they will wilfully pollute a limpid stream that babbles along their path. The fact that she brought smiles and friendliness to everyone devalued her, rather than elevated her, even in the eyes of those who benefited from her. Her sociability and her lack of pride were interpreted to her detriment; even though no one caught her out in anything that might have compromised her girlish honour, they did not exclude the possibility of some misstep, and entirely on account of her smiling, open countenance.

'However, she knew nothing of this, and perhaps never realized that many were looking askance at her through their fingers. Of course I would have been able to tell her and to save her from some ill-considered actions: she was glad to obey the first noble impulse; but judge for yourself, what pleasure is there in exposing people's meanness?

'Besides, I had other interests of my own at that time, and had not become a humble supplicant; I was seeing less of her later, too, but I never ceased watching her and taking pleasure in her joys.

'Then I heard, as a titillating piece of news, that B., a teacher, had fallen in love with Markéta. It was recounted as if it were an uproarious joke, anticipating the scenes and incidents which would inevitably follow as a consequence of this match. B. was known as an insanely jealous man. Hilarious anecdotes circulated about his outbursts, such as that concerning an unknown girl, whom he had watched every day and seen in his mind's eye as his wife, but whom he had never approached: he had become mortally angry and offended when he once met her with another man.

'The news fascinated me, and I rushed to pay Markéta a visit. I knew I would immediately find out the truth from her.

'She lived alone; I think this was the reason why public opinion distrusted her. Our own day loves the idea of a free-thinking woman, but woe to her who is taken in by fine words. Let a girl have a constant chaperone to guard her virtue – otherwise she is suspect. Markéta had no one of the sort. Two of her aunts, old maids from the country, used to imagine themselves her benefactors; they did not approve of her studies, but, as they claimed, tolerated them as a lesser evil to prevent a greater one. They frequently enquired about her conduct, and asked with displeasure about her male escorts, about her lone attendances at the theatre and at concerts, and about her intimate conversations in her little rented room.

'I found her at home. She was at work. She was particularly fond of artwork in the folk style, and was just then getting several vignettes of that type ready for L.'s book; her work was to be published first.

'If she had seemed like a spark before, I found her a flame. At the first mention of B., she blushed fiercely. Her blue eyes were blazing with ardour; she did not look at me, but sparkled; she did not speak, but showered me with flowers; she did not walk, but soared. She confided to me that she would take her examination at the end of the year and that she would go on holiday to Italy with B.; there would be no need to take account of her aunts, because the teaching post at the school was already virtually certain, and in any case they would get married as soon as B. received definite word of his appointment.

'Of course, she did not tell me this as dryly as I am repeating it to you now. The divine pathos of love clothed every word with radiance, so that it seemed a wonderful dream.

'Love is a miracle, she said, but she did not convince me that day, just as she had not convinced me in earlier conversations when she had asserted the exact opposite. The sad story of her life has proved me right: it has shown that love is an irony of fate, a trap that fate sets for people, to confuse their logic, to tame their self-confidence, and to punish their rebelliousness.

'While I was listening in silence to her words, and watching her wielding the pen with her fair hand, B. came in. He entered as if he were at home; it was evident from all his movements that he regarded himself as master of the apartment and of this woman. He gave me to understand that I should say nothing – there was no need for that, as I was about to leave in any case.

'Outside the house I met Verner. He was fluttering like a butterfly. He always gave me the impression of a little butterfly: a cane in his hand, eyeglasses, a loosely tied cravat, the flying lapels of his coat, his curls gracefully escaping under his broad-brimmed hat. He was all aflutter.

'"Did he go there? Did he go there?" he repeated, frantically. "But he won't get her, he won't get her, I'll warrant you. You'll remember me!"

'I paid no attention to his outburst. He had always loved great gestures and exaggerated verbiage.

'Later I forgot completely about this meeting; it was he himself who brought it back to my mind, and only after the funeral.

'Of course, Markéta travelled nowhere that year. The war closed off all routes and all plans, and B. donned the uniform of a reserve officer. Before he went into the field, Markéta and he were married. Everything was done quietly, almost in secret; there were only two witnesses who knew about the matter, B.'s brother and myself.

'I did not exchange words with Markéta after that; it was as though she had disappeared without trace. She was not to be seen at the theatre, at concerts, at exhibitions – nowhere. She was living in the strictest seclusion. I had occasion to meet her twice, but each time she crossed to the other side of the road, either by accident or on purpose, and I did not follow her because of a sort of shy, embarrassed expression, which I disliked in her.

'That expression on her face came back to my mind at the news of her death. And will you believe me if I tell you that I was not surprised – that I did not even exclaim, as perhaps everyone else did, "It's impossible! Such a lively girl!"

'I was not astonished, nor was I sorry for her. To me, it was as if I had seen the curtain fall at the end of a play. On the one hand, the war had taught me to regard more lightly the misfortunes and sufferings of individuals; on the other, I had in fact always expected something of the sort from her, and I was unsurprised, as one is unsurprised when a blind man falls over.

'It was only at the funeral that I saw that B. had returned home; I closely observed his obduracy, which seemed to me an unpleasant, secret hostility to the dead woman.

'I knew that expression of his; he had looked like that when he encountered that unknown woman with the young man; he had always looked like that when he thought himself offended.

'Without showing him sympathy – I felt that it would be out of place to do so, though I could not justify the feeling in any way – I left the Olšany cemetery, and at the gate leading to the Strašnice road I saw Verner.

'At a single glance I could see that some misfortune had befallen him. He looked pitiful; his airy elegance was all gone, his irresistibility was all gone; a sad, sodden little butterfly with no lustre and blurred colours; he was leaning against the gate in a posture that was, above all, picturesque.

'He had totally forgotten his pose as a seducer; it seemed that he had also forgotten about his external appearance. He was very carelessly dressed, and his clothes were bespattered with mud.

'He stared at me vacantly, almost like a man dead drunk. I took him under my arm, not too graciously, and growled:

'"What are you gaping at? Come with me."

'He offered no resistance and let me lead him. I put him in the first carriage that appeared. It was one returning from the funeral procession of a child; the coachman still had a buttonhole with a myrtle sprig and a black ribbon.

'We did not speak on the way. Verner sat there, oblivious, and his head nodded intermittently as if he were dozing.

'His spirit did not manifest itself until we had arrived at his house and I was paying the coachman: in a flamboyant gesture he took the coachman's myrtle sprig and placed it slowly and theatrically behind his hat. The coachman smiled indulgently.

'I avoided questioning him, and waited, sure that he would start speaking – and so he did.

'Preparing me with duly deep sighs and a tragic expression, he began.

'"You think I'm a cad, don't you?" he demanded. "You do think so, don't you?"

'Eventually I cut him short.

'"Now I think you are well out of sight, and that you won't be making a scene. I'm entirely happy with that."

'But Verner had not only suffered his misfortune, he had been its cause himself. He went on talking, and the more of his deeds that he mentioned, the greater his flood of words became, the murkier his delivery seemed, and finally Verner grew intoxicated by his own dramatic narrative, and forgot he was a tragic hero.

'In brief, this was how everything had taken place:

'As soon as B. left, Verner had resolved to make a conquest of Markéta at all costs; he still did not believe that he could possibly be resisted. He looked neither to right nor left, pursuing his goal like a horse with blinkers. B.'s love was nothing to him; Markéta's resistance was nothing to him. On the contrary, the cooler she was, the more he exerted pressure on her. The whole trouble lay, I think, in the fact that he regarded Markéta with the eyes of the majority of people: he thought her a credulous, accessible girl, simply the sort of girl with whom "possibilities" could not be "excluded".

'He paid her visits; she was still living in her old way in her little rented room. He must have thoroughly disgusted her, though she mastered herself, not mustering enough unkindness to drive him away. Then he lurked at her house and at the school, strolling through the streets at the time she was due to pass that way; he pretended to be pleasantly surprised, stroking his moustache, leaning over intimately, and speaking petty courtesies, at which she laughed. She could not bring herself to say, "Sir, how dare you?" with a solemnly offended face. Such words were not current among us, and in any case he was not "daring", but merely offering and carrying out small favours that required further meetings; that satisfied him in the meantime. His "devilish plan", as he termed it, was to discredit B. and then to achieve his success. He was simply waiting until B. came on leave.

'He waited it out.

'Markéta rushed out of school, beaming and happy. He ran up to her. Very weightily and urgently, he began to tell her a story about some "little girl" from his family who had arrived in Prague, in need of her advice and protection. She agreed readily; if at other times she might have been willing, that day she would have torn her heart asunder. They reached the crossroads on Na Můstku Street, and suddenly Markéta announced:

'"B. is waiting for me in front of the Koruna Palác shopping centre on Wenceslas Square. Go away."

'Her hesitant phrase, "Go away", encouraged Verner. It sounded like a secret pact, like an involuntary admission of some kind of shared guilt.

'I can imagine her saying it, prodded by thoughts about B.'s jealousy. She would certainly have had the shy, embarrassed look on her face that I disliked in her.

'But Verner with his blinkers saw only "Go away!" in flaming letters, and, beyond them, B., irascibly looking out on the pavement in front of the Koruna. He had already seen them – that was clear. And for that reason Verner went on with his "devilish plan", bending over towards Markéta in unexpected intimacy, and whispering "Don't forget, then!" with a significant wink. She hesitated briefly before offering him her hand; he clasped it in his own as long as he could, and when he finally parted from Markéta, who was now impatient, he was still calling after her so loudly and insistently that B. heard him, and she was obliged to turn around:

'"Yes?"

'She did indeed turn around. Her kindness and willingness had made a slave of her; she smiled mechanically, saying "Yes" with her usual simplicity, and flew towards B. in the fullness of her heart.

'Verner was satisfied for the time being. He came home, sat down straight away and drafted a letter, copied it out and put it in the post the same evening. He showed it to me in his notebook.

'"Markétka," he wrote, "I kiss your hand for your kindness. Thank you, thank you! On Tuesday, then, at three in the afternoon, at your house. Yours, in body and soul, Verner."

'He always had winged words with which to spice up his speeches. At that time, everything was "in body and soul" with him. There was of course no "little girl": he had merely invented her on the spur of the moment as a ploy.

'Are we able to imagine the effect this letter had on B. next morning? In no way. Even he himself would not have believed the day before how much coarseness, fury and callousness would be unleashed by it, as if in a cornered animal. Verner might well rejoice, for his plan had succeeded. And yet he was not rejoicing: he still seemed an idiot on the third day after the catastrophe.

'When he had told me all this, he paused for a while, and suddenly spoke in a very low, uncertain voice.

"'I'm a cad, that's obvious, but I wouldn't have expected that!"

"'And what would you have expected?" I grinned.

"'That B. would get angry and simply leave her, or that she would leave him."

"'Do you think a husband would leave his wife for the sake of a mere suspicion?"

'Verner thrust his hands into his pockets, straightened up from his crumpled position, and muttered:

"'Husband? B. was her husband?"

'Then I too straightened up.

"'And did you not know that?"

'We looked at one another for a moment, not finding it very funny.

"'But why did you send Markéta that 'devilish letter', if you did not know about their marriage?"

'He shrugged his shoulders.

"'So – I just presumed that he would be with her."

"'Pre-SUMED!" I yelled into his ear, and I had a thousand urges to punch him. "Hat, coat!" I ordered him, putting my own on as well. He acquiesced without demur. And once more we were wandering in silence, this time to Markéta's apartment.

'It was now evening, and every corner was dark. Her little room in no way called to mind the death that had visited it. The bed was covered with a dark batik shawl, an easel bore a pastel that was new to me, evidently a surprise for B.; on the table were her books, including the one with the vignettes, Indian ink, pens, and a drawing board; on the hat rack hung her velvet hat and cloak; it was as if she had merely left for a moment and would be returning straight away.

'"And she won't ever be returning," said the landlady, a lonely lady who had grown warmly attached to Markéta during her years of study. "I'm left here alone, like an orphan. Do you gentlemen know where the lieutenant is?"

'"We are looking for him ourselves," I replied. "Dear lady, we don't know anything at all about exactly what has happened."

'She knew both of us and was glad to talk. Between her sighs and tears she told us that the B.s had returned in a state of excitement on Monday, the lieutenant had sent her to get wine, had poured her a glass as well, and she had drunk a toast to him; and that he had then asked her, half in jest and half in earnest, whether it were true that women were unfaithful to soldiers.

'They were still asleep the next day when the postman delivered the letter.

'She heard them talking. He knocked, and said jokingly:

'"A letter for Miss Markéta!" It was really addressed to her as "Miss".

'From that moment, the noise was deafening. They did not stop talking until lunchtime, and barely touched their food. They did not go out; around three o'clock the door burst open and the lieutenant shouted, "As soon as the little girl arrives, just bring her in immediately!" I have no idea what "little girl"; no one arrived. Both of them were waiting for her; they did not stir from the house until the evening. But their talk grew louder and louder; I was not trying to listen, but it was impossible not to hear what was said. He was screaming and pouring out abuse, and accusing the good lady of such things as I am ashamed to repeat. Everyone knew, he said, what sort of woman she was, everyone knew about her laughter and her "merry" disposition; only a fool could be taken in by her. Oh, sirs, I can't repeat it. I could not bear it, either, and I stood up for her; I knew her best myself, and I know how lovely she was.

'"Well, where is the 'little girl'? That pretty 'little girl'?" he answered, though I had said nothing about a little girl. His wife had changed completely. She was sitting there in her chair, silent and white-faced, simply following him with her eyes; she was emaciated and seemed to have aged. He was shouting at me and also at her, but she was no longer answering him. Then suddenly he put on his coat, slammed the door, and left.

'Immediately I rushed over to her to comfort and calm her. For a long time she did not listen to me at all, and kept looking at the wall, though there was nothing there. Then suddenly she looked at me and sent me to the chemist for some antipyrin. And when I got back, she was already lying in a pool of blood; the lieutenant had forgotten about the loaded revolver here.

'Verner wept and wrung his hands; he knelt down before the table, before the bed. Such a hypocrite – he disgusted me. I said to him:

'"Off you go, and exculpate the memory of the dead."

'At first, he agreed, even showing eagerness to go immediately. We left. But where were we to look for a deceived husband on the evening after his wife's funeral, who had been convinced that her guilt had caused her to condemn herself to a cruel punishment? We ended up not finding him. Only later did I discover that he had left at about the time when we were sitting in her little room.

'"You'll write a letter," I insisted.

'He brought me several drafts, but I approved of none of them. "Her exoneration must be absolute and perfect; not the least shadow of doubt must remain."

'But suddenly he stopped bringing me sheets of paper with his letter, and entirely ceased visiting me. I sought him out myself, told him off in some form of words or other, and because it seemed to me that he was suddenly judging the matter differently from me, and hiding that from me, I tried to irritate him by saying:

'"You have stained your hands with her blood."

'"No one can see that blood," he replied, with a wry smile. "In any case, I'll get my hands clean, don't you worry. I know now what to do."

'I acknowledged in my mind that it was his business, and suddenly I lost the desire to be concerned in it. Time had done its work: the grass of spring was budding on Markéta's grave, and the flagrant injustice of her death was half overlaid with awkward what-ifs, buts, and what's-the-uses. I found myself reflecting that B. would not have benefited by such a revelation, but would have only found his life made harder. In this way one is constantly making compromises between the ideal and one's own convenience.

'But Verner astonished me and almost embarrassed me by his action. I had always regarded myself as above him, and now I suddenly felt the scales move, and my arrogance sink.

'He volunteered for the army; after a few weeks' training he left for the front. He summoned me to the railway station; he was resplendent in uniform, everything about him glittered, and he himself was glowing with a kind of sparkling cheerfulness, whose affectation pained me strangely.

'I took my leave of him in a tender mood; his mother fainted as the train moved off. A week later, news was received at home that he had fallen in a heroic death on Italian soil.

'There is no reason to conceal his story; I am not bound by any promise, and yet I have never told it to anyone until now. But I have thought all the more about him, and from the tangle of feelings, doubts and reflections excusing me, one single question has arisen, which occupies me and torments me at night when I cannot sleep.

'Verner was guilty, but he served his sentence. He paid for Markéta's blood with his own blood; he is no longer guilty before her. But is he guilty before B.? I have recounted the whole affair to you, because the question is now weighing me down, and the responsibility is becoming unbearable to me. I am laying a piece of torment on you too; you think of a way out, of an answer: is B. to be told about everything, or is he not to be told, when he returns?'

With this thorny question, his narrative came to an end.

A REMARKABLE INCIDENT

ANNA MARIA TILSCHOVÁ

The Ohnes family was totally uninteresting; it was as if the name that they had brought with them from Germany several generations earlier had not been merely a name, but also a sign of emptiness. Old Ohnes and both of his sons were not people of any kind at all – rich and miserly, without flair, ambition or moral compass, and without goodness of heart, like their name, 'ohne', 'without', which was simply a symbol of negation. They were not evil, nor were they good; they showed no enterprise, they had no plans and no broad interests; they did not even have great, unconstrained vices – in short, they had nothing at all. And a remarkable incident that occurred in their family arose from completely commonplace infidelity, without passion, interest, or piquancy.

Although both brothers had gained doctoral degrees, these in no way reflected an ambition for education or for work, for exciting and exhausting employment; they wished merely to do everything entirely without effort, as if something were simply being thrown away. Such things could be done, but there was no need to do them. The brothers squandered and danced away their youth, though they were bored at every turn. Boredom! They valued and judged things, matters, even people, that crossed their path, only according to how much of a bore they were. And Richard, the younger of the two, had already exceeded the age of Jesus Christ when his elder brother finally married an elegant Jewess from Vienna.

A marriage of love – that is what it was called in the family and in society. But it meant merely that they were not antagonistic to one another. The human interest that the young couple took in each other was fragmented into a thousand tiny interests, about their residence, their clothes, their box in the theatre, or the pedigree of their thorough-bred dog, so that there remained only the merest fragment, or poor residue, of feeling in their actual relationship as husband and wife. The young lady brought a dowry into the household, one of conventional worldly affability, under which her true self lay safely concealed from everyone, as if tied up with pink ribbons. And yet, even if Emil, her husband, and also Richard, her brother-in-law, and their old father were such bland and uninteresting people, and the sumptuous apartment, with its long vista of rooms, seemed cold, the young woman brought a kind of tantalizing uneasiness and a gleam of amorous smiles into the boredom and soberness of the owners of the chemical factory, with the scent of her skin and her perfumes, with her clothes, and with the click of her high heels.

Long before Emil's wedding, and long before the old man had transferred the flourishing enterprise, the crowning glory of his life, to them, in order to save on death duties, the brothers used to appear everywhere in tandem. It would be too much to suppose, perhaps, that concord – or at least masculine friendship – reigned between the brothers; it suffices to state baldly that no one, not even the servants, had ever heard the two of them quarrel. They attended auctions together, they patronized poor artists together, and they maintained a lavish private gallery, commensurate with their considerable means; they even made joint excursions to the mountains or to spas, whether from boredom, from convenience or from habit; in short, they were always standing or sitting side by side somewhere, as if they were Siamese twins.

And so people became accustomed to seeing the profiles of the two Ohneses behind them against the purple background of a loge at floor level, outlined as sharply as on a bronze medal – the profile of the nose of the elder, with a sharp line from the nose to the mouth on his clean-shaven face, and close to it the face of the younger, the profile of a bird of prey, perhaps a condor. One might also have imagined Voltaire like that in his youth, with those thin, pursed lips, with that cool sneer, and with that strange sallow skin, full of golden freckles in summer. Richard, the younger brother, though truly ungainly, was nevertheless elegant and impeccable, heedless of all his surroundings, and careless in his bearing.

The communal life of the three men and the young Viennese lady was so uninteresting, and apparently so tranquil, that even people's gossip made no inroads on it. Apart from tittle-tattle about the enormous profits the brothers were making from the war, or that they had become members of the Masonic lodge, not a single rumour touched the reputation of the young lady, though she had risked it precisely with her worldly appearance and her Parisian toilette. And then, suddenly, there burst like a bombshell into this greyness, this boredom and this blasé indifference of wealth, an alarming report in the newspaper: a great explosion at the factory of the Ohnes brothers in Libeň.

The evening papers carried only a vague report of an accident at the chemical factory, but the morning papers were more precise. It was known that there had been no carelessness among the workers, and also that none of the workers had been injured, but that the explosion and the mishap had occurred in a laboratory, where the brothers who owned the factory had been testing something with aniline paints, with no witnesses, and that both of the Ohneses had been taken, severely injured and burnt, to a sanatorium in Podolí. And the public, avid for sensational events, and always sympathetic to misfortune when there was no reason for envy, was feverishly interested in the health and further fate of the two brothers, as also in the young lady, who had been sitting in her loge only three days earlier, with the smile of a modern Empress Messalina, and with her naked shoulders and her pregnant body wrapped in expensive furs.

Evil tongues began to wag, though no one had ever previously suggested such a thing, alleging that the igniting of the explosive had not been due to an accident or mistake – that the two brothers must simply have been settling an ugly, indeed perhaps tragic, score between each other. And when their old father indignantly rejected the tactless allegations of the gossips, and eagerly began supporting his daughter-in-law, there sprang up into the darkness of these mysterious rumours reports that he too, though a septuagenarian with one foot in the grave, was head over heels in love with the voluptuous Jewess and her worldly charms and cool smile.

The fickle sympathies which had hitherto been on the side of the lawful husband, began to turn and waver when word spread that Richard, the younger, unmarried, brother, was in mortal danger. His high fever and his delirium were spoken of with sympathy, and sensitive young ladies were quoting his remarks with sentimental fondness, as if he had had an evil premonition beforehand. And all their spiteful scorn descended in a hailstorm exclusively on the head of the young lady, on her Jewishness, and on the irresponsibility of Vienna – on the same young lady in whose belly a child's little heart was already beating regularly.

This passionless and embarrassing story of a woman caught between two brothers might be a modern variant, empty and ironic, of that of the tragic Francesca da Rimini, who had been reading a book with her brother-in-law, when suddenly the adulterous lips of the two met over the book and kissed with irreversible consequences. 'Quel giorno più non vi leggemmo avante!', 'that day we read no further!'[2] The horror lay here elsewhere: in that there had in fact been no

2 The quotation is from Dante, *Inferno*, 5.138.

passion, and that both the misfortune and the betrayal of a brother by his own brother had not been unavoidable – that even this had been a matter of no consequence with the younger Ohnes, without any elemental necessity. And the public, stern and yet unjudgmental, believing itself to represent a general conscience, wept cheap, uncritical tears, and covered itself with a funereal wreath of emotion, when the announcement appeared in the papers of the death of Richard, the younger of the two heads of the vast factory.

Now, when death had removed Richard from the scene as peremptorily as if he had been a knight or castle taken in chess, it seemed that the affair had somehow been settled and simplified, and was, perhaps, even in the past. And yet it is only here that the remarkable incident began. The other brother, the betrayed, badly cheated husband, had also been close to death. The doctors had been stretching all their ingenuity, and trying out the newest methods. And what they had striven for with such tenacity had come to pass: part of the burnt skin was replaced with different skin. And when, six weeks later, Emil Ohnes, now sole owner of the estate, the name, and the factory, returned to the family home near the Písecká brána, the newspapers were agog with the glorious success of Czech medical science.

There were only a few old ladies pressed against the railings of the large garden when young Ohnes alighted from an automobile, with the wan face of an unremarkable blond made paler than ever in the shade. A young woman came out on to the steps, in billowing drapery concealing her pregnancy, and suddenly there rang out a scream across the blossoming spring garden across the breadth of the Letná hill – a scream to penetrate bone and marrow, a scream of enormous horror. Slowly, one step after another, but as irrevocably as fate, the man walked across the ground up to the young woman, who was clinging convulsively to the railings.

The door of the house immediately slammed shut, and no one knew what else passed between the couple. The doctors had forbidden the young lady to visit the sanatorium, and for long weeks neither of the two had seen the other since the great accident in the factory. The master of the house had returned from the threshold of death to a disgraced house. Had an explanation perhaps been exchanged between the couple? The husband had returned to the family – had he forgiven his unfaithful wife? The child she was expecting – was that his, or that of the dead man? All these outraged notions and agonizing human questions were echoing against the locked doors of the excessively opulent villa surrounded by pink flowering hawthorn and fragrant lilac, against the elegant lacquered doors that were as silent as lips clenched in defiance.

No scandal ensued, and the swollen waves of malicious enjoyment in participation in this embarrassing adulterous history, without any redeeming or mitigating feeling, subsided and grew calm, since nothing new was emerging. Summer was approaching in the city, the dead season, and clouds of Prague dust were obscuring the city with a grey veil of boredom and dirt. The young lady was hardly venturing out at all, and the couple were seen only perhaps twice together in the theatre. The Viennese lady, all wrapped in lace and costly jewels, reclined wearily in the dim background of her loge, beside the old man in his second childhood, who played the gallant by plying her continually with sweets. A broad hat shielded her white face; people attributed her pallor to the heat, as also her altered, glazed expression, which did not suit her frivolous face, now close to motherhood. Attention was mainly directed, however, at young Ohnes, who was sitting in front alone. He seemed to be as deficient in blood and colour as if he had risen from the grave. And society people, who had been accustomed to seeing the sharp profiles of the Ohnes brothers in that same loge behind them, even though different from each other, yet with that marked family resemblance – such people had the impression that the heads of the two brothers had been rolled into one. Of course it was Emil, the elder Ohnes, and yet it was *he* who now had the pursed lips and the Voltaire-like sneer of the younger one. Indeed – he had changed. But just as this appearance of the couple in public was startling, and an ostentatious rebuttal of damaging rumours, it was also a proof that the couple wished to live together once more in harmony.

In early July the child was born, a boy. And now the tongues that had been silenced began to whisper once more, and to relish the gossip. After all, the child was the product of nature – and who was its father? The cream of society showered the young mother with baskets of flowers and little favours of lace and embroidery, simply in order that they might see with their own malicious eyes the unique picture of a worldly mother bending over the ornate cradle of a child with two fathers – brothers. The child was in no way out of the ordinary, and its small sleeping face betrayed nothing; it was only the Viennese lady who seemed very strange. She was dressed from her head down to her silk stockings and alluring red slippers in clothes worth thousands and thousands, and yet with her nervous movements she only made an unpleasant impression on all her visitors, and an impression doubly unsettling in the frivolous package she represented of powder, perfume and chic little items from Paris. Those dilated, anxious eyes of hers were conspicuous not only to visitors, but also to the doctors in the house. God forbid, it was not the look of a guilty woman who felt, perhaps in secret, remorse and moral distress at the misfortune that was her lot. No, in those eyes, fixed on the door to her husband's room, there was only some undefined horror; the talkative old man came and caressed his grandson with the indulgence of an old man who understood no more than a quarter of what was going on around him. He bowed to his daughter-in-law with old-fashioned courtesy, but she was not listening to him at all, and her eyes were darting God knows where. Her Jewish eyes were free of onerous moral responsibility, and glittered only with the unease of a hunted animal. And when the father – whether real or supposed – entered the room, which was completely filled with flowers like the dressing-room of a prima donna, the doctor sensed from the unnatural laughter of the lady, who did not even look round, that she was feeling his presence in the room entirely with frayed nerves. He realized that the same young woman who had seemed a heartless, perverse beast to him previously, and had now changed into a blend of morbid unrest and nervous agony, was connected by a gloomy mystery with her present husband, whom she had welcomed back to his house from his brother's grave.

The old doctor was a true altruist – one who would go straight out from a long trip in the mountains to deal with a difficult birth. From the outset he had not liked this pampered lady, who had brought her own millions as a dowry to a house that was already rich. Indeed he disliked the whole atmosphere, that with the raw weight of its gold quenched both the kindling glow and the white-hot flame of human moral strength; he disliked the artificial atmosphere where all human nature seemed to be standing on its head; and he disliked the traces of blood clinging to the elegant Jewess. But now, when he observed how altered the superficial woman was, who had previously commanded all three Ohneses with the capricious riding-switch of her exotic ideas, and had tormented them with the wildest demands of a moneyed princess, this strange, mysterious case began to interest him.

He observed both of them – the woman and also her husband, with that cold, sardonic laugh, which was haughtily disparaging everything and itself was amused by nothing.

He had already encountered unbelievably ridiculous things in his practice, and also many heartless tragedies, and yet he was surprised how markedly the illness had altered young Ohnes, even *physically*. Surprisingly enough, the burns had healed – there was only a slight scar remaining on his chin – but his hands had suffered most, those white, idle, manicured hands in their immaculate cuffs. They were not mutilated, and even the fingernails were not damaged, but they exhibited skin that was unevenly coloured, and their appearance had changed. These hands, once merely indolent and blasé, even now appeared calm – and yet, whether they were lying on a book or rolling a cigarette, they seemed as if they were idly grimacing and in fact lying in wait for something.

Besides, it may have been no more than a fancy, but one to which all outsiders, including the old, wise doctor, were subject, that young Ohnes, since his recovery from his dangerous illness, was coming more and more to resemble his brother, the deceased Richard. Otherwise, however much the doctor strained, he could perceive no changes in his behaviour, that is, in his conduct towards his own wife, which was always courteous, always unconcerned, apart from those hands and apart from that laugh. Only once, when the young husband was supporting his wife as she was ascending the stone steps to the greenhouse, the doctor saw distinctly that she was turning away and shuddering all over, as if she had been touched not by a human being, but by a monster. But he still did not know what was the matter, though it was clear to him that here, in this orderly house with its elegant servants and chambermaids, and with its wealth of gold and diamonds, there was slumbering not an everyday tragedy of love, but a uniquely strange horror, hitherto carefully concealed.

The half-crazed scream with which the young woman had greeted the father-to-be had long since fallen silent, and was now only a piquant spice in the bloodthirsty history which had enveloped the family as well as the house in its huge garden as if in an envious shadow. It was only the human core that interested the old doctor: what had been going on before, and what was still going on, in the young husband. Even though he knew how boring the family was, and admitted the most extreme superficiality of all the Ohneses, without a shred of true human feeling, he could not imagine anyone returning to a wife who had deceived him, especially with his own brother, as if he had merely returned from a stroll in the park.

Only two things seemed possible to him: either all of it was nothing but a swamp of evil gossip, though he did not himself believe this as he looked into those Jewish eyes, so cold and sensual; or – and he returned to the point from which he had started out, once more confronting that dumb, insistent horror that he sensed pervading the whole house.

Once in August in an intense sultry heat in the city, when it seemed that the sun was burning the park of the Ohneses into nothing but a Sahara, he caught sight of the eyes of the young woman wide open to the point of discomfort. He followed the direction of her gaze – she was staring at her husband's hand as it was toying with the newspaper on the table. And he saw a strange thing: the whole hand was faintly and wearily white, as if washed out with the sweltering heat of summer, and the thumb alone was brimfull of golden freckles. And in the same moment, as it flashed through his mind that the hand seemed as if it had been artificially put together from two different and mismatched hands, he heard a strangled cry, which a lace handkerchief vainly attempted to seize and suppress. The Viennese woman was barely holding on to the garden table, and on the face of her husband was playing the same sneer that had changed the face of the elder brother into that of Richard, who had now been dead for months.

Vacuous heads always concern themselves with other people's affairs, and, to be sure, there was too much chatter about the marriage of the young people over ices and also over tea. The women attributed her irritable condition to her confinement, and the men also to the strain, and tendency to psychoses, endemic in old, decadent Jewish families. But otherwise, the defiant waves, and the floods of slander, were crashing on a firm shore – on the completely solid wealth of the whole family, attested in the land registry. Indeed, the whole of high society had a two-edged and immoral relationship with the Ohneses as if with some aristocratic family: on the one hand they disseminated rumours so damaging that a decent person would not have taken a poor crust of bread with salt from their hands, and on the other they were obsequious before them, happy when they acknowledged one of them with a smile or with a greeting.

The wise old doctor was shaking his head more and more over the decline in health of the shapely lady who had been drinking the sparkling wine of her twenty-five years to the full only a year before. Although she went riding in Stromovka every morning on a beautiful bay horse, although she went swimming and also rowing, she was nonetheless continually pestering him simply for bromides and new medicines, and for ever stronger sleeping pills. It was not merely that she had stubbornly refused any explanation, but she had so far evaded his medical queries and subterfuges. It was not until he accidentally blurted out something about marital relations that she had suddenly fixed her burning gaze on the door of her husband's room with hate-filled flames. So that is it! thought the doctor to himself privately. The bedroom, nest of flattering love, and the most intimate of retreats, had been and still was a torture-chamber for this Jewish Messalina! And he looked in surprise and also curiosity at the figure of this insatiable lady, who a year ago, while the younger brother was still alive, had loved, and cheerfully alternated between, the two brothers, and now was trembling with hate-filled revulsion from her husband.

Yes, he had lifted and indeed perhaps even drawn back its corner, but he had not removed the opaque veil covering the mystery of the sumptuous bedroom. And again nothing happened for a long time, and the days passed in a series like buttons on clothes. And the end, or rather the explanation of this strange and almost cynical episode, bereft of all tragedy and ethics, was not vouchsafed to the old doctor by his perspicacity, but by capricious Lady Chance, who dropped it into his lap one autumn evening like a shuttle-cock. At other times he used to come by in the morning, but that day he had been detained by an autopsy on a poor seamstress who had died in desperation, and he entered the house when twilight was already stretching out and unravelling the grey threads of the evening's sorrow. He crossed the carpeted passage and entered the anxiety-inducing room that separated the bedrooms of the couple. He already had his hand on the doorknob when he heard the lady's voice from the room, trying to resist something, a quiet, impatient, and once more tortured, voice.

He realized that he had come upon an intimate scene between the young couple, and he hesitated to enter. The invisible couple were speaking so quietly that he did not understand their words, but he could easily hear that the laugh of young Ohnes, that joyless and yet patronizingly triumphant voice, was corresponding with the fearful and exasperated voice of the lady.

'So – when?' asked the man behind the doors suddenly, as decisively as if he were not asking a question but putting a knife to her throat.

'Ah, what do I know, today!' replied the young lady impatiently.

'These are all simply excuses and – your aristocratic whims,' replied the man courteously, and yet it could be heard that *he* was master of the whole affair and of the whole situation.

'What would I be making excuses about! I simply don't want to go today – it's too early to go!'

'*With me!*' uttered the man, with a cold sneer, and the word was as hard as when a stone falls.

Now the Viennese woman was muttering something rapidly and feverishly, which the old doctor did not understand, and to it her young husband replied, sharply and distinctly:

'Why do you not tell things as they are? Why – do you hold yourself back so rigidly?'

'Ah!' she gasped arduously, and then it could be heard through the door how the voice of the young woman was trembling. 'You are so terrible again today, you – *Richard!*'

The old doctor was startled to hear her call her living husband by the name of his dead brother, with whom she had cheated on him. He trembled to know what would happen next, expecting an outburst of jealousy or a wild eruption. But her husband was not offended, did not become angry, did not shout; indeed what happened was what he had expected the least – he burst out laughing. And that laugh of young Ohnes was an ugly laugh!

After the ugly, cold laugh, there was a long, long silence in the bedroom. Then it was the invisible husband, who continued to question his invisible wife with the intrusive tones of a torturer.

'What are you raving about *again!*'

Now the old doctor could understand that Richard's name had not been a slip of the tongue by an adulterous woman. Although he understood neither its meaning nor its strange connection, he realized that ugly outbursts of this type must often have been repeated behind the curtains and the closed doors in the silence of the bedroom, and that the name of the deceased man had often been spoken, and was alive, between the couple.

'Am I raving?' the voice of the distressed lady again trembled behind the door, a voice choked, rising impotently and almost leaping with fury: 'But why then have you no answer? Why then?'

Her husband indeed gave no answer, merely crossing the room with the dry, sharp steps of a former officer.

'Would you be alive today if he had not died?' The young lady spoke, slurred her words and babbled feverishly. 'Yes, you look like him . . . you have his hands – and you speak and walk like Emil, my husband, too! But just tell me this: *who* are you today? Are you Richard – or is it he who is you? Or have the two of you merged into a new unknown person? For pity's sake, just tell me the truth for once!'

The sharp soldierly steps ceased, and young Ohnes laughed, a short brief laugh; it was the icy laugh of a victorious, fully self-aware tormentor, a persecutor of his wife. 'Darling!' He called her that cajolingly, using the English word, after that ugly laugh, and immediately after that outburst. And then a pitiful cry was heard, or rather the yelp of a dog that has been stamped on – he was embracing her, the woman tormented by those freckled hands, those hands of his dead brother.

It was almost dark when the door opened. The doctor, completely shaken, cowered in a chair in the corner, watching him pass against the curtains with the profile of a bird of prey. And in the bedroom next door the Viennese lady was sitting, the insatiable Messalina was sitting, with dishevelled hair, her dress half undone. And on her well-groomed face, under a layer of powder and rouge, as if under a frivolous, decrepit mask, lay only horror, dumb and insane, with the question: What can happen next?

MARIE AND MARTA
LÍDA MERLÍNOVÁ

They were striding towards one another along the wide boulevard . . . Their eyes locked – and they recognized one another. At the same time they turned around to look at each other, and stood face to face. In that first moment, neither spoke a word. And when Marie stepped out again, Marta joined her. So they walked together through the December night far beyond the city, where only they and the bright stars were alive. They said all that was necessary to one another, and they met again and again – and yet again, when the fields were clothed with emerald green, and the trees with blossom.

They did not promise friendship to one another. They never spoke of love. They were not disrespectful. But Marie was beautiful – as beautiful as the spring, as cherry blossom, as birdsong, as youthful sunshine – and the strange charm of Marta, as if of a young man, her rare intelligence, and her doglike devotion, undermined Marie's serenity. And the more the spring was filled with beauty and song, the more timid and fearful Marta became, and the more restive Marie became. But beware of the time when the moon is full, when there is not a soul about, and the soft grass is full of flowers . . . There were billions of stars above them, a hallowed silence around them, and the approval and benediction of God!

Marta, completely overwhelmed, wept silent tears. And Marie's cynical spirit was astounded. If anyone had recounted something of the sort to her, she would have called it kitsch. But it was not kitsch . . . It was something that was so beautiful, so simple, so straightforward and natural – the most beautiful thing Marie had ever experienced, and the most powerful.

She rose from the grass, gave Marta her hand and said to her, simply:

'Come with me! Come to me! I feel that you belong to me. I don't wish to be without you now!'

And of course Marta went. She went, and she stayed. And there was beauty not only in the earth, but also, and especially, in her. All her previous sorrows were drowned in the face of this new happiness. And she lived only so that she could love Marie with her immense love.

In beautiful quiet evenings *à deux*, she used to listen to their breathing and their heartbeat, and would whisper happily:

'Tell me, Marie, what do you think is lacking if we love one another?'

Marie stroked her boyish, close-cropped head thoughtfully, and Marta felt: She lacks so much, so very much! Marie was thirsty for life's sensations – eternally hungry, eternally curious about new faces, new characters, new embraces, new incidents. She wished to get to know women of every race and nationality. She wished to live in the magnificent simplicity of a mud hut in a Negro village, but was longing immediately afterwards for the fabulous luxury of the palaces of Indian maharajas.

In fact Marie did not know what she was wishing for, and the instability of her character caused the devoted Marta ever new worries about their fragile happiness.

Naturally, this contentment of theirs, with two natures that were so heterogeneous, could not last for long. Marta found she had a rival.

She was younger. She was more beautiful. She was far richer. She craved to have Marie's beauty close to her. It was her whim, as a bored, dissatisfied woman, to destroy their friendship, to prove her superiority, to triumph, to play at being Fate. And the heedless Marie did not resist.

Marta realized all this. When Marie went out to pursue her affair, she went to the window and gazed after her for a long time, as she was disappearing with eager steps . . .

Marta closed her eyes and surrendered involuntarily to logical ideas. She saw her rival – young, beautiful, self-confident, and proud of her victory; surrounded by the refinement of luxury; much more amusing, because simply flirtatious and not loving; much more enchanting, because she was something forbidden, stolen, lied about. And then she saw Marie – her adored girl, dazzled by this glamour, by all the expensive and luxurious things that Marta would never be able to provide for her . . . How would she speak about her, about Marta, her comrade? About her simple, poor lover? Surely with compassion? She would be explaining that she could not simply leave her empty-handed . . . Ah, the agony! Such shame and humiliation.

It was now four o'clock in the morning, and the sky was beginning to grow light, calmly and without haste. Marta was still standing at the window, as if turned to stone, gazing with weary eyes into the grey dawn. Then she wept the desperate, coarse, masculine sobs of the female invert.

'She will not return now!'

But she did return! Stealthily, like a thief, and shamefacedly, like a dog with its tail between its legs. She stood before the door of Marta's room, and trembled with inner mortification at the deed she had committed, and with desperate fear whether she would be able to explain it and make amends.

. . . I shall go down on my knees before her – she whispered to herself – and Marta must understand and must forgive. I have been irresponsible, have been damaged goods; I have not appreciated her . . . I have not been mature enough to understand all that I have in my Marta. I shall say to her: Forget that I defiled myself with that painted beauty. I have wounded you terribly, but I have redeemed my soul.

I have discovered you and I have also discovered myself. Now I shall no longer chase after every gilded temptation, but I shall tremble on your account, my love! You must understand: a human being is not born instantly perfect; so forgive me for this betrayal. It will be for the last time, Marta! Now I know what I want: only you, only you, my darling Marta! You, until I draw my last breath! Remember where we began, there beyond the city, in the meadows, under the stars. God loved us – he loved us so. He granted you to me! I shall lie at your feet my whole life long – because I have caused you pain; because I have realized that you are the only one I have loved and still love; because I have finally now come to understand that I cannot make love without being in love . . .

But Marie did not in fact say any of this. When she entered quietly with eyes downcast, the room was too quiet for there to be any living soul there. When she raised her startled eyes, she saw that the bed had not been slept in, and instead of Marta, there was a white sheet of paper, inscribed in her pedantic, well-formed handwriting.

'Marie – I am leaving – and you know why. I forgive you, and I understand you! You are beautiful, Marie, too beautiful to be capable of great love. You were made for laughter, for flirtation, for colour, and for music. I gave you love. Your spirit longs for liveliness and a glamorous life, just as your beauty longs for expensive luxury.

'I am taking myself out of your way, Marie, and making easier something that would soon be happening in any case.

'I kiss you for the last time, with all the tenderness of which I am capable.

'*Farewell!*'

In these brief notes I give only the barest of outlines of the authors' lives, in order to place them chronologically and socially. Biographical dictionaries and critical studies can usually be relied on for further details.

BOŽENA BENEŠOVÁ, née Zapletalová (b Neutitschein [Nový Jičín], 30 Nov 1873; d Prague, 8 Apr 1936). Author and editor. Although she was from a lawyer's family, her parents prevented her from receiving formal education beyond the age of sixteen, and she was largely self-taught. In 1902 she was befriended by Růžena Svobodová and in 1903 by the eminent critic F. X. Šalda, subsequently making journeys to Italy, studying art history and concentrating on literature. Her marriage in 1896 with a railway official, Josef Beneš, was legally dissolved after a domestic crisis in 1912, but she remained bound to her husband. From 1908 she lived in Prague, writing and editing literary journals; she was also involved in leftist politics.

LILA BUBELOVÁ [pseud. Lila B. Nováková] (b Krempna, Galicia, 12 Feb 1886; d Prague, 13 Sep 1974). Author and dramatist. A daughter of the manager of a Galician branch of a small Moravian family timber firm, she spent her early childhood at Kroměříž in Moravia, and then lived with her mother on the charity of relatives in Prague after her father's death in 1900. Her ambition to become a teacher was thwarted, and she undertook menial work in Prague offices, but she turned to writing drama after receiving support from Jaroslav Kvapil, who produced two one-act plays of hers at the National Theatre in Prague in 1924.

MARIE VON EBNER-ESCHENBACH, née Dubsky von Třebomyslice [Dubská z Třebomyslic] (b Zdislawitz [Zdislavice] near Kroměříž, 13 Sep 1830; d Vienna, 12 Mar 1916). Author. Born into an old Bohemian aristocratic family, she was encouraged in her education (undertaken by a series of governesses) by her father's cultivated fourth wife, Countess Xaverine Kolowrat-Krakowsky, and read widely as a child during the summer months in the castle library at Zdislavice in Moravia, mastering several languages, including Czech. At the age of eighteen she married her cousin, Moritz von Ebner-Eschenbach, a university professor fifteen years her senior, who disapproved of her literary activity and tried to limit it; but for many years she persevered in aspiring to a professional standard despite illness and persistent unfavourable criticism, both private and public. In 1898 she was awarded the *k.u.k. Österreichisches Ehrenzeichen* ('litteris et artibus') for her work, as the composer Brahms had been for his, and in 1900 she became the first woman to be awarded an honorary doctorate by Vienna University.

VLADIMÍRA JEDLIČKOVÁ, née Marie Krombholcová [pseud. Edvard Klas] (*b* Kleintschitschowitz [Malé Číčovice] near Středokluky, 20 Mar 1878; *d* Prague, 24 Mar 1953). Author. She married Jaromír Jedlička, a classical philologist, corresponded with the Decadent author Jiří Karásek ze Lvovic, and was the mother of Jaromír Jedlička, a translator.

RŮŽENA JESENSKÁ (*b* Prague, 17 Jun 1863; *d* Prague, 14 Jul 1940). Author, teacher and editor. The daughter of a petty clerk and shopkeeper, she was trained as a teacher during the 1880s, and taught at schools in Jungbunzlau [Mladá Boleslav] and Prague until her retirement in 1907, in consequence never marrying. She wrote for numerous magazines for women and children, and her literary output was quite voluminous and eclectic, in genres ranging from lyric poetry to novels and dramas.

ANNA LAUERMANNOVÁ-MIKSCHOVÁ, née Mikschová [pseud. Felix Tèver] (*b* Prague, 15 Dec 1852; *d* Prague, 16 Jun 1932). Author and organizer of the most important Bohemian literary salon of the period. Her father, a physician, was on friendly terms with František Ladislav Rieger, one of the most prominent members of the Czech National Revival, and in 1877 she married Josef Lauermann, the rich grandson of the equally distinguished Czech patriot Josef Jungmann; in 1880 she inaugurated her literary salon, and she maintained it for fifty years. Her marriage ended in divorce in 1888; the themes in her work of women's lack of freedom and romantic disillusion have been related to her personal experience as also to her admiration for the author Karolina Světlá. The prominent author Julius Zeyer was a close friend of hers.

MARIE MAJEROVÁ, née Bartošová (*b* Auwal [Úvaly], 1 Feb 1882; *d* Prague, 16 Jan 1967). Author, journalist, and editor. Her childhood was spent mainly in the Kladno region, where her stepfather was employed at the steelworks. Lacking any university education, she was self-taught; under the influence of such writers as S. K. Neumann she espoused anarchism, but had abandoned it by 1907 and moved towards communism. She contributed to the communist press and edited magazines until she was temporarily expelled from the Communist Party in 1929 after signing the so-called 'Manifesto of the Seven' (a protest against the alignment of the Party with the Bolshevist politics of the Comintern and against its leadership by Klement Gottwald). Her writing in the 1930s approaches Socialist Realism on the Soviet model, and after World War II she became a prominent member of the communist establishment.

HELENA MALÍŘOVÁ, née Nosková (*b* Prague, 31 Oct 1877; *d* Prague, 17 Feb 1940). Author, journalist and communist activist. The elder of the two daughters of a city official, she entered the circle of anarchist intellectuals around S. K. Neumann after her father's death in 1899, and began publishing articles and short stories. Jan Malíř, her husband, died in 1909; in 1910 she left the Roman Catholic Church, and in 1912 she acted as a reporter and nurse during the First Balkan War. Under the influence of the prominent author Ivan Olbracht, who was her partner from 1913 until 1935, she took part in left-wing politics, travelling illegally to Russia in 1920, where she attended the second World Congress of the Comintern, becoming a founder member of the Communist Party of Czechoslovakia in 1921, and spending time in prison. Together with Marie Majerová, she signed the 'Manifesto of the Seven' in 1929 against the Bolshevization of the Party, and was expelled from it for a time, but achieved posthumous recognition.

LÍDA MERLÍNOVÁ, née Ludmila Skokanová (b Prague, 3 Feb 1906; d Prague, 11 Jul 1988). Author, actress and journalist. She trained initially as an actress and dancer, founding her own dance school in Olomouc by 1928. In that year she married Cyril Pecháček, the conductor of the Olomouc theatre orchestra, in what may have been a marriage of convenience, though surviving until his death in 1949: her writings from that period play with 'inverted' (lesbian) sexuality. From 1934 she turned towards a more conventional career as a writer of stories for modern women and girls, though still avoiding conventional notions of love and marriage; her writings were entirely suppressed under postwar communism.

TERÉZA NOVÁKOVÁ, née Lanhausová (b Prague, 31 Jul 1853; d Prague, 13 Nov 1912). Author and feminist activist. Her father was a Czech bank official; although her mother, who was from a wealthy German-Jewish family from Iglau [Jihlava], spoke no Czech, Teréza was educated in Czech, and was encouraged by Karolina Světlá, who provided her with a role model. In 1876, after her marriage with Josef Novák, a teacher, she moved to Leitomischl [Litomyšl]; cut off from Prague, she undertook ethnographic study, focusing on folk culture, and she founded and chaired an Association of Czech Women and Girls (Spolek paní a dívek českých, 1885–95). The eminent critic Arne Novák was her son.

TEREZA SVATOVÁ, née Albertová (b Senftenberg [Žamberk], 31 Mar 1858; d Vysoké Mýto, 19 Feb 1940). Author and journalist. Born into a provincial professional family, she was brought up by an aunt at the nearby small town of Wildenschwert [Ústí nad Orlicí] after the family house burned down in 1860. At the age of 16 she married Josef Svata, a tax official; from 1880, encouraged by editors, including the prominent journalist and author Jan Neruda, she began publishing articles and short stories in various journals and newspapers.

RŮŽENA SVOBODOVÁ, née Čápová (b Niklowitz [Mikulovice] near Znaim [Znojmo], 10 Jul 1868; d Prague, 1 Jan 1920). Author and organizer of a literary salon. She was the daughter of the administrator of a monastic estate, and was educated in a monastery school, also familiarizing herself with European literature through wide reading. In 1890 she married the author F. X. Svoboda, organized an influential literary salon which attracted many leading personalities (for example, Božena Benešová), and undertook travel widely within Europe. The critic F. X. Šalda was a close friend, and strongly influenced her work.

ANNA MARIA TILSCHOVÁ (b Prague, 11 Nov 1873; d Dobříš, 18 Jun 1957). The daughter of wealthy parents, she was educated in Prague at the Girls' High School (Vyšší dívčí škola), and at the Charles University as an external (mimořádná) student. In 1895 she married her cousin, Emanuel Tilsch, thus retaining her maiden surname. Her early writing, arguably some of her best, was originally published under the half-pseudonym Anna Maria, which encouraged early critics to find resemblances to George Eliot. Her novels include *Alma mater* (1933), a psychological study of the Prague academic world and of urban bourgeois society. Under postwar communism she was admired, and probably most for her *Haldy* (1927), a novel set in the industrial society of the Ostrava region; she was made a National Artist in 1947.

BOŽENA VIKOVÁ-KUNĚTICKÁ (b Pardubitz [Pardubice], 30 Jul 1862; d Libočany near Žatec, 18 Mar 1934). Author, politician and feminist campaigner. An innkeeper's daughter, she married a clerk in a sugar factory, and in 1912 became the first woman to be elected to the Bohemian Diet, for the 'Young Czech', or National Liberal, Party; later she became a senator in the new Czechoslovak Republic, for the Czechoslovak National Democratic Party. In novels she defended free love and unmarried motherhood, while opposing male Decadence; and in polemical writings she argued strongly for the rights of women.

MODERN CZECH CLASSICS

Published titles
Zdeněk Jirotka: *Saturnin* (2003, 2005, 2009, 2013; pb 2016)
Vladislav Vančura: *Summer of Caprice* (2006; pb 2016)
Karel Poláček: *We Were a Handful* (2007; pb 2016)
Bohumil Hrabal: *Pirouettes on a Postage Stamp* (2008)
Karel Michal: *Everyday Spooks* (2008)
Eduard Bass: *The Chattertooth Eleven* (2009)
Jaroslav Hašek: *Behind the Lines: Bugulma and Other Stories* (2012; pb 2016)
Bohumil Hrabal: *Rambling On* (2014; pb 2016)
Ladislav Fuks: *Of Mice and Mooshaber* (2014)
Josef Jedlička: *Midway upon the Journey of Our Life* (2016)
Jaroslav Durych: *God's Rainbow* (2016)
Ladislav Fuks: *The Cremator* (2016)
Bohuslav Reynek: *The Well at Morning* (2017)
Viktor Dyk: *The Pied Piper* (2017)
Jiří R. Pick: *Society for the Prevention of Cruelty to Animals* (2018)
Views from the Inside: Czech Underground Literature and Culture (1948–1989), ed. M. Machovec (2018)
Ladislav Grosman: *The Shop on Main Street* (2019)
Bohumil Hrabal: *Why I Write? The Early Prose from 1945 to 1952* (2019)
*Jiří Pelán: *Bohumil Hrabal: A Full-length Portrait* (2019)
*Martin Machovec: *Writing Underground* (2019)
Ludvík Vaculík: *A Czech Dreambook* (2019)
Jaroslav Kvapil: *Rusalka* (2020)
Jiří Weil: *Lamentation for 77,297 Victims* (2021)
Vladislav Vančura: *Ploughshares into Swords* (2021)
Siegfried Kapper: *Tales from the Prague Ghetto* (2022)
Jan Zábrana: *The Lesser Histories* (2022)
Jan Procházka: *Ear* (2022)
A World Apart and Other Stories: Czech Women Writers at the Fin de Siècle (2022)
Libuše Moníková: *Transfigured Night* (2023)

Forthcoming
Jiří Weil: *Moscow – Border*
Ivan M. Jirous: *End of the World. Poetry and Prose*
Jan Čep: *Common Rue*
Egon Bondy: *Invalidní sourozenci*
Jaroslav Hašek: *The Good Soldier Schweik*

*Scholarship

MODERN SLOVAK CLASSICS

Published titles
Ján Johanides: *But Crime Does Punish* (2022)

Forthcoming
Ján Rozner: *Seven Days to the Funeral*
Alfonz Bednár: *Hodiny a minúty*
Gejza Vamoš: *Atómy Boha*